Carola Dunn is the author of several mysteries featuring Daisy Dalrymple, as well as numerous historical novels. Born and raised in England, she lives in Eugene, Oregon.

The Daisy Dalrymple Series

Death at Wentwater Court
The Winter Garden Mystery
Requiem for a Mezzo
Murder on the Flying Scotsman
Damsel in Distress
Dead in the Water
Styx and Stones
Rattle His Bones
To Davy Jones Below
The Case of the Murdered Muckraker
Mistletoe and Murder
Die Laughing
A Mourning Wedding
Fall of a Philanderer*
Gunpowder Plot*
The Bloody Tower*
The Black Ship
Sheer Folly
Anthem for Doomed Youth

*Coming soon from Constable & Robinson

Die Laughing

A Daisy Dalrymple Mystery

CAROLA DUNN

ROBINSON

Constable & Robinson Ltd
3 The Lanchesters
162 Fulham Palace Road
London W6 9ER
www.constablerobinson.com

First published in the US by St Martin's Press, 2003

This edition published in the UK by Robinson,
an imprint of Constable & Robinson Ltd, 2011

A copy of the British Library Cataloguing in
Publication Data is available from the British Library

ISBN: 978-1-84901-707-7

Typeset by TW Typesetting, Plymouth, Devon

Printed and bound in the UK

1 3 5 7 9 10 8 6 4 2

To the multitude of dentists who have struggled to cope with my teeth over the years, especially the latest – Dr Terri Baarstad – with thanks.

ACKNOWLEDGEMENTS

My thanks are due to Stephanie Walker and Dr Anne Dale of the University of Toronto; Heather Thompson, Deputy Coroner, Franklin County, Washington; and Alice Ford-Smith of the Wellcome Library, for their invaluable assistance in finding obscure technical information for me and their patience in enduring my endless questions.

CHAPTER 1

As Daisy took her hat from the wardrobe shelf and turned to the looking glass, Nana capered hopefully around her heels. Daisy looked down and sighed.

'Sorry,' she said. The little dog's feathery tail and ears drooped. 'Believe me, I'd much rather take you up Primrose Hill than go to the dentist, but I've put it off too long already. I can't pretend I've forgotten the appointment when the blasted tooth aches like billy-o.' With the tip of her tongue she probed the hole – big enough to swallow a dinosaur, or at least to trip one.

Setting the cloche on her shingled curls, she straightened it and admired her reflection. Lilac coloured, with a cluster of pale yellow primroses to one side of the narrow brim, it was new for spring, 'And rather dashing, don't you think, Nana?'

She had acquired vast quantities of new clothes since her wedding six months ago. Her mother-in-law and her friend Lucy, though disapproving of each other on sight, agreed on one thing: Daisy's wardrobe was a disgrace. She had gone from the nursery to earning her own meagre living via school uniform and the exigencies of wartime shortages, and fashion had never been one of her priorities.

It was difficult to be enthusiastic when today's styles

stressed the straight-up-and-down boyish figure which she would never attain. She did have decent legs, though, and the latest spring hemlines for 1924 had risen again to near the knee, to the elder Mrs Fletcher's outrage.

Still, Daisy felt she had quite successfully split the difference between the expectations of her mama-in-law, widow of a bank manager, and Lucy, a smart young woman-about-town. At least, Lucy considered her new clothes dowdy, while Mrs Fletcher thought them far too modish for a respectable suburban matron. Alec seemed satisfied, and in the end that was all that mattered.

Belinda had chosen the hat. Daisy, always clad in daisy-print dresses and daisy-decked hats in nursery days, had continued to follow the path of least resistance in that regard. Her ten-year-old stepdaughter was more adventurous on her behalf. On a joint shopping expedition, she had spotted the lilac cloche with its primroses and insisted that it was perfect for Daisy.

Its purchase had necessitated the ordering of a new spring costume to match, in lilac jersey, with a pale yellow silk blouse. Though it was tailored instead of off-the-rack in Selfridge's Bargain Basement, Alec had not even blinked at the bill. 'Worth every penny,' he had said appreciatively the first time she wore it.

'Yes, quite fetching,' Daisy said now, and powdered her nose. Lip rouge? No, it would only come off all over the dentist's hands.

The dentist . . . ugh! At the thought, the tooth gave a particularly vicious twinge. She moaned, and Nana licked her hand anxiously.

'I'd better get going. Mustn't risk annoying Mr Talmadge

by being late when I'm going to be entirely at his mercy. What a way to start off a new week!'

She hurried downstairs. The sun was shining outside, but the April morning had alternated between sun and showers so she took a light coat from the coat closet at the back of the hall. On the way to the front door, pulling on her gloves, she stuck her head into the sitting room to say, 'I'm just on my way to the dentist, Mother.'

It still felt strange to call Mrs Fletcher 'Mother'. Not for any sentimental reason – her own mother, Lady Dalrymple, had rarely visited the nursery, and now Daisy visited the dowager viscountess as rarely as she could get away with. Mrs Fletcher, on the other hand, was ever-present. Admittedly, having her continue to run the household allowed Daisy to pursue her journalistic career, but she was definitely a damper.

'Don't forget your umbrella,' Mrs Fletcher said, looking up from the menus she was planning for the next day. 'You'll have to hurry if you're not to be late for your appointment. You won't want to offend Mr Talmadge. He's a neighbour as well as a dentist, remember. An excellent dentist. Where's the dog? Put it out before you go, please, Daisy. I don't want it making a mess in here, burying bones under the carpet.'

The bone burying had been a single incident, several weeks ago, but Nana was a bone of contention. Mrs Fletcher regarded her every misdeed as entirely Daisy's fault, since she had persuaded Alec to let Belinda adopt the puppy. Daisy took her to the kitchen, where Dobson, busy with the lunch dishes, welcomed her with a crust of toast.

'She can go out while it's sunny, ma'am. If she does trample a few daffies, well, there's plenty, and at least she isn't a digger, I'll say that for her. I'll call her in if it rains.'

'Thank you, Dobson. I shan't be more than an hour or so. I hope.'

'The dentist, isn't it, ma'am? Rotten luck, but Mr Talmadge is ever so good. Everybody says so.'

Everyone said Raymond Talmadge was a good dentist, Daisy thought as she hurried, pillar-box red umbrella in hand, down the front path to the tree-lined street. In his middle thirties, Talmadge was presumably experienced at his profession without being out of touch with the latest techniques. He was also extremely good-looking, in a pale blond, square jawed, rather Nordic way. She had met him and his wife at someone's dinner party, and again for cocktails at someone else's house. Also, the Fletchers had been invited to their house once, for drinks before Sunday lunch.

The demands of Alec's profession enabled the two of them to avoid a good deal of the St John's Wood entertaining circuit. The demands of Alec's mother ensured that they did not escape altogether. Mrs Fletcher was determined to introduce Daisy to her circle.

Good neighbourliness also played a part. Daisy didn't want to be thought above her company, labouring as she did under the disadvantage of the 'Honourable' before her name. It had inevitably become known, though she rarely used it. (After all, a distant cousin was now Viscount Dalrymple of Fairacres, since Gervaise was killed in Flanders and their father had succumbed to the flu pandemic.) So, while reserving her mornings for work and declining invitations to morning coffee, she accepted those for lunch and afternoon tea when her schedule allowed. Naturally, these were usually hen parties, their unstated purpose the exchange of gossip.

Daisy was quite surprised at the innocuous nature of the gossip. Apparently the professional middle class were as solidly respectable as their reputation.

She had made two new friends, mothers of school friends of Belinda, but she didn't feel she had come to know any of the other women well. Mrs Talmadge, the dentist's wife, she recalled as one of the smart set, always impeccably dressed.

Daisy returned to the present as she turned onto the street where they lived. Mr Talmadge's surgery was in his house. Many of the large, detached houses were half-hidden from the street by laurels and hollies, behind railings. The Talmadges' was separated from the pavement by a low brick wall fronting a lawn with a big chestnut, not yet in bloom. Brick gateposts framed the gravel carriage drive, and on one of these was a brass plate: Raymond Talmadge, Dental Surgeon LRCS 9.30–12.30, 2.00–5.30.

The sight of it made Daisy's tooth throb, and butterflies started frisking about in her stomach.

She glanced at her wristwatch. Dead on two. She was just in time. She crunched up the drive, flanked by a neat bed of daffodils and crocuses. A paved path led off to the front door, but a sign on the corner of the building sternly admonished her to continue around the side for the surgery.

Ahead, the drive continued past the house to a garage at the bottom of the garden. To Daisy's left, the house had two side doors, some yards apart. She stopped at the first, which announced Surgery – Enter. The door was unlocked so she obeyed.

The waiting room was deserted. The chairs against the white-painted walls looked reasonably comfortable, but Daisy felt much too fidgety to sit still. She noted without interest a rack with a selection of magazines, including a

Punch she hadn't read and an old *Town and Country* with one of her articles. The view from the window was less than engrossing: the yellow gravel drive and a high brick wall, covered with greenish bronze Virginia creeper, just beginning to leaf out.

Daisy turned back to the room. The wall to her right had a door in it, guarded by a desk with a modern, glass-fronted cabinet full of files behind it. On the desktop were a telephone, an open appointment book and a stack of three or four manila folders.

She went to look. The top folder had her name on it, so she flipped it open. Inside was nothing but a blank invoice form. Naturally – she hadn't seen Talmadge before. She wondered vaguely whether she ought to try to track down the dental records from her childhood and get them sent to him. It was ages since she'd seen a dentist.

And now she was here, she wanted to get the horrid business over with. Her watch said nearly ten past. She knocked on the door of the torture chamber.

No response. At that moment, she realized that the nagging pain which had driven her hither had vanished. Obviously the hole in her tooth was nowhere near as large as her tongue had led her to believe. Anyway, no one was here to deal with it, so she might as well go home. If the ache returned, she could always make another appointment. She'd better make her escape while the going was good, and ring up from home to explain why she had left.

Daisy was halfway across the waiting room when she heard hasty footsteps crunching on the gravel outside. The door swung open and a young woman in a grey cloak and white nurse's cap appeared, high-coloured and breathing hard.

'I'm so sorry I'm late,' she cried. Even in her flustered state she was quite pretty, though rather sharp featured. She stripped off her gloves, dropped them on the desk and cast off her cloak to reveal a neat navy frock with white collar and cuffs. 'I'm Nurse Hensted, and you must be Mrs Fletcher. Mr Talmadge hasn't called you through?'

'No. I knocked and there was no answer.'

'That's odd. He's usually ever so punctual. But so am I, and look at me.' Miss Hensted checked the watch pinned to her bodice. 'Nearly ten minutes late! Lucky for me he is too. I'll just go set everything ready for you and by that time he'll be here.'

Daisy resigned herself to going through with the dreaded business.

The nurse turned the handle of the connecting door, but it didn't open. 'Oh dear! I wonder why he locked it? Maybe he decided to go out to lunch. He usually leaves it unlocked when he's in the house.'

'He must have been delayed,' said Daisy, seizing the chance of a reprieve. 'I can come back another time.'

'Oh no, Mrs Fletcher, I'm sure he'll be here any minute. There'll be plenty of time for an examination at least, even if you should need another appointment. I'll tell you what, I'll go round to the front door and check if he's just got busy with something and not noticed the time. I expect that's it. Why don't you come with me?'

By this time Daisy was beginning to be distinctly annoyed with Talmadge. She was, after all, a neighbour as well as a patient, and he ought to have had the courtesy to be on time for her. Rather than twiddle her thumbs in the depressing waiting room, she accompanied Nurse Hensted, hoping for another opportunity to flee without looking like a coward.

A shower began to spatter down as they turned onto the paved path.

'Botheration,' said Daisy, 'I've left my umbrella in the waiting room. I'd better fetch it.'

'It will wait,' Miss Hensted pointed out, apparently without humorous intent. 'We'll be inside in a moment, if you come along. Otherwise I may get left on the doorstep while the maid goes to find Mr Talmadge. They all know Mrs Talmadge gets snippy at me going through the house.'

She seemed quite apprehensive, so Daisy, with an internal sigh, agreed. They hurried to the front door and had just reached it when a taxicab turned into the drive.

Mrs Talmadge emerged. She wore a smart fawn coat, its shawl collar and wide cuffs trimmed with dark bands of astrakhan, as was her cloche hat. Even her handbag had astrakhan trimmings. As she approached, she put up the hat's short veil and Daisy saw in her face signs of agitation or distress, a redness around the eyes, not quite concealed by careful make-up.

'What is going on, Nurse?' she asked sharply, and then, 'Oh, it's you, Mrs Fletcher, good afternoon. Is there something I can do for you?'

'Good afternoon,' said Daisy.

Before she could explain, Miss Hensted interrupted, sounding quite antagonistic. 'It's Mr Talmadge. Mrs Fletcher came for her appointment and he's not there. The door's locked so we came round to see if maybe he's overslept his forty winks or something.'

Mrs Talmadge, her hand on the door handle, glanced back. A brief look passed between the two women. A shared secret, with no trace of liking, Daisy thought. Did Raymond

Talmadge sometimes drink too much at lunch? But no, his reputation as a first-class dentist would never have survived that kind of overindulgence.

'We had a difficult morning,' the nurse continued. 'Two screaming kiddies, and old Mr Pettigrew, who's set on keeping all his teeth though half of them ought to be pulled.'

'My husband will be so sorry to have kept you waiting, Mrs Fletcher. Do come in out of the rain.'

'Thank you, but I won't stay. I can make another appointment and come back another day.'

'Oh no, you mustn't do that. I know how difficult it is to nerve oneself to see a dentist. Raymond will certainly fit you in this afternoon.'

Curses, foiled again! Daisy meekly followed Mrs Talmadge into the house, Nurse Hensted at her heels.

On her previous visit, Daisy had been too busy trying to recall the names and faces of new acquaintances to pay the house much heed. The hall was welcoming, parquet floored, with daffodils in a green glass vase on the glossy walnut half-moon table. Reflected in the looking glass hanging over the table, the flowers glowed like an indoor sun. Beside the vase, a silver tray held a couple of calling cards and three or four unopened letters. Ignoring these, Mrs Talmadge opened a door on the left and glanced into the room beyond.

'He's not in his study. Surely he's not still eating lunch. It's Cook's day off, so she left him a cold lunch.' As she spoke, Mrs Talmadge crossed to the opposite door and opened it. 'He hasn't eaten it. I wonder if he decided to go out instead and something delayed him? Just let me check the drawing room.'

They all trooped into the drawing room, a large room at the back of the house, furnished in the elegantly simple style of Sheraton or Hepplewhite – Daisy could never remember the difference. The wallpaper, striped in muted tones of lilac and blue, was perfectly complemented by two vases of vibrant Dutch iris. Yet the overall effect was lifeless, almost museumlike, wonderful for entertaining but unattractive for a cosy evening at home. No books or magazines lay about, no chess or draughts board with a half-played game, no jigsaw puzzle begun and temporarily abandoned, not even a record left out on the gramophone.

It reminded Daisy of the Fletcher house before she had moved in and subverted the rigid order imposed by Alec's mother. Unlike Alec, though, the Talmadges had no children, so excessive tidiness was more understandable, if not more inviting.

It had not, apparently, invited Raymond Talmadge to snooze on one of those stiff brocaded sofas. His wife turned back, looking upset.

'I'm so sorry, Mrs Fletcher. Perhaps he wasn't feeling well and lay down upstairs. Otherwise I'm afraid he must have gone out to lunch, though I can't imagine what might have delayed him. Oh, Gladys,' she said to a maid who was coming down the stairs at the rear of the hall, 'have you seen the master?'

'No, ma'am, not since breakfast. We've been upstairs doing some mending, me and Miss Kidd. I was coming down to clear the table. If you just came in the front door, I 'spect you just missed him and he's in the surgery by now.'

'Of course, we must have just missed him!' Mrs Talmadge went on past the stairs, her heels tapping on the parquet.

Daisy followed. A short passage to the right, leading to an outside door, had a door on each side, one to the kitchen and one to the surgery.

Opening the latter, Mrs Talmadge stepped in. 'Oh!' she exclaimed, turning as if to bar the way.

But Daisy was already through the door. There was the dentist's chair. In it slumped the dentist, his pale hair unmistakable above the mask of the nitrous oxide apparatus clamped to his nostrils, half hiding his moustache. His eyes were closed, his lips curved in a happy smile, almost a grin.

Not a drinker but a dope fiend! Or perhaps laughing gas didn't quite count as 'dope', but if his patients found out he was addicted to the stuff, his practice was bound to suffer.

Realizing she was too late to stop Daisy from seeing him, Mrs Talmadge turned back, saying sharply, 'Raymond, this is no time for . . . Raymond?' She clutched Daisy's arm. 'He's awfully still!'

Daisy tore her gaze from Talmadge's silly smirk. With a sinking feeling in the pit of her stomach, she observed that his chest did not perceptibly rise and fall. She extracted her sleeve from his wife's grip and moved forward, her only thought to remove the mask from his face.

But would that release the gas into the room and put them all under? She glanced back. Mrs Talmadge stood stock-still, eyes wide, her hand to her mouth. Where was the nurse when she was needed? 'Call Miss Hensted,' Daisy ordered, and reached for Talmadge's wrist.

The dentist's skin was chill to the touch, and try as she might, she could find no pulse.

'He's killed himself!' shrieked Mrs Talmadge.

CHAPTER 2

Nurse Hensted arrived at last. 'What's going on? Oh lord, is . . . ?'

'I think he's dead,' Daisy faltered.

Pushing past Mrs Talmadge, who seemed incapable of movement, Miss Hensted scanned the anaesthetic apparatus. 'He didn't turn on the oxygen. I knew he'd bungle it sooner or later.' She turned a couple of valves, then reached for the wrist Daisy had dropped.

'Shouldn't we take off the mask?' Daisy asked.

'No. I've turned off the nitrous. He's getting pure oxygen now, or would be if he was breathing. It's the only antidote, but the gas bag's full and the dial's not moving. It's too late.' Grim faced, she laid the limp hand on the arm of the chair. 'He's long gone.'

'Dead!' Mrs Talmadge burst into noisy sobs, mixed with hiccuping laughter.

The nurse slapped her face, hard. The laughter stopped abruptly, but she started gasping and clutching at her throat, while tears ran down her face, streaking her face-powder and making her eye shadow blotch.

'Hysteria. I'll deal with her,' said Miss Hensted, 'if you wouldn't mind ringing up the doctor, Mrs Fletcher. Not that he can do anything, but it's got to be reported.'

Not waiting for an answer, she hustled Mrs Talmadge out. Daisy heard her in the passage, calling, 'Gladys! Gladys, come and help me get your mistress upstairs.'

Accident or suicide? Daisy wondered. Why had Mrs Talmadge jumped to the conclusion that her husband had killed himself? Whichever, Talmadge's death had to be reported to the police as well as to his doctor. Alec wouldn't believe his ears when he heard she'd found herself mixed up in another unnatural death.

Accident or suicide, not murder. She nerved herself to take another look at the dead man's face. He looked too cheerful to have committed suicide, but of course that was the effect of the gas. Odd how he had a discoloured, pinkish brown patch around that horribly smiling mouth, in the otherwise pallid face. A rectangular patch.

Steeling herself, Daisy bent to sniff at the discoloration. The cinnamony odour of benzoin tincture was faint but plain.

Suddenly cold, she looked again at Talmadge's arms, laid so neatly on the arms of his chair. Wouldn't a man who was going to kill himself, or one who planned a few minutes of gas-induced euphoria, relax with his hands in his lap? And what were those creases in the sleeves of his white jacket, an inch or two up from the wrists? The sleeve she and the nurse had not disarranged, in feeling for a pulse, also showed a sort of dent or furrow, as if something had compressed the material.

Daisy wildly scanned the room, hoping for something – anything – to dispel her suspicions. She saw all the paraphernalia of a dental surgery: adjustable light, electric drill, a rack of vicious steel implements, sinks for spitting and hand washing, a sterilizer, a mahogany cabinet with dozens of miniature drawers for supplies, a waste bin and a small table with a blank loose-leaf ledger page on it, headed with her name, waiting in vain for notes on the state of her teeth.

The cupboard with a red cross on the door presumably held a first-aid kit, a kit containing the simple tools necessary for this particular murder.

The evidence might be in the waste bin, but Daisy couldn't bring herself to look. That was a job for the police. No one must touch anything until they arrived. She checked that the key was in the keyhole on this side of the locked connecting door to the waiting room. Without another glance at the dead man, so much more pathetic now she thought of him as a murder victim, she went to the door to the side passage.

The door stood wide open. The key was on the inside. With her gloved hand, Daisy took it out and put it in the outside. She pulled the door closed and locked it, doing her best not to smudge any 'fingerprints'. Sergeant Tring would be proud of her, she hoped. Then she wrapped the key in her hankie and dropped it in her handbag.

She mustn't give herself time to think about what she had shut away. Time to ring up the doctor and the police. She recalled seeing a phone in the waiting room, but by now more patients might have arrived and she didn't feel up to coping with them. Surely there was one in the house.

As she passed the stairs, the maid came dashing down, pink faced with excitement, the ribbons on her cap floating behind her. She slowed to a more decorous pace on seeing Daisy.

'Can I help you, madam?'

'Yes – Gladys, isn't it? – I'm looking for a telephone. Do you know who is the Talmadges' doctor?'

'Dr Curtis, ma'am. There's a telephone in the study, in there. The mistress is in such a state, I never seen the like in all me born days! Miss Hensted sent me to put on a kettle for tea and Miss Kidd said fetch the brandy, but I'm sure, ma'am, she ought to have the doctor to her, right enough.' Her voice sank to a whisper. 'Screaming and crying she is that the master's dead!'

'I'm afraid Mr Talmadge has met with an accident. When you have done as Nurse Hensted told you, you had better go around to the waiting room and tell people there will be no appointments because of an emergency. Put up a notice.'

'Yes, ma'am.' The girl bobbed a curtsy.

'Thank you, Gladys.' Daisy nodded dismissal and hurried to the study.

More of an office than a comfortable retreat, this was apparently where Talmadge did the business of his practice. Daisy sat down at the utilitarian desk, pulled the telephone apparatus towards her and asked the operator to put her through to Dr Curtis. The doctor was another local man she had met socially, an elderly GP who had been the Fletchers' family practitioner for donkey's years.

The phone rang and rang. At last Dr Curtis's maid answered. The doctor was out on his rounds.

'Blast!' Daisy muttered. But it wasn't really an emergency. Raymond Talmadge was beyond help, and Miss Hensted was surely capable of coping with Daphne Talmadge's hysterics. The police would send their own doctor anyway.

The police. Taking a deep breath, Daisy asked the operator for Whitehall 1212. Alec was not going to be happy when he heard that after four peaceful months – well, three and a half – she had once again enmeshed herself in a murder enquiry. Or was she imagining the whole thing?

'Scotland Yard.'

'I'd like to speak to Detective Chief Inspector Fletcher, please.'

'Who's speaking?'

'This is Mrs Fletcher. It's urgent.'

'Right you are, ma'am, I'll see if the Chief Inspector is in.'

Over the wire came the sound of whispering and a snicker. Daisy felt herself blushing, a despicable affliction even when there was no one to see. The whole Metropolitan Police force probably knew by now that she was in the Assistant Commissioner (Crime)'s black books for her meddling in a number of cases.

'Sorry, ma'am, the Chief Inspector's out.'

'Sergeant Tring?'

'Went with him. If it's police business, ma'am, not personal, you'd better tell me about it and I'll put you through to someone else.'

'I . . .' Daisy hesitated. She didn't want to speak to someone else, she wanted Alec. 'It's . . . I'm afraid it's a suspicious death.'

'Where are you, Mrs Fletcher?' the voice asked sharply.

She gave the address. 'It's . . .'

'You need to ring division HQ, Mrs Fletcher. Have you got a pencil? Here's the telephone number. I'll see a message gets to the Chief Inspector when he comes in.'

A message and a lot of ragging, Daisy thought resentfully as she wrote down the number and thanked the officer. It wasn't her fault, let alone Alec's, that dead bodies bestrewed her path through life. She'd much rather they didn't.

She clicked the hook a couple of times to disconnect the call and summon the operator, and gave the girl the new number. On the first ring a bored voice asked her business.

'I want to report a suspicious death.' It sounded sillier and less likely each time she said it.

'Suspicious?'

'Well, unnatural, anyway.'

'Your name, please, madam, and the number you're ringing from.'

'Mrs Fletcher.' Daisy gave the Talmadges' number, and added their address.

'Is that your residence, madam?'

'No, it's the victim's residence, and his dental office. I'm just a patient. A would-be patient, rather. Mr Talmadge, Raymond Talmadge, has died of an overdose of laughing gas. Or maybe suffocation,' she said doubtfully, remembering the turned-off oxygen.

'You can leave that to the medicos to decide, madam.' Boredom banished, the voice was quite cheerful now. 'I'll send the police surgeon and one of our detective officers round right away. Hold on a minute, please, madam.'

This time, no whispers or snickers reached Daisy's ears. Either the Yard gossip had not reached the divisions, or they had not realized that she was *that* Mrs Fletcher.

'Mrs Fletcher? You stay right there, if you please, madam. Detective Sergeant Mackinnon is on his way and he'll want to ask you a few questions. Can you keep everyone away from the scene of the . . . incident?'

'I've locked the surgery.'

'Good for you! DS Mackinnon will be with you shortly. I need to clear the line now, but you ring me right back if you need to.'

Daisy hung up the earpiece. She considered ringing up her mother-in-law to say she'd be delayed, but then she would have to explain why. Mrs Fletcher knew she had been mixed up in several of Alec's cases, though they had managed to keep some from her. Not unnaturally, she strongly disapproved. What she would feel about Daisy's involvement in the local murder of an acquaintance didn't bear thinking of.

In fact, Daisy really didn't want to think at all, but she had run out of useful things to do. She longed for a cup of tea.

Gladys had probably made a pot and taken it upstairs by now. Mrs Talmadge was only a slight acquaintance so it would be frightfully improper to invade the upper reaches of the house. To barge into the kitchen to make tea for oneself would be almost equally unacceptable. Not quite, though, and she might get away without being caught: Cook's day off, Mrs Talmadge had said. Daisy headed for the kitchen.

She had just reached the stairs when she remembered that the kitchen door was right opposite the door to the surgery. Feeling sick, chilled and weak at the knees, she sat down on the next to bottom step and hugged herself.

'Are you all right, Mrs Fletcher?' Miss Hensted's voice came from behind her.

She looked back to see the nurse coming down the carpeted stairs. 'Yes. Yes, quite all right.' She stood up to let the woman by. 'How is Mrs Talmadge?'

'In a bad way. If that Hilda Kidd, that's her maid, thinks she can cope without my help,' she said resentfully, 'well, all I can say is she's got another think coming. All she is is a glorified parlourmaid, and the silly woman needs a doctor.'

The nurse, as a medical professional, should give a decent show of sympathy, Daisy felt. 'She's had a terrible shock,' she pointed out, 'finding her husband dead.'

'It's little enough she cared when he was alive, so she's got no call now to carry on like the end of the world. And slandering him, saying he killed himself when it was obviously an accident! Dr Curtis'll have to give her something good and strong to calm her down.'

'Dr Curtis was out. I left a message. I expect the police surgeon will be able to help Mrs Talmadge when he arrives.'

'Police! Don't say you called in the police?' Miss Hensted looked quite put out. After a frowning moment she said, 'That'll do her a lot of good, that will, having them stirring things up, making a mountain out of a molehill. It's bound to convince her it actually was suicide. Dr Curtis could have given a certificate nice and quiet, kept it out of the papers. She'll have reporters hounding her and—'

'Accident or suicide, it had to be reported to the police,' said Daisy. 'I'm sure Dr Curtis would have insisted, in the circumstances.'

'Oh well, least said, soonest mended, and it's no good crying over spilt milk.' She gave Daisy a critical appraisal. 'You're looking a bit seedy yourself. Better go and sit in the drawing room and I'll make you a nice strong cuppa.'

'I'll come with you,' Daisy said gratefully.

She sat down at the oilcloth covered table, while Miss Hensted filled a kettle, set it on the gas stove and struck a match. At that moment a bell rang. They both looked up at the bell board over the kitchen door.

'Front door,' said Daisy.

'That'll be the police.'

As the nurse made no move, Daisy stood up. 'I'll get it.'

'No need for that, Mrs Fletcher. It's Gladys's job and if she doesn't go it won't hurt him to – Ouch!' She dropped the match on the stovetop and rushed to stick her fingers under the tap. For all her veneer of professional coolness, she was more upset than she wished to let anyone see, Daisy thought.

'Are you all right?' she asked, going over to light the gas under the kettle.

'Yes, it was nothing. I was just saying, it won't hurt him to wait while I make the tea.'

The bell rang again.

'It looks as if Gladys is otherwise occupied.' Though the Dowager Lady Dalrymple would have strongly objected to either course, in the circumstances Daisy decided making tea was less infra dig than answering the door. 'I think you should go and let him in. I'll do the tea.'

Lips pursed, Nurse Hensted regarded Daisy with a slight frown. 'Yes, perhaps I will,' she said, and went off, her rubber-soled shoes squeaking slightly on the linoleum in the passage.

Daisy found a big brown earthenware teapot and a pair of japanned canisters, one smelling of Earl Grey, the other of Darjeeling. There was a packet of a cheap brand of tea, too, but she didn't feel obliged to lower herself to that extent just because she would be drinking from a thick white china cup. She set out cups and saucers for Miss Hensted and Detective Sergeant Mackinnon as well. The kettle was steaming so she poured hot water into the teapot to warm it.

As she swirled the water in the pot, she heard voices approaching. She moved closer to the open door to listen.

'. . . Mrs Fletcher, she's a patient who just happened to be here. Oh, and Gladys, the housemaid. I don't know where the dratted girl has got to! But there was no need to call you out, Sergeant. It was an accident, for sure.'

'That's for the Coroner's jury to decide, miss.'

'You see, I'm afraid Mr Talmadge was in the habit of taking a little sniff of laughing gas when we'd had a run of difficult patients, just to relax. No harm in that!' The nurse gave a forced laugh. 'I never thought anything of it, but looking back, I suppose it was bound to happen sooner or later, that he'd forget to switch on the oxygen. There's no reason to think he did it on purpose.'

'That'll be for the Coroner to decide, miss.' The rolling Scottish *r* confirmed the speaker to be Mackinnon. 'In here, is he?'

'That's right.' Miss Hensted's hand came into view, reaching for the doorknob. The plainclothes detective officer gripped her white-cuffed wrist.

'Don't touch, please, miss. It'll have to be done for fingerprints.'

'Why on earth . . . ?'

'Standard procedure, miss, in any unexpected death. Did you touch this handle when you found the deceased?'

'Yes, I—'

'No,' said Daisy. 'Mrs Talmadge opened the door and I closed it, when you had to help her upstairs.'

'Oh yes, that's right.'

Sergeant Mackinnon, a tall, rawboned redhead who looked even more Scottish than he sounded, eyed Daisy and her teapot askance. 'And you are . . . ?'

'Mrs Fletcher. I telephoned.'

'Ah yes.' He took out his notebook. 'I have a few questions to ask you, madam' – he pronounced the last word dubiously, with another look at the teapot – 'before I take a look at—'

'Miss Hensted!' Gladys came tearing along from the front

hall. 'Miss Hensted, Miss Kidd says if the doctor's not come yet will you come and see to the mistress. She's fallen into a fit!'

'What did I say? I told her she couldn't manage without me.' Miss Hensted hurried off.

The maid hesitated, obviously agog with curiosity over the stranger downstairs while not wanting to miss any of the excitement upstairs.

'This is Gladys, the housemaid, Sergeant,' said Daisy.

'A pleeceman?' Gladys squeaked.

'Yes, and I'll want to have a word with you later, my girl, but you can take yourself off now. You listen out for the doorbell, mind. There'll be more people coming.'

With another inarticulate squeak, Gladys scuttled away.

'I think you ought to go and look at . . . him first, Sergeant,' Daisy suggested. 'The signs I saw may fade. I'll explain what to look for.'

Mackinnon cast an uneasy glance behind him at the surgery door. 'That can wait till the doctor comes,' he said.

'But—'

'I'll just do things my own way, if you don't mind.'

Daisy sighed. 'Then you'd better come into the kitchen and sit down. The kettle's boiling and I really do need a cup of tea. Will you have one?'

'Not just now, thank you, madam.' He closed the kitchen door and sat down at the table, the notebook before him. 'Your full name, please.'

'Daisy Fletcher.'

'Mrs Fletcher, please describe in your own words what occurred leading to your telephone call.'

So while Daisy made tea, she quickly explained how the dentist had not turned up for her appointment and she and the nurse had gone to look for him. 'We found him lying in his reclining chair, with the laughing-gas mask on. His hands were cold and he wasn't breathing, and Miss Hensted couldn't find a pulse. She turned the gas off and the oxygen on, just in case.'

'The gas off and the oxygen on?'

'She said oxygen was the only remedy, but she was pretty sure it was too late. Then Mrs Talmadge went into strong hysterics and Miss Hensted had to deal with that. She and Gladys took her upstairs. That was when I noticed the things that made me wonder if it really was either an accident or suicide. There was a sort of pinkish patch around his—'

'Pinkish patch,' Sergeant Mackinnon said skeptically, not writing it down.

'Yes, squarish, around—'

'No doubt the police doctor will take note of anything significant in the appearance of the deceased.'

'But if he doesn't come soon—'

'Thank you for your statement, Mrs Fletcher. It will be transcribed for you to sign, and there may be further questions. Where may I get hold of you?'

As Daisy gave her address, she was trying to decide what to do next. The sergeant obviously wasn't going to listen to her. Should she phone the Yard again, or just give up and let some maniac run loose hither and yon murdering dentists?

The notion was undeniably attractive.

CHAPTER 3

A bell rang – the front door again. With any luck it was the police surgeon. Maybe he would listen to Daisy, or notice the anomalies for himself.

'Here they are now.' With evident relief, Mackinnon jumped up and opened the kitchen door.

They heard heavy footsteps approaching and Gladys's voice. 'Oh yes, Mr Atkinson, the sergeant's in the kitchen. Isn't it awful? The mistress is in such a taking you wouldn't believe.'

A large bobby with his helmet in his hands appeared in the doorway, Mackinnon giving way before him. 'Constable Atkinson, Sergeant. This is my beat and they told me to come and see is there anything I can do to help. Afternoon, Mrs Fletcher. A sorry business, ma'am!'

'Yes, ghastly,' Daisy said feelingly. 'Do you know if the police surgeon will be here soon? I'd like a word with him.'

'No need for that, madam,' said Mackinnon, annoyed. 'You're free to leave, and I have your address if we need to trouble you further.'

Atkinson looked from one to the other. 'Half a mo', Sergeant, a word in your ear.' He whispered. Daisy caught the words 'Honourable', 'Dalrymple as was', and 'Chief Inspector'.

Mackinnon turned a red, aghast face to her. Maybe she should have warned him, but she hated to flaunt either her own courtesy title or Alec's more substantial rank.

'Gosh,' she said quickly, 'I nearly forgot, Sergeant. I have the key to the surgery in my handbag. I must have left it in the study, where I telephoned. I'll get it for you.' She headed for the door.

They parted to let her through, then followed her into the passage. 'Thank you, ma'am,' said Mackinnon weakly.

'I wrapped it in my hankie. I didn't touch it, or the doorknob, with my bare hands.'

'Knows all about dabs, see,' came the constable's loud whisper behind her.

'I was going to tell the medico what I noticed in there,' Daisy continued, entering the hall, 'but as he's still not here, I dare say I ought to tell you.'

'If you please, Mrs Fletcher.' Drawing abreast of her, Mackinnon cast her a look of fervent gratitude.

She described the discoloured mark around Talmadge's mouth and the lingering odour of the antiseptic adhesive benzoin. As long as she didn't actually think about it, she could talk about it quite calmly. 'There's a first-aid cabinet which surely includes sticking plaster, though I didn't look. It could have been used to stop him breathing through his mouth, couldn't it?'

'More than likely,' agreed the sergeant with the devoutness of the converted.

'Then there are the peculiar creases in his sleeves, as if his wrists were tied to the arms of the chair.'

'With bandages, maybe, from the first-aid kit!'

'That's what I'd guess,' said Daisy approvingly. 'His arms

were on the arms of the chair unnaturally neatly. I mean, if you were going to relax for a few minutes, with or without the aid of the gas, with or without the intention of killing yourself, wouldn't you fold your arms comfortably, or clasp your hands in your lap? Or at most put your elbows on the arms of the chair and let your hands sort of droop?'

'Umm . . . I expect so,' said Mackinnon, making a visible effort to picture himself in that situation.

Having won her point with her observations, Daisy refrained from pushing her theories, a decision Alec would have heartily approved. She turned into the study. Her handbag was on the desk. She extracted the wrapped key, careful not to rub it, and handed it to the detective.

'I'd like my handkerchief back, please, when you don't need it any longer.'

He felt in the pockets of his brown serge suit. Constable Atkinson handed him a huge cotton square, blue polka-dotted with white. The key was transferred and Daisy's hankie returned to her. Now she had no excuse for lingering, except that she still hadn't had any tea.

'If there's a chance it could be murder,' said the sergeant, going to the telephone, 'I'd better ring up the station and get them to send a photographer, and report to my super.'

'I'll just pop up and see how Mrs Talmadge is doing.' Daisy made her escape.

On the first-floor landing, faced with a number of closed doors, she didn't know which way to turn. Despite her refusal to abide by the strict rules of propriety instilled by her nanny and her school, she couldn't quite bring herself to listen at the doors. Her dilemma was solved when one of them opened.

Miss Hensted stalked out, her face a study in outrage, yanking the door after her. Just before it slammed she caught it and closed it with the excessive care of repressed violence.

Then she noticed Daisy. 'Oh, Mrs Fletcher, can I help you?'

'I wondered whether Mrs Talmadge is well enough for me to see her for a moment to express my sympathy.'

'*I* would say so, but what that woman will say . . . Well! I'm not one to take offence, but really, when an ignorant servant thinks she knows better than a registered nurse, what's the world coming to? Wanting to give Mrs Talmadge brandy for shock, like in the bad old days, instead of strong tea. Sending for me because she took a fit, then arguing about what's best to do, then after I bring her out of it, telling me I'm not wanted to look after her! I ask you, did you ever?'

'Everyone's upset,' Daisy said soothingly. 'The doctor's bound to get here soon, and he can decide whether Mrs Talmadge needs your professional care. In the meantime, why don't you go down and have a cup of tea?'

'I could do with one, and that's a fact.'

'And in your opinion it's all right for me to see Mrs Talmadge?'

'Nothing wrong with her bar hysterics. It'll do her good to have a friend of her own sort to talk to, instead of no one but that Hilda Kidd that's been coddling her since the year dot.' Still stiff with indignation, Miss Hensted marched off towards the stairs.

Daisy knocked on the door. The tall, spare woman who opened it wore a black dress with no white collar and cuffs and no cap on her grey hair. She was vaguely familiar to Daisy. The nurse had called her a 'glorified parlourmaid', so she probably put on collar, cuffs and cap on occasion to admit guests to the house and hand round trays of drinks. Apparently she acted also as lady's maid in this post-war world where servants were so hard to come by.

'Yes?' she said suspiciously.

'I'm Mrs Fletcher. I've come to see Mrs Talmadge.'

'She's not seeing anyone.' Hilda Kidd started to close the door in Daisy's face.

'Hilda, who is it?' Mrs Talmadge's voice sounded exhausted, blurry with tears.

'Mrs Fletcher, ma'am.'

'Of course I'll see her. Ask her in.'

'There's no call to go worrying yourself with people who—'

'That's enough, Hilda!'

Grim faced, the maid opened the door and stood aside to let Daisy enter. If looks could kill, Daisy would have dropped dead before she got halfway across the room.

It was a spacious, very feminine room, rose pink and white with gold touches, all ruffles and frills and broderie anglaise. Almost defiantly feminine, Daisy thought, as if daring any male to profane it. No masculine touch was visible anywhere. The only bed, though comfortable for one, would be cramped for two.

Mrs Talmadge reclined on a chaise longue. With the ruined make-up washed off and eyes red rimmed, the expensively marcelled bob tousled, her pale face was quite plain. She had one of those oddly flat faces, all in one plane except for a button nose, though clever cosmetics usually disguised the lack of any distinguishing features.

As Daisy approached, she made an effort to sit straight.

'No, don't get up,' said Daisy, holding out her hand. 'I don't want to disturb you. I just wanted to say how very sorry I am.'

'Thank you,' Mrs Talmadge said on a half sob. 'I can't quite believe it's happened, somehow. Do sit down. You'll have some tea, won't you?'

'It's cold,' Hilda announced, her tone mutinous.

'Then go and make some more. Nurse Hensted said I should have some and I never drank it.'

'A drop of brandy's what you need.'

'I gather tea is preferred for shock these days,' said Daisy. 'Strong, hot and sweet, they say.'

'Tea, please, Hilda.'

Muttering, 'Well, if you want to take *her* word against them that's cared for you all these years!' the maid at last departed.

'I'm afraid Hilda can be awfully rude sometimes,' Mrs Talmadge apologized. 'She was a nursery maid when I was a child, and she's been with me ever since. It's difficult to stop her taking liberties.'

'Old retainers tend to be like that, unless they're stiff and starchy and frightfully proper. She naturally feels a need to protect you at this dreadful time.'

'How *could* he do this to me! Just when I thought we had it all sorted out. Everyone will say it's my fault.'

'Why should they?'

'Because I . . . Because that's the sort of thing people say. People always assume the worst. They don't need a reason for it. Of course there's no reason to blame me. Poor Raymond was feeling rather depressed.'

'What a shame.' Daisy's tone held a hint of a question.

'Yes, he . . . A professional disappointment.' Mrs Talmadge didn't quite look around wildly for inspiration, but she sounded as if she were finding it as she went along. 'He . . . he had hoped to buy into a practice in Harley Street. Unfortunately, they are asking rather more than we can afford.'

'How frustrating!'

'Yes, poor Raymond was quite shattered. You know how men are, so anxious about rising in their professions. Is your husband likely to be called in, do you think? Nurse Hensted said the police had to be notified about . . . poor Raymond.'

'They wouldn't call Alec in for an accident or suicide,' Daisy replied evasively.

'I don't believe it,' groaned the Assistant Commissioner for Crime.

'I'm afraid it's true, sir.' Superintendent Crane was no happier.

'I did hope that once the Honourable Daisy Dalrymple became Mrs Chief Inspector Fletcher, she'd stop this nonsense.'

'To be fair, sir, it's been five months since Mrs Fletcher found herself on the scene of a crime. And that was in America.'

'Four months. Remember Cornwall.'

'I've been trying to forget it, sir! How does she do it?'

'I suppose it's what the young people call an affinity.'

'Isn't that a term used by young women of unsuitable young men they wish to marry?' Crane asked, puzzled.

'Only in Mrs Fletcher's case it's unsuitable murders she's involved with. It *is* murder, is it?'

'The divisional super says his man assumed accident, sir, or at worst suicide, but Mrs Fletcher suspects it's murder.'

'Damnation!'

'Yes, sir. In the circumstances, Superintendent Willoughby's asking for our assistance. I take it you want me to assign Fletcher to the case?'

Heaving a sigh, the AC nodded.

The arrival of Dr Curtis, a slight, grey-haired GP with gold-rimmed spectacles, drove Daisy from Daphne Talmadge's room. She was not unwilling to leave. Having expounded the fairy tale about 'poor Raymond's' disappointment, Daphne had grown teary again. She developed a tendency to regard Daisy as her only true friend and insisted on first name terms. Had she not turned down brandy in favour of tea, Daisy would have guessed she was just a trifle tiddly.

Hilda and the tea arrived simultaneously with the doctor, so once again Daisy went without. Dr Curtis dismissed the maid along with Daisy. They went downstairs together.

'Mrs Talmadge told me you've been with her since she was a child,' said Daisy. 'You must be fearfully worried about her.'

'Well, and I am, there's no denying. She's ever so upset. Who wouldn't be?' Hilda demanded, then added sotto voce, 'Though there's some might think she's well rid of him!'

Pretending not to hear this last, Daisy said, 'Of course, she's had a frightful shock.'

'And it's not very nice having the police in the house, not at all what we're used to. Poking and prying when anyone can see it was an accident.'

'So you agree with Nurse Hensted.'

'About that,' the maid agreed grudgingly, 'and not much else. The mistress used to beg the master not to use that nasty gas. Have a whisky and soda, she'd say, or gin-and-It, like everyone else. It was bound to happen sooner or later and we don't need any police upsetting everybody with their nosey-parkering.'

Gladys was closing the front door as they reached the hall. 'More pleecemen, Miss Kidd,' she said, quite blasé by now. 'One of 'em's got a great big camera. I sent them round to the side door.'

'Good girl! They've no call to come tramping through the house. But they could quite well get to the surgery through the waiting room. Nurse Hensted should have told them to go that way.'

'The pleece doctor came with Dr Curtis. He's in there now, with the sergeant, looking at the—'

'That's quite enough of that, Gladys, thank you very much! You'd better stay here in the hall to answer the door in case any more of them turn up.'

'Sergeant Mackinnon said he's going to ask me some questions.'

'No doubt he'll send for you when he wants you,' Hilda said repressively. She turned to Daisy. 'I expect you'd better stay, madam, till they've finished with their questions. If you'd like a cup of tea, I'll bring a tray to the drawing room.'

As long as there was a chance of learning something new, Daisy was not about to reveal that Detective Sergeant Mackinnon had already said she could leave. Besides, every mention of tea made her thirstier. But if she waited in the drawing room, it might never arrive. 'I'll come with you to the kitchen,' she said firmly.

The door to the surgery was ajar. Daisy kept her face turned away, not wanting either to see or to be seen. As she hurried into the kitchen, the latest arrivals knocked on the door at the end of the passage. Hilda went to let them in.

'Don't touch that knob!' warned Mackinnon, coming out of the surgery. He was too late.

From the safety of the kitchen, Daisy saw the maid turn and scowl at him. 'You'd better open it yourself!' she snapped. 'And it'd be a sight easier for everyone if you used the door to the waiting room.'

His handkerchief over his hand, Mackinnon passed Hilda and gingerly turned the handle. 'Not locked,' he observed with satisfaction, pulling the door open. 'Warren, you'd better check this door for dabs first, though I don't suppose it's much use now. Ardmore, bring the camera through this way.'

Hilda came to the kitchen door and said to Daisy, 'I'll put the kettle on in half a mo', madam. I'm just going to tell Gladys to send the rest through the waiting room if there's more coming.'

Nurse Hensted jumped up from her seat at the table. 'Who goes through the waiting room's my affair, not yours,' she said belligerently.

'They'll be going in there in the end anyway,' Daisy pointed out, 'from one end or the other, if they haven't already. Why don't *you* go and tell Gladys, Miss Hensted.'

Hilda instantly protested, 'She's got no right to give orders to—'

'She will convey *my* order.' Daisy employed the tone of

voice her mother used at her haughtiest. She tried it rarely, and was always surprised when it worked, as it did now, though she had no conceivable right to give orders to either Gladys or these two. However, Miss Hensted headed for the door and Hilda for the kettle.

'Chinese or Indian, ma'am?' enquired the latter.

'Indian, please.' Maybe she really was going to get a cup of tea in the end. 'I hope you and Nurse Hensted will join me. I'm sure you both need some too.'

'Well, ma'am, I can't say I wouldn't be glad of it, and I s'pose if I'm making it, that woman might as well have a drop.' Hilda set out one 'good' cup and saucer, Royal Doulton, beside the kitchenware Daisy had left on the table earlier.

Miss Hensted came back. 'What a lot of fuss and bother over an accident!' she said irritably, plumping down on one of the chairs at the table.

'Mrs Talmadge doesn't think it was an accident,' said Daisy.

'I don't know what call *he* had to do himself in,' Hilda snapped.

'I gather he was in despair because he'd wanted to buy into a Harley Street practice but couldn't afford the price.'

'Because *she* spends every penny he earns,' Miss Hensted asserted.

Hilda bridled. 'Rubbish, it was her money in the first place, that he bought this practice with. And what's he do but waste it on hiring a nurse, like he was already in a fancy practice in Harley Street.'

Red in the face, Miss Hensted demanded, 'Are you saying I don't earn my wages?'

'All I'm saying is you don't need a registered nurse in an ordinary practice like here. People don't expect it.' Hilda jumped as the kettle hissed and rattled its lid. Busy making the tea, she added, 'He only married her for her money. She ought to of married Lord Henry, I always said, and I'll stand by that to my dying day!'

'Lord Henry?' Daisy queried.

'Lord Henry Creighton, that was courting her before she met Mr Talmadge. A proper gentleman, he was, treated her lovely. They were mad for each other. But her father wouldn't hear of her marrying a man-about-town, a useless drone he called him, without two pennies to rub together if it wasn't for an allowance from his father, and no more idea how to earn his living than a babe in arms.'

Miss Hensted snorted. Daisy, who was slightly acquainted with Lord Henry, tried not to smile at this all-too-accurate description.

'Miss Daphne's father was a nerve specialist, see,' Hilda continued. 'A consultant. He sent her to a fancy school, and she made friends with lots of toffs and got invited to parties. But he didn't like the men she met. He was pleased when she took up with another medical man, even if he was only a dentist.'

'But he couldn't force her to marry him,' Daisy said.

'He didn't have to. Raymond Talmadge turned her head, didn't he. There's no denying he's . . . he was a smasher. Poor Lord Henry couldn't compete in that department, him having no chin to speak of. Always reminded me of a ferret, he did. But handsome is as handsome does, I say. He treated her right, and there's no harm in it if she has lunch in town with him now and then and goes to a show.'

'No harm!' Miss Hensted's fist crashed on the table, rattling the cups and saucers. 'She goes on seeing another man behind his back, and you expect him to take it sitting down? No wonder he needed a bit of gas now and then to keep his spirits up!'

'Gas wasn't all he had,' said Hilda grimly, 'and don't tell me you didn't know it. That's what drove her to it, if you ask me. What's sauce for the goose is sauce for the gander!'

With that triumphant, if somewhat confusing, statement, she poured the tea.

CHAPTER 4

'I don't believe it,' said Alec, narrowly missing the rear of an omnibus as he swung the Austin Seven around Marble Arch.

Beside him, massive in maroon and bottle-green checks, Tom Tring chuckled. The little car shook. 'Don't want to believe, more like, Chief.'

'I 'spect Mrs Fletcher'll know who did it by the time we get there,' put in Detective Constable Ernie Piper from the back seat. 'All we'll have to do is pick him up. Though I can't say I blame anyone that does in a dentist, do you, Sarge? Self-defence, I'd call it.'

'That's why they have those chest straps on the chairs, laddie,' Tom rumbled, 'so's the patients don't throttle the dentist. Do we know how it was done, Chief?'

'All Superintendent Crane could bring himself to tell me was that Daisy found her dentist dead and told the local man, a DS Mackinnon, that it's murder. I dare say we'll find it was a heart attack. Admittedly Talmadge was rather young to drop dead unexpectedly of natural causes, but it does happen.' *Just my age*, he thought.

'If Mrs Fletcher thinks it's murder, Chief,' said Piper, whose faith in Daisy was unbounded, 'then you can bet your boots that's what it is.'

'Knew him, did you, Chief?'

'I met him now and then socially, and consulted him several times in his professional capacity.'

'I reckon that makes you our first suspect, Chief,' said Piper.

'You watch your cheek, my lad,' Tom reproved him. 'You're getting too big for your boots.'

'Fortunately,' Alec said dryly, 'I spent the morning and half the afternoon in the East End rounding up the last of the Newbolt gang, with several unimpeachable witnesses, including both of you. Here we are.'

The ambulance was in the drive, so he left the Austin in the street. The local beat constable stood by the gate, surrounded by three uniformed nursemaids with perambulators.

Getting out of the car, Alec heard PC Atkinson say benevolently, 'No, nothing to see. Now you be off home to your tea.' He saluted Alec. 'Glad to see you, sir.'

'Not much of a crowd yet,' Alec said, chiefly to forestall any comment on Daisy's involvement.

'Not in a posh area like this, sir. The neighbours aren't the sort to stand about in the street staring.'

'True.' He glanced up and down the street. It was a cut above his own street of large but semi-detached houses. Half the inhabitants probably didn't even know anything was going on, unable to see past the trees and shrubbery in their front gardens. Not much hope of anyone having spotted an intruder.

'Dead-end street,' Tom commented, as usual in tune with Alec's thoughts.

So casual passers-by were unlikely, and even errand boys and delivery men would not cut through on their way elsewhere. Anyway, Alec needed more information before he sent a man door-to-door to question the neighbours, let alone started looking for nonresident witnesses.

'Round the side, sir, the waiting room entrance,' Atkinson said as Alec started up the drive, followed by Tom and Ernie.

Entering the dentist's waiting room, he recognized the local police surgeon. He had worked with Dr Ridgeway once or twice, as well as meeting him occasionally on the St John's Wood social circuit. Ridgeway was talking to a tall, lanky redhead, obviously a Scot, presumably DS Mackinnon.

'You canna narrow it down a bit, Doctor?' he was pleading. 'We already know it happened between quarter to one, when the nurse left, and ten past two, when he was found.'

'That's already a shorter period than I'd care to commit myself to. Hello, Fletcher. Come to bail out your wife?'

Ridgeway was a bachelor. Gritting his teeth, Alec managed to smile. 'I hope that won't be necessary.'

'Oh no, sir!' blurted the Scot, beetroot red, saluting. 'Detective Sergeant Mackinnon, sir. Mrs Fletcher's been verra cooperative. I let her go home, sir.'

'Good man!' Alec said with heartfelt relief. 'I've brought Detective Sergeant Tring and Detective Constable Piper with me from the Yard, but I hope your super will let you assist with the case. Let me hear what Dr Ridgeway has to say, then you can give me your report.'

'You know Talmadge died in his dental chair?' said Ridgeway. 'With the anaesthetic mask over his nose. He died laughing. I see nothing to contradict death by nitrous oxide poisoning, though asphyxiation probably played a part. The post mortem should be able to say for sure. Time of death: between noon and two p.m. The good sergeant can place it closer than I can.'

'No sign of injury?'

'Not exactly,' the doctor said cautiously. 'He wasn't hit on the head and stuffed into the chair. There are slight – very slight – indications of abrasion around the mouth, which will probably fade before the autopsy. On the other hand, without a microscope I won't commit myself as to whether a few moustache hairs have been pulled out, as Sergeant Mackinnon wanted to know. But the pathologist may be able to tell you, though I rather doubt it.'

From the corner of his eye, Alec saw Tom Tring's luxuriant moustache twitch, usually a sign of amusement. A glance at Piper showed him industriously taking shorthand notes with one of his endless supply of newly sharpened pencils. His smirk said as clear as day, 'Mrs Fletcher's right again!'

'Perhaps Talmadge shaved with a blunt razor this morning,' Alec suggested.

Ridgeway shook his head. 'Not like that at all. Mackinnon also asked me to look at the arms.'

'I'm sorry, sir,' the sergeant broke in anxiously. 'It meant disarranging his clothes, taking off his jacket, which you ought to've seen, but we got plenty of photographs. I was afraid any marks on the skin would be gone before you got here.'

'Were there any?'

'Too faint to be anything but corroborative evidence, but yes, I found traces of bruising just where the sergeant expected to see them.'

'Thanks to Mrs —'

Alec glared him to silence. The less said about Daisy's part in all this the happier he'd be – not that there was much hope of Ridgeway forgetting if not reminded. No doubt the entire neighbourhood would find out sooner or later, but the later the better.

'That's about it,' the doctor concluded. 'You'll get my report in the morning, Fletcher.'

'Thank you. I won't keep you any longer, then. See you at the inquest.'

The doctor departed.

'It was his sleeves, sir,' said Mackinnon. 'That and the square around his mouth. Rectangle, rather. I don't know that I'd've noticed anything amiss if it hadna been for . . . if it hadna been drawn to my attention.'

'By Mrs Fletcher,' Tom supplied, eyes twinkling below the vast, hairless dome of his head.

'You can speak freely in front of DS Tring and DC Piper,' Alec said resignedly. 'But while you talk, I want to look at what's left of the scene of the crime.' He made for the connecting door to the surgery. 'I take it you've fingerprinted the door handles?'

'Yes, sir, and everything else in there. My photographer's gone to develop the plates. But I took the dabs of the deceased and the nurse for comparison, and the only place there's any others is on the arms of the chair, where you'd expect patients to put their hands.'

'Pity.' Alec contemplated the limp body in the reclining chair. Unnatural death was always disturbing and he had known Talmadge – not well, and not to like him particularly, but for a good many years. Yet what made his gorge rise was the euphoric smile on the man's face.

That was no meaningless rictus of death. Talmadge had died happy. If this was murder, it was the most bizarre murder he had ever seen.

Forcing his attention from the horrible grin, he scrutinized the area around the lips. The faint brownish patch would scarcely have been visible had not the skin paled to an ivory white as blood drained from the face.

'It was pink, before,' said Mackinnon, who had moved to the opposite side of the chair. 'Around the mouth, I mean. Pinkish brown. Mrs Fletcher said it smelt of benzoin.'

'Sticking plaster,' said Piper. 'Tincture of benzoin and isinglass.' It was the sort of obscure detail he excelled in.

Mackinnon nodded. 'That's what she said. The marks on the arms have pretty much faded too, sir. There wasna much to see in the first place. Here at the wrists, and just above the elbows.' He turned on the adjustable electric light poised over the chair.

Talmadge was in his shirtsleeves, the sleeves rolled up well above the elbow. Alec inspected the areas of his arms indicated by Mackinnon. 'Piper, your eyes are better than mine.'

Piper bent low. 'I'm not saying I can't see nothing, Chief,' he said dubiously, straightening, 'but nothing I'd swear to in court.'

'What exactly is it you can't see?'

'It looks to me sort of like as if he might've been tied to the chair.'

'That's what Mrs Fletcher thought!' Mackinnon said. 'She noticed the creases in the sleeves of his jacket.'

'Which you had to take off,' Alec sighed. 'I realize it was necessary, but it's a pity. Even if the photographs come out well, evidence will have been lost. Where is it?'

Mackinnon pointed to a small table in one corner. On it lay a parcel, wrapped in brown paper but not tied. 'I took a brush to the creases, sir, before we took it off, and put the dust in envelopes. If there's any fibres to be found, we should've got them.'

'Well done. Any idea what he might have been tied with?'

'Bandages, maybe, sir, and that's Mrs Fletcher's guess. I think they're there in the waste bin, but when I heard you were coming, I thought I'd best leave 'em for you. That's the ties for the wrists, ready to hand in the first-aid cupboard. The elbows . . . Mrs Fletcher didna mention it, but I reckon the murderer would just use the chest strap. This here, that the dentist puts around you to keep you from trying to stop what he's doing to you.'

The broad canvas strap was neatly hooked in place at the back of the chair.

'Wouldn't that have been enough on its own?' Piper wondered. 'I s'pose he might've managed to reach up and pull off the mask.'

'Better safe than sorry,' said Tom, taking a pair of forceps from the rack of instruments. He delved into the waste bin and brought forth a wad of bandage. 'Any more envelopes, Sergeant?'

Mackinnon turned pink. 'I took them from the desk in the waiting room,' he muttered. 'I'll get more.'

Tom grinned at him. 'They're talking about giving us a "murder bag" with everything we need for an investigation. I hope I'll live to see the day. In the meantime, I didn't bring any envelopes meself, and I had a better idea than you did that this might be murder.'

'A nasty one,' Alec said soberly. 'The poor chap must have been under the gas already, or he wouldn't have sat still to be tied down. And then the murderer must have stayed to watch him die, so as to be there to untie him. What sort of cold-blooded bastard could stand there and watch a man die?'

CHAPTER 5

The kitchen door opened. Daisy looked round in considerable relief, which redoubled when she saw Alec. She jumped up, and would have run to hug him except that one simply didn't hug in public. Especially in someone else's kitchen with servants looking on.

'Darling!'

'Daisy! I thought you'd gone home.'

'Not quite,' said Daisy, hoping she didn't look frightfully guilty. 'Sergeant Mackinnon did say I could leave, but I absolutely had to speak to Mrs Talmadge. She's a neighbour and an acquaintance, after all. Besides,' she added, being now close enough to hiss in his ear, 'I rather dreaded having to explain things to your mother. Hello, Mr Tring.'

Tom Tring grinned at her. Reminded of his presence, and Sergeant Mackinnon behind him, Alec closed his mouth on whatever expression of sympathy, or blistering reproof, he had been about to utter.

'I see,' he said forebodingly, looking beyond her to the two women at the table.

'Alec, these are Nurse Hensted and Miss Kidd, Mrs Talmadge's maid. I expect you both recognize my husband, Chief Inspector Fletcher. Miss Hensted was with me and Mrs

Talmadge when we discovered . . . him. Which of us do you want to talk to first?'

'Mrs Talmadge,' Alec said.

'Oh, darling, I'm afraid you can't. Dr Curtis was here a moment ago. He's given Mrs Talmadge a sedative. Actually, he wants someone with her at all times. Miss Hensted and Hilda have been . . . discussing who should go up first.'

The nurse stood up, tight-lipped. 'I'm sure you'll agree, sir, Mrs Talmadge will obviously need more professional care during the day than at night, when she's sleeping natural. *She* will do for the night watch, but I must go to her now. She needs someone competent.'

'Don't make me laugh!' cried Hilda Kidd. 'Haven't I looked after her through thick and thin since she was a tot? She don't hardly know you, and you're nothing but a fancy receptionist. Call yourself a nurse, ha-ha.'

Miss Hensted's fists clenched and she leant forward, red with fury. 'Don't you laugh at me, you sanctimonious old bitch! If my patient was to wake up and see your sour face—'

'Enough!' Alec snapped. 'Miss Kidd, you go up to your mistress now.' The nurse subsided, but Hilda's triumph was short-lived. 'Miss Hensted will take over from you when I've asked her a few questions. What other servants are there?'

'There's Gladys, the housemaid, sir. It's Cook's day off. Mrs Thorpe, she is.'

'Gardener? Chauffeur?'

'Just a jobbing gardener comes twice a week. Not today.'

'Thank you. Send the housemaid along, please, then you may go up to Mrs Talmadge.'

'And mind you observe Dr Curtis's directions,' said Miss Hensted. 'I'll be up to relieve you shortly.'

With a glare at the nurse, Hilda took herself off.

'Tom, you'll see Gladys when she arrives,' Alec said. Tom, despite his devotion to his equally mountainous wife, had a way with female servants. 'Not in here, I think. Take her somewhere else.' Daisy expected to be sent out also, but he ignored her and went on, 'Mackinnon, take notes, please.'

'Yes, sir.' Mackinnon already had his notebook in his hand – Daisy assumed he had just reported his findings so far to Alec – but he fumbled for a sharpened pencil. Where was Piper with his ever-ready supply? she wondered.

'Miss Hensted, may I have your full name and address, please?'

'Brenda Mabel Hensted. I have a room in Marylebone.' She gave the street and number. With Hilda's departure, she had quite recovered her cool, professional demeanour.

'And your position in the household? This is for official purposes, you understand.'

'I'm not part of the household, not really, sir. I work . . . worked for Mr Talmadge in his practice, as nurse and whatever else he needed. I'm a registered nurse, but I don't care for hospital work, you see, having been in a military hospital all through the war. Though come to that, hospital's a sight better than being at an invalid's beck and call! Most dentists don't employ a registered nurse, but Mr Talmadge had a high-class practice – people like yourself and Mrs Fletcher – and what with giving the patients gas and doing all the latest procedures—'

'Yes, thank you. How long have you been here?'

'Three years come the fifth of May.'

'You liked the position, I assume. Nurses can always find a job.'

'Oh yes, it was smashing. At least, it was till I realized Mr Talmadge was . . .' She hesitated. 'I realized he was using the nitrous oxide himself. It's ever so dangerous, using it regularly, like he did. You can damage your brain, you know.'

'Do you think Talmadge had damaged his brain?'

'I wouldn't like to say. You'd have to ask a doctor. Not so you'd notice normally, but maybe enough to make him careless. It would explain this accident, wouldn't it?'

'Ah yes, you told Sergeant Mackinnon you were sure his death was an accident. Could you explain just how that could happen?'

'I've been thinking, and there's two ways it might happen. Maybe he just forgot to switch on the oxygen. You have to breathe oxygen along with the laughing gas, you know. Or maybe he was just going to take a quick whiff, so he didn't bother with the oxygen, and then he breathed deeper than he meant to and got too happy to care.'

'I see. You don't think it could have been suicide, as Mrs Talmadge assumed?'

'Not likely,' said Miss Hensted scornfully. 'She thought he was upset because of her carrying on with that Lord Henry Creighton, but I can tell you, he didn't mind. You've got to care for someone a lot before you mind about stuff like that. He didn't care two pins for *her*.'

'For whom, then?' Alec enquired.

The nurse laughed unconvincingly. 'I'm sure I don't know. Nobody, I suppose.'

'Lord Henry Creighton . . .'

'All I know about *him* is what that Hilda's let drop. You'll have to ask her about him.'

'I shall. You left the surgery at twelve forty-five, I think Sergeant Mackinnon said?'

'That's right, sir,' the sergeant confirmed.

'Yes. I went to the ABC in the High Street for a bite to eat, same as usual. I got back a bit late, about ten past two. In a bit of a fluster I was, after rushing. Mrs Fletcher was already waiting.'

'Thank you, Miss Hensted, you've been most helpful. I may need to see you again, but you'd better go and see to Mrs Talmadge now. Send Miss Kidd down, will you? Tell her to find Sergeant Tring, who'll have some questions for her.'

Miss Hensted left, looking smug, which Daisy put down to her having been interviewed by a chief inspector while Hilda Kidd was going to have to make do with a mere sergeant.

'Right-o, Daisy, your turn. You had an appointment to see Talmadge.'

'Yes, at two o'clock. I had a toothache,' Daisy explained for the record, as though her tossing and turning with pain had not kept him awake at night until he insisted that she see a dentist. 'I arrived on time. The waiting-room door was unlocked so I went in, but no one was there.'

'Did you hear anything?'

'From the surgery? No, not a whisper. Of course, I didn't listen at the door,' she said regretfully. Had Tom Tring or Piper been taking notes, instead of Mackinnon, she might have confessed that her tooth had stopped hurting and she'd nearly turned tail. Instead, she simply described what had happened and how her suspicions had been aroused.

'Mrs Talmadge was first into the surgery?' Alec asked. 'I somehow had the impression it was the nurse. You're sure of that?'

'Quite sure. It was natural for her to lead the way in her own house, looking for her husband. Now I come to think of it, though, I was a bit surprised, when we found him, that she hadn't asked me to wait in the hall.'

'Why?'

'Well, she obviously didn't want me to see him indulging in his secret vice. It wouldn't have done his reputation any good if I'd talked about it. I suppose it was wishful thinking: she wanted to believe he'd just gone through to the surgery a bit late.'

'She told you she knew about his habit?'

'Yes. No, actually, I don't think she did.' Try as she might, Daisy couldn't actually remember where the impression had come from. 'Anyway, when she saw him, her immediate reaction was to block my view.'

'And then, you say, she realized he was dead and claimed he had killed himself.'

'"Claimed" is much too restrained a word. She fell into strong hysterics. Thank heaven the nurse was there to take charge.'

'What happened exactly?'

Daisy put almost as much effort into picturing the scene as she had previously put into evading the memory. 'Miss Hensted slapped her face. No, first she – the nurse – turned off the gas and turned on the oxygen. She said something about knowing he'd make a mess of it sooner or later. Then she felt his wrist. Oh, I'd already done that. She said pure oxygen was the antidote but it was too late and that's when Mrs Talmadge had hysterics and Nurse Hensted hustled her away.'

'And you left with them?'

'I looked around. I didn't touch anything, and I put on a glove to close and lock the door and take the key, because I suspected he'd been murdered.' Daisy suddenly felt as cold and clammy all over as his skin had felt to her probing fingers.

'Sorry, love!' Alec sprang to her side. 'Here, put your head down on the table for a moment.'

'I must be out of practice,' she mumbled feebly.

'You'd better have some tea, with plenty of sugar.' He reached for the pot. 'Damn, it's cold.'

DS Mackinnon appeared on her other side, wielding a bottle. 'Cooking sherry?' he offered. 'It's all I can find.'

'Ugh,' said Daisy, who wasn't frightfully keen on even the best sherry.

However, Alec poured a dollop into the clean kitchen cup that Mackinnon produced, so she sipped it. It was just about as disgusting as she expected, but it did warm her.

'I'm all right,' she said after a few more sips, pushing the cup away. 'Thank you, Sergeant. But Nurse Hensted says alcohol for shock is outdated.'

'It seems to have worked,' Alec pointed out. 'Are you able to go on?'

'Yes, darling, and I've told you every tiniest detail about the surgery, so we can drop the subject. After I spoke to Sergeant Mackinnon, I went up to see Daphne – Mrs Talmadge.'

Alec's dark eyebrows met over steel grey eyes, but after casting a glance at Mackinnon, he didn't tell her she was a meddlesome wretch.

As if he had, she excused herself. 'The Talmadges are neighbours, after all, as your mother reminded me before I came. I couldn't just walk out without a word.'

'Hmm.'

'She repeated, more calmly, that her husband must have committed suicide. She told me he'd been depressed because he couldn't afford to buy into a Harley Street practice, but I must say, she didn't say it as if she believed it. Lord Henry Creighton is a much more likely reason, but I can't tell you about him because it's just hearsay, and anyway, Talmadge didn't commit suicide, did he?' Daisy said, fixing Alec with what he persisted in calling her 'misleadingly guileless' blue eyes.

'No, he was killed all right,' he answered incautiously.

'Then I was right!'

'Dash it, Daisy, I shouldn't have—'

'Don't worry, darling, it's perfectly obvious. You wouldn't be here asking me all these questions if it wasn't murder.' From the corner of her eye, she noticed Mackinnon biting his lip. She could only hope he would prove as discreet as Ernie Piper as to how much he wrote down in his official notebook. She smiled at him, and went on, 'It was Hilda Kidd who talked about Lord Henry, so you'll have to ask her, until Daphne is fit to be interviewed.'

'Mackinnon, go and find Sergeant Tring and tell him to ask the parlourmaid about Lord Henry Creighton.'

'And he'd better ask what she meant by "What's sauce for the goose is sauce for the gander."'

Mackinnon looked to Alec, who shrugged and nodded. 'He'd better phone the Yard, too, and get hold of DC Piper, or leave him a message. Tell him to find out where Creighton lives and ring back.' Alec waited till the door closed, then said, 'Off the record, because I shouldn't be sharing speculations with a witness, am I to take it that Mrs Talmadge was having an affair with Creighton?'

'Quite likely. He was an old flame. Hilda said Daphne would meet him in town for lunch and a show, how often I don't know.'

'Why on earth would Hilda give away a thing like that? I had the impression she's devoted to her mistress.'

'She is, darling, beyond the bounds of common sense, but she was too upset to be discreet. When she dropped Lord Henry's name, she was actually trying to defend Daphne against Miss Hensted's aspersions.'

'No love lost there.'

'No, I thought for a minute they were actually going to come to blows over who should look after her. I was never so glad to see you in my life.'

'"What, never?"'

'"No, never!"'

'"What, *never*?"'

'"Hardly ever!"' (They had recently taken Bel to see *HMS Pinafore*.) 'Seriously, though, Hilda blurted out that Daphne should have married Lord Henry, then felt obliged to explain it to me. I suppose the title – though it's only a courtesy title, like mine – must be an attraction. Lord Henry hasn't much else going for him.'

'You know him?'

'Slightly, but I wouldn't dream of prejudicing you for or against him. I assume you're going to see him?'

'Yes, of course,' said Alec. 'The lover doing away with the husband is the oldest tale in the book.'

'As old,' Daisy asked, 'as the husband doing away with the lover?'

CHAPTER 6

Mackinnon returned to the kitchen and took up his notebook again. 'DS Tring will ask about Lord Henry and about the goose and gander, sir,' he reported.

Alec had a feeling the sergeant was having a hard time keeping a straight face. That was always the way when Daisy got involved in a case. Either other police officers concerned strongly objected to her meddling, or they fell for her, hook, line and sinker. Just as well it was usually the latter, he thought with a sigh.

Mackinnon was also obviously bursting with curiosity. Alec asked the question for him.

'Daisy, what's this about sauce for the goose and gander?'

'It was a bit confusing at the time, because what Hilda really meant was "what's sauce for the gander is sauce for the goose". She was excusing Daphne's carrying-on by hinting that she was getting back at her husband for his own peccadillos. Who sinned first I can't guess, but it wouldn't surprise me if he had a mistress.'

'Why not?' Alec asked, resigned to venturing into the dangerous territory of Daisy's speculations.

'Well, he really was devastatingly handsome, wasn't he? I heard – at some of those local parties we've been to – that women swoon when he bends over them with that intent look on his face, even though what he's intent on is their rotting teeth.'

Alec momentarily forgot Mackinnon's presence. 'Is that why you made your appointment with him?' he asked, with more interest than jealousy, he hoped.

'Darling, he's . . . he was your dentist, Belinda's dentist and yet more important, your mother's dentist. I wouldn't have dared go to anyone else. Besides, I'm far too frightened of dentists to care about their looks. And everyone said he was a very good dentist.'

'He was.'

'I was just making the point that any man so attractive would have to beat off the applicants for the position of mistress. Which is a shockingly vulgar thing to say and I hope you're not writing it down, Sergeant.'

'Not me, ma'am.'

'Good. Incidentally, as an additional indication, I think you'll find the Talmadges have . . . had separate bedrooms.'

'I suppose we'll have to go through all his records and pick out the eligible patients,' Alec groaned.

'Yes. What fun for you, darling. Now I really think I've told you everything I can remember—'

'And a good deal else besides!'

She wrinkled her nose at him in the way that begged for a kiss, but this time he remembered Mackinnon's presence. 'I'd rather like to go home now. Bel's bringing a couple of school friends home for tea and I promised I'd be there. If I think of anything else, I'll write it down so I don't forget.'

'Right-o, love, off you go. Do you want a taxi?'

'No, I'd rather walk. I shall contemplate the daffodils and

put everything that's happened this afternoon out of my mind for a while.'

Alec wondered momentarily why she needed to be home when Belinda brought her friends home from school. His straitlaced mother had not been an ideal person to bring up his daughter after Joan's death, but that was one thing she had never cavilled at.

What, never?

Hardly ever.

That one time had driven Belinda to run away. If this was the same child visiting again, he was glad to have Daisy to sort out the situation. He dismissed it from his mind and returned to the case before him.

By that time, the dead dentist, daffodils and her mother-in-law had already ceased to claim Daisy's immediate attention. When she reached the Talmadges' front hall, she saw Gladys peering out through the coloured glass panel beside the front door. The housemaid swung round.

'Are you leaving, ma'am? You don't want to go this way. A reporter come knocking on the door, bold as you please, and Constable Atkinson, he come running after and says he's trespassing. Seems he climbed over the wall! Did you ever? Mr A shooed him back to the street and he's closed the gates, ma'am, and there's more people there now, too, so if I was you I'd go out the back way.'

'Thank you, Gladys, I will, if you'll explain how to get there.'

'It's easy, ma'am. Just go out the back door by the kitchen and down the drive and past the garridge. You'll see a gate.

There's an old alley or lane, not much more'n a footpath. A ginnel Cook calls it, that's from Yorkshire.'

'I'll try it. Thank you.'

As Daisy turned back, the rumble of Tom Tring's voice came from the dining room. Gladys giggled.

'He's a caution, that Sergeant Tring. Ever so nice, really. I don't mind telling you, ma'am, I was shaking in my shoes when Miss Kidd said he wanted to see me, but he wasn't a bit scary. He was even nice when I had to say I don't know nothing. I wish I could've helped him,' she added regretfully, 'but Miss Kidd, she never tells me nothing. Cook and her stop talking when I come in.'

'Where were you around midday?'

'Me and Miss Kidd had our dinner around noon, in the kitchen, and I laid Mr Talmadge's lunch in the dining room, then we went up to the sewing room. It's up on the second floor by our bedrooms, and it's only got one window, the opposite side from the drive. We didn't hear nothing nor see nobody.'

'What a pity.'

Daisy returned down the hall to the back door. Passing the kitchen door, she nearly went in to tell Alec about the alley, and also that Cook might be privy to any secrets known to Hilda Kidd. But a glance at her watch made her hurry on. She didn't know how far out of her way the alley would take her, and no doubt Alec would find out about it for himself.

The back garden was bright with tulips, hyacinths and pansies, growing in ranks in formal beds surrounded by low box hedges. It reminded Daisy of the formal, comfortless drawing room, though pansies are incapable of real formality. The whole added up to a show place, not a home, suggesting the residents' emotional needs were satisfied elsewhere – if at all.

When she reached the garage, she saw that the gravel continued in a narrower path around the side. Until she came to the rear corner of the small building, it hid the wooden gate in the garden wall. In the narrow space between the garage and the wall lurked a compost heap and a rubbish incinerator, which emitted a trickle of noisome smoke.

The bandages and sticking plaster which had killed Talmadge might even now be smouldering there. She hesitated, wondering if she ought to take a look.

A choking wisp of smoke reached her nostrils and dissuaded her. If she went back to Alec, she'd only find that Mackinnon already knew all about it. In any case, it was a very slow fire. Anything not already consumed could wait another ten minutes. She'd ring up from home and ask Alec whether anyone had looked in there.

The wooden gate in the wall had a bolt, but it was held firmly in the open position by rust. The latch worked easily, though, and the gate swung on its hinges without a squeak. Before she stepped through, Daisy checked that there were no footprints approaching the gate for her to spoil.

The alley was about six feet wide, between walls, fences and hedges separating it from the gardens on either side. It was cobbled, the mortar between the stones long crumbled away. Grass and dandelions grew along the sides, but the centre was clear, so presumably used regularly. The cobbles showed no footprints, and a patch of gravel from the path, spreading in a fan beyond the gate, was equally unhelpful.

As she approached the end of the alley, a whistling errand

boy on a bicycle turned in from the street. Seeing her, he stopped and backed out again to leave room for her to pass.

'Afternoon, miss,' he called, touching his cap. 'Beautiful day, eh?'

'Lovely. Do you often ride this way?'

'Now an' then. It's a good shortcut, see, 'cause of them dead-end streets.'

'Most convenient,' Daisy agreed, taking note of the shop name on the packages in his basket: J. Witherbee, Chemist. Alec might want to ask J. Witherbee's boy if he'd seen anyone unusual in the alley earlier today.

She hurried on. Halfway home, the beautiful day dissolved in another shower. At that point she remembered that her umbrella was waiting for her in the waiting room – always supposing it hadn't been impounded by the police as a valuable clue. Far from providing shelter, the plane trees lining the streets simply gathered the rain and deposited it in great splotches instead of small drops.

Feeling damp, Daisy turned into Gardenia Grove. A dark red Sunbeam tourer with gleaming brass and a dark-skinned chauffeur passed her and pulled up before the Fletchers' garden gate. Before the chauffeur could get out to open the doors, three little girls in navy blue school uniforms scrambled out of the rear. After them, at a more leisurely pace, came a flamboyant figure in a yellow sari embroidered with green leaves, a shawl covering her glossy black hair. The chauffeur raised a large black umbrella over her.

'Poor Mummy, have you been at the dentist all this time?' cried Belinda, ginger pigtails flying as she ran to hug Daisy.

'Sort of, darling. Hello, Deva. Hello, Lizzie. Sakari, too sweet of you to bring the girls from school.'

'Thank you very much, Mrs Prasad,' said Belinda, echoed by Lizzie.

'Go on into the house, girls,' Daisy said. 'I hope you'll stay for a cup of tea, Sakari?' She touched cheeks with the plump Indian woman, conscious of the exotic fragrance of her.

Sakari murmured, 'Ulterior motive, I am afraid, Daisy.' She spoke excellent English, her accent making her sound formal even at her most colloquial. Her dark eyes sparkled with mischief. 'I brought Melanie, also. She is cowering in the car, hoping you will not think us too vulgarly inquisitive for words.'

'So you've heard already.' Daisy sighed, going to peer into the hooded back of the car. 'Mel, come along, do. I'm getting wet. I'll tell you what I can, and probably more than I ought.'

'Oh, Daisy dear, how dreadful for you!' Melanie Germond's husband was the local bank manager, as Alec's father had been. As his wife, Mel was eminently acceptable to St John's Wood society, but she was frightfully shy.

Despite this handicap, she had championed the Prasads' entrée into the social life of the neighbourhood, though there were still plenty of houses where the Indian couple were not invited. These had, until Daisy's marriage, included the Fletcher household under old Mrs Fletcher's sway. Daisy had met both women through Belinda's school, and had grown very fond them.

'Kesin,' Daisy said to the chauffeur, 'if you go to the kitchen, Dobson will give you a cup of tea.'

'Sank you, madam.' He bowed to her, hands folded together, and looked to Sakari, who nodded. He went off to the kitchen door while Daisy took her friends into the house.

The girls were already in the dining room, chattering over

a lavish spread laid out in advance by Dobson. Daisy, pausing
in the doorway, hoped the cook-maid had saved some cake
and biscuits for the grown-ups.

Belinda saw her. 'I told Gran I'm home, Mummy, and I
said you are too, so she needn't bother with us.'

'Right-o, darling. Don't forget to take Nana out, between
showers.'

So Bel had neatly evaded a confrontation with her
grandmother over Deva, leaving Daisy to face her unprepared
mother-in-law with Sakari in tow. Daisy wondered whether
Mrs Fletcher had already heard about the murder. Her
involvement was bound to be another bone of contention.
Not that there would be a vulgar row, just pointed arrows
sent her way at every opportunity.

Swallowing a sigh, she led the way to the sitting room.

Mrs Fletcher's lips tightened when she saw the Indian
woman. Her cold 'How do you do' was aimed somewhere
between Sakari and Mel. Placing a bookmark in the book she
had been reading, she stood up. 'I'm glad you're home at last,
Daisy. Will you keep an eye on the children? I have one or
two errands to run.'

'Have you had tea, Mother?'

'I shall have mine at the tea shop in the High Street.' Thus
making it plain – and no doubt telling any cronies she met
there – that she had been driven from her home by her
daughter-in-law's insistence on entertaining unsuitable
people. She stalked out, her drab silk skirts rustling reproachfully.

The room seemed the warmer for her absence. It was a
pleasant room, looking southwest over the back garden, now
sunny again. Alec's first wife had had the ponderous 'good'

Victorian furniture re-upholstered in gay prints and the walls painted white. A cheerful view of Paris hung over the fireplace, in front of which, on a low table, Alec and Belinda's unfinished chess game from last night awaited them.

'Sit down,' Daisy invited. 'I simply must ring up Alec, but I won't be a moment.'

'Clues!' Sakari pronounced gleefully. 'You have thought of some clues which he missed.'

'I'm sure Detective Chief Inspector Fletcher wouldn't miss any clues,' Mel protested.

'I can't be sure, that's why I must ring him. I'll tell Dobson to bring tea.'

'Then you will return and tell us all.'

'Some of it, anyway,' Daisy promised, laughing.

Tom Tring answered the Talmadges' phone. London operators were usually too busy to listen in, but she chose her words with care, just in case, as she told him about the alley and the errand boy and the incinerator.

'Maybe I should have come back to the house to tell you right away. If there was anything burning, it might be gone by now.'

'I shouldn't worry, Mrs Fletcher. Those things burn slow. We'll have a look, but – I'll tell you, though the Chief may have my hide for it – we found what I expect you're thinking of in the waste bin in the surgery.'

'Oh, good. I nearly looked in there, but I couldn't face it.'

'Nor should you have,' he said in what was supposed to be a reproving voice. Daisy could practically hear his splendid moustache twitching as it covered a grin. 'The Chief sent young Ernie off with the stuff to the lab at the Yard, to make sure it's what we were looking for.'

'I should think it must be. Dentists can't have much use for that sort of thing.'

'Not unless they let the drill slip and—'

'Don't, Tom!' Daisy exclaimed, reminded that she still had to see a dentist. 'Did the servants have anything interesting to say?'

'Now, that I can't tell you, Mrs Fletcher, or the Chief really will have my hide. If that's all, I'd better go and see to that incinerator. There might be something in it we haven't thought of.'

'Just one thing more. Gladys told me Hilda Kidd and Cook – Mrs Thorpe – often stopped talking when she went into the kitchen.'

'So Miss Gladys told me.'

'Right-o, Tom. Cheerio, then.'

''Bye, Mrs Fletcher, and thanks for the tips.'

Daisy said goodbye, hung up and returned to the sitting room. Dobson had brought tea and biscuits, but Daisy was not allowed to enjoy them in peace. Though she tried not to tell her friends more than she ought, she was too tired to guard her tongue. She most definitely should not have let slip that Alec was looking for patients who might have been having an affair with Raymond Talmadge.

'Oh dear, I hope neither of you was a patient of his?'

Sakari and Mel exchanged a look.

'We both went to him once or twice,' said Sakari. 'And we both, independently, disliked his attitude more than we liked his expertise.'

'His attitude?'

'Condescending,' Mel said in her soft voice.

'He thought he was the cat's pyjamas. What is more to the

point, he did not trouble to hide his contempt for those of us who have not been blessed with perfect teeth. I am sure – do you not agree, Mel? – that Raymond Talmadge would never make love to a woman with whose rotting teeth he was intimately acquainted.'

CHAPTER 7

The telephone bell rang in the front hall. Daisy heard Belinda go to answer it, and a moment later her stepdaughter appeared in the doorway.

'It's for you, Mummy. Mrs Grantchester. I told her you are entertaining guests.' Belinda pronounced this newly acquired phrase with pride. 'She said it's urgent.'

'Thank you, darling. What on earth can she want? I hardly know her. Excuse me a minute,' Daisy said to Mel and Sakari. She went out to the hall. 'Hello, this is Daisy Fletcher.'

'*Oh*, Mrs Fletcher, I *do* hope you'll excuse the short notice. I was wondering whether you could *possibly* come to luncheon tomorrow, *quite* informal, just a few local ladies, I'm sure you know most of them.'

Daisy's immediate impulse was to hunt for an excuse. She didn't particularly like Mrs Grantchester, a large, gushing woman, and she suspected her company was wanted mostly for what she could tell of Talmadge's death. On the other hand, she might pick up useful gossip about the Talmadges for Alec, though middle-class matrons didn't gossip half as much as she had expected before becoming one of them. Also her usual excuse was invalid: she had just finished an article and her next was not due for a fortnight.

Her pause for thought had lasted long enough to be noticed.

'Oh, *please* say you'll come,' Mrs Grantchester begged. 'I know you write – so *adventurous* of you. I *always* read your articles – but we won't keep you *long*, just an hour or so. All *work* and no *play* . . . you know what they say.'

Definitely Daisy didn't like Mrs Grantchester. She started to beg off: 'It's very kind of you, but—'

'*Splendid!*' the beastly woman overrode her. 'We'll see you at one o'clock. Oh, and I nearly forgot, of *course* your dear mama-in-law is invited too.' She rang off before Daisy could protest.

Her mama-in-law's inclusion in no way reconciled her to the luncheon, but now that her acceptance was assumed, it was impossible to back out without giving offence. Sighing, she jiggled the hook on the telephone apparatus to call the operator. She must let Alec know that Talmadge's mistress, if any, was probably not a patient.

'Hello, caller, you have an incoming call. Do you want to take it or make your own call?'

'I'll take it,' said Daisy. 'Hello? St John's Wood 2351.'

'Hello, Mrs Fletcher? This is Marianne Randall. I do hope this isn't a bad time to ring?'

Mrs Randall, with apologies for the short notice, wanted Daisy and Alec to come to dinner tomorrow. Alec might well have to work late? Never mind, her brother could always be called in at the last minute to make up the numbers if necessary. Daisy simply must come anyway.

On the spur of the moment, Daisy failed to think up a better excuse.

Marianne Randall hung up at last and Daisy phoned Alec.

He groaned when he heard that Talmadge's lover probably was not a patient.

'The prospect of digging through his files was bad enough. We'll still have to do that, but if your friends are right, the field is wide open. We'll just have to hope someone will report having seen him with a lady-friend.'

'Don't despair, darling. I'll see what I can find out.'

'Daisy, don't—'

'I must run. They're waiting. Bye-bye, darling.' Prohibition averted, Daisy returned to the sitting room.

In the next hour, she received another five invitations for the next two days. She managed to decline three, only because they arrived in the form of servant-borne notes, not telephone calls.

'Gosh! I've never been so popular in my life,' she said as she penned an answer to the latest note. 'I thought the ladies of St John's Wood were unnaturally immune to gossip, but this puts paid to that theory.'

'It is the murder of one of their own,' Sakari declared. 'It has overcome their inhibitions.' She was an inveterate attender of public lectures, including a recent series on Freud.

'Few of them have any inhibitions about gossiping,' said Mel. 'If you haven't heard much, Daisy, it's because they don't indulge when you're around.'

'Why?' Daisy demanded, astonished. 'Do they think I'm not interested? A writer is always interested in people.'

'That's one reason I've heard mentioned,' Mel told her. 'That you're a writer, I mean. A journalist, if not a reporter. I think they're afraid you might write about them.'

'What else?'

'Well, I know you don't like it mentioned, but you *are* an Honourable.'

'This I have heard,' said Sakari: '"Servants talk about people, ladies and gentlemen talk about things."'

'So my nanny used to tell us,' Daisy admitted, 'but if it's true, I know very few true ladies and gentlemen. I can't believe people think I'd disapprove, just because I've got an honorary title in front of my name, which I don't even use. Except when my editors insist, but I insist on still using Dalrymple with it, not my married name.'

'There is another reason people are reticent, Daisy. You are married to a police detective.'

'But . . .' Daisy stared at Sakari. 'As if Alec would care about common or garden gossip! Honestly, anyone would think they were all criminals.'

'I suppose lots of people have something they'd rather the police didn't know,' Melanie murmured.

'In that case, it's very odd of them to come out of the woodwork just when Alec *will* be interested in their secrets, in case they have some bearing on the murder. Maybe they expect to pump me without giving anything away.'

Sakari shook her head. 'That is part of it, perhaps, but I suspect it is rather that they look on you as an intermediary. If I had possibly useful information, I should much prefer to reveal it to you rather than the police. Many people know that you have assisted Mr Fletcher in a number of his murder cases.'

'How?' Daisy demanded indignantly. 'I've never breathed a word, not even to you two, and Alec certainly wouldn't, let alone his mother. Oh – Belinda?'

'I'm afraid she told Lizzie,' Mel confirmed.

'And Deva.' Sakari smiled, in a friendly way enjoying Daisy's discomfiture.

'The girls told us. Naturally, we haven't spoken of it, but they must have chattered to other friends. You know what girls are.'

At least they could know only about the few cases Bel had been involved in, Daisy realized with relief. 'No use crying over spilt milk,' she said. 'The only question is, will it make people more likely or less likely to tell me things?'

'Then you *are* sleuthing?' cried Sakari. 'What did I tell you, Melanie? May we help?'

'Sorry, Alec would kill me if I let you get mixed up in it. He's always trying to keep me out.'

'Men are so often unreasonable, even Englishmen,' the Indian woman sighed.

'I'm sure Mr Fletcher is only trying to keep Daisy safe,' said Mel, the peacemaker. 'After all, there is a murderer somewhere about. I hope people won't give you information which will endanger you, Daisy, but I rather think they're all secretly thrilled and dying to bare their souls.'

When Daisy hung up on him, Alec nearly rang her right back to order her not to meddle in the case. That was undoubtedly what Superintendent Crane and the AC would expect him to do. What they didn't comprehend was that at the best of times a modern young woman like Daisy didn't take kindly to orders. Now, with the bit between her teeth, there wasn't the slightest hope of Alec's reining her in.

He consoled himself with the thought that she had so far remained somewhat aloof from such society as St John's Wood afforded.

Not that Daisy was a snob. Alec had seen her take up arms

on behalf of an undergardener and chat happily with a shop girl. But her only real friends in the neighbourhood were Mrs Germond and Mrs Prasad, neither of whom he expected to find on his suspect list – though one could never be sure.

The rest of the Talmadges' social circle were mere acquaintances. Daisy couldn't very well approach them with leading questions about Raymond Talmadge's mistress. For once she would have to stay out of his investigation in spite of having found the body.

Alec surveyed the study where he had been when Daisy's call came through. It was really an office, not the sort of place where a man could retire to smoke a pipe and sip a glass of whisky and soda with a friend. The bookcase contained only dental reference books and journals. A quick look through the drawers of the desk had turned up nothing but stationery supplies, bank statements and a locked cash box small enough for any burglar to pocket. The cabinet held ledgers with the financial records of Talmadge's practice.

Sooner or later, someone would have to go through the records, looking for a financial motive for murder. It was a job for Ernie Piper, who was good with figures, good at spotting numbers that didn't quite fit. Fraud seemed improbable in a dental practice, but blackmail was always a possibility.

'Any love letters, Chief?' Tom came in, his bulk making the small room seem even smaller.

'Nothing but business as far as I can see. No locked . . .' Alec sniffed. 'Tom, what *have* you been doing?'

'Raking through a bonfire Mrs Fletcher came across at the bottom of the garden. I didn't touch anything, just raked it over, but the smoke must've got into my clothes. Smells a bit, doesn't it?'

'Just a bit.' Alec fanned the air with the blotter. 'I suppose it will wear off. Did you find anything of interest?'

Tom shook his head. 'Garden rubbish and kitchen scraps. No luck in here?'

'Not even a locked drawer. I doubt there's much in this.' He pushed the cash box across the desk. 'You have the keys we found on the body.'

The box contained a chequebook and nearly fifty pounds in coins, notes and cheques. 'Cor, that the morning's take, d'you think? I'm in the wrong job.'

'He probably doesn't go to the bank every day. Is that the lot?'

'Not a love letter to be seen.'

'Hilda Kidd confirmed that Talmadge had a lady friend, did she?'

'Not exactly. That is, she swears he did – says she's prepared to swear to it in court if she has to – but when you ask how she knows, it all comes down to a "feeling". Could be she just hasn't worked out what gives her that feeling, or could be plain spite. She detested Talmadge.'

'So I gathered. To the point of doing him in?'

Tom's boundless forehead creased in a frown. 'I don't think so. I mean, if she'd caught him knocking his wife about she might've picked up a poker and whopped him over the head. Not the sort of nasty, cold-blooded business we've got here, even if she knew how. But if Mrs Talmadge did it, Hilda Kidd would cover up for her like a shot. She's kicking herself for having mentioned Creighton. Tried to make out she'd been joking.'

'So you didn't get anything useful from her? What about the other girl, the housemaid?'

'Quite a bright girl, that. She reckoned she'd have noticed if there was any carrying-on here in the house. The Talmadges never had a row, not that she heard, just mostly went their own ways. They never spent an evening at home together unless they were entertaining. She did say Miss Kidd and Cook likely know more than she does. They often stopped talking when she went into the kitchen.'

'When is the cook due back?'

'Six o'clock.'

'Right-o, Tom, you wait here for her, and in the meantime take a look around the rest of the house. I wish I could talk to Mrs Talmadge. Failing that, I'll have a go at Creighton. Mackinnon is checking with the neighbours. When Ernie gets back, he can start on the patient files.'

'Making a list of all the eligible females?'

'All those between eighteen and forty, at least. Though unfortunately it has been suggested that Talmadge probably wouldn't fall for a patient.'

'Pity! Where do we start looking?'

'We may have to ask the press for help,' Alec said reluctantly. 'See if you can find a photograph of Talmadge so that we don't have to use one of the body. He was distinctive enough for people to remember seeing him and with luck someone will be able to describe his companion.'

'Let's hope.'

'We won't do it unless we have to.'

'You going to have a word with the press boys out front now?'

'No, it can wait till tomorrow. Maybe by then we'll have more idea of whom we're looking for. Anything else?'

'When Mrs Fletcher rang up about the bonfire, she also

told me there's an alley out the back that errand boys use for a shortcut, and she gave me the name of the employer of a lad she met there. I took a look at the path, but it's paved, so no help there.'

Alec checked his watch. 'The shops'll be closing any minute. You'd better get on to the boy first thing in the morning.'

'Right, Chief.'

Tom went off to search the rest of the house. While Alec waited to hear from Ernie Piper, he had a closer look at the contents of the cabinet. At the end of the top shelf, he found two file boxes marked Personal.

One contained documents pertaining to the ownership of the house, showing that Mrs Talmadge had inherited the freehold from her father. The other contained various other papers, including Talmadge's discharge from the Royal Army Medical Corps and two wills. The latter were dated just after the beginning of the war, nearly ten years ago. Raymond Talmadge's will left everything to his wife; hers left everything to him except for two hundred pounds to Hilda Kidd.

Alec wondered whether either had made a new will since then. He was noting down the solicitor's name when the phone rang. It was Piper, reporting that Lord Henry Creighton, youngest son of the Marquess of Addlestoke, resided in a service flat in Mayfair.

'I talked to the man who valets Creighton, Chief. He says his lordship is generally home between six and half past seven, preparing for an evening out. His lordship dines out practically every evening during the Season. A very popular and sociable gentleman, his lordship is.'

Always willing to make up a hostess' numbers at the last minute, Alec guessed cynically. 'Good job,' he said. 'I'd better get over there right away. And I want you back here to go through the files.'

'Now, Chief? Have a heart, it's rush hour.'

'Get something to eat in the canteen before you come. It's going to be a long evening.' Alec explained what he wanted Ernie to look for, then hung up.

He went to tell Tom he was leaving. Tom had found a studio portrait of Talmadge in Medical Corps uniform. The cap hid the pale hair which was his most conspicuous feature.

'It'll do in a pinch, but see if you can find something without a hat. I'm off to see Creighton. Ernie should be here soon. When Mackinnon comes in, he'd better go back to his station and write up a report. Do you think you can work with him?'

'Seems like a good enough lad. As long as he exhibits the deference due to the position of a Yard man—'

'And to your age and girth, of course. Right-o, I'll put in a request to have him seconded to me for the case. I'll phone here after I've talked to Creighton, and either come back here or meet you at the Yard, depending on what we've discovered.'

'Why do these things always happen on steak-and-kidney pud night?' Tom mourned.

'Be nice to Mrs Thorpe,' Alec advised, 'and maybe you'll get whatever she'd planned for the Talmadges.'

He had left the Baby Austin in the street at the front, so he had to leave that way. A glance from the window of the study had shown him that the throng of gentlemen of the press had thinned somewhat.

Assisted by Constable Atkinson, Alec ploughed through the diminished crowd. He placated them with confirmation that Scotland Yard was investigating a suspicious death and a promise of a statement in the morning. As he drove off, they scattered to quiz the neighbours. In this affluent neighbourhood they were not likely to get much satisfaction except, perhaps, from the servants.

Thinking back on the faces he had recognized, he realized that those who had departed earlier were the evening rags' reporters. The late editions' stop-press columns would be full of the death of a dentist, sinister or mysterious, according to taste. Neither the *Evening Standard* nor the *Evening News* was noted for waiting for official confirmation. They would undoubtedly announce that the Yard was on the spot.

If Creighton was involved in Talmadge's death, he would surely have bought a paper. By now he knew that – largely thanks to Daisy, Alec admitted – the police had not been fooled into dismissing murder as an unfortunate but foreseeable accident.

CHAPTER 8

Creighton lived in Mayfair, in one of the blocks of flats erected where a Zeppelin raid had levelled most of a street of gracious Georgian town houses. The marble lobby, too cramped to be elegant, was guarded by a Commissionaire in the full glory of his braided, brass-buttoned and bemedalled uniform.

Alec asked for Lord Henry Creighton.

'Is his lordship expecting you, sir?'

'No.' At least, he hoped not.

'I'll just ring through on the house phone.'

'No, don't do that. I'm a police officer. I have a few questions to ask Lord Henry and I'd prefer to do so without prior warning.' He presented his credential.

One hand that reached for it had two fingers missing and both were badly scarred. The man shook his head dubiously. 'Well, I'm sure I dunno, sir. As a general rule we don't like police in the house. When we get 'em, it's usually a summons for driving a motorcar without due care and attention, or pinching a bobby's helmet on Boat Race night, or summat like that.' He studied the warrant card with a worried frown. 'Detective Chief Inspector— This wouldn't be anything like that, I s'pose.'

'Not exactly.'

Looking up, the man noticed Alec's tie and his face cleared. 'Royal Flying Corps, sir? That's where I ended up, transferred out of the Navy. Flight Sergeant Cummings, sir.'

'Happy to see you've fallen on your feet, Sergeant.'

'Wait a bit – Fletcher – not Arrow Fletcher, sir? The only spotter that always brought home the goods?'

'Usually,' Alec amended. Flying a single-seater observer aeroplane during the war, he had become renowned as one of the few who actually found their objectives most of the time.

He was glad that he had dashed home to change his tie. Failing a public school Old Boys' tie, he found his RFC colours often made his intrusions just a trifle less obnoxious to the upper levels of society.

'What's this Lord Henry like, Sergeant?'

'A nice, quiet gentleman, sir, always a pleasant word. Can't see him doing nothing as'd interest a Scotland Yard 'tec.'

'He probably hasn't. We spend as much time clearing the innocent as catching the guilty. Does Lord Henry do much entertaining?'

'Not what you might call a lot, sir. These here service flats, they've got dining rooms you couldn't swing a cat in – if so be you was wanting to do such a nasty, cruel thing – and the kitchens is no more than a place to boil a kettle or wash up a few glasses. His lordship has a friend or two in for drinks now and then, and maybe once or twice a month a luncheon or dinner for four sent up from our restaurant. We got all the facilities right here on the premises.'

'Very convenient.'

'If that's what you likes. I'm a family man meself.'

'So am I,' Alec hastened to assure him. 'Any ladies visiting Lord Henry?'

'His mother, the Marchioness, and his sisters, Lady Ann and Lady Alice. Then there's a married couple, Captain and Mrs Dixon.' Flight Sergeant Cummings's craggy face managed to look coy. 'And there's another lady comes with 'em, often as not. I never heard her name.'

'A looker, is she?'

'Dunno, sir. She always wears this veil on her hat that hides her face, like ladies wear for motoring. As for the rest of her, as you might say, she dresses very smart and her shape's what's fashionable nowadays, though we'd've called it skinny in my young day.'

Alec thought with gratitude of Daisy's cuddlesome curves. 'This mysterious lady always arrives with the Dixons?' he asked. Dixon! – the name might almost as well be Smith, even with the 'Captain' before it, if he had to run the couple to earth.

'Ah, now, as to that I can only speak to my shift, which is eight in the morning till eight at night, Tuesdays off and half day Saturday. *I* never seen her without them, coming or going, which ain't to say Bert, that's on night shift, hasn't. Which ain't to say he'll tell you if he has, being PBI and sour as an unripe gooseberry.'

A Poor Bloody Infantryman, looked down on by every other branch of the services, was not to be won over by an RFC tie, Cummings implied. Alec grinned at him. 'I came at the right time. You've been most helpful, Sergeant. I'll go on up now and see what Lord Henry has to say.'

'Right you are, sir. Fifth floor, second door to your right'

Alec went on to the lift, where a cheeky-looking lift boy

had been standing watching his conversation with Cummings. 'Fifth floor, guv? 'Ang on tight!'

The lift cage jerked into motion and they moved with ponderous stateliness upwards past floor after floor. The corridors visible through the door were narrow but carpeted, with prints on the walls. This was definitely an expensive place to live. Creighton might be a younger son but he was not a poor man.

Alec considered asking the lift boy for further information about Creighton. Better not, he decided. The lad couldn't be expected to adhere to the code of discretion required of the old soldiers of the Corps of Commissionaires. If he knew, the world would soon hear of Scotland Yard's interest in the Marquess of Addlestoke's youngest son. Alec wasn't unduly impressed by aristocratic rank, but unnecessary tittle-tattle would not please his superiors, already annoyed by Daisy's involvement.

He could always question the lift boy later if the information he needed was not forthcoming directly from Creighton.

Delivered to the fifth floor, Alec rang Creighton's doorbell. The man who opened the door could have stepped straight from a *Punch* caricature. Tall and thin, with too much nose, not enough chin and a pronounced widow's peak, he wore a midnight blue silk dressing gown over his shirt, waistcoat and trousers. He peered at Alec through a gold-rimmed monocle.

'I say, my dear fellow, am I expecting you?'

'Not exactly, sir.' Alec handed over his card.

'Oh, right-o. The fact is, I've a rotten memory for appointments – need to get a secretary, eh, what? – and people do get upset if you don't remember they're coming. As a matter of fact,' he went on apologetically, 'I usually take my bath about this time.'

'I hope I shan't have to take up much of your time, sir.' Alec advanced into the small entrance hall.

He thought Creighton was going to stand firm, but after a moment his lordship took a step backwards. Then he turned away with a gentle sigh, raising Alec's card towards his face. Pushing the door shut behind him, Alec watched and thought he saw Creighton stiffen but could not be sure.

'New Scotland Yard?' he murmured. 'Do come in and sit down, Chief Inspector. To what do I owe the honour?' His tone was gently ironic, the first hint that the man was not the fool he appeared.

Alec glanced around the spacious room. One long wall was entirely occupied by theatrical memorabilia. Playbills and posters vied with photographs of actors and actresses in and out of costume. Lord Henry appeared in some of the photos, and some were inscribed, presumably to him, in showy handwriting.

Below this display, low shelves ran the length of the room. On top stood a number of busts. Thanks to his university studies of the Georgian age, Alec recognized three nearby as Goldsmith, Sheridan and Edmund Kean; presumably the rest were also theatrical luminaries. The lower shelves held books. The few titles Alec could read without going closer were plays and books about the theatre.

The opposite wall had two doors with a fireplace between them where a welcoming fire flickered. Above the mantelpiece hung a portrait of Sarah Bernhardt as Cleopatra. Comfortable chairs were grouped about the fireplace.

Alec walked the length of the room to take a seat on the straight chair at the escritoire between the two tall windows. He turned it to face an easy chair placed to catch the light from the window. On the occasional table beside the armchair lay a book with a leather bookmark protruding.

After a moment's hesitation, Creighton followed and sat in the designated seat. 'Well?' he asked.

'Have you read an evening paper, sir?'

'No. As a rule I only see the *Morning Post*, unless I have a review in one of the others. I review plays. Er . . . Was there something of interest to me in the late news?'

Alec said bluntly, 'The death of a suburban dentist.'

Creighton blinked. His face, naturally pale, was very hard to read because of the monocle, which made one eye look smaller than the other and distorted the whole picture. Behind the impassive façade his brain was alert, for only a few seconds passed before he sighed and said, 'I assume I can guess the dentist's name, and that he did not die a natural death, or you would not be here. Mrs Talmadge told me her husband occasionally indulged in a whiff of laughing gas. I suppose he took an accidental overdose.'

'Not exactly.'

'Don't tell me he killed himself? How perfectly dreadful!'

'I'm afraid not, sir. We are fairly certain it was murder.'

'Murder.' Creighton pronounced the word without a tremor, then fell silent, contemplating it. Alec waited. 'Mrs Talmadge told you we lunched together?'

That was easy, Alec thought. 'I'm glad to have confirmation of that, sir. I hope you can also confirm times and places?' He took out his fountain pen and notebook, wishing he had Piper, or even Daisy, to take notes for him.

Creighton's face remained calm, but he started to tap steadily with one finger on the arm of his chair. He was beginning to realize the complications of his position.

If he had been unaware of Talmadge's death, he could have no idea when it took place or whether the dentist's wife was involved. Thus, assuming he cared for her deeply, he could not know whether he ought to try to provide an alibi for her, and if so, for what period.

On the other hand, if Creighton had been involved in the planning or execution of the murder, he and Daphne Talmadge would surely have concocted a credible story. In that case, he only had to worry about her remembering the details correctly. It would have been easiest to cover as brief a period as possible. So if Creighton presented an alibi covering only luncheon, that would seem to point to his guilt, or at least to knowledge of his mistress's guilt.

'We met at eleven,' he said, 'or a few minutes after. Mrs Talmadge took a taxi to New Bond Street and I was waiting when she arrived.'

'New Bond Street?'

'Yes, we went to a preview of an auction at Sotheby's. As you may be aware, Sarah Bernhardt died last year. Her collection is to come under the hammer, including the manuscripts of the two plays she herself wrote. Here.' He took a catalogue from under the book on the table beside him, and handed it to Alec. 'You'll see my notes on the various items.'

Alec riffled through the pages. 'I see, sir, but I'm afraid this doesn't prove that you were there today. Did you see anyone you know?'

'Most people one knows go in the afternoon.'

'So no one can confirm your whereabouts.'

'Oh, I expect Truscott, their theatre expert, will remember me. I spoke to him. I thought you meant the sort of people one knows.'

'Truscott.' Alec wrote down the name. 'An auction room seems an odd place for a rendezvous with a lady.'

'Daph – Mrs Talmadge is as great an aficionado of the theatre as I am. She found the preview fascinating. Her husband, alas, is not interested, so I take her to a matinée now and then. She is an old friend.'

'You went to a matinée this afternoon?'

The tapping finger stilled. Alec guessed the questions racing through Creighton's mind: Did Daphne go straight home? What time did she get there, and do the police know it? What time did Raymond Talmadge die? *What time did Raymond Talmadge die?*

Unless, of course, he was actually thinking: How did they know it wasn't an accident or suicide? What went wrong?

Creighton played for time, the tapping finger resuming its betrayal. 'Let's take things in their proper order. When we had seen enough at Sotheby's, we decided to lunch, although it was still rather early.'

'Where did you go?'

'We strolled up to Oxford Street and popped into the first restaurant which appealed to her.'

'Which was . . . ?'

'I haven't the faintest idea, Chief Inspector. I seldom eat in that part of town and I didn't notice the name of the establishment. Nor can I recall what we ate. She . . . We had a great deal to talk about.'

Murder? 'I see, sir. Well, I dare say we can find the place. And which theatre did you go on to?'

'The New Theatre, to see Shaw's *Saint Joan*. A superb play, well worth seeing twice. Mrs Talmadge had missed the first night.'

'Did she enjoy it?'

'She . . .' A pause, then Creighton rose and stepped forward to stand facing the window, his fists clenched at his sides. The silence stretched.

'The truth is generally the best policy,' Alec said gently.

A long sigh followed, as if squeezed from Creighton's lanky frame like lava from a volcano, by intolerable internal pressures. Yet, as he turned back to Alec, he managed an ironic comment: 'I notice you say "generally", not always, Chief Inspector. However, being uncertain what lie may serve in the circumstances, which remain unclear to me, I find myself driven back upon the truth. Mrs Talmadge did not attend the theatre with me.'

Alec's sigh was silent. He had manoeuvred Lord Henry into a position where he had either to lie about the theatre or to confine himself to the feeble lunchtime alibi. Choosing the latter might mean that he was aware of the time of death – or it might mean that he was innocent and felt that a lie was likely to be disproved and therefore to arouse unwarranted suspicion.

In either case, Alec was convinced that his lordship was concealing something more than an illicit relationship with a married woman. Otherwise a man of his social rank would surely not have answered with such patience questions he must regard as impertinent.

'One of my men will be speaking to Mr Truscott at

Sotheby's, sir, and of course we'll be trying to find the restaurant you patronized. I don't suppose you have a photograph you could let me have, of you and Mrs Talmadge?'

'Only a very old . . . one of myself. I'll fetch it.' He hurried out through the nearer door.

There were plenty of recent photos on the wall, though Creighton might be reluctant to part with one. So his pause and quick recovery meant he had kept a photo of the two of them, probably from before her marriage, which argued that he had at least a deep affection for her. Deep enough to try to protect her, knowing she was a murderess? Deep enough to murder her husband for her sake?

Creighton returned with a faded, blurred photo of a school cricket team. He had to point out to Alec his own likeness, standing in the back row.

'Useless for identification, I'm afraid, sir. Perhaps you could spare me one of these?' Alec gestured at the theatrical wall.

For the first time, Creighton showed annoyance. 'One of my collection?'

'I'll do my best to see it's not damaged. We'll make copies to show around and return the original to you.'

'Oh, very well, if you must.' He chose an unsigned photograph of himself with an actor who had enjoyed a brief success three or four years ago, before sinking back into obscurity.

A passion for the theatre might be the link between him and Daphne Talmadge, but Alec wasn't prepared to bet on which he'd pick if forced to choose between his beloved and his memorabilia.

'Thank you, sir.' Alec started towards the entrance hall. 'We'll take good care of it. I may have some more questions for you later, so if you leave London I'd be grateful if you'd let me know your whereabouts.'

'I'm not going anywhere. Is ... is Mrs Talmadge greatly distressed?'

'Naturally.' His hand on the front-door knob, Alec turned to observe Creighton's reaction as he continued, 'As any woman would be having found her husband's murdered body.'

'My God! I must—'

'Mrs Talmadge is under heavy sedation, sir,' Alec added with some satisfaction. 'I'm afraid it's no good your trying to see her.'

It was frustrating not to be able to question his chief suspect, but at least the second on his list couldn't speak to her either.

CHAPTER 9

For Daisy, Mrs Grantchester's luncheon party started badly before she even left home. When she came downstairs, her mother-in-law was already waiting in the hall, toe tapping impatiently though Daisy had left plenty of time.

She took one look at Daisy, and asked, 'Is that what you're wearing to Mrs Grantchester's?'

'Yes,' said Daisy. She considered the plain amber crêpe frock a neat compromise, less dressy than would be appropriate to lunch in the West End, but more formal than a country house party. Maybe it was the hemline just below the knee Mrs Fletcher took exception to; or the hip-level belt – *she* still kept her waist where her waist had once been; or maybe the flesh-coloured stockings, though only old ladies wore black or white these days, and not all did.

Whatever her objection, she merely uttered a disapproving 'Hmm.'

Paying this as little heed as it deserved, Daisy went to the coat closet to get her coat. It was a beastly day, cold and rainy, the sullen drizzle quite unlike yesterday's smiling showers. She turned to the umbrella stand, and remembered she'd left her umbrella in Talmadge's waiting room.

'Blast!' Her mild epithet earned a pursed mouth from Mrs Fletcher.

Both Alec's and Belinda's umbrellas were gone. With a choice of sharing with her mother-in-law or getting wet, Daisy resigned herself to the latter. Thus she arrived at Mrs Grantchester's with her hat dripping and drooping over her ears and the shoulders of her coat soaked through.

The parlourmaid took their coats. On impulse, Daisy handed over her hat, too. The maid's eyes widened, and Mrs Fletcher's lips pursed so tight Daisy wondered if they would ever unknot again. Lunching out without a hat simply wasn't done, but she'd rather be thought eccentric than have it drip in her soup. No doubt her hostess and the other guests would blame her aristocratic background for the lapse. They might be right.

She felt entirely justified when, after her mother-in-law gave their names as 'Mrs Fletcher and Mrs Alec Fletcher,' the maid announced them as 'Mrs Fletcher and the Honourable Mrs Alec Fletcher.' She must have done so on prior instructions from Mrs Grantchester, with intent to impress.

Mrs Grantchester surged forward to greet them. Dressed in pale silk, she made Daisy think of a battleship swishing through the waves. She blinked at Daisy's bare head, but at least she didn't comment. She was far too keen to start on the topic of the day.

'My dear, it's too, too *brave* of you to join us. I'm sure I should be quite *prostrate* after what you went through yesterday.'

Daisy refrained from asking why, then, she had been invited. The room had fallen silent, awaiting her response. Trying to look brave, she said bravely, 'It's no good brooding, is it?'

An elderly lady sitting nearby said in a loud voice,

'Admirable, if you ask me. In my day we were expected to brood. You don't see these modern young things going into a decline over a lost lover.'

'Her dentist, Mother!' said the woman next to her in an agony of embarrassment. Daisy recognized Mrs and Miss Tebbit, and gave the latter a reassuring smile. When Mrs Tebbit responded with a wink, Daisy realized she had been deliberately outrageous and immediately wanted to know her better.

'An excellent dentist,' young Mrs Ledway lamented. 'So good with the children.'

Mrs Grantchester ignored this by-play. Having succeeded in snaring Daisy for her luncheon party, she abandoned restraint and asked bluntly, 'It was murder, I suppose? A chief inspector would hardly be called in for anything else.'

'We shall all be murdered in our beds!' That was Miss Petherington, who was given to premonitions of disaster.

'Better to be murdered in bed,' observed Mrs Tebbit, 'than anywhere else. So much more comfortable.'

'Nonsense,' said Mrs Grantchester. 'No doubt Mr Fletcher will very soon arrest the perfect *monster* who killed Raymond Talmadge. It must be quite *obvious* to him who did the *dreadful deed*, and it will be equally clear to us once Mrs Fletcher has told us all about it, won't it, Mrs Fletcher?'

The question was addressed to Daisy, as her mama-in-law had abandoned her to join a crony on the other side of the room, where they muttered darkly together.

Daisy had decided earlier that the best way to deflect questions she couldn't or shouldn't answer was to float a red herring. 'I'm sure we're all safe, Miss Petherington,' she said, 'not being dentists.'

Several people gasped.

'You mean there's a maniac going around killing dentists?' Mrs Grantchester asked, all agog.

'Who can blame him!' said Mrs Tebbit. 'I've always thought you have to be a bit of a sadist, in the modern idiom, to become a dentist.'

'Oh, Mother, how can you say such a thing?'

At that moment, the parlourmaid came in to announce luncheon.

Miss Cobb, a particular friend of the hostess, glanced around the company and asked, 'Didn't you say you were going to invite Mrs Walker, Julia?'

'I did, Ettie,' said Mrs Grantchester in a voice heavy with significance, 'but she *declined*. Shall we go through, ladies?'

Shepherded into the dining room with the rest of the flock, Daisy pondered the significance of Mrs Walker. There might well be more than one lady of that name in the neighbourhood, but the one her memory turned up was the wife of a Major Walker. Offhand, Daisy couldn't remember anything else about her.

Over luncheon, to her relief, the subjects of murder and dentists were studiously avoided. She was not lulled into imagining either had been abandoned. It was just the effect of the middle-class belief, not shared by the aristocracy, that if one didn't mention something in front of the servants they would not find out.

The talk was mostly of bridge and the relative merits of various resorts for summer holidays. To liven things up, Miss Petherington had a premonition that the south coast would be hit by a tidal wave in August. Hearing this, the parlourmaid almost dropped the sauceboat. However, under the eagle eye of her mistress, she recovered herself after merely dripping parsley sauce on Miss Cobb's sleeve.

Fortunately Miss Cobb didn't notice, being intent on proclaiming the superiority of her favourite resort, Buxton Spa, well out of reach of tidal waves.

Miss Tebbit, sitting beside Daisy, ventured to mention that she had enjoyed her last article in *Town and Country* magazine and to ask her about her next. Before Daisy could respond, Mrs Fletcher said from across the table, 'Such a nice hobby for Daisy, since she doesn't care for bridge.'

Daisy was tempted to respond that writing was her profession and sleuthing her hobby. She decided it was better not to remind people of the sleuthing. They might take fright and not tell her things if they couldn't pretend they were just exchanging gossip with someone like themselves.

So she held her peace, unlike Mrs Tebbit, who said, 'Writing is a dashed sight less of a waste of time than bridge. More lucrative too, I should hope. Though there are those who make a good thing of bridge.' She glared at her hostess.

Mrs Grantchester bridled and changed the subject to the new dressmaker in the High Street. Over treacle tart and custard, it was agreed that the competition with Delia's, the current favourite, ought to lower prices but probably would not. The conversation moved naturally to the pros and cons of the High Street hairdressing salon.

'I don't believe I've ever seen Mrs Alec Fletcher at our local *Salon de Beauté*,' observed Miss Cobb.

'I go to a hairdresser in Chelsea,' said Daisy. 'It's where I had my hair cut short, just last year. They did a good job with the shingle, and besides, it gives me an excuse to visit friends in the neighbourhood.'

'Such *interesting* people live in Chelsea,' said Mrs Grant-chester.

'It's not nearly as bohemian as it was in my young day,' Mrs Tebbit said regretfully.

'It's not a good place to bring up children,' Mrs Ledway contributed, 'or so I've heard. But I suppose you didn't have any to worry about then?'

'Not a single one,' Daisy agreed with a straight face, aware of her mother-in-law's outraged face but avoiding her eye. 'I enjoyed living there and I like going back now and then.'

'But you miss all our local news,' said Miss Cobb. 'The High Street salon is quite the best place for—'

'Shall we have coffee in the drawing room?' interrupted Mrs Grantchester, rising in a determined way. Everyone trailed after her obediently, back to the drawing room.

The parlourmaid brought in coffee. As the door closed behind her, Miss Cobb sat down beside Daisy. 'We're all dying to hear what happened yesterday,' she said.

A sudden silence attested to the accuracy of her words.

Daisy had already considered what she could say, knowing it would not satisfy them. 'I had an appointment with Mr Talmadge,' she explained. Her tooth gave a reminiscent twinge and she realized it hadn't made itself felt since yesterday. 'That's why I happened to be at his house when . . . when he was discovered. I telephoned for the doctor. And I happen to know that the police have to be notified of any unexpected death, so I rang them up, too. That's really about all I can tell you.'

'Did you see the body?' asked Miss Petherington ghoulishly. 'The papers say it was murder, but they don't know how he was killed.'

'No doubt Mrs Talmadge *seemed* very upset?'

'How lucky they have no children!' That was Mrs Ledway, of course.

'Naturally Daphne Talmadge was upset,' said Mrs Tebbit, 'whatever her feelings for her husband.'

'Not as upset as Gwen Walker, I imagine,' Miss Cobb said just loud enough for Daisy to hear.

'Does Mrs Walker have bad teeth? Poor thing, it must be dismaying to lose one's dentist in the middle of a course of treatment, but she can always find another.'

Daisy's wilful misunderstanding vexed Miss Cobb. 'Teeth! For all I know she has perfect teeth,' she exclaimed rather snappishly, then tittered. 'Oh, my dear, you really miss a great deal by not having your hair done locally. One has heard that Raymond Talmadge and Gwen Walker were seen dining together. Tête-à-tête!'

'Who saw them? And where?'

'In *Soho*, I believe! At a club! No one respectable would admit to going to a nightclub in Soho, so I don't know who saw them. Simply shocking!'

'An anonymous rumour is hardly worthy of credit.' Though Daisy would report it to Alec anyway.

'No smoke without a fire. And she hasn't come today. She doesn't want us to see how upset she is.'

'I dare say she had a prior engagement.'

Miss Cobb tittered again behind her hand. 'Not with Mr Talmadge this time.'

Daisy couldn't help giving her a disgusted look, one which she knew made her look like her mother, the Dowager Viscountess, at her most *grande dame.* She was disgusted with herself, too, for encouraging such a spiteful scandal-monger to pass on her malicious tale.

At least she had the best of motives, to help find a murderer. It was up to Alec to discover whether the rumour was true.

Catching Mrs Grantchester's gaze, she wondered whether her hostess had induced Miss Cobb to recount the gossip. Perhaps Mrs Grantchester didn't want to be caught telling tales.

'Excuse me, Miss Cobb,' Daisy said, 'it looks as if my mother-in-law is ready to leave.'

After a round of goodbyes, Daisy, Mrs Fletcher and the latter's friend, Mrs Harbison, departed together. In the hall, the parlourmaid returned Daisy's hat to her, dry but rather droopy about the brim. Outside it was still raining, though not quite as hard as earlier.

'Thoroughly distasteful!' fumed Mrs Fletcher as the front door shut behind them. 'Alec is frequently involved in such cases, alas, but I have never before been subjected to such impertinent inquisitiveness.' She didn't need to spell out that it was all Daisy's fault.

'How lucky I haven't told you anything about it,' said Daisy, following the older ladies down the garden path. 'You could truthfully say you didn't know any more than was reported in the papers.'

'Perhaps you should go away, Enid, till it all blows over,' suggested Mrs Harbison. 'The talk of summer resorts put it into my mind. You could go and stay with your sister in Bournemouth.'

'How can I abandon my son and my granddaughter at such a time?'

Daisy fumed, but managed to ignore this innuendo also. 'As you said, Mother, dealing with murder is nothing out of the ordinary for Alec. And it will be no different for Belinda from any other of his cases.' She was pretty sure Bel had told her grandmother a great deal less than she had told her friends. 'You and I are the ones who face the questions of our nosy neighbours. I'm a witness, so I can't escape, but there's no reason you shouldn't.'

'Well . . . Bournemouth is very pleasant in April, before the crowds arrive. But people will say—'

'What business is it of anyone else's if you choose to take a spring holiday?' Daisy demanded. 'You haven't seen your sister since Christmas. I'm sure Dobson and I between us can manage not to let Alec and Belinda starve in your absence. If anyone dares to say anything, we'll say you've been feeling a bit run down and the sea breezes will buck you up, won't we, Mrs Harbison?'

'It is a very healthy place,' said Mrs Harbison, 'but I thought I might go as well. I know a very comfortable boarding house near the front . . .'

'Good, that's settled then. You can send your sister a wire today, Mother, and go down tomorrow morning.'

'But—'

'And by the time you come home, Alec will have caught the culprit and everyone will have found something else to talk about. I'm going to look for my umbrella now. I'll see you later.'

Without waiting for any further protests, Daisy turned into the Talmadges' street. Perhaps she had been a bit high-handed; perhaps Mrs Fletcher would decide not to go; but the chance of a few days without her carping was worth the attempt.

At the Talmadges' house the front blinds were down. Daisy

went round the side to the waiting room, but the door was locked. She'd have to go to the front door, and she could hardly do that without asking after Mrs Talmadge. Even Alec couldn't possibly call it meddling.

CHAPTER 10

Gladys opened the door. 'I'm sorry, madam,' she said, 'Mrs Talmadge is not— Oh, it's you, ma'am. Lor, ma'am, you're ever so wet.'

'I've come for my umbrella,' Daisy explained. 'I left it in the waiting room.'

'Oh dear, the pleece took away the keys. They maybe took your brolly, too, ma'am, thinking it was a clue. Nurse might know. They was asking her about stuff in there. I'll go ask her, ma'am, if you'll just step in. She's upstairs with the mistress.'

'How is Mrs Talmadge?' Daisy asked, stepping in.

'I'm s'posed to say "As well as can be expected", ma'am, when people call or ring up. But you being here yesterday, well, I heard Nurse telling Cook the mistress slept right through till noon, what with the doctor's med'cine and all. And when she woke up, she felt sick and didn't want no lunch. Nurse made her eat some consommy and a bit of dry toast, just to keep up her strength, like.'

'That sounds like a good idea.'

'She didn't have no breakfast, being asleep, nor dinner last night neither. The chief pleeceman – him that's your husband, isn't he, ma'am? – he came this morning and wanted to see the mistress, but Nurse wouldn't let him. I'll go ask her about your brolly, ma'am.'

'Thank you, Gladys. Tell her I enquired after her patient, and I'd be grateful for the latest news.'

The housemaid left Daisy standing in the hall, as no well-trained parlourmaid would have. The wilting daffodils in the vase on the half-moon table were another sign of a household at sixes and sevens. Hilda Kidd must be sleeping after watching over Daphne Talmadge all night.

Daisy badly wanted to talk to the cook – Mrs Thorpe, if she recalled correctly – but she couldn't think of an excuse to go to the kitchen. Or rather, she came up with a couple that might satisfy the cook, but there wasn't a chance they would pass muster with Alec. Instead, she hurried into the study, telephoned Scotland Yard, and left a message about Gwen Walker. She put a couple of pennies on the desk to pay for the call, then returned to the hall to wait for Gladys.

The silver tray on the table now held a large number of visiting cards, with written messages of sympathy visible on the top layer. This morning, callers must have been queuing up to leave their condolences. Daisy wasn't sure whether she ought to add her own card to the heap. What on earth was the proper etiquette when one had been present at the discovery by the bereaved of the murdered body of the deceased? Even the Dowager Viscountess would be hard-pressed to come up with an answer to that conundrum.

Lady Dalrymple would certainly not approve of her daughter's present appearance. Daisy regarded her droopily damp image in the looking glass over the table, wondering whether her hat would ever recover. Thank heaven she had put on an old one to go out in the rain.

'The pleece took your brolly, ma'am,' Gladys announced from halfway down the stairs. Continuing down, she went on, 'The mistress says to lend you one to go home, but she wants to see you first. Would you be so kind, ma'am, she says, as to step up to her room. Nurse says she's too ill to see anyone, but she says she won't take her med'cine till she's seen you. Miss Kidd says it smells ever so nasty. If you please, ma'am.'

'Of course I'll go up.'

Daphne Talmadge was in bed, propped up on several frilly pillows. Her starkly pale face rose from a froth of lace adorning a pink quilted satin bedjacket. Miss Hensted stood by the bed, a neat figure in her uniform dress and cap, a brown medicine bottle in one hand. It occurred to Daisy that the nurse would already be looking for a new job if it weren't for Daphne's breakdown.

'Daisy, how good of you to c-come!' Daphne's voice broke on a sob.

'There now, what did I say, you're getting all upset again,' Nurse Hensted reproved her. 'Better take your dose like the doctor said.'

'Not now. Later. I want to talk to Mrs Fletcher. Go away, Nurse. I'll ring when you can come back.'

The nurse set down the bottle with rather a thump on the bedside table beside a glass of white liquid, milk perhaps. But she looked less annoyed than anxious. 'Don't let her keep you long, Mrs Fletcher,' she said in a low voice as she passed Daisy. 'Call me if she gets agitated.'

Daisy gave her a nod, and made sure the door was properly latched behind her. Whatever Daphne wanted to say, it was none of Miss Hensted's business, and Daisy didn't quite trust the nurse not to listen.

'She's never liked me,' Daphne moaned. 'I hate her hovering over me.'

'Dismiss her,' said Daisy, moving a chair to a convenient position near the bed. 'If the doctor wants you to have a nurse for a few days, hire someone else.'

'I couldn't. She . . . she knows things. If I send her away she might tell . . . people.'

'A nurse who spreads rumours about her employers isn't likely to get any decent jobs. Has she threatened to talk if you don't go on paying her? If so, that's blackmail, and the police don't like it at all.'

'Oh no, nothing like that,' Daphne gabbled. 'It's just a feeling, nothing the police would be interested in.'

'If you're worried about what the police might find out, I think it's too late for that.'

'You mean they know? About Harry? Lord Henry?'

Daisy was a bit disappointed. Was the illicit liaison the only misdeed Miss Hensted might have discovered? 'Alec went to see Lord Henry last night,' she said. Arriving home very late and dog-tired, he had told her no more than that before falling asleep.

'But he hasn't been arrested?'

'Did you expect him to be?'

'No! He didn't kill Raymond!' Daphne buried her face in her hands and started to cry in great, gasping sobs.

'There, what did I say?' Hilda Kidd rushed in, in a buttercup yellow dressing gown and carpet slippers, Nurse Hensted at her heels. 'You're a fine one to be taking care of her, I don't think! Good job I came down to check. Letting people in to bully her!'

'Rubbish,' Miss Hensted retorted angrily. 'She's just

overwrought, which isn't surprising, considering. It's time she took her medicine.'

'Oh yes, give it to me. I'll take it now. I don't want to remember. I don't want to think!'

'Stands to reason you don't. That's why Dr Curtis left the Paral.' Picking up the bottle from the bedside table, the nurse unscrewed the top and picked up a measuring spoon.

Daisy had moved out of the way, but made no move to leave. Hilda rounded on her.

'See what you've done? I hope you're—'

'Hilda, that will do! Daisy, I'm sorry, I didn't mean to get so weepy. It's just—' Daphne choked up.

'Altogether too much.'

'Yes. Will you ... Would you mind staying till I go to sleep?'

'Of course.' At least she could stop the nurse and the maid squabbling, Daisy thought.

Hilda scowled. Miss Hensted, her nose wrinkling slightly, measured a spoonful of liquid and stirred it into the milk. She handed it to Daphne, who gulped down the mixture with a grimace.

'Horrid stuff.' Leaning back against the pillows with a little sigh, she closed her eyes.

Daisy was wondering how she would know when to leave, when Daphne grimaced again.

'My stomach hurts,' she mumbled.

Then suddenly she sat bolt upright, clutched her abdomen, and with a cry of pain doubled over.

'You witch, you've poisoned her!' Hilda screeched, rushing at the nurse. 'I'll kill you!'

As Daisy jumped to grab the maid, from the corner of her

eye she saw Miss Hensted wrench the bedcovers off Daphne. She didn't for a moment believe the nurse would commit murder in front of two witnesses, so she averted her gaze. Not for nothing had she chosen to work in a hospital office during the war, rather than as a VAD nurse.

Anyway, she had no attention to spare for what was going on elsewhere. She had Hilda around the waist. For what seemed like forever, the maid clawed at her hands, still screeching imprecations.

The nurse's cold, businesslike voice cut through the shrieks. 'You're bleeding. It looks like a miscarriage to me. Are you—?'

'My baby!' wailed Daphne.

'Lie down flat. I don't care if it hurts, it just may save the poor little beggar and stop you bleeding to death. Miss Kidd, I need clean linen and a basin of cold water. Mrs Fletcher, please go and telephone for the doctor. If you can't get Dr Curtis, find someone else. Lie flat, I tell you!'

Daisy fled. She had to assume Hilda would come to her senses and help Miss Hensted instead of attacking her. At least no screams followed her as she raced down the stairs. With any luck, that also meant the drug Daphne had taken was dulling her pain.

Could the drug have caused the miscarriage? Although her sister had had one, Daisy didn't know much about the subject. She did know her brother-in-law had worried that any emotional upset might lead to another, and what Daphne had gone through was a huge emotional upset.

The doctor's telephone was engaged. Daisy told the operator it was an emergency, and the girl broke in on the call. Mrs Curtis, sounding a bit cross, said her husband was just setting out on his rounds.

'Oh, please try to catch him! It's Mrs Talmadge. The nurse thinks she's having a miscarriage.'

'My dear, I'll run. Hold the line.'

Daisy held on. She heard quick footsteps, a motorcar engine, a shout. The engine noise subsided to an idle. It sounded as if Mrs Curtis had managed to stop the doctor as he drove down the drive.

A minute later she was on the line again. 'He's on his way,' she panted. 'Just a moment while I catch my breath.'

'Thank you so much.'

'I'm getting too old for these emergencies! He says to keep her lying flat on her back with cold compresses to the abdomen. She mustn't take any more of the Paral he prescribed. And keep her calm, though I know that's a tall order in the circumstances.'

'I'll tell Nurse Hensted. Thanks, Mrs Curtis.'

'I do hope she doesn't lose her baby. Or perhaps, in the circumstances . . . Oh dear!' Unable to decide what to hope for, the doctor's wife rang off.

In the circumstances— How long since Daphne had shared a bed with her murdered husband? The baby was almost certainly her lover's. Their motive for doing away with the inconvenient dentist was doubled with a vengeance.

CHAPTER 11

Arriving panting on the upper landing, Daisy met Hilda coming out of the bathroom with a bowl of water and followed her into the bedroom. Carefully averting her eyes from the bed, though she couldn't avoid hearing Daphne's moans, she passed on Dr Curtis's instructions.

'Just what I'm doing,' said Miss Hensted complacently. 'It might stop the bleeding, you never can tell. At least she's vomited up the Paral, for a mercy.'

'Unless there's something I can do to help,' said Daisy, feeling cowardly, 'I'll wait downstairs.'

The nurse gave her the cheerfully pitying glance of one to whom blood and vomit are nothing. 'Off you go, then, dear,' she advised. 'You might send up some tea, if you don't mind.'

'I will,' Daisy promised, and once again fled, this time with an excuse to go and speak to Cook.

The kitchen smelt of fried onions – the servants had to eat regardless of their master's death and their mistress' lack of appetite. Daisy found Gladys there with Mrs Thorpe, and sent her to wait at the front door to admit the doctor. The cook was a short, thin woman with a face as dour as Hilda Kidd's. She turned from a simmering pan on the stove to stand with her hands on her white-aproned hips waiting for Daisy to explain her presence.

'Nurse Hensted asked for a pot of tea to be sent up, please, Cook.'

'Oh aye? What kind? For that woman or t'mistress?'

Daisy didn't know. Daphne was in no state to enjoy a drink of fragrant China tea, and the nurse surely had her hands too full to stop for a cuppa. Conceivably what was needed was a stimulant to counteract any of the sedative Daphne had absorbed before she . . . in which case, the stronger the better.

'Indian. Strong. It's medicinal.'

'And t'doctor?' said Mrs Thorpe, putting on the kettle. 'What's gone wrong, that's what I want to know?'

Daisy sat down at the table. 'I'm not exactly sure. Miss Hensted seems to have everything in hand.'

''Tis not like Mrs Talmadge were ever ill, not one to coddle herself. Not one o' these gaumless ladies always fussing over their food and fancying themselves at death's door. Hilda didn't ought to have never let that woman get her hands on her.'

'After such a shock as she had yesterday, it's hardly surprising that she's not well. I know it was your day out, Mrs Thorpe, but have you any idea about what might have happened?'

'Ideas?' The cook looked blank, as if she'd never heard of such things. 'I'm sure 'tis not my place to have ideas, madam. I wasn't here and I didn't see nowt and that's that.' Her mouth set in an uncompromising line, she set about making the tea.

Daisy knew when she was beaten. It wasn't often that even the most unlikely people failed to confide in her. She wondered whether Tom Tring had had better luck.

As long as she was here, though, there was a chance of

learning something. Anyway, she couldn't leave until she knew what was happening upstairs.

'Pour me a cup before it gets too strong, would you, please?'

Reluctantly Cook obliged. 'I'll have Gladys bring it to you in t' drawing room, madam.'

'Oh no, I want her to stay at the door to admit Dr Curtis, so there's no delay. I'm quite comfortable here. Won't you sit down and have a cup with me?'

'I couldn't do that, madam.' Mrs Thorpe was stiff with disapproval. ''Twouldn't be proper.'

Another of those middle-class taboos, Daisy thought with a sigh. Growing up at Fairacres she and Gervaise and even Violet, the best behaved of the three, had often gone to the kitchens for a snack, and Cook would join them if she wasn't extra busy. And in Chelsea, before she married, Daisy had often sat down at the kitchen table with the daily help for elevenses and what Mrs Potter called 'a nice bit of chin-wag'.

Muttering, 'I only hope 'tis for t'mistress,' Mrs Thorpe spread an embroidered cloth on a tray. She had made the tea in the Royal Doulton pot, and set out milk, sugar and hot water in the matching jugs and basin. Now she hesitated with the cup and saucer in her hand, as if the thought of Miss Hensted drinking from the good china appalled her.

'Why do you dislike the nurse so?' Daisy ventured.

'Dead chuffed wi' herself, isn't she? Right stuck-up, fancies herself as good as t'gentry and a sight too good for us servants. Some people, you give 'em an inch and they'll take an ell. If there's anything I can't abide, 'tis someone that doesn't know her own place.' She glared at Daisy, who decided not to offer to take the tray up, as she had intended.

Gladys came in. 'The doctor's come, madam.'

'Good, that was quick. Mrs Thorpe, you'd better put out a cup for him.' And one for Hilda Kidd? No, it would only upset Cook still more to suggest the maid might drink with Mrs Talmadge and the doctor. 'Then Gladys can take it.'

With an air of triumph, the cook set out two Doulton cups and saucers and one of the white kitchen china. 'That'll show her,' she gloated, turning back to the stove as Gladys carried the tray out.

Almost simultaneously three bells rang: the side door, the telephone and Daphne Talmadge's bedroom. Gladys, already on her way, could take care of the last.

'That'll be t'butcher's boy,' said Cook. 'He's late again, t'good-for-nowt.'

Daisy would have liked to ask the butcher's boy whether he had noticed anything the day before, but Mrs Thorpe was already on her way to the door. No doubt Tom had taken the names of all deliverymen and interviewed them by now – that might even be why the boy was late.

'I'll get the phone,' Daisy offered.

'Let it ring. 'Twill stop. Just some nosey parker, think on.'

A reporter, maybe, but it could be another emergency for the doctor. Daisy hurried to the study, picked up the apparatus and gave the number.

'Daisy?'

'Alec!'

'What the dickens are you doing there?'

'I came to get my umbrella, darling. I didn't know you had impounded it as a clue.'

'So Mother said. But she expected you home long ago.'

'Well, once here I couldn't very well leave without asking after Daphne, and she wanted to see me, so—'

'What's this message you left for me?' he interrupted. 'Something about Mrs Walker being the missing factor.'

'I didn't want to be too explicit, darling, because it's only a rumour and you never know who's listening. In fact, hold on while I close the door.' She did so. 'There. It was at the ghastly luncheon your mother and I went to today. I'm inclined to think Mrs Grantchester set it up just so that her mouthpiece, Miss Cobb, could enlighten me.'

'About what, for pity's sake?'

'Gwen Walker was seen dining in Soho with Raymond Talmadge.'

'Mrs Major Walker? Well I'll be . . . dashed. I have to admit you've beaten us to it there. We had no leads so far.'

'Maybe, but it's just High Street salon gossip. Miss Cobb didn't even know who was supposed to have seen them. Something much more significant is going on here right now.'

'More significant than discovering Talmadge's lover? Do stop being so mysterious, Daisy!'

'Stop interrupting and give me a chance. It looks as if Daphne's having a miscarriage.'

'A mis— Great Scott, she's pregnant?'

'Is or was. The doctor's with her now, poor thing.'

Alec snorted. 'Poor thing! Tom's pretty sure after talking to the servants that she and Talmadge hadn't slept together for at least a couple of years. It's Lord Henry's baby, and I can't think offhand of a better motive for either or both to do in her husband. Assuming she knew.'

'She knew,' said Daisy. 'Which doesn't mean she'd told him.'

'How do you know she knew?'

'Ummm. I'm not sure, darling, but I definitely have that impression.'

'An impression's not evidence, Daisy.'

'It must have been something she said. I expect I'll remember if I just think through the scene again – which I'd far rather not. It was dreadful.'

'Poor love, but you do rather let yourself in for these things when you start meddling,' Alec said callously. 'All right, I'll accept your impression for the moment. I wonder if she consulted Curtis? Or some other practitioner? I must talk to her as soon as possible. Is she still under sedation?'

'No, but she's in the middle of a medical emergency!'

'Oh, right-o. I'll send Mackinnon over to keep an eye on the situation, and I'll have another go at Lord Henry.'

'He doesn't have an alibi?'

'Not one that's easy to check. Ernie's working on it now. Didn't I tell you about it?'

'By the time you came in last night, you were dog-tired and only said you'd seen him. Then you fell asleep.'

'Strictly speaking I shouldn't even have said that. And I'd better ring off before I say any more. You go home.'

'Darling, I can't possibly. I'd feel as if I was deserting a sinking ship. I must at least wait to find out if she lost the baby. What about Gwen Walker? Do you think she's a red herring?'

'I've no idea. Daisy, don't you dare go and call on her next.'

'I can't go running about the neighbourhood without an umbrella. Try and bring mine home with you, will you? Do you think you'll make it for the Randalls' dinner tonight?'

'The Randalls?'

'I did tell you, but I suppose you were already half asleep.'

'In the unlikely event that I get home for dinner,' Alec said grimly, 'I'll be damned if I turn out again before morning.'

'Right-o, darling. Toodle-oo, then,' said Daisy, and rang off, her own red herrings having succeeded admirably. She rang Marianne Randall and left a message with a maid, then, with a sigh, rang home.

'Still looking for your umbrella?' enquired her mother-in-law waspishly.

'Alec's men impounded it. I hope he'll be able to get it back for me, or I'll have to buy another. I'm still at the Talmadges', though. I'm going to be here a while yet, I'm afraid. There's a bit of an emergency and—'

'Not another murder!'

'Gosh, no! A medical emergency. I can't in good conscience leave till I find out how Mrs Talmadge is doing.'

A muted 'Conscience? Pshaw!' came over the wire. Daisy had never heard anyone say 'pshaw' before, though they were always doing it in books, to indicate contempt or incredulity.

Fortunately Mrs Fletcher muttered it softly enough to allow Daisy to ignore it. 'The doctor's come already,' she said. 'I don't suppose I'll be here much longer. 'Bye.'

She sat for a moment examining her conscience. Of course it was mostly the ''satiable curtiosity' she shared with Kipling's Elephant's Child which urged her to stay, but she did feel desperately sorry for Daphne. To lose a baby must be perfectly dreadful. She had never really understood when Johnnie was so worried about Violet; since Vi had presented her with an adorable baby niece, she had been thinking about giving Belinda a brother or sister. Now the whole business had become a matter of personal concern.

Yes, to lose a baby must be perfectly dreadful – whoever

the father. Perhaps because Daphne's secret life with Lord Henry had precluded close friendships, she had chosen to confide in Daisy, although she knew Alec was a policeman. Either Daphne was innocent of her husband's murder, or she was confident of her ability to mislead Daisy.

Or else she was just in such a state she was quite unable to think clearly.

Whichever way Daisy looked at the situation, sympathy, curiosity and a duty to find out what she could for Alec all led to the same course of action. She headed back to the kitchen.

'Your tea's cold,' Mrs Thorpe growled at her. 'I've made another pot.'

'How kind.' Meekly Daisy sat down and drank a cup of Earl Grey, which she didn't care for at all.

The cook was opening a package neatly wrapped in newspaper, with an inner wrap of butcher's paper. 'Them newspapermen, were it, on t'telephone?' She took out a pound of pale pink chipolata sausages.

'Don't worry, I wouldn't dream of telling the press anything.'

Staring at the sausages, Mrs Thorpe turned pale and sat down suddenly. 'Ooh, I've come over all queer. The master liked his sausages for breakfast, well browned he liked 'em. "They're best if the skins split," he used to tell me, "so's they get a bit crispy." So I wouldn't prick 'em afore I cooked 'em. "You do 'em just the way I like 'em, Cook," he'd say. Ee, he won't be saying that to me niver again, will he?'

'I'm afraid not.'

'What am I going to do with these here, that's what I want to know. T'mistress don't care for 'em much. They'll go off afore they get ate. I better parboil 'em.' Her queer turn apparently over, she set a pot of water on the stove to heat and started to snip apart the string of sausages.

'Mr Talmadge was a good master, was he?' Daisy asked.

'I've known worse. Niffy-naffy about his food but if you did it to his liking, he'd say so. Careful of his figure, he were. No cakes and pies for him. He were getting to t'age when men start to get a bit of a belly on, if you know what I mean, madam, and he didn't want to go that way.'

'A ladies' man?'

'Nay, I niver said so! Don't you go putting words in my mouth. Him and Mrs T. had their differences, I don't deny, but there wasn't never any funny business in this house and to that I'll give my affydavy.' She stabbed viciously at the sausages with a fork. 'I'm a respectable woman, I am. I wouldn't stay at a house where there was carryings-on.'

'I'm sure you wouldn't,' Daisy said soothingly.

'And I don't hold wi' murder in t'house, neither. If it wasn't that the mistress is poorly, I'd be thinking about giving my notice.'

'Oh, don't do that.'

'Well, I won't. But she needn't think I'll put up with carryings-on in the house now t'master's gone, lord or no lord, for I won't, and so I've told Hilda.'

The now-pricked sausages went into the boiling water with a hiss. Daisy poured herself another cup of the pale, scented tea. If she sat here making sympathetic noises for long enough, she might learn something useful.

'If you ask me— Drat that doorbell! Back door. Who can it be? I'm not expecting no more deliveries today.'

'I'll get it. You keep your eye on those sausages.' Standing up, Daisy saw them bobbing amid the roiling water like so many pallid sea bathers. Would she ever be able to eat sausages again?

She opened the door to Detective Sergeant Mackinnon. 'Hello, Sergeant! I forgot, Alec said he'd send you over.'

'I got a message from the Chief Inspector, ma'am. They didn't say you'd be here. Just something about . . .' He turned fiery red. 'About . . . I mean . . . They said Mrs Talmadge . . . That is . . .'

Daisy rescued him. 'She's not at all well. You won't be able to talk to her.'

'Oh no!' said Mackinnon, aghast. 'I wouldna dream . . . I'm just supposed to make sure she doesna get in touch with Lord Henry Creighton. And just sort of generally keep an eye on things. Though I'm not quite sure what he means by that. The message wasna very clear.'

'I expect it got garbled in transmission,' said Daisy. She suspected Alec wanted the sergeant to keep an eye on her in particular rather than 'things' in general, but he couldn't very well have said so to whoever passed on the message.

'And I'm to talk to the doctor, if he's still here.'

'He's with her, upstairs. I expect you have to make sure she's really having a . . . that what I told Alec is what's actually going on?'

'Yes,' he said, grateful for her circumlocutions. 'We have to consider the possibility that she's faking a . . . pretending to be ill to avoid being questioned.'

'She's not faking,' Daisy asserted, remembering all too clearly Daphne's agonized face. 'Apart from anything else, she'd never have persuaded Nurse Hensted to go along. They hate each other.'

'The nurse was there when . . . it happened?'

'Yes. It was she who realized Mrs Talmadge was having a . . . what was happening. You'd better come into the hall to catch Dr Curtis when he comes down. Oh, blast, is that the phone ringing *again*?'

'I'll get it,' Mackinnon volunteered. 'Maybe it's the Chief Inspector. I'll leave the door open so I see the doctor when he passes.' He headed for the front of the house.

About to turn back into the kitchen, Daisy paused as she heard him speaking to someone. A moment later, Gladys arrived.

'Oh, good, you're still here, ma'am. The doctor wants to speak to you.'

'Upstairs?'

'No, ma'am, he's just coming down. In the droring room, maybe?'

'Right-o, tell him I'm expecting him there, Gladys.'

She went into that oddly impersonal room, a room to take pride in for entertaining, but not one to relax in. Crossing to the French windows onto the garden, she gazed out at the ranks of flowers. The tulips were closed against the rain, the hyacinths bowing before its onslaught, the pansies downright bedraggled.

At the sound of footsteps, she turned, as Dr Curtis came in.

'How is Daphne, Doctor?'

'She'll do. We saved the baby, though she's not out of the woods yet.' Frowning at Daisy, he took off his gold-rimmed eyeglasses and stabbed towards her with the earpiece to punctuate his words. 'If I'd known she was pregnant, I'd never have prescribed Paral. Not that I've ever heard of it producing an abortion, but severe stomach cramps are not unknown. Violent contractions of the abdomen – but any strong drug is to be avoided, especially in the early months, and when you add the horror of Talmadge's death . . . Did you know she was expecting a child?'

'I? Heavens, no! She knew, I take it?'

'She consulted a Harley Street man,' he said with a touch of resentment. 'I'll have to write up my notes and send him a copy, I suppose. Common courtesy, though she says she doesn't intend to continue seeing him. It's all most unfortunate, her husband dying at such a time. She ought to have a relative to stay with her. I know she was an only child, and her parents have both passed on, but there must be someone suitable?'

'I'm sorry, I know nothing about her family. Hilda Kidd would be the one to ask.'

'She says there's no one. But I wondered . . . umm . . .'

'Whether she just doesn't want anyone horning in between her and Daphne? She does seem to be frightfully jealous of their relationship. You didn't ask Daphne about relatives?'

'Not after the maid said there are none. She is not to be emotionally disturbed.' The doctor eyed Daisy with some severity.

'I'm afraid that's a bit of a nonstarter, considering her husband was murdered yesterday!'

'Yes, well, as I said, it's all most unfortunate.'

'The police are going to want to talk to her, if you don't absolutely forbid it.'

'She may see your husband. I would take him to be capable of delicacy in the situation. But you should be present to make sure she doesn't become agitated, and that she stays lying flat in bed.'

'And for propriety's sake,' Daisy said primly, tongue in cheek.

To her surprise, Dr Curtis gave her a wry smile. 'If anyone cares for propriety in this degenerate day and age.'

'But I can't imagine Daphne will want me there when she's being questioned.'

'Perhaps not. At any rate, she would like to see you now. I left her quite calm but very tired, so don't stay long. Good day, Mrs Fletcher.' He bowed slightly and departed.

So Daphne wanted to see her? What luck! Daisy followed him out and made for the stairs.

Since the baby had been saved, she didn't have to feel quite so sympathetic. And according to the doctor, the mother-to-be was now calm, no longer in such a state she couldn't think straight. Daisy could concentrate on trying to decide whether Daphne was actually innocent of murder or just sure she'd be able to hoodwink Daisy.

CHAPTER 12

On her way upstairs, Daisy thought of another possibility. Even if Daphne was herself innocent, she still could know, suspect, or simply fear that Lord Henry had killed her husband, in which case she must be desperate to protect him.

Daisy tapped on the bedroom door and was invited to enter. In spite of her resolve, she felt a pang of sympathy at the sight of Daphne's wan face, pale as her pillows, with its pitiful attempt at a smile.

'I'm so glad the baby is all right.'

'Yes, we managed to save the poor, fatherless little mite,' said Miss Hensted complacently.

Hilda Kidd glared at her. The maid's face was creased with fatigue after the emotions of the past hour following her watchful night. She opened her mouth to retort, but Daphne forestalled her, her tone authoritative despite the weakness of her voice.

'Hilda, you really must get some rest. Bring that chair over here for Mrs Fletcher, then off to bed with you. And Nurse, you can leave me with Mrs Fletcher. I promise I won't try to sit up.'

'I'll stop her if she does.' Daisy reopened the door she had closed behind her and stood holding it to usher out the reluctant pair.

The door firmly shut again, Daisy went to sit on the chair Hilda had moved close to the bed.

'I suppose I must be grateful to Nurse Hensted,' said Daphne, 'much as I dislike her. Dr Curtis says she may have stopped me bleeding to death, as well as saving my baby. Oh, Daisy, what must you think of me?'

'I think you've got yourself into a fearful mess,' Daisy said candidly. 'And I know that now you're no longer under sedation, you're going to have to talk to the police.'

'Even if I tell you everything?'

'Gosh, yes. I may have given Alec a hand with one or two cases, and he does *occasionally* listen to what I have to say, but I have no official standing. You'll have to see him. Or he'd send someone else if you prefer, I expect. I can see it might be a bit awkward baring your soul to a policeman you've been socially acquainted with for ages.'

'Very, but probably no worse than to a stranger. On the whole I'd rather have your husband, especially if you can stay with me. But I want to explain to you first anyway. You've been so kind.'

Daisy thought guiltily of her ulterior motives. 'Not really,' she felt obliged to demur.

'Kinder than anyone else.'

'There are stacks of condolence cards downstairs.'

Daphne pulled a face. 'All of which I'll have to answer politely though I can guess what some of those cats are saying behind my back. I can't imagine you going off and repeating what I've told you to the neighbours.'

'No, I wouldn't do that.' Daisy recalled with distaste Miss Cobb's glee as she passed on her tidbit of gossip, while Mrs Grantchester watched avidly. 'I wouldn't even tell Alec in ordinary circumstances, but—'

'Poor Raymond! I still can't quite believe it's happened.' She sounded more bewildered than shattered. 'Are the police absolutely sure it wasn't an accident?'

'Pretty sure. You said something before about it happening just when you thought you'd sorted everything out. Did you mean he'd agreed to let you divorce him?'

'No, on the contrary. Divorce would have ruined his practice, and having a divorced mother would be a rotten start in life for my baby. No, he'd agreed to accept the child as his own.'

'Did he really?'

'Noble of him, wasn't it?' Daphne's smile was twisted. 'He wasn't a bad man. I was madly in love with him once. And, you know, not having children was one of the things that drove us apart in the first place. No, not drove. We weren't driven, we drifted. Don't let it happen to you, Daisy.'

Daisy couldn't imagine drifting apart from Alec, but she said, 'I'll do my best.'

'We were going to try to put our marriage back together. He promised to drop his latest mistress, and I told Harry I couldn't see him again.' Her eyes filling with tears, Daphne turned her head away.

'Oh, please, you mustn't upset yourself. Dr Curtis said . . . I'd better go.'

'No, please stay. I'll go mad if I can't talk about it. I'll try to be calm. Only it was perfectly awful, you can't imagine.'

'You told him everything? I mean, about why you and your husband were going to try to salvage the marriage? About the baby?'

'His baby, as I expect you must have guessed. Yes, I told him. We've known each other for nearly twenty years, you see. I would have married him, but Father wouldn't let me. He said he was an effete aristocrat barely capable of tying his own shoelaces.'

'Oh dear!'

'It's not true. And I can tell Harry anything, knowing he'll understand. He was so kind, and so sad.'

'It must have been very painful.' Daisy tried to imagine the dilettante-about-town finding himself in that awkward situation. She would expect him to be extremely relieved that his mistress intended to stay with her husband rather than attempting to saddle him with the responsibility for the child. Nothing seemed less likely than that he should rush off to murder said husband.

Admittedly Daisy didn't know Lord Henry at all well. His long liaison with Daphne Talmadge was surprising enough in itself. One would have expected him to dally with actresses.

Reaching out a pleading hand, Daphne said passionately, 'I have to see him!'

'Oh dear, I don't see how—'

'I can't go out, so Harry must come here.'

Daisy tried to work out how to say politely that a man visiting his mistress in her bedroom at home on the day after her husband was murdered was simply not on. Especially as he'd been murdered in that very house. 'I really don't think—'

'I don't care what people say. It's too late to worry about that. Will you go down and telephone him for me?'

'As a matter of fact, there's a policeman down there for the express purpose of stopping you getting in touch with Lord Henry until Alec has talked to you. And please don't ask me to write a note or something. I may not always agree with

Alec, but I couldn't deliberately thwart him like that.' At least, not unless she was absolutely certain he was wrong.

At present, the only certainties were that Daphne was tired, upset and worried about Lord Henry. Daisy hoped she wasn't deluding herself that he cared equally for her. Or was she worried because she was afraid he might desert her?

She could even be making up the whole story to divert suspicion from herself to him. A reconciliation with her husband eliminated her motive for killing him, but intensified Lord Henry's – always supposing he really was devoted to her.

'I wish he'd hurry up and come, then,' Daphne sighed. 'Mr Fletcher, I mean. But I want you to tell him first what I've told you. It won't be quite so difficult if he already knows the worst.'

'I could try to phone him at the Yard, and if he's not there, leave a message that you're ready to see him.'

'Would you? Please?'

'Right-o. Then I'll wait and come up with him, if you're sure that's what you want. He can't very well object to your having a chaperone.'

'I'm afraid I'm taking up a great deal of your time. I know you're awfully busy with your writing. I do envy you for having something really worthwhile to do, and I admire you for going on with it in spite of what people say. I sometimes think if I had had more to do . . .' She sighed again. 'You've been very kind, and I don't want to ask anything more of you, but . . . I don't think I can bear the Hensted woman brooding over me any longer. Her squabbles with Hilda alone are intolerable.'

'You really must brace yourself to dismiss her. Did Dr Curtis say you ought to have a nurse on hand?'

'For a few days, at least.'

'Well, if you like I'll call an agency and get them to send someone, but I can't chuck Miss Hensted out for you. I don't see why she should mind, given pay in lieu of notice. After all, the job she was hired for no longer exists, and she told Alec she abhors waiting on an invalid.'

Daphne brightened. 'She did? Then maybe I can make it seem as if I'm doing her a favour by letting her go.'

'Try it,' Daisy advised. 'I'll send her in. I'm off to phone Alec.'

When Daisy left the bedroom, Nurse Hensted was on the landing waiting to return to her patient. Hilda Kidd, thank heaven, was nowhere in sight.

Lost in thought, the nurse didn't notice Daisy for a moment. Judging by her heavy frown and downturned mouth her thoughts were not pleasant. It must be hard to lose a position she had no doubt expected to keep for years, particularly one where the work was not exactly exacting. Even if Daphne kept her on, it could only be a few days before she'd have to start pounding the pavements again in search of a new job. She would probably end up either in a hospital or looking after an invalid.

She looked up, saw Daisy and started forward. 'I hope you didn't upset her, Mrs Fletcher,' she said belligerently. 'We don't want another emergency.'

'Mrs Talmadge is quite calm at present. You'll see that she stays calm, won't you?'

'That's my job. It's Hilda Kidd gets her all worked up.'

Daisy nodded, but she paused to listen before going downstairs.

Miss Hensted pushed the door to after her, but it didn't

latch, bouncing back to leave a crack. Daisy heard professionally soothing sounds, but without putting her ear to the crack she couldn't make out the words. Not that it mattered; she just wanted to make sure there wasn't going to be a battle royal.

Daphne's voice came next, in firm tones. Then the nurse said clearly, 'Oh yes, Mrs Talmadge, I'd be ever so grateful. I didn't want to leave you in the lurch, but it'll suit me down to the ground. You'll write me a reference? I'm sure I've always given satisfaction.'

All was well. Daisy went on down the stairs. She found DS Mackinnon perched uneasily on the shield-back chair in the hall. He jumped up when he saw her.

'How is the lady, Mrs Fletcher?'

'Much better. I was just going to ring up my husband and tell him he can come and see her.'

He flushed. 'I already did,' he said guiltily. 'The doctor said it was all right.'

Daisy smiled at him kindly. The poor man must hate the tendency to blush even more than she did. It would make life very difficult for a police officer, so the fact that he had reached the rank of detective sergeant meant he was pretty competent at his job. Alec's keeping a division man on the case when the Yard had taken over also spoke well of Mackinnon.

So he probably had a good grasp of what was going on, and with any luck she might wheedle some information out of him before Alec arrived.

'That's good,' she said. 'When I last spoke to him, he said he was going to see Lord Henry again, so I thought I'd have to leave a message. Lord Henry wasn't exactly forthcoming last night.' That seemed a fairly safe deduction. 'As for his alibi, it sounds pretty vague.'

'Yes,' agreed the obliging sergeant. 'DC Piper canna find the restaurant his lordship said he and the lady lunched at. Not a single waiter in any restaurant in or near Oxford Street recognized his photograph.'

'And his looks are rather distinctive,' Daisy mused. So Creighton had admitted to being with Daphne at lunchtime yesterday, and had attempted to give them both an alibi. 'Do you know if Tom – Sergeant Tring – managed to get hold of the errand boy I found for him?'

'Yes indeed, easily, with the information you provided, ma'am. He hadna seen anything useful, but he gave the names of others who use the alley regularly, and some of them provided more names. Last I heard, Sergeant Tring was working his way through a list as long as your arm, and most of them out and about on their bicycles.'

'Poor Tom!'

'Dinna fash yoursel', as we say in my part of the world. He's sitting still and letting them come to him.'

'While you've been slogging round all the neighbours, and I'd bet none of them have seen anything.'

'You'd win the bet hands down, Mrs Fletcher. This is the worst sort of place from our point of view. The houses are hidden from each other and the servants aren't local people, as they would be in the country.'

'Each house is an island, entire of itself,' Daisy misquoted, doubtless making John Donne spin in his grave. Compounding the offence, she went on, 'Never send to know for whom the bell tolls, they all know by now it tolls for poor Raymond Talmadge.'

'So they do.' Mackinnon, with a thorough Scots education behind him, was less successful than Tom Tring in concealing his amusement, not having a moustache to hide behind. 'However, I did get the names of all the shops that delivered to this street yesterday, and those also are on Sergeant Tring's list.'

'The butcher, the baker, the candlestick maker. I hope some of them overlap with the alley users. Oh, there goes the phone again.'

Mackinnon was closer to the study and beat her to it. He gave the number, listened, then said, 'Detective Sergeant Mackinnon, sir.'

All Daisy could hear was a distant quack-quack.

'The doctor says the lady is out of danger, sir.'

'Danger!' That came through loud and clear.

'*Out* of danger, sir,' Mackinnon said soothingly.

Quack-quack.

'I havena seen Mrs Talmadge myself, sir, but I assure you I wouldna dream of bullying her, or anyone else. Nor would Detective Chief Inspector Fletcher . . . Now just hold on a minute, sir. Hold the line, please.' He put his hand over the mouthpiece and turned to Daisy. 'Lord Henry Creighton, Mrs Fletcher, as you'll doubtless have guessed. He says he's coming right over.'

'Bringing his solicitor?'

'He didn't say so.'

'Well, that could mean they're both innocent,' Daisy said thoughtfully, 'or it could be an oversight.'

'What do you think the Chief Inspector would want me to tell his lordship?'

'I can't see it matters if he comes. You and Alec between

you should be able to keep them apart as long as you want, and Alec might even find it useful to bring them together.'

The sergeant grinned. 'In his presence. Verra well, I'll say he can come.' He turned back to the apparatus. 'My lord? Hello?' Shrugging, he hung up the earpiece. 'It seems his lordship didna wait for permission. I hope Mr Fletcher will get here first.'

'Dinna fash yoursel',' Daisy said with a smile. 'If Alec left right away, he'll have missed the rush hour, whereas Lord Henry should land right in the thick of it. And if he should somehow happen to arrive first, I'll be frightfully chatty and clinging and he'll be far too polite to brush me off.'

CHAPTER 13

Daisy didn't have to display her talent for adhesive loquacity. She just had time to ring up a nurses' agency before Alec arrived.

Sergeant Mackinnon reported apologetically that his lordship was on the way. Alec frowned.

'It's not his fault,' said Daisy. 'Lord Henry hung up without giving him a chance to say he mustn't come. But if you think about it, darling, it's really very convenient. You wanted to see him anyway. Now you won't have to chase after him. And if you want, you can see the two of them together.'

'True,' Alec grunted. His look conveyed that while she might be telling the truth and nothing but the truth, he didn't for a moment believe it was the whole truth. 'I must go and talk to Mrs Talmadge before he turns up.' He started towards the stairs.

Daisy caught his arm. 'Hang on, darling. I have news for you.'

'Can't it wait, Daisy?'

'Not really. Daphne asked me to tell you before you go to her. And it's no good looking at me like that. She insisted on seeing me, and Dr Curtis said she wasn't to be upset.'

'All right,' he sighed. 'Let's have it.'

'She claims she told her husband about the baby – which she admitted is Lord Henry's, by the way – and that he – Talmadge, that is – agreed to accept it as his own.'

'That seems excessively noble of him,' Alec said sceptically.

'No, quite reasonable actually, darling. They neither of them wanted the scandal of a divorce, for the sake of the child and his career. She says they intended to make a new start with their marriage, to try to patch it together. He was to break off with his mistress—'

'Does she know who that was?'

'She didn't mention a name. She said his *current* mistress. No, his *latest*, I think. I didn't have Piper and his notebook with me, but I'd remember if she'd given a name. Though that doesn't mean she doesn't know, of course. I could hardly ask. Her part of the bargain was to tell Lord Henry she could never see him again, which she claims to have done.'

'She told him she's pregnant?'

'So she says.'

'And that it's his child?'

'So she says.'

Mackinnon looked as if he were bursting to speak. Alec raised an eyebrow at him.

'I'd've thought his lordship'd be delighted, sir, her not wanting him to take responsibility for the bairn. Surely he wouldna go off and murder her husband!'

'So one would expect,' Alec agreed. 'However, it's so obvious that he had only to claim that such was the case and all the world would believe him. I'd certainly be inclined to. Yet he didn't.'

'Chivalry,' Daisy suggested. 'After all, it would have cast

even more suspicion on Daphne if she could hope that Raymond's death would force Lord Henry to take care of her and his child. Did he say anything about her being pregnant?'

'No. He said nothing that could be construed as an admission that she was his mistress.'

'More chivalry. Or else he didn't know and she made up that story out of whole cloth.'

'I noticed that you said she "claims" this and that, and "so she says". You didn't believe her?'

'She was very convincing, darling, but I must admit I wouldn't be surprised if there was no reconciliation, or there was but she didn't tell Lord Henry about it, or that she didn't tell him the baby's his. I think your scepticism must be rubbing off on me.'

Alec laughed. 'And vice versa. I'm inclined to believe most of what Creighton told me and to credit his reticence, and even his lies, to chivalry. I shan't let it influence me, of course. He's very high on my list.'

'Just below Daphne, I take it.'

'They're about equal, now you've told me about the reconciliation with Talmadge. If true, and if Creighton's passion for her is genuine, that vastly increases his motive.'

'Yes, I wondered if she realizes that.'

'I'd better go and see if I can find out, before he turns up breathing fire.'

'She'd like me to be with her,' Daisy said tentatively. She didn't want to ruin her present rapport with Alec.

He raised his eyes to heaven, but said, 'Right-o, if you'll take notes and keep your mouth shut. But only because I must leave Sergeant Mackinnon down here to stop Creighton barging up the stairs when he arrives.'

'I'll do my best, sir,' said the sergeant.

On the way upstairs, Daisy said, 'Remember, darling, whether she's telling the truth or not, Daphne's been under heavy sedation followed by a medical emergency. She's pretty fragile.'

'I promise not to put her through the "third degree". But any questions I ask are bound to be upsetting. This is a murder investigation and she's one of the chief suspects.'

'And it's just possible that she's innocent, and that her lover has just murdered her husband, with whom she's just reconciled. Just be careful.'

'I'll be just,' he said with a grin. 'I see I was not mistaken in thinking you'd taken her under your wing.'

She turned her head to wrinkle her nose at him. 'Not exactly. I'm sorry for her, but ... Well, here we are.' She knocked on Daphne's bedroom door.

Nurse Hensted came to the door. She looked resigned when she saw Daisy, but the sight of Alec obviously dismayed her. 'Mrs Talmadge isn't fit,' she said fiercely.

'I know,' he said. 'I'm sorry, but I can't put off interviewing her any longer. I'll disturb her as little as I possibly can.'

'Don't worry, I'll see to it,' said Daisy.

'I'd better stay,' said the nurse.

'I'm afraid that won't be possible,' Alec said firmly, and ushered the nurse out. He went over to the bed, where Daphne lay flat, only her head raised an inch or two by a single thin pillow. Daisy could tell he was trying to conceal his shock at Daphne's ravaged face. He hadn't seen her since the murder, had never seen her without her usual immaculate make-up. 'I'm very sorry to trouble you at such a time, Mrs Talmadge,' he said, his voice gentle. 'I'm afraid I have to ask you a few questions.'

She gave him a pitiful smile. 'I'll do my best to answer, Mr Fletcher. Or should I call you Chief Inspector today?'

'Mr Fletcher will do nicely. I gather you asked Daisy to be present at this interview? I am not at this time taking an official statement which you would be asked to sign, but if you don't mind she will take notes for me.'

'Not at all. I'd much rather her than anyone else.'

'Thank you.' He sat down, and Daisy perched with her notebook on the dressing-table stool. 'Will you tell me, please, exactly what you did yesterday from about nine o'clock in the morning on?'

'Nine? That's when I got up. I usually have breakfast in bed while I open the post, but I've been feeling rather unwell first thing in the morning. I went downstairs after my bath, and Hilda brought me some tea and toast. I was too upset to eat, though.'

'Why was that? No,' he went on as she cast a pleading glance at Daisy, 'I need you to tell me yourself.'

'I . . . You see, the day before, I went to see a doctor, because of feeling sick in the morning and . . . and other things.'

'Dr Curtis?'

'No, a friend of my father's. He practises in Harley Street.'

'His name, please.'

'Pettibone. Arthur Pettibone. When I was a child, I used to call him Uncle Arthur. He told me I was expecting a baby, and he said my father would have been delighted to have a grandchild. My father died several years ago, you see. Only, of course, Father wouldn't have been pleased at all, because . . . because it's not my husband's child.'

'You're quite certain of that?'

'Absolutely. We've had separate bedrooms for years and . . . and each gone our own way. Believe me, if I could have claimed it as Raymond's child, I would have.'

'So the next morning you were still so upset about the news as to be unable to eat.'

'No, it wasn't that. I . . . in spite of everything, I was happy that I was going to have a baby. I've always wanted children, more than one. I was an only child, you see.'

'I see. Then what upset you?'

'It was the night before. I . . . I told Raymond about the baby.' Daphne's voice was so faint Daisy had to lean forward to hear her. 'He asked if I wanted a divorce. I said no, for the baby's sake, and he said that was lucky because a divorce would ruin him. He said . . . he said he'd accept the baby as his own, as long as I promised never to see Harry again.'

'Harry?' Alec asked, for the record.

'Lord Henry Creighton,' Daphne whispered. 'I agreed.' Then her voice grew stronger as she went on, 'But only on condition that he also would be true to his vows.'

What's sauce for the goose is sauce for the gander, Daisy thought, scribbling away in her own idiosyncratic version of Pitman's shorthand.

'You're quite certain he wasn't faithful?' Alec asked.

'Quite certain. He wasn't even faithful to one mistress, but he swore never to start a new liaison and to tell his present lover it was all over between them.'

'His present lover – do you know who she was?'

'I didn't, and I'm not sure now. But he sat down at the escritoire in the drawing room and wrote to her right then and there – it wasn't too late to catch the last post at the post office in the High Street. He left the letter on the table in the hall while he went to put on his coat to go out and post it. I didn't pick up the envelope and read it, but I glanced at it from a little distance and I think it was addressed to Mrs Francis Walker.'

Major Francis Walker? Daisy wondered. She didn't think she'd ever heard the major's Christian name. The coincidence of surname was too great to be pure chance, though. It must be Gwen Walker. Besides, Alec looked satisfied, insofar as his impassive-policeman face allowed such an emotion.

'Thank you,' he said. 'It was your interview with your husband, then, that made you lose your appetite for breakfast yesterday?'

'Yes. Well, not exactly. It was the p-prospect of saying g-goodbye to Harry.' Daphne sounded on the edge of tears, as if she had a lump in her throat.

Alec handed her a handkerchief. He went through vast numbers of hankies, as weeping suspects rarely laundered and returned them to him. She sniffed into it and dabbed her eyes.

'You already had an appointment with Lord Henry?' Alec asked.

'Yes. There was a preview at Sotheby's, the auction house, of Sarah Bernhardt's effects. She collected the most marvellously exotic objets d'art, and they had some of her own paintings, too, and the manuscripts of her plays. She wrote and painted, as well as acting. Did you ever see her on the stage?'

'Yes, in France during the war. She came to entertain the troops, though by then she was over seventy and missing a leg. You enjoyed the preview, then, Mrs Talmadge?'

Daphne's enthusiasm vanished. 'Harry did. He couldn't help it, though he saw that I was unhappy. It's just the sort of stuff he likes best. I didn't want to spoil it for him so I paid attention and I suppose I found it impossible not to appreciate such wonderful things. I couldn't tell him there, anyway. About the baby. It wasn't busy, but there were always people around.'

'How long were you at Sotheby's?'

'I took a taxi and got there just at eleven, which was when we'd arranged to meet. I think it was about noon when we left.'

'And then?'

'Oh, we walked for a bit, while I ... while I told him everything.'

'Everything?' Alec asked sharply.

'That ... that I was going to have his baby, and that Raymond and I were going to patch things up and try to make a go of it. And that I couldn't see him again. He was devastated. He wanted me to go abroad with him, to let Raymond divorce me and then we'd be married. Perhaps I'm a coward, but I couldn't face the scandal, not just for my own sake but for his, and our child's. I know lots of people don't snub divorcees the way they did even ten years ago, but plenty still do. We'd live under a cloud for the rest of our lives.'

Daisy wondered whether Daphne was deliberately making a play for Alec's sympathy, or just wallowing in her own self justification. And the question recurred: was she deceiving herself or attempting to deceive Alec? Did she or did she not realize that the more desperate she painted Lord Henry, the more suspicion must fall on him?

'I'm doing my best to stay calm now,' Daphne went on, 'but I was as upset as Harry then. We had intended to lunch together but neither of us felt like eating. We went ...'

After a long pause, Alec said, 'You went?'

'We went . . . We went to Regent's Park.' This statement had the same air of inspired improvisation as when she had told Daisy about her husband's imaginary disappointment. 'He accepted my decision to stay with Raymond, you see, but we just wanted a little more time together before we parted forever.'

'You walked to the park?'

'No, I . . . we took a taxi. We sat on a bench by the lake and talked.'

'In the rain.'

'It wasn't really raining, just an occasional shower. We had umbrellas.'

But she hadn't been carrying an umbrella when she stepped out of the taxi yesterday. Daisy particularly remembered, having just discovered she'd left her own behind. Of course, Daphne might have forgotten hers in the taxi, but women who habitually took taxis, rather than buses or the Tube, often didn't bother with an umbrella.

Anyway, her story of sitting in the park conflicted with Lord Henry's of going to a restaurant. Either they had not been together and were trying, ineptly, to give each other alibis, or they were together – committing murder.

While Daisy pondered, Alec had asked something to which Daphne responded, 'I don't know exactly. I didn't look at my watch, but it didn't seem very long. Daisy knows what time I got home, and I came straight by taxi from . . . the park.'

'Ten past two,' Daisy said. Wherever Daphne had been, it wasn't Regent's Park. 'No, call it twelve or thirteen minutes past, if you want precision. It was ten past when I checked the time a couple of minutes before Daphne arrived.'

'Thank you,' said Alec, giving her an I-told-you-to-keep-quiet look. 'Mrs Talmadge, I understand you jumped to the conclusion that your husband had committed suicide. Do you mind telling me what you thought might have driven him to take his own life?'

No drivel about a Harley Street practice this time. 'Everything.' Tears started again. 'I thought he must have been brooding about the baby not being his and . . . oh, everything! I felt that way myself.' Her voice quavered. 'If it wasn't for the baby, I might have tried to kill myself.'

To Daisy's wifely eyes, Alec looked torn between disbelief in Daphne's melodramatic statement and concern over her emotional condition. With outward equanimity he said, 'I'm very glad you didn't, and I trust the impulse has passed. Just one or two more questions, if you feel up to it.' Not waiting for an answer, he went on, 'Did you know your husband was in the habit of inhaling laughing gas?'

'Yes. I asked him to stop, but he said he knew what he was doing so it wasn't at all dangerous. I don't think he did it very often.'

'Who else knew?'

'Just Nurse Hensted, I think. I never told anyone, of course, and I doubt she did. It wouldn't do his practice any good.'

'I dare say. Can you suggest anyone who might have a motive for hating or fearing your husband?'

Daphne gave a short, unamused laugh. 'I suppose most of his patients feared him. The only person I can think of who might have hated him enough to murder him is his mistress' husband.'

CHAPTER 14

'She's right, darling, don't you think?' Daisy led the way downstairs. From above, her shingled head looked like a bronze chrysanthemum, Alec thought. He recalled how she had jammed her hat down over her head when she had her hair cut short, for fear he'd hate it. Her next words, however, were of a kind to dispel tender memories: 'If Major Walker discovered his wife was having an *affaire* with Raymond Talmadge, he'd burst a blood vessel. At least, I've only met him a couple of times, but he struck me as a bit of a fire-eater.'

'You're assuming Gwen Walker is the woman in question. All we have is an unsubstantiated and unattributed rumour provided by a noted scandalmonger, and an address Mrs Talmadge herself admits she may have misread.'

'But they coincide.'

'I shall have to go and see her,' Alec conceded with a sigh. 'No sign of Creighton?' he asked Mackinnon as they reached the hall.

'I reckon he's stuck in traffic, sir. Likely he's not the sort to take the Tube.'

'Most unlikely,' said Daisy. 'Well, that clears up one puzzle, at least.'

Though Alec recognized a tactic intended to lead to a discussion of her theories of the crime he asked, 'What puzzle is that?'

'I've been wondering why, when she so obviously didn't want people to know about the gas-sniffing, she led me right to the surgery.'

'That's a good point. What's the answer?'

'She was so distraught after saying goodbye to Lord Henry forever, she just wasn't thinking clearly. Of course, that's assuming she actually did tell him it was all over.'

'You still suspect she made it up?'

'I don't know about that, but I'll tell you something I'm quite sure she made up. I don't believe for a moment that she and Lord Henry spent well over an hour sitting on a bench in Regent's Park; with or without umbrellas!'

'No,' Alec agreed.

'We might find the taxi man who brought her home, sir,' said Mackinnon. 'Then we'd know where he picked her up, and if there was a gentleman with her then.'

'It's worth a try. Get on to it when we finish here, will you? But I can't help thinking that if they were murdering Raymond Talmadge, both together or either one with the other's knowledge, they would have done a better job coordinating alibis! I wonder what they were doing?'

'I bet they were—' Mackinnon cut himself off, his face turning scarlet as he glanced shamefacedly at Daisy.

'You could be right, Sergeant,' she said. 'It wouldn't surprise me in the least if they went to a hotel for a final fling.'

Mackinnon gazed at Daisy with mingled embarrassment and awe. Apparently she had read his mind.

The last thing Alec needed was another detective officer

who believed Daisy to be infallible! Suppressing a groan, he said, 'I suppose it would explain why neither of them wants to admit where they were. And even if it's not true, the possibility gives me a point of attack when Creighton gets here. You don't mind walking home, do you, Daisy? Your umbrella's in the car.'

'I'll fetch it, Mrs Fletcher,' Mackinnon offered eagerly, and was gone before she could say yea or nay.

For once she didn't argue. 'I'll get these notes typed for you before I go out, darling.'

'That would be a help.' Alec thought she looked a bit tired. 'Do you really have to go to this dinner party tonight, love?'

'Yes, I told Mrs Randall I would and one can't let people down at the last minute. How lucky I said you couldn't make it.'

'Not a chance, thank heaven. First Creighton, then him and Mrs Talmadge together, if the nurse thinks she's up to it, and then I'd better go and have a word with Mrs Walker.'

'I hope the major doesn't shoot you for suggesting his wife is unfaithful. Come to think of it, doesn't death by laughing gas seem a bit subtle for a military man?'

'He'd hardly bring a pistol with him if he came to have it out with Talmadge. A horsewhip more likely. But if he found Talmadge already under the influence, perhaps laughing at his remonstrances, he might seize the opportunity. I'll worry about that if I find out Gwen Walker actually was Talmadge's mistress. Keep your ears open this evening.'

'I will, darling. Oh, by the way, Daphne's giving the nurse pay in lieu of notice. She can't stand her. In fact they can't stand each other and Miss Hensted is keen to be off. There'll be an agency nurse coming in the morning. Just in case you need to talk to her again.'

'That's all right, we have Miss Hensted's address.'

'I thought so. Thank you, Sergeant Mackinnon.' Taking from him her red umbrella – endearingly audacious in a world of black ones, Alec thought, especially as it clashed with her lilac costume – she pulled on her gloves. 'Do try to make sure the Chief gets something to eat, won't you? Even if it's just a sandwich. Cheerio, darling, and good luck.'

As the door closed behind her, Mackinnon said admiringly, 'Maybe we could do with a few lady detectives on the force.'

'No doubt the day will come,' Alec said dryly. 'The women constables we got last year seem to be working out quite well. While we wait, I'd better bring you up to date on what Mrs Talmadge said.'

Before he had quite finished, the doorbell rang, followed immediately by the rat-tat of the knocker. Gladys appeared from the nether regions. Alec waved her away and went to open the door himself.

'Good evening, Lord Henry.'

'Oh, it's you, Inspector.' No sign of the cool, even nonchalant façade Alec had met yesterday. In his agitation, Creighton had rushed out in his smoking jacket, embroidered crimson silk and most unsuitable for wearing in the street. He glanced wildly from Alec to Mackinnon and back. 'It wasn't you who told me Daphne is in danger?'

'*Out* of danger, sir,' said Mackinnon in a soothing tone Alec couldn't have bettered.

'You spoke to Detective Sergeant Mackinnon here, Lord Henry. Mrs Talmadge is resting comfortably.'

'But what happened? I must see her at once!'

'If Mrs Talmadge wishes to see you, and the nurse doesn't

forbid it, you shall go up as soon as you've answered a few questions.'

'Questions! I told you everything yesterday.'

'I think not, sir. Shall we go into the dining room?' Alec led the way, confident that Mackinnon, like a Scottish sheepdog, could be relied upon to herd Creighton after him. He pulled out a chair at the table, waited till Creighton sank onto it, then seated himself at the head of the table.

The sergeant, sitting down opposite Creighton, took his notebook from his pocket with a deliberation intended to impress his lordship with the serious nature of the interview.

'Perhaps you would like to . . . ah . . . amend your version of where you and Mrs Talmadge went yesterday,' Alec suggested.

'We went to Sotheby's, and then out to lunch.'

'I'm afraid Mrs Talmadge disagrees.'

'Have you been bullying her?' Creighton rose, angry yet weary, planting his fists on the table as much to help himself up as in a gesture of outrage. 'Ill as she is!'

'Certainly not.' Suspecting the man had spent a long night pacing the floor, Alec raised his hand palm down. Creighton collapsed back onto his chair. 'I talked to Mrs Talmadge in the presence of . . . a friend, a female friend, at her request. The nurse was within easy call.'

'But what happened to her? Tell me that, and I'll tell you anything you like!'

'She nearly lost her baby. Your baby.'

Creighton seemed to crumple. 'If you know that, you know everything. You know why I couldn't tell the truth before. No gentleman could.'

He'd rather be suspected of murder than of being ungentlemanly? Alec wondered. 'So let's hear it now.'

'We did go to Sotheby's and we were there from eleven till about noon. We would have left sooner, because I could tell Daphne was in distress though she tried to hide it, but she insisted that I must see everything I was interested in. Afterwards, we could not talk in the street, and she didn't want to go to a restaurant, so we went to a friend's flat.'

Alec had to suppress a smile at Sergeant Mackinnon's disappointed expression. A flat, not a hotel – Daisy had missed the mark, though she was right that the park story was pure fabrication. No doubt Mrs Talmadge had been too embarrassed to confess to the love nest.

Creighton continued. 'There, she told me . . . I expect you know what she told me.'

'I need to hear it in your own words, sir.'

'Oh, very well.' He removed his monocle from his eye and started to polish it on a silk handkerchief. Without it he looked much more human, haggard and defenceless. His gaze remained fixed on the mechanical motion of his fingers as he continued. 'She told me she was going to bear my child. She had already spoken to her husband, who apparently was willing to accept the child as long as she never saw me again. Except to say goodbye – I suppose that was generous of him. He could have made her write to me.'

As he had written his farewell to his lady-friend, Alec thought. Or had he? Perhaps the letter Mrs Talmadge watched him write had been to arrange a final rendezvous.

'I begged her to come away with me. We could go to the Continent, where people are more tolerant of such arrangements, and let Talmadge divorce her. I would have married her like a shot, but she was adamant . . .' He looked up, his expression lightening. 'I *will* marry her. She's free now, after all these years!'

'Free because her husband has been murdered.'

Creighton's busy hands instantly stilled and his face went blank. After a frozen moment, he returned the monocle to his eye and his face resumed its usual lopsided inscrutability. With studied care he tucked the handkerchief into his pocket. 'It must have been an accident,' he asserted.

'It was not an accident, Lord Henry. I warned you that honesty really is the best policy, in spite of which you lied to me. And now I find you have an excellent and immediate motive for wanting Raymond Talmadge dead. I must now warn you that anything you say will be written down and may be used in evidence. Do you wish to ring up your lawyer?'

'Lord, no! The old buzzard would have a fit if he found out the mess I seem to have got myself into. Been the family's man for centuries, don't you know. He'd go straight to m'father. No, I didn't do Talmadge in, and you seem to know the worst already. I'll "come clean", as I believe they say in America. Fire away.'

Oddly, the official warning seemed to have restored his lordship to the breezy manner with which he had first greeted Alec yesterday.

'The address of the Dixons' flat, please.'

'The Dix— Devil take it, how did you know?'

'The address, please.'

'Six J, Oxford and Cambridge Mansions, Old Marylebone Road.'

'Was Captain Dixon at home when you arrived? Or Mrs Dixon?'

'No. They've gone down to Henley for the week. They have a place on the river.'

'Address, please.'

'Dabchick Cottage, Wargrave Road.'

'Telephone?'

'No, they don't have one down there. They don't know we were at the flat yesterday. I've got a key, you see.'

'I'll just take charge of that for now, sir. Sergeant, write out a receipt. So no one saw you at the flat?'

'Oh yes, their cleaning woman was there. Mrs ... uh ... Mrs Simpkins. She can tell you when we arrived.'

'And when you left?'

'No. She goes home at one. We were there till nearly two o'clock. It . . .' The breeziness dropped away. 'It isn't easy to say goodbye forever after eighteen years.'

'No doubt the doorkeeper or lift boy will be able to confirm the time.'

'No doorkeeper, no lift,' Creighton said uneasily.

Very convenient for an illicit rendezvous; less so if you wanted to prove an alibi. 'What did you do when you reached the street?'

'We walked round the corner to the taxi rank in the Edgware Road. Mrs Talmadge took a cab home. I went to the New Theatre, as I told you before.'

'In St Martin's Lane?'

'Yes. I just wanted to be somewhere where I didn't have to talk to people. Look here, Chief Inspector, can't you trace the taxi drivers?'

'We'll do our best, sir. Did you see anyone you know at the theatre?'

'The girl in the box office. She'll tell you I arrived just in time for the first act. Mrs Talmadge probably reached home a bit earlier than . . . Oh, Lord, when did he die?'

Alec decided there was no harm now in letting him know. 'The body was found at about quarter past two.'

'Aahh!' Creighton looked as if he'd just been given the crown worn by Edmund Kean in his celebrated *Richard III*.

'By Mrs Talmadge.'

'Yes, horrible! Shattering!' Relief forgotten, his lordship started up. 'I *must* go to her.'

Alec stood. 'Just another minute or two, sir. If you'll wait here, I'll go and check with the nurse.' Though an inch or two shorter, he dominated the other by force of will and authority. Lord Henry sat down.

A slight motion of Alec's head brought Mackinnon from the room in his train. 'Sergeant, I want enquiries started right away to try and trace those taxicabs. It's a bit late in the day but we might catch some cabbies who don't work mornings.'

'You don't reckon they had time after the char left to pop over here and do Talmadge in?'

'At a pinch. It would take planning and very precise timing, and that's not how I see this crime. For one thing, they couldn't expect Talmadge to carefully arrange himself in the chair at just the right time, and take enough gas to prevent his resisting. And for another, the nurse was due back at two o'clock, remember, which would cut the timing even closer.'

'And you canna count on getting a taxi just when you want it, not in these parts anyway, to get back to Marylebone Road after.'

'Nor ask a driver to wait. He'd be sure to report it as soon as he read about the murder. Those fellows are always up on the latest news, gossiping and reading the papers while they wait for fares.'

'Maybe one of the two left before the charwoman, without her knowledge. If she saw the other, she'd assume both were still there.'

'Might be possible. We'll get Tom Tring onto the woman. For the rest, DC Piper can help you track down the cabmen. It's the sort of exercise in logistics he's good at. If you have time before our meeting this evening, go to Oxford and Cambridge Mansions and have a word with the neighbours. Someone might have seen something. Here's the key to Six J. Should you get caught popping in to take a look around, I don't know you. It's not worth taking risks for, mind. We'll get the Dixons' permission tomorrow if necessary. I'll leave the job to you.'

'Right, Chief,' Mackinnon said with a grin. 'I mean, yes, sir!'

'Chief will do, while we're on this job. As long as no one else is around except Tring and Piper. Or my wife.'

Struggling to keep a straight face, Mackinnon repeated, 'Right, Chief,' and headed for the study.

Alec went upstairs and found Miss Hensted sitting on a chair at Daphne Talmadge's bedroom door.

'She won't have me in there,' the nurse said resentfully. 'Who's that just arrived, then? Her fancy man?'

'Lord Henry Creighton. He wants a word with her, if she's fit enough.'

'I don't suppose it'll hurt her, as long as I'm in there to see he don't get her worked up.'

'That won't be necessary, Miss Hensted. I shall be present.'

'I ought to be there. I'm her nurse, after all. I can tell when she's had enough.'

'I shan't let him stay long, and you will be just outside the door.'

She subsided, looking vexed. Alec had the impression that she was less interested in her patient's welfare than in hearing what was said. She disliked Mrs Talmadge, he recalled, her allegiance being given to her late employer. Perhaps she hoped Mrs Talmadge and Lord Henry would accuse each other of killing the dentist, or still better, one would incriminate the other. Death was no horror to a nurse, and witnessing an arrest would no doubt crown the ghoulish tale of her employer's murder.

'Will you warn her, please, that we'll be up in a couple of minutes?'

'I'll tell her *you're* coming. Best if she doesn't have time to get too excited about *him*.'

Alec didn't argue. It suited him quite well that the confrontation should be unexpected on one side at least. He went back down.

Creighton was coming out of the dining room. 'Well?' he demanded.

'Nurse Hensted says it's all right for you to see Mrs Talmadge for a few minutes. I'll take you up.' He turned and led the way.

Nurse Hensted met them at the top of the stairs. 'She's to stay flat on her back,' she commanded his lordship, 'and don't you go getting her wrought up or she'll lose that baby yet.'

'Righty-o, Nurse,' he said meekly.

'Just a few minutes, mind!'

Creighton looked disconcerted when Alec went first into the room but he didn't protest.

'I've brought Lord Henry to see you, Mrs Talmadge.'

'Harry!' Her pale cheeks flushed and she started to sit up.

'Lie down, or he'll have to leave.'

Obeying, she reached out both her hands. Creighton loped across the pink carpet to take them.

'Oh, Harry!'

'My poor dear!'

They gazed at each other, bemused. Less and less satisfied with either or both of them as murderers, Alec was now impatient to interview Mrs Walker. A wife and her lover were usually the prime suspects in the death of a husband, but as Congreve so nearly said, Hell has no fury like a woman scorned. Perhaps Gwen Walker had not accepted her dismissal gracefully – if, in fact, she had been Talmadge's mistress. Alec wished he had more definite information in that regard.

At the window, he leaned half seated on the sill. Creighton and Daphne Talmadge seemed to have forgotten his presence. She was telling him about the miscarriage she hadn't quite had. Neither mentioned nor even apparently gave a thought to the death of Raymond Talmadge and her discovery of his lifeless corpse in the dentist's chair.

'Daisy Fletcher was so very kind,' said Mrs Talmadge. 'I don't know what I'd have done without her.'

'Fletcher?' Creighton looked a startled query at Alec, who looked back with his blandest expression, the one Daisy accused him of practising in the looking glass.

'Yes, the Chief Inspector's wife. She had an appointment with poor Raymond and she was with me when I . . . when . . .'

'Don't talk about it, dearest. Don't even think about it. We'll be married as soon as you are well enough and then you can forget all about the unhappy past. I'll see about getting a licence right away.'

'Oh, Harry!'

Alec averted his eyes. A loud knocking came to his relief, followed by Miss Hensted's neatly capped head appearing around the door.

'Time's up!' she cried with a jollity ill suited to her piquant features. 'Now, now, my lord, that's enough of that or we'll be having a relapse.' She chivvied Creighton and Alec out and closed the door on them.

Creighton turned to Alec. 'No startling revelations for you, Chief Inspector,' he said sardonically.

'Not startling, no.' Alec matched his tone. 'But your obvious fondness for one another and your desire to marry can only be regarded as confirmation of your motive for disposing of Talmadge.'

'"A hit, a very palpable hit!" I can only assure you that neither of us did so, and I'm sure I'm wasting my breath.'

'Afraid so, sir.' He looked around as Hilda Kidd came along the passage from the stairs to the second floor. 'Good evening, Miss Kidd.'

'Have you been bothering Mrs Talmadge?' the sour-faced maid demanded, then she saw Creighton, and bobbed a curtsy. 'Oh, it's you, my lord! I hope you've come to stop them police h'rassing my mistress.'

'I'm doing my best ... Hilda, isn't it? I'm sure you're taking good care of her.'

'I do what I can, my lord, but that nurse, she's been interfering something awful. It's my turn to take over now. You see, there'll be a great argument over it.'

'I believe Miss Hensted is leaving tonight, for good,' said Alec.

'Does Daphne not need a nurse any longer?' Creighton asked anxiously.

'I understand there's an agency nurse coming in the morning. Miss Hensted is taking pay in lieu of notice.'

'Then I'll make so bold, my lord, as to ask will you pay her off right now?' the maid implored. 'I don't want Mrs Talmadge being troubled for money, she's got enough troubles in her dish already.'

'Of course.' Creighton took out his wallet. 'How much?'

'That I don't know, being none of my business. And you don't want to take *her* word for it, neither.' Hilda disappeared into the bedroom.

Creighton looked at Alec, who shrugged. 'I expect the records of her pay are down in the study. We'll take her down there and have a look.'

The sound of raised voices filtered through the door. A moment later Nurse Hensted flounced out. She turned for a Parthian shot: 'You'll be bloody lucky if the new nurse'll put up with your squabble-some ways! Pardon my language, my lord, I'm sure,' she added primly.

Creighton explained that he was going to give her a cheque for wages due, since Mrs Talmadge was out of commission. As they went down to the study, Miss Hensted pointed out that she needed a recommendation, too.

'How long did you work for Talmadge?' his lordship enquired. 'Three years? Then I believe I can truthfully assume you gave entire satisfaction. I'll write you a reference. No one will wonder, in the sad event of the death of your employer.'

Alec, reading over his shoulder, was filled with admiration at the way he managed to write nothing but the truth while giving the impression he was personally acquainted with Nurse Hensted's admirable qualities. It reminded him of Creighton's attempt to imply that Mrs Talmadge had gone with him to the theatre. A slippery customer!

As for Nurse Hensted, she went off more than satisfied. A reference from a lord was not to be sneezed at, she said.

'Shall I ring up for a taxi for you or did you keep yours waiting?' Alec asked Creighton.

'Taxi? No, I brought the Bentley. But I was going to stay here.'

'I don't think that would be a very good idea, sir. After all the pain caused by Mrs Talmadge's determination to avoid scandal . . .'

'You're right, of course. I wasn't thinking. She'll be all right, won't she, with the maid to take care of her?'

'I'm sure she will.'

They went out together. His lordship's Bentley sports car stood in the drive, its hood up against the persistent rain, which had spotted the royal blue paint. A neat and fast machine, of whose existence Alec had been unaware. In that, Creighton could easily have dashed over from Marylebone Road, quarrelled with Talmadge, killed him and returned to Oxford and Cambridge Mansions in time to put his lady-love in a cab for home.

CHAPTER 15

The spring evening was drawing towards dusk when Alec stopped the Baby Austin outside the Walkers' house. Major and Mrs Francis Walker lived in a street not far from and very similar to Gardenia Grove. The semi-detached houses were slightly smaller and newer, with smaller gardens, but attractive enough. A military pension would hardly stretch to so desirable a residence, so the major must have a private source of income, unless it was his wife's money.

In that case, if rumour spoke true, the Walkers matched the Talmadges as an advertisement against men marrying for money.

But that was jumping the gun. Alec had no real evidence that the Walkers' marriage was less than perfect, and none at all that the money came from the distaff side of the family.

He had met them socially, quite a few times over the past few years, he supposed, but he could not say he knew them. The major, an irascible man, played bridge and golf. Gwen Walker was a fashionable beauty some fifteen years younger than her husband. Goodness only knew what her interests and pastimes were if they did not include Raymond Talmadge.

Very likely Alec's mother could tell him a good deal about the couple, but she wouldn't appreciate being asked, not for such a reason. No doubt she was already furious because Daisy had got herself involved in the present case.

Cravenly, Alec prayed he would not have to intervene between the two Mrs Fletchers. He'd far rather face the major, even with such a thin excuse for questioning him.

He rang the doorbell and was not surprised to be left standing on the step for a few minutes. Like the Fletchers, the Walkers probably had just one live-in servant, who would be busy in the kitchen at this hour. In fact, the elderly cook-housekeeper came to the door wiping her hands on her apron, looking harassed. In case he didn't cotton on, she glowered at him to remind him that this was neither a conventional nor a convenient hour for an unexpected visitor.

'I'm sorry to call at such an awkward time,' he said. 'I was hoping for a word with Mrs Walker. Detective Chief Inspector Fletcher.'

'I'll see.'

The door shut in his face. A couple of minutes later, Mrs Walker herself reopened it.

'So sorry, Mr Fletcher.' Her scarlet smile was bright but her blue eyes were wary. 'Very naughty of Bates to shut you out, and in the rain, too! She's a frightful grouch but her cooking is divine, and it's terribly hard to find good servants these days, isn't it? Do come in.'

Only one possible reason for such a warm welcome sprang to mind: Gwen Walker had some more than ordinary cause for interest in Talmadge's death.

'Thank you.' Alec hung his damp hat on the hat rack and followed her into the front room. Her black hair was unbobbed, pinned up behind in a complicated chignon. She was wearing a chiffon tea gown, green and gold, which made the most of her fashionably boyish figure. The wide sash around her hips swayed enticingly as she moved, but not, he thought, with deliberate provocation. It was her natural walk.

The sitting room they entered was furnished in post-war modernist style, with a good deal of glass, tubular steel and black leather. The starkness of the decor was offset by the room's untidiness. Tea things, for three people, had not been cleared and a half-empty cocktail glass had joined them on the glass-topped table. Beside one chair, a stack of fashion magazines sprawled across the white carpet while a copy of *Vogue*, open and facedown, crowned the chair's arm. A partly smoked cigar, cold and dead, balanced on the rim of an ashtray heaped with ash and cigarette ends, most of them lipstick stained.

She turned to face him. 'I assume this is a business, not a social visit, Mr Fletcher? I've heard about . . . what happened, of course. But I hardly knew poor Mr Talmadge.' The slightest of tremors shook her cool voice as she pronounced the name. 'Just the usual dinner parties and so on. He wasn't even my dentist.'

'We often glean useful details from the merest acquaintances, Mrs Walker. You don't mind if I ask a few questions?'

'No, of course not. Do you care for a cocktail?'

'Thanks, not on duty.'

She picked up the half-full glass. 'Won't you sit down?'

The awkward-looking chair of woven leather strips slung between bent pipes was surprisingly comfortable. So comfortable, in fact, that Alec found it impossible to sit straight with the formality proper to an interview. He doubted it mattered. Mrs Walker's tension was clear in the way her fingers turned the glass around and around. No stiffness on his part was necessary to establish the gravity of the situation, though she might not acknowledge it openly.

'I expect you want to know where I was at the crucial time?' She managed to laugh. 'I've read a few detective novels.'

'That's the first question we have to ask everyone. Where were you between, say, noon and two-thirty yesterday?'

'I went to lunch with a friend in Denham, an old schoolfriend.'

'Is she on the telephone?'

'No, she lives with her aged mother in rather poor circumstances, I'm afraid. I try to get down to see her as often as I can.'

'I'll have to have her name and address, but we shan't bother her unnecessarily.'

'Jennifer Crouch, Five Station Row. I arrived about half past twelve. I can't remember the exact time of the train. What . . .' She moistened her lips. 'What time did he die?'

'The medical evidence is never precise. How long have you known Raymond Talmadge, Mrs Walker?'

'Four or five years, I suppose. Francis and I came to live here when we were married, in 1919, after he was demobbed. I can't recall whether I met Daphne Talmadge at some hen party or Francis met . . . him, at the golf club, perhaps. Francis might remember. That must be him now.'

From the hall came sounds of the arrival of the master of the house. Alec cursed silently as the sitting-room door swung open.

'Hello, darling!'

'What the devil's going on here?' Major Walker was the very pattern of a retired army officer, ramrod straight, brusque, his greying toothbrush moustache as bushy as his *en-brosse* hair. He wore damp plus fours in a greenish herringbone tweed, and a matching Norfolk jacket open over a Fair Isle pullover. His face, ruddy from hours on the golf links rain or shine, tended to empurple under the stress of annoyance. 'Oh, it's you, Fletcher. What d'ye want?'

Alec heaved himself from his chair. 'Good evening, Major. I'm making enquiries with regard to the death of Raymond Talmadge. We have to talk to everyone who knew him.'

'Barely acquainted with the fellow. Dare say Gwen's sat next to him at dinner a couple of times. Sorry, we can't help you.'

'Just for the record, I must ask you where you were yesterday at lunchtime.'

'Yesterday? Lunched at my club. Army and Navy, Pall Mall. Now if you'll excuse us, Fletcher, we're dining out tonight. Got to change.'

At least he had a couple of alibis to check, Alec thought, accepting his dismissal. Time enough for more persistent questioning if they didn't pan out.

Mrs Walker had produced her alibi with the air of one who had planned it beforehand, though that did not mean it was not true. Alec decided he'd better run down to Denham himself to speak to Miss Crouch. If he had learnt anything at all, it was that Gwen Walker was badly disturbed by the dentist's death.

The rain had stopped at last. He drove home. Nana, in exile in the hall, greeted him ecstatically and her yip brought Belinda from the sitting room.

'Daddy! Mummy said you were going to be late home today. Nana, be quiet or Gran will never let you in the sitting room again.'

'What's she done now?'

'Nothing. Nothing much. She just saw a cat in the garden and shouted at it a bit, but she didn't try very hard to get out or she would have broken the glass, wouldn't she? Daddy, are you going out to dinner with Mummy, or staying with Gran and me?'

'I have to go on to the Yard later, pet. I'll have supper with you first, though, if it's soon. Daisy's not left yet?'

No, she's primping. That's what Gran calls it when she puts on powder and lip rouge and stuff. She said I could watch but Gran said I have to do my homework before supper. I've nearly finished. Will you look at it, Daddy? I wrote a story about Nana.'

'I'll read it before I go. Ask Dobson to have something on the table for me within ten minutes, will you? Even if it's just bread and cheese. I must have a word with Daisy now.'

Daisy was in their bedroom, seated at the dressing table, scowling at her image in the looking glass.

'What's wrong, love?' He kissed the back of her neck, nuzzling the feathery curls.

She waved an eyebrow pencil at him. 'Just wondering whether the result can possibly be worth all the trouble.'

'It's no good asking me. You look wonderful to me with or without all the trouble. You're not still worrying over that little mole by your mouth, are you?'

'No, not for ages, not since you told me about the "Kissing" patch eighteenth-century ladies used to wear just there. How lucky you specialized in the Georgians at university! Don't kiss me like that, Alec, or I'll drag you to bed here and now. Are you finished for the day? Shall I ring up Mrs Randall and say I've broken my leg and can't come to dinner?'

'No, alas, I'm due at the Yard shortly.'

'Darling, don't tell me you've solved the case without me?'

'No such luck. Nowhere near.'

'Good. Because the only reason I'm going to the Randalls' is to see if I can get some definite information about Gwen Walker for you.'

'Having seen her, I'm pretty certain you're right about her relationship with Talmadge. Needless to say, she denies more than a casual acquaintance, so if you can find me a witness to anything closer it would be extremely useful.'

'I'll do my best, darling, short of interrogating everyone at the table. Does she have an alibi? And the major?'

'Of sorts. They'll have to be checked.'

'What else have you found out?'

'Mrs Talmadge and Creighton lied about their where-abouts, and their new story may well be equally mendacious. But they make no bones about being in love.'

'Which they would surely attempt to hide if they were guilty – unless that's what they want you to think.'

'What a tortuous mind you have, my love!'

'I've learnt from you,' Daisy retorted. 'Did Tom find out anything from the errand boys?'

'I haven't heard from him yet. He's been all day at it so I hope it isn't turning out a sheer waste of time.'

'I expect each boy he talks to mentions another who uses the shortcut. Then he has to run that one to earth, when they're all buzzing all over the place all day.'

'Yes, and he may even have had to catch some at home after they finished work for the day, the lucky brats. No quitting time for us guardians of the law. We're all meeting in my office in about half an hour. I've got to get moving.'

'I wish I could go with you.'

'The super would scream blue murder, to put it mildly. Are you ready? Come down and sit with me while I have a quick bite and I'll give you a lift to the Randalls' on my way.'

She preceded him out of the room, no coquetry in her walk, conscious or unconscious. She was wearing her dark blue charmeuse, a thigh-length tunic over a straight under-skirt, a style, she had explained, intended to flatter her unfashionable figure. It didn't disguise anything from Alec, who found her gentle curves infinitely more enticing than the no-bosom-no-bottom look she so envied.

'You look delectable,' he said, stopping her with his arms around her waist. 'I hope Mrs Randall has invited all the dullest men in St John's Wood.'

She turned her head to look up and back at him, laughing. 'Beast! If you're not there, I'll need all the wittiest men to make up for your absence. No, don't kiss my nose or I'll have to powder it again. Come on, come and eat. I told Dobson to have something ready in case you managed to dash in.'

'There are advantages to murder in one's own neighbour-hood.'

'Yes, but I'm afraid your mother doesn't quite see it in that light.'

'Oh?' Alec enquired warily, but they had reached the hall. His mother and Belinda came out of the sitting room and Dobson appeared from the kitchen with a tray, and they all converged on the dining room.

'I thought you were dining out, Daisy.'

'I am, Mother. Alec has to go out again, so he's going to drop me off on his way.'

'It's only a five-minute walk. And the rain has stopped.'

'It's my pleasure to drive Daisy, Mother. What's that you have there, Dobson? It smells delicious.'

'It's a rag-out, sir. Leastways, what I'd call it's a fancy stew, but I cut out the recipe from the ladies' page in the *Sunday Graphic*, and rag-out's what they call it, with a little squiggle over the *u*.'

'That's because it's French, Dobson,' said Belinda. 'I think it's pronounced ra-goo, isn't it, Mummy?'

'More or less, darling.'

'Well, fancy you knowing that, Miss Bel, and you just starting French at school last September. Ra-goo, I'll remember that.'

'It smells heavenly,' said Daisy. 'I wish I wasn't going out.'

'I'll make it again, madam, when you're home for dinner.'

'I see,' said Alec, laughing, 'you're just trying it out on the rest of us to see if it's good enough for Daisy'

'Well, madam's used to the best, isn't she. I wouldn't want to let her down.'

Alec's mother sniffed, and it wasn't a sniff of appreciation of the savoury aroma. 'There's nothing wrong with a good Irish stew. I believe I ordered stew for supper today. That will be all, Dobson.'

'I love Irish stew,' said Daisy pacifically, 'but a change is nice. And anything is a change for the better after the eggs and sardines and cheese I survived on in Chelsea. Thank you, Dobson.'

'My pleasure, madam.'

The ragoût tasted as good as it smelled, but Alec was not allowed to enjoy it in peace. His mother poked and prodded suspiciously at the small helping she had taken, though such indecorum in Belinda would have drawn instant censure. She ate a boiled potato uncontaminated by the sauce, then laid down her knife and fork.

'Alec, I suppose you will be far too busy in the morning to give *me* a lift in the motorcar.'

'Where to, Mother? I'm not quite sure what I'll be doing first thing tomorrow, but if you're leaving early and it's not too far out of my way, you know I'll be happy to take you.'

'Waterloo Station.'

'Waterloo! Why on earth—?'

'I'm going to Bournemouth.'

'I hope my aunt hasn't fallen ill?'

'Darling, your mother is uncomfortable with an investigation so close to home, so to speak.' Daisy's eyes begged, *Don't kick up a dust!*

'Impertinent questions! And Daisy in the thick of things – it's intolerable!'

'Of course, Mother,' Alec soothed, 'there's no reason why you should have to suffer. I'll get you to Waterloo in plenty of time for your train, never fear.'

'Gertrude Harbison is going with me.'

'Then we shall pick up Mrs Harbison on the way, unless you're taking a lot of luggage. It's a small car, remember.'

'Granny's packed her big trunk,' Belinda announced, 'and a basket and an overnight case and three hatboxes.'

'There's no knowing how long I'll have to stay,' her grandmother said defensively. 'If Gertrude has to take a taxicab, I might as well share it with her.'

'I think you'll find it more convenient all around,' Alec agreed. He certainly would.

He finished his dinner – a staid rolypoly pudding followed

the ragoût – and while hastily drinking a cup of coffee he read Belinda's story. It made him laugh, to her delight.

'Maybe I'll be a writer like Mummy,' she said, handing him his hat. 'You will come and kiss me good night in bed, won't you, Daddy, however late you get home and even if I'm fast asleep?'

'Of course, pet. Ready, Daisy? Let's go.'

As he settled behind the wheel and reached for the self-starter, Daisy heaved a gigantic sigh.

'What's up, love? You know, if you really desperately don't want to go to this dinner party, I'd hate you to feel you must just because you might happen to find me a witness. The chances are pretty low. I could ring up Mrs Randall and say you've broken your leg, or more believably that your tooth is in agony. They all know all too well that you didn't manage to see the dentist.'

'Well, I can't say I'm looking forward to being interrogated about the murder, but I shan't cry off. Isn't it extraordinary that the blasted tooth hasn't given me a single twinge since then? Simply being in his waiting room seems to have cured it.'

'Most extraordinary.' The car, kept in good order by Scotland Yard's mechanics, started smoothly. Letting out the clutch and moving off, he asked, 'If the sigh wasn't for the dinner party, what's bothering you?'

'Guilt,' she said mournfully. 'It's all my fault that your poor mother's running away from home.'

'Great Scott, Daisy, don't talk such bosh!' Not that it wasn't true, but red-hot wild horses – as Belinda had once proclaimed – would never draw that admission from him.

'No, it's true, darling. She doesn't like the way I do things, and I ought to have tried to compromise more than I have. After all, it's been her home for simply ages, and I've just moved in and changed things. No wonder she's not happy.'

'But I am, love, and so is Belinda.'

'And that's another thing: she's brought Belinda up since she was four and now Bel tends to turn to me before her. It must seem frightfully unfair.'

'Daisy, I wasn't going to tell you this, because it seems to me unfair to you to talk about Joan, as well as not quite fair to Mother, but—'

'In that case, perhaps you shouldn't tell me.'

'But I can't have the situation making you unhappy. The fact is, Mother went to Bournemouth a few months after Joan and I married and didn't come back except for visits till Joan died.' He stopped the car outside the Randalls' house and turned to her.

'Really?'

'Mother is old-fashioned and not very flexible in her ideas. She didn't get on with Joan any better than she does with you. And grateful as I am to her for her care of Bel, to see Bel blossoming since you became her mother has been a pure joy to me.'

'Oh, darling!' Teardrops sparkled on her lashes in the light of the streetlamp. 'Right-o, I'll stop feeling guilty, except for a little bit because I'm relieved that she's going. After all it's only for a few days, this time, isn't it? Till we catch Talmadge's murderer. I haven't driven her away for good.'

'Well, we can always hope—'

'Alec!' She put her hand across his mouth. 'Don't say it. I'm very sorry for her. It's much the same with my mother. I love her, but in a dreadfully dutiful sort of way and I'd rather not have to spend too much time with her. I hope I won't be like that when I'm older.'

'You couldn't possibly!'

'Thank you, darling, and thank you for telling me about Joan. I suspect I'd have liked her no end. I'd better enter the lions' den now or they'll start the soup without me.'

He went round to open the car door for her, kissing her as she stepped onto the pavement. 'Don't walk home alone in the dark, love. Ring for a taxi.'

'I expect someone will give me a lift home. Toodle-oo, darling, don't work too hard. My best to Tom and Piper.'

He watched her go up the garden path and ring the doorbell. Joan would have liked her, too, he thought, and loved her for being a loving mother to Belinda. She was having a hard time trying to adjust to life in St John's Wood. Thank heaven she had her writing to fall back on.

His mother, who disapproved of the writing, was not helping Daisy's adjustment. As he drove towards Whitehall, Alec started to calculate. Suppose she were tactfully encouraged to go to live permanently with his aunt. His father had died young, in his early forties, but heavily insured. Alec had never allowed his mother to pay any of the household expenses while she resided with him, and she was not an extravagant person. She must have been living well below her income for years. She could well afford to share with her sister or even to live independently if she chose.

His father had left the Gardenia Grove house to him, unmortgaged, along with a decent sum in debentures. With Daisy earning her own spending money, they could promote Dobson to housekeeper and hire another maid to help her, thus relieving Daisy of numerous dull chores.

Then they might think about starting a family. Turning into the Yard, Alec wondered how Daisy felt about having children of her own, and how he did. Babies again, at his age? At least these days it was possible for even respectable women to avoid having them if they didn't want them.

Which made him wonder about Mrs Talmadge and her pregnancy – intentional or accidental? His thoughts turned back to the case of the murdered dentist.

CHAPTER 16

Alec reached his office a few minutes early for the meeting he'd set up. Tom Tring was already at his desk, reading the pathology report.

'Any luck, Tom?'

'If you're talking about the canteen coffee, Chief, no.' He waved a disgusted hand at the disgusting dregs in the mug at his side. 'If it's them cheeky buggers I've been after all day you mean, well, in a manner of speaking.'

'Stop being oracular.' Alec sat down at his desk, on which reposed several discouragingly large piles of papers. 'You've been at it all day. What have you got to show for it?'

'Have a heart, Chief. I managed to nab eleven likely lads that use the shortcut, and there's a few more I've heard about but didn't get ahold of. It's like trying to catch minnows with your bare hands.'

'And?'

Tom grinned. 'And one of 'em saw a veiled lady going in through the Talmadges' back gate at about one o'clock.'

'A veiled lady? He's sure of the time and place?'

'Sure of the time, within a few minutes either way. He'd just delivered a pair of lamb cutlets and got a wigging because it was too late to cook 'em for lunch. And sure of the place because I took him to the alley and he picked out the right gate. But he couldn't see her face because of the veil on her hat, and all he can say about her hat and coat and shoes is that they were sort of brown.'

'So near and yet so far,' Alec groaned. 'Tall, short, fat, thin?'

'He was in a hurry, being late back to the shop, too. He remembered her because it was unusual to see a lady in the alley and because of her surreptitious behaviour – acting sneaky, he called it. He particularly noticed the veil because it added to the impression of furtiveness.'

'Watch it, Sarge,' said Ernie Piper, coming in, 'your fancy vocab's showing.'

'That's vocabulary to you, young whippersnapper. Like constabulary.'

'"When constabulary duty's to be done, to be done,"' Piper warbled, '"the policeman's lot is not a happy one."'

The divisional sergeant entered behind him.

'Evening, Mackinnon,' Alec greeted him. 'You're very full of yourself, Ernie.'

'It's the only thing I am full of, Chief. No time for tea, the sergeant and me.'

'You ought to go on the music halls, you ought,' said Tom, reaching for his telephone. 'All right if I ring down to the canteen for sandwiches, Chief?'

'Do. Are you starving too?' Alec thought guiltily of his ragoût and jam pudding.

'Not me. I stopped in the canteen before I came up, not that their steak-and-kidney pud's worth a farthing compared to the wife's.'

'All right, Ernie, your stomach's empty, but I hope your brain's full. What have you got?'

'Three cabbies, Chief. Leastways, I only talked to one of 'em, but I checked the logs of the other two that they turned in to the company at the end of their shifts. One picked up a couple in New Bond Street around twenty past twelve and took them to Oxford and Cambridge Mansions, Old Marylebone Road. The other took one person from the rank in the Edgware Road to the New Theatre, leaving at five to two.'

'And the one you talked to?'

'Took a lady in a veil from the Edgware Road rank to the Talmadge house. Left at seven minutes to two, arrived ten past. The lady was put in the taxi by a tall thin gentleman with a monocle and no chin, who gave him a fiver. He'd not likely forget that! Blimey, Chief, I reckon I'm in the wrong business. Some bloke offers me a fiver, I have to arrest him.'

'Talk to the other two tomorrow and make sure it's our pair, though there seems little doubt. Good work, Ernie, and quick work.'

'But I never found whoever took 'em there and back in between,' said Piper disconsolately.

'Try again tomorrow, but there's another factor. Creighton owns a very nippy three-litre Bentley, royal blue. He wouldn't want to leave it in New Bond Street, but suppose he always intended the stop at the Dixons' flat and then, perhaps, to take Mrs Talmadge for a spin in the country.'

'He could have driven it over earlier and parked it in one of those side streets,' said Mackinnon, catching on at once. 'With that, he'd have plenty of time to dash over to talk to the victim and finish him off.'

'What about my veiled lady?' Tom demanded.

Piper and Mackinnon stared at him.

Alec gestured to Tom to explain. When he finished, Piper said thoughtfully, 'So either Mrs Talmadge did take a taxi, in which case I'll find it, or she can drive. But it don't seem likely, somehow, that he'd lend her the car to hurry home and murder her old man.'

'Ah,' said Tom, 'but he might have driven her there – not gone in himself – so she could tell hubby it was all off and she was going to run off with his lordship. It's always looked like a spur-of-the-moment job to me.'

'Me too, Tom,' Alec agreed. 'We'll have to see if we can trace the car. Ernie, add that to your taxi-tracing chores.'

'Right, Chief.'

'Before we discuss any further, let's make sure we all know all there is to know or we'll be talking at cross-purposes. Mackinnon, let's hear from you. Tell them about the interview with Creighton, and then report on the Dixons' flat.'

Skimming the relevant reports on his desk as he listened to his men, Alec gathered together the threads of the investigation. Unfortunately, they showed no sign as yet of entwining in a knot.

The pathology report held no surprises. Talmadge had died of a combination of the suffocating and toxic effects of breathing pure nitrous oxide. Any pressure marks caused by his being bound and gagged had disappeared before the autopsy. However, traces of isinglass and benzoin were found around his mouth. Also, the lab confirmed moustache hairs on the sticking plaster from the waste bin and an exchange of fibres from his white coat with those of the bandages and chest strap.

Daisy had got it exactly right.

Ernie Piper had gone through Talmadge's personal and business accounts, all very orderly. He had found nothing to suggest blackmail or gambling or any other irregularity. Scanning his list of female patients from eighteen to forty, Alec saw many names of people he knew. It wouldn't be needed, though, unless Gwen Walker was definitively eliminated.

Either she or Daphne Talmadge was almost certainly Tom's veiled lady. Alec was going to have to go down to Denham to check the old-school-friend alibi.

As for Mrs Talmadge's alibi, Mackinnon had not had to sneak into 6J to study the possibilities. When he knocked on the door of the flat below, to ask if the resident had seen or heard anything at the relevant times, he was invited in. The elderly widow, delighted to have a visitor, had assured him the flats were all identical in design and shown him around her own. Though there was no back door, the rooms all led off a passage and the cleaner could easily have left without seeing Creighton or Mrs Talmadge.

'You'll see her tomorrow, Tom,' said Alec. 'Mrs Simpson, isn't it, Mackinnon?'

'Simpkins, Chief.'

'That's it.' Another good mark for the sergeant. 'On second thoughts, you can deal with her. I want Tom to tackle the Army and Navy Club. If Major Walker lunched there, he probably signed a chit. Times may be more difficult to establish.'

'What's he look like, Chief?' Tom rumbled. Alec gave a description. 'Ah! Sounds like ninety per cent of retired army officers that go on calling themselves by their rank.'

'I'm afraid so. You'll have to hope he's well known at the club. Any questions or ideas, anyone?'

The discussion continued for another half hour or so, without any new facts or insights emerging. Alec sent the others home. He stayed on for just long enough to flip through the pile of papers marked Urgent, concerned with other cases and general directives. Deciding to come in early to deal with those that really were urgent, he went home.

Daisy was still up. As he hung up his hat and coat, she came out of the sitting room and into his arms. He kissed her. 'Any luck?' he asked.

'Well, in a manner of speaking, darling.'

'Don't you be oracular, too!'

'Too?'

'That's exactly what Tom said when I asked him if he'd learned anything from his errand boys.'

'And what did he say next?'

'One lad saw a veiled lady going through the back gate in a furtive manner. He'll swear to the time, but didn't see her well enough to recognize her. He was in a hurry.'

'Oh dear, Daphne was wearing a veiled hat when she arrived home. Cocoa, darling? Or a whisky?'

'Cocoa, please.' He followed her to the kitchen and sat down at the scrubbed wood table. 'What else was Mrs Talmadge wearing?'

'A fawn coat with astrakhan trimmings.' Daisy fetched a bottle of milk from the larder and took down a small pan with a lip from its hook.

'General description: brownish?'

'Good enough, though I'd have thought he'd at least notice the contrast of light cloth with dark collar and cuffs.'

'Yes, he'll have to be asked about that. I should have found out from you yesterday what she was wearing. What's your news?'

'Another rumour about Gwen Walker and Raymond Talmadge, a new one. They were seen having breakfast together at a hotel in Brighton. No mention of who saw them, I'm afraid, or when, or which hotel, and it may be pure fantasy or even a deliberate fabrication. But I do think it's significant, as it's not just repeating the Soho story.'

'Watch the milk!'

'Oh, blast!' The froth had risen in the pan and bubbled over the sides. Daisy snatched it from the flame before too much spilt, but a smell of burning permeated the kitchen. 'Oh dear, I don't think I shall ever be frightfully good at domestic things, darling. There's enough left for half a mug each.'

'Fill mine up with cold. I don't mind it lukewarm as long as it hasn't got a skin on it.'

'Right-o. Did you see Gwen Walker this evening?'

'Yes. Naturally she denied any more than a casual acquaintance with Talmadge. Not convincingly.'

'Here, try this. Here's the sugar if you want more. You believe she was involved with him, then?'

'Delicious.' A vast improvement on canteen coffee, at least. 'I'm working on the assumption that such is the case. I've got to go down to Denham tomorrow morning to check her alibi.'

'I bet she has a hat with a veil, too, if she's been sneaking around seeing Talmadge on the sly. And everyone has a brown coat. I was going to ask you about the major, but Tom's veiled woman must have done it, mustn't she?' Daisy gulped the last of her half cup of cocoa and smothered a huge yawn.

'Seems likely. I've got Tom checking the major's alibi tomorrow, and Creighton's not altogether out of the running yet. Come on, love, time for bed.'

They went upstairs. Alec popped into Belinda's room. His daughter lay sprawled on her back, her loose nighttime braid gleaming redly against the pillow by the light from the landing. Her arms were flung every which way in utter abandon, her face relaxed in a slight smile. Tucking her arms under the bedclothes, he recalled a time when her freckled face in repose had contrasted with her usually anxious expression. Nowadays there was not much difference. Since Daisy moved in, Bel had found less worry and much more fun in her young life.

Dropping a light kiss on her forehead, Alec wondered how he was going to persuade his mother to move out – without her realizing she was being persuaded.

CHAPTER 17

The quantity of luggage loaded into Mrs Fletcher's taxi next morning showed a lamentable lack of faith in her son's ability to solve the dentist's murder. As well as her large trunk, the basket and overnight case and three hatboxes, she added a Gladstone bag at the last minute. Daisy almost hoped the latter contained the family silver, such as it was, as that must surely indicate a lack of intent to return.

The last half hour before her departure Mrs Fletcher spent giving orders to Dobson and advice to Daisy. The advice differed from the orders only in being couched in slightly more conciliatory language. Daisy listened, willing to learn, horrified at how much there was to learn, and resentful of her mama-in-law's smug certainty that she would do it all wrong.

Daisy went out to the curb to wave goodbye. The moment the square black back of the cab disappeared around the corner of the street, she hurried back indoors to consult Dobson.

The cook-housekeeper was seething with indignation. 'I'm sure I don't need to be told how to do things after all these years, madam,' she burst out. 'And there's no call for you to worry your head about what to have for dinner, 'less you want to, nor yet when to send the sheets to the laundry!'

'Really?'

'As if Mr Wu don't send his boy to pick 'em up reg'lar as clockwork, for all he's a heathen. And no one knows better'n me what Mr Fletcher and Miss Belinda likes to eat and what veg is in season and where to get the best lamb chops. And Mrs Twickle knows as well as me what rooms to turn out when, and if there's summat needs doing different she'll do it as I says, won't you, dearie?' she added menacingly as the daily help came in through the kitchen door.

'Yes, Mrs Dobson,' said the stout charwoman timidly. 'Whatever you says.'

'I know I can rely on you, Mrs Twickle,' said Daisy.

'Yes, ma'am.' Looking to Dobson, who nodded a regal permission to leave, Mrs Twickle scuttled to the scullery for a bucket and scrubbing brush.

'So you go do your typewriting, madam, and don't you worry about a thing. *Some* ladies haven't got nothing better to do than poke their noses in where they're not w— needed, but them as has talent didn't ought to waste it on ordering liver and bacon for dinner!'

'Thank you, Mrs Dobson,' Daisy said, much moved. 'Fried onions with the liver and bacon, I hope?'

'If onions is what you like, madam, onions there'll be. Mrs . . . T'other Mrs Fletcher couldn't abide 'em. I hope you don't think I meant you wasn't to tell me what you like, madam. You've only to give the word. But Mrs I'm not, not if it was ever so, never having been married.'

'Married or not, a housekeeper is always addressed as Mrs.'

'Well, thank you, madam. I've heard that's what real ladies do. I dare say it's a compliment.'

'It's meant to be.'

'Thank you, madam. And if I was to try summat a bit different, like as if it was a recipe Mr Kesin gave me, I'd be sure to ask you first,' Mrs Dobson promised.

'Oh, Mr Fletcher and Miss Belinda and I have all had Indian food at Mrs Prasad's and liked it, as long as it's not too spicy-hot. But you'd better not try serving it to Mrs Fletcher.'

'As if I'd dare, madam! I'll make this recipe of Mr Kesin's tomorrow, shall I? He brought me a little jar of the curry mixture.'

'O-ho, did he indeed? Perhaps we'll end up calling you Mrs Kesin!'

'I couldn't marry a heathen, madam,' said the housekeeper regretfully, 'not but what Mr Kesin is ever so gentlemanly in his foreign way. Well, I'd best be getting on if there's to be anything got done today.'

Thus dismissed, Daisy went up to the spare bedroom, where her Underwood typewriter sat incongruously on an elegant Regency writing table from Fairacres. Her conversation in the kitchen had sparked an idea for an article on 'the servant problem'.

No one who lamented the difficulty of finding good servants since the war ever seemed to wonder if the cause might be the way they were treated. Daisy's mother, for instance, left everything to her staff and complained constantly and bitterly about the results. Her mother-in-law, on the other hand, had a finger in every pie, never trusting the housekeeper or the part-time gardener to use their initiative.

Servants were expected to be competent, obedient, deferential, loyal and hard-working, all for minimal wages and very little free time. No wonder the young women who had cheerfully gone to work in the factories of England during the war were reluctant to re-embrace servitude.

Daisy sketched out an article on the subject. If she managed to sell it, she'd have to make sure the Dowager Lady Dalrymple and Mrs Fletcher were unrecognizable. Though both heartily disapproved of her writing, both made a point of reading her work so as to be able to criticize it.

Perhaps she should write it pseudonymously, but the sad fact was that it would sell more easily and probably have more impact from the pen of the Honourable Daisy Dalrymple. It was a pity, but no doubt other writers used their connections to get published.

Sighing, she put a paperweight on her notes and went to get ready to go out to morning coffee.

After nearly three hours clearing the arrears of papers from his desk at the Yard, Alec took the train from Marylebone to Denham.

The station was perched on a railway embankment above the flat surrounding countryside. The village was visible about a mile away. Alec crossed the bridge over the line and asked the ticket collector for Station Row. He was directed to an isolated terrace of tiny brick cottages at the bottom of the station access road, facing the main road.

Probably provided for workers building the railway, Alec thought as he approached. The brick might once have been red, but soot smuts had long since blackened it. Every time a train went by up above, the windows rattled in their grimy frames.

Alec simply couldn't see the elegant Mrs Walker dropping

in for lunch in such shabby surroundings, quite apart from the strain on the Crouches' budget of feeding a guest.

No pavement. The blue front door was about a yard from the edge of the road, which continued under a bridge beneath the railway line. In the intervening space, potted pink hyacinths struggled against soot and coal dust and the shadow of the towering embankment. The brick step was neatly swept and some ineffectual effort had been made to wash the smuts off the paint, Alec noted as he raised the iron knocker.

A sharp rat tat brought no response. He waited a couple of minutes, then knocked again.

The next front door, defiant scarlet beneath its coat of soot, opened and a head tied up in a scarlet polka-dotted scarf poked out to peer around the downspout in between. 'It's no good banging away, dear. Miss Crouch went into the village to the shops and the old lady's stone deaf. You can try stepping over to the window and waving. She mostly sits in the front room and there's nothing wrong with her eyes.'

'Thank you, madam.'

The neighbour came out onto her front step, feather duster in hand, to watch. A couple of steps took Alec to the centre of the window. Lace curtains, their original whiteness compromised by age, not dirt, hid the interior. Feeling a bit of an ass, he gesticulated at the glass, which reflected a gibbering monkey in a charcoal grey suit.

It worked, however. A moment later the blue door opened on a chain and an elderly, well-bred voice asked, 'Who is it?'

He passed his papers through the gap. The door closed. He heard the chink of the chain and it reopened wide to show a small, wrinkled woman with an amazing quantity of silvery white hair done up on top of her head.

'Police? Has something happened to Jennifer?'

Alec shook his head vigorously. He made a discreet gesture towards the neighbour, who had moved closer on hearing the fascinating word 'police'.

Mrs Crouch put her hand on his arm and drew him forward into the postage-stamp hall. 'Come in, Mr Fletcher.' She closed the door. 'Inquisitive as a robin, but she has a kind heart. Come in.'

She led him into a tiny room crammed with overstuffed furniture which had once been good. Not a speck of dust marred the polished wood, but the quantities of cross-stitchery failed to hide all the worn patches in the upholstery. Mrs Crouch sat down in a wing chair to one side of the sole window, waved Alec to the sofa and offered him a pad of paper and a pencil.

'What can I do for you, Chief Inspector?' she asked, picking up a piece of embroidery.

I am trying to trace the movements of a number of people, he wrote. *You and your daughter may be able to help me*. He showed it to her.

'I do watch the coming and going to the station,' she admitted. 'I rarely go out. It's so difficult when one can't hear what people are saying. Of course I'll help if I can.'

Did Mrs Francis Walker lunch with you this week?

'Gwen Walker? No, she never comes to lunch. Now and then she'll pop in for a cup of tea, while her husband is playing golf at Denham Golf Club, I understand. She always brings a treat, knowing I have something of a sweet tooth. She was at school with Jennifer, you know, and used to come to stay in the holidays, in better times. Gwennie and Jenny, they called themselves. I hope she's not in serious trouble?'

We're trying to trace several *people.*

'She's a good girl, Gwen. She never forgets Christmas or birthday cards, and she often gives Jennifer clothes, some of them almost new.'

Have you seen her or heard from her at all this week?

'I have not, but Jennifer might have had a letter without showing it to me. Don't tell me Gwen has disappeared, Mr Fletcher?' the old lady asked anxiously. A passing train forced Alec to concentrate to catch her next words. 'One hears such dreadful stories, and her husband the major is quite an irascible gentleman, Jennifer tells me.'

Mrs Walker is alive and well. You've known her a long time. Tell me a bit about her background.

Delighted by the opportunity to talk without needing to hear, Mrs Crouch became garrulous. Gwen Walker's father, James Garrity, was a barrister, she said, a junior partner in her own husband's chambers. They had flourished as acknowledged experts in a certain obscure branch of the law.

Garrity married and his wife was soon expecting a child. Mrs Crouch, considerably younger than her husband and married for over ten years, had given up hoping for a child but to her joyful surprise found herself in the same condition. The two girls were born within a few weeks of each other.

Then that obscure law, dating from medieval times, was unexpectedly repealed. The practice gradually dwindled away. Mr Crouch died, leaving his wife and daughter in difficult circumstances.

Garrity, in no better case, quit the law and retired to his family's farm in Ireland, where he still eked out a livelihood of sorts. When the war came, Gwen returned to London to work in a ministry, where she met Francis Walker. Mrs

Crouch did not presume to say whether it had been a love match, on either side. The fact was that Gwen was beautiful and Major Walker had enough money to whisk her back to the sort of life she had grown up enjoying.

'And good luck to her,' said Mrs Crouch. 'I only wish Jennifer . . . but never mind that. After all I've told you, do you still need to talk to her?'

Alec nodded.

'I wonder where she has got to? Would you care for a cup of tea while you wait?'

He didn't want to put her to the trouble, nor to diminish whatever meagre store of tea lurked in the Crouches' larder. But he was thirsty and didn't want to offend her by rejecting her hospitality. Before he had quite made up his mind, he heard the sound of a key turning in the front door.

The woman who came in looked ten years older than Gwen Walker's thirty years, and had probably never been pretty. She appeared in the sitting-room doorway with a little wave to attract her mother's attention, then noticed Alec as he stood.

'Oh, I beg your pardon. Who . . . ?'

'This is Detective Chief Inspector Fletcher, dear, from Scotland Yard. He's come to ask you one or two questions.'

Miss Crouch looked at him in astonishment. 'What on earth about?'

Mrs Crouch continued placidly, 'I'll go and put on the kettle and put away the shopping while you talk to him.'

'Allow me.' Alec took the heavy basket from Miss Crouch's arm and followed the old lady back to the kitchen. It appeared to be the only other room on the ground floor, no doubt matched by two bedrooms above.

Returning to the hall, he found Jennifer Crouch hanging up her once expensive, now shabby Burberry on a hook behind the front door. She preceded him into the front room, where she sat down in the chair opposite her mother's, on the other side of the window, and picked up a piece of needle-work. An automatic action, Alec thought. He wondered whether they supplemented an inadequate income by selling their work.

'I can't imagine how I can possibly help you, Mr Fletcher,' she said. 'Do sit down.'

But he remained standing, asking without further ado, 'Have you seen Gwen Walker this week?'

She looked taken aback, then, after a momentary hesitation, she said warily, 'Yes.'

'Yesterday?'

'Y-yes. You told Mother you're from Scotland Yard!'

'I am.' He held out his papers, which she gave a cursory glance.

'But—'

'What time was she here?'

'Midday, for lunch. The train arrives at about half past twelve, and I suppose she was here for about an hour and a half.'

'Your mother says she hasn't seen Mrs Walker this week, and that she never comes to lunch.'

'Oh dear.' She bowed her head over her embroidery. 'I'm afraid Mother is confused. She is . . . getting on in years.'

'Mrs Crouch strikes me as perfectly *compos mentis.* Was Mrs Walker here for lunch the day before yesterday also?'

'The day before . . . No. Yes. I mean . . .'

'What exactly do you mean, Miss Crouch?'

'I suppose I may have confused the days. Are you sure you're not a private investigator?'

'Ah!' His guess as good as confirmed, Alec sat down on the sofa. 'I begin to see the light. I'm quite sure I'm not a private investigator. I'm from the Criminal Investigation Department of the Metropolitan Police, and this matter is a good deal more important than protecting your friend from her husband's suspicions. Was she here at midday the day before yesterday?'

Miss Crouch moistened her lips. 'What's happened?'

'Was she here the day before yesterday?'

'N-no.'

'Thank you. Has she explained to you why she wanted you to lie for her?'

'She said she was seeing a man. I know it's dreadfully wrong of her, but she's like a sister to me, you see. And the major is . . . is not a sympathetic person.'

'Did she tell you whom she was seeing?'

'No. Only that he had a very unromantic profession, but she'd had her fill of romance when she married the gallant major. What's happened? Is the major . . . He isn't dead, is he?'

Alec shook his head. 'No, alive and kicking at last sight. How long had this been going on? Her liaison?'

'A little over a year. She's never asked such a thing before. You needn't think she only kept in with us because of that.'

Mrs Crouch came in, a tea tray in her precarious grasp, from which Alec hastened to deliver it. He had no more questions to ask, and in her mother's presence Miss Crouch swallowed those he saw on the tip of her tongue, though the old lady would not have heard.

'I'm afraid we finished the tin of biscuits Gwen brought last month,' Mrs Crouch apologized.

Alec had just time for a cup of tea before the next train back to town. In fact, he left in a bit of a rush, glad of an excuse not to face Miss Crouch's questions as she showed him out. She was obviously deeply unhappy at having betrayed her friend. Alec wished he had brought Daisy with him. She would have known how to comfort the poor woman.

Daisy expected to have quite enough on her hands with the morning coffee gathering. The day was cloudy but mild and dry, and she quite enjoyed her walk through the tree-lined streets. When she arrived, she was happy to find both Sakari and Melanie among the guests. Between the two of them, they managed to shield her from the worst of the interrogation. The rumour about Gwen Walker dining with Raymond Talmadge in Soho surfaced again, this time quite openly.

Daisy finished off a Banbury tart, followed it with a sip of coffee, and asked bluntly, 'Who saw them?'

Everyone looked at each other. No one knew.

'My dear Daisy,' said Sakari, a wicked twinkle in her eye, 'none of the respectable ladies here would visit a Soho nightclub. I am driven to the conclusion that someone has a less-than-respectable acquaintance whom, naturally, she does not care to acknowledge.'

The respectable ladies looked askance at each other. Each protested that she had heard the story at third or fourth hand, and some even named their informants, all equally respectable ladies.

Daisy dug out her notebook from her handbag and wrote

down these names and those who had given them, who watched in dismay. 'Of course, I'll have to tell my husband,' she said. The subject of the dead dentist died a swifter death than he had.

The party ended soon after. Sakari was whirled away in the red Sunbeam to a diplomatic luncheon. Daisy and Mel walked homeward together.

'Vultures!' said Daisy.

'It's only natural to be interested when someone you know is murdered,' Mel protested. 'Don't tell me people haven't wanted to know the details in the other cases you've been mixed up in.'

Thinking back over past cases, Daisy was startled by how many there had been. She had always dealt with them as they happened and tried to forget the horrid details as soon as they were over. No wonder Superintendent Crane and the AC (Crime) were aghast at her propensity for stumbling across bodies!

But she shook her head. 'I've never before been besieged with questions by so many people who are not themselves personally involved. And if they think they have evidence, they should take it to Alec, not filter it through me.'

'You're so much easier to talk to, Daisy. I can imagine Alec being rather fierce.'

'He can be a bit intimidating,' she admitted, remembering times when he had fixed her with the icy grey gaze which made erring subordinates shiver, suspects shudder and malefactors think they'd be better off at the North Pole. Not that it bothered Daisy. She looked at her friend, who was nervously nibbling her lower lip. 'Mel, is there something you want to tell me?'

'You just said . . .'

'That doesn't apply to my *friends*, darling. What's up?'

'It's something Robert told me, in complete confidence, of course. Is Alec quite certain that Mrs Walker was seeing Talmadge?'

'He hasn't any real evidence, if that's what you mean. He's . . . I suppose I'd have to say he's fairly sure. Do you know something definite?'

Not about that, Daisy. I'd have told you, or him. No, on the whole I think I'd better not mention what Robert said. It's probably nothing to do with the murder at all.'

'How can you be sure?'

'It's nothing to do with Talmadge, at any rate. Just . . . just something which made Robert suggest that I shouldn't become too friendly with Gwen Walker. I promise I'll tell you if Alec finds out she really was his mistress. Oh, here's where we go our different ways. Cheerio, Daisy.' Melanie turned the corner and dashed off at a fast walk.

Dying of curiosity, Daisy stared after her, then turned in the opposite direction towards Gardenia Grove. If Robert had told Melanie something confidential, it was probably something to do with his bank. Were the Walkers desperately in debt and vastly overdrawn? Doubtless it would reflect badly on the bank manager if his wife was intimate friends with a customer who went bankrupt.

Could the Walkers' impending bankruptcy have any bearing on Talmadge's death? Suppose Gwen had counted on him to rescue her from prospective destitution, and instead he bade her farewell forever?

That would certainly add fuel to the flames of the notorious fury of a woman scorned!

Alec came home to lunch, a rare occurrence. 'I was at Marylebone,' he explained, 'so it seemed silly to go back to the Yard and suffer canteen food.'

Mrs Dobson was equal to the challenge. She stretched the chicken consommé with top of the milk, added bread and butter and cheese to the cold ham and salad, and dressed up the stewed rhubarb with a quickly browned crumbly topping.

'This soup is delicious,' Alec said.

'I'll tell Mrs Dobson.'

'Mrs?'

'From now on,' Daisy said firmly. 'Calling a woman by her surname just because she's a servant is frightfully Victorian.' Not wanting to get involved in a discussion which must inevitably lead to his mother, she asked, 'What were you doing at Marylebone?'

He told her about his interview with Gwen Walker's indigent friend Miss Crouch and her mother.

'I'm told Mrs Walker never forgets Christmas or birthday cards, and she often passes on bundles of clothes, some of them almost new.'

Daisy shuddered. 'I'd absolutely loathe wearing a friend's castoffs. I'd rather go to the Salvation Army. But I suppose she's being kind.'

'I can't believe the frock Mrs Walker was wearing when I saw her would be much use to a woman in Miss Crouch's circumstances.'

'Why, what was it like?'

'Oh, one of those floaty tea-gown things, all green and gold. Chiffon, I think.' Alec, as a trained observer, was remarkably good at women's clothes, for a man.

'I expect she gives Miss Crouch her more practical stuff. Skirts and blouses and woollies.'

'Yes, there was a Burberry coat. I suppose it's to Mrs Walker's credit that she didn't altogether abandon old friends when she moved back up in the world and they stayed behind.'

'You liked the Crouches, didn't you, darling?'

'They're pleasant, straightforward people, making the best of what life has dealt them, without complaint.'

'I'd like to meet them.'

'Daisy, you are not to go calling on them!'

'I don't know their address,' she said regretfully. 'Why? Because Miss Crouch lied to you? You're not going to charge her, are you?'

'Great Scott, no! She did it so badly she obviously doesn't make a practice of it. Besides, if we charged everyone who lies to the police, half the population would be in gaol.'

Daisy was annoyed to feel herself blushing, though she couldn't at present recall any downright thundering lies she'd told the police, at least not recently. A little prevarication or suppression of probably irrelevant facts, long ago, was quite another matter. 'Are you going to see Mrs Walker this afternoon?' she asked quickly.

'Yes, later on. The fact that she gave a false alibi doesn't prove her a murderer, alas. Nor are the rest of the suspects by any means in the clear. I'm meeting Tom and the others at the Yard and it's always possible one of them will have come across some real evidence.' He pushed back his chair. 'I must run.'

'No coffee?'

'No time, love.' He stooped to kiss her goodbye and was gone.

Daisy sat on at the table for a few minutes, pondering. She was awfully tempted to call on Gwen Walker, but couldn't think of any excuse. On the other hand, she really must drop in to see how Daphne Talmadge was doing. She could work for a couple of hours, then pop round at about four, as Belinda had a music lesson after school, so would be late home.

Bel was quite old enough to manage without Daisy for a while, especially as the housekeeper was always there. But Mrs Fletcher had always made a point of being at home when her granddaughter got back from school, and in her absence Daisy could do no less.

Sighing, she started to stack the dishes for Mrs Dobson.

CHAPTER 18

'Mrs Walker's alibi is exploded,' Alec told the two sergeants and Ernie Piper. He explained how he had trapped Miss Crouch into contradicting herself.

'Cor, that was neat, Chief.'

'Listen and learn, lad,' said Tom. He was wearing the sober dark suit he had donned to impress the Army and Navy Club. It made him look less bulky and more formidable than his usual loud checks. He always swore villains were so stunned by the latter they didn't realize who was wearing them until he'd clapped on the darbies. 'Listen and learn,' he repeated sententiously.

'I do, Sarge. Even to you.'

'Tom, did you get anywhere at the Army and Navy?'

'The major ate lunch there all right, Chief. The club secretary showed me his signed chit. It's dated, but there's no time on it, as you'd expect. They serve lunch till half two.'

'So he could easily have followed his wife to the house at one o'clock, done Talmadge in and turned up in the club dining room in plenty of time to eat. Anyone remember him?'

'Not a soul, not to swear to. I spoke to the porter and the waiters but they have five Major Walkers and hordes of members who look just like my description of our Major Walker. They were extra busy that day, too, because there was some sort of reunion in the evening and a lot of members came up from the country.'

'Damn!'

'No better luck with the errand boy, neither. I sent DC Ross to ask him about the astrakhan coat Mrs Fletcher described. The lad thought he might've noticed, but then again he might not.'

'Your veiled lady could still be either Mrs Walker or Mrs Talmadge, then.'

'Or someone else entirely, Chief.'

'Or someone else entirely,' Alec agreed gloomily. 'What about you, Mackinnon?'

'I went to the Dixons' flat, Chief, but the charwoman wasna there. I couldna think of any way to trace her wi'out getting in touch with the Dixons, so I telephoned the Henley police to send someone out to their cottage. But it seems it's on the wrong side o' the river so they had to ring up the Berkshire police—'

'Ah yes, I remember, three counties meet there.'

'Well, after a deal o' havering, I ended up wi' Mrs Simpkins's address in Islington. I took the Tube there, but she wasna at home. Her neighbour said she was at work, but she didn't know where.' Mackinnon apparently wanted to prove himself by describing all his difficulties and how he had overcome them.

'I take it you found her?' Alec said.

'Aye, Chief, in the end. She only does for the Dixons two mornings a week. When she left their flat that day, at one o'clock, she opened the door of the sitting room to say she was going. She saw the gentleman sitting with the lady in his lap, crying on his shoulder. She backed out in a hurry without speaking, so they might not have seen her.'

'Even if they'd jumped up the moment she left,' said Alec, 'they'd have had to rush to get to St John's Wood and back. Ernie?'

'No sign of a taxi taking one or both of 'em there or back, Chief, or there *and* back. I covered pretty well all the possibles. I talked to the other two cabbies, too. It was our two for sure that was taken from Bond Street to Oxford and Cambridge Mansions, and his lordship that was taken to the theatre.'

'And the Bentley?'

'I found the garridge where his lordship keeps it. There's a group of toffs keep their motors there and they pay a bloke to keep 'em filled up, and polish 'em and do minor repairs and gen'rally keep an eye on things. He checks the oil and water and petrol whenever someone brings one back, and keeps a log to bill 'em.'

'There's a bit of luck!' said Tom.

''Fraid not, Sarge. The Bentley's not in his log for that day, but it could mean it went out but didn't go far enough to need filling. He's pretty sure it wasn't taken out, but not prepared to swear to it.'

'St John's Wood and back wouldn't take much petrol,' observed Mackinnon.

'It wasn't parked near the alley, anyway,' said Piper. 'I asked DC Ross, seeing he was going to talk to Sarge's errand boy, to ask him about it. It's the sort of car any boy couldn't help noticing, and he didn't. He's going to ask around his friends, though.'

'Good work, Ernie. I think we'll leave it at that for the moment, wait and see if anything turns up. It would take more manpower than the AC's likely to allow me to do a door-to-door in both Marylebone and St John's Wood, though it may come to that. However, my feeling is that those two were not involved in the murder. I don't want to waste time flogging a dead horse.'

'So we concentrate on—' The phone on Tom's desk rang and he stopped to answer it. 'DS Tring ... Yes, put her through, please ... Hello, Mrs Fletcher. Do you want to speak to the Chief? ... Go ahead.' Still listening, he reached for pad and pencil and wrote. 'Thank you, Mrs Fletcher ... Yes, I'll give them to him, and he can decide whether they're worth following up ... Bye.'

'Well?' Alec asked impatiently.

'She forgot to give you these names, Chief, but they're probably not worth much, she says.'

'What names?'

'Ladies who passed on rumours about Talmadge and Mrs Walker to the ladies who passed them on to Mrs Fletcher. She asked them where they'd heard the story in hopes of tracking down a source.'

From the corner of his eye, Alec saw Piper and Mackinnon exchange grins and nods that said as clearly as words, 'Mrs Fletcher does it again!'

'We'll have to talk to them,' Alec said with a sigh. 'I'm pretty sure Mrs Walker was Talmadge's mistress but until we have more to go on than rumours and guesses, we're hobbled. I'm going to talk to her again. Tom, as you're wearing your best bib and tucker, you can deal with the ladies Daisy's named.'

'Right, Chief.'

'Mackinnon, I'm putting you onto the Walkers' cook-housekeeper, Bates. See if you can get a line on where she goes on her day off, whether she has any particular friend she might have gossiped with about her mistress. Without more evidence I prefer not to question her officially yet. There's probably a cleaning woman, too, and a gardener, possibly another maid. Find out. Ernie, you stay here and go through all the reports. See if you can spot any discrepancies, anything we've overlooked, any obscure connections.'

'Have a heart, Chief!'

'Sorry, but you have the best eye for details. I'll be back a bit before five to see if you've come up with anything. At five I have to report our progress or lack thereof to Superintendent Crane. Tom, Mackinnon, if you find out something worth telling the super, telephone here before my appointment. Otherwise we'll meet here at six to exchange news.'

On his way out, Alec was buttonholed by a colleague who had taken over one of his less urgent cases when the murder became his first priority. When at last he managed to tear himself away, he drove straight to the Walkers'. He parked a little way down the street. If Mrs Walker was not at home – and he prayed she was there as he was now somewhat pressed for time – she might recognize his car and turn tail if it was right outside her house.

Like last time he stood on that doorstep, he was left there for several minutes after ringing the bell. This time the door was opened, just as he was about to ring again, by a short, wiry woman in a flowered overall and carpet slippers. Wisps of henna'd hair peeked out from beneath a purple paisley headscarf knotted in front. In one hand she bore a mop, the regimental standard of her profession.

'Nobody's home, ducks,' she announced. Though there was no reason the Walkers should be home waiting for him, Alec was annoyed. Their absence typified the investigation, which seemed to consist so far of one petty irritation after another. As yet he had not even succeeded in eliminating a single suspect.

'When are Major and Mrs Walker expected back?' he asked.

'Dunno 'bout madam. Nora – that's the cook-housekeeper, Nora Bates, it's 'er 'alf day – she left tea things out for the major's tea, so I specks he'll be back soon.'

'I'll come in and wait then,' Alec said authoritatively. 'I'm a police officer.' He showed her his credentials.

'Coo, that's nice!' she said, admiring the seal. 'You read it to me, ducks. I left me glasses at 'ome.'

Can't read, Alec interpreted, amused and appalled. 'Detective Chief Inspector Fletcher, CID, Metropolitan Police,' he told her gravely, though for all she knew it could have read 'Sewer Inspector' or 'Confidence Trickster'.

'Ooh, that's Scotland Yard, innit? Well, I never! Come on in, ducks, and sit yerself down in the front parlour 'ere. I was just goin' to make meself a cuppa if you fancy one. Awready put the kettle on.'

'That sounds good, but I'll come along and save you a step or two.' He might as well try and get her talking about her employers.

'To the kitchen?' she said dubiously. 'Well, I s'pose it's all right. I've always been respectable, ain't got nuffink against the rozzers. And I don't mind if I get the weight off me bunions for a bit.'

Sitting down at the kitchen table, Alec knew himself in this situation less capable than Tom Tring. By now Tom would be laughing, teasing, maybe flirting a little, certainly calling the woman by her Christian name. Alec didn't even know her surname yet. His visit to the kitchen was regarded as condescension, not because of his rank – a chief inspector was after all still just a rozzer – but because of the way he spoke.

Still, though she had ushered him towards the sitting room, she had called him ducks, not sir, so maybe there was hope.

'This is very kind of you, Mrs . . . ?'

'Davies, ducks, wiv an *e*. Me dear departed was a Welshman, bought it in the Fusiliers. What was you wanting to see the major for, if you don't mind me arstin'? They don't send a chief inspector round 'cause he busted the taillight on his motor car, I don't think! He lose his temper and sock summun on the jaw, did 'e?'

'You sound as if you wouldn't be surprised if he had.'

'No more I would. Got a nasty temper, 'as the major, which ain't to say he ain't got nuffink to aggravate him. But there, we're none of us perfect, are we? Sugar?'

'No, thanks. Just a spot of milk.'

Even with milk, the tea was as dark as mahogany. Sipping, Alec felt the tannin eroding the enamel from his teeth. More work for his dentist – he'd have to find a new one.

Mrs Davies swigged down half her mugful in one long draught. 'Ah, that's a bit of all right, that is. Puts the life back into you, don't it? Yes, the major 'as his troubles like the rest of us.' She leant forward and said in a thrilling whisper, 'Madam!'

'The major has troubles with his wife?' Alec asked hopefully.

'Messy like you wouldn't believe. Never puts nuffink

away, and it stands to reason that don't suit a military gentleman like the major, all shipshape and Bristol fashion. Well, that'd be the Navy, wouldn't it, but a place for everything and everything in its place, that's what I say.'

'They rowed about Mrs Walker's untidiness?'

'Like cat and dog. I don't say he hit 'er, mind, bein' a gentleman. Leastways, I ain't never seen 'er wiv a shiner, and I does for 'em every day 'ceptin' Sunday. I likes me Sundays off.'

'Who doesn't? You'd know, then, if they rowed about anything else.'

'Money. She spends too much, 'e says, but what I say is, if you've got it you may as well spend it. It don't do you much good otherwise, does it? Why shouldn't she 'ave pretty clothes, I arst you! She's a real looker, sure enough, and when she gets dolled up, she'd turn any man's head.'

'Could that be the real reason for the trouble between them: that she turns men's heads, or perhaps one particular man's?'

Mrs Davies gave him a sharp look. 'Is that what you're after? You want to know 'as she got a fancy bloke? What's that to the perlice, I'd like to know?'

Alec decided to tell her. 'It may be relevant to a murder case.'

'I don't 'old wiv murder,' she said, in tones of deepest disapproval. 'That dentist, is it? Well, I dunno, I'm sure. There's times when she'll be talkin' soft like on the telephone and 'e'll come 'ome and she'll 'ang up double quick. And I've seen 'er hurry to get the post and take summat out before 'e comes downstairs of a morning. That sort of thing. But I don't know as it's a gentleman friend. Could be a bookie for all I knows.'

'What about Nora? I expect you have a good gossip over a cuppa. She hasn't mentioned anyone?'

'Her! A good gossip I don't think! Wouldn't pass the time of day wiv the Duke of York, was 'e to tip 'is 'at to 'er nice and polite. Tells me what to do and I does it, and 'ardly another word out of 'er all day. I specks that's why I'm sitting 'ere gabbing with a rozzer as shouldn't. Not but what I'm sorry I can't be much 'elp. Like I said, I don't 'old wiv murder.' She stood up and collected their mugs. 'I better get back to me work. The major'll be 'ome for 'is tea any minute, I shouldn't wonder.'

'Thanks for mine. I'll go and wait for him in the hall,' Alec said, swallowing a sigh. Though he hadn't got any useful information from her, he didn't think she had any for even Tom to extract. He hadn't done too badly. Could it be Daisy's influence? She talked with equal ease to a dustman or a duchess, so why shouldn't he?

He left the kitchen, then, on impulse, stuck his head back in. 'By the way, Mrs Davies, have you ever seen Mr Talmadge?'

'The dentist what was done in? Just the once. 'E come to a dinner party, 'im and 'is missus, one time when I stayed late to wash up, just to oblige. Cor lumme, what a smasher! If 'e'd been mine, I wouldn't've let 'im out of me sight. All the girls after 'im, I shouldn't wonder. Can't 'ardly blame madam if she was carryin' on wiv 'im!'

Alec had a feeling that she had at last said something helpful. Before he could go over her words with a fine-tooth comb to extract any hidden significance, he heard the front door closing and brisk footsteps in the hall. He hurried from the back passage to meet the major.

Major Walker greeted him with a thunderous scowl, not undeserved. 'Fletcher! What the devil are you doing here?'

'I came to see your wife, Major. Since she isn't in, Mrs Davies kindly allowed me to wait and gave me a cup of tea.'

'My wife?' Walker asked suspiciously.

'And you. I'm afraid we've been unable to find corroboration of the times you were at your club.' Alec took out his notebook. 'Would you be so kind as to give me the names of the people you talked to or lunched with?'

'I certainly will not! As it happens I didn't see anyone I know. Some regiment or other was having a big reunion and the place was a madhouse. If I'd known, I wouldn't have gone at all.'

'What time did you arrive and leave?'

'I'll be damned if I know. I'm no clock watcher, dammit. And if you're pestering everyone who ever passed the time of day with Talmadge, you must be working the clock round, with little to show for it. I've said everything I have to say and I'll thank you to leave us alone!'

'When do you expect your wife back, Major?'

Alec's calm persistence provoked another, still more explosive outburst.

'Leave Gwen out of this! How dare you harass us? I'll report you to your superiors. And now get the hell out of my house!' Walker opened the front door and stood holding it. His moustache bristled, his face was red with fury, but Alec detected a definite uneasiness that no amount of bluster could quite conceal.

'As you wish. But I'll be back. Please try to remember the times you arrived at and left your club.'

'Get out!'

Alec got.

Daisy rang the Talmadges' doorbell with some trepidation. She had no qualms about going to see Daphne, but it would be too, too embarrassing to meet Lord Henry. Should she pretend not to know he was Daphne's baby's father? The situation was not one her teachers had covered in their lectures on deportment and etiquette.

Hilda Kidd came to the door, in her parlourmaid get-up. 'Mrs Talmadge isn't seeing— Oh, it's you, ma'am. We've had that many callers, half of 'em strangers. Ghouls, I call 'em.'

'I just wanted to ask how Mrs Talmadge is doing.'

'Much better today, ma'am, but she's to stay lying down for a couple of days yet. Step in and I'll see if she'd like to see you.'

Astonished at the maid's affability, Daisy stepped in. No doubt Hilda's surliness had been caused by the shock of her master's death, worry over her mistress and perhaps the presence of her enemy Brenda Hensted. Nurse Hensted should be gone by now, a relief to all concerned.

Or was she gone? Coming down the stairs were familiar black shoes and stockings, navy dress with white cuffs and collar, and lastly a white cap.

But the figure inside the dress was plump. The face, illuminated now by the the fanlight over the front door, was round and rosy and cheery, and the hair peeking out from beneath the cap was grey.

'Mrs Fletcher? I'm Nurse Biddlecome. Mrs Talmadge is ever so pleased you dropped by. She's doing nicely, but just as a precaution for the dear baby's sake, she's to stay flat on her back. I'm sure you won't upset her, will you, dear. Just have a nice cheerful chat.'

'Right-o.'

'I'll have Cook send Gladys up with a tea tray in a few minutes, and I'll be up to help her drink as she's not allowed to sit up properly, poor dear. You know your way, don't you?' With a friendly nod, Nurse Biddlecome whisked past Daisy and disappeared towards the kitchen.

Daisy went up to find Daphne looking much changed from the ill, miserable woman she had been the day before. Her hair was neatly brushed, her face made up lightly but thoroughly, her smile happy and welcoming, very different from yesterday's pitiful attempt.

'Daisy, how kind of you to come.'

'I'm glad to see you so much better.'

'I feel wonderful.' Daphne sobered. 'I know it's dreadful of me after what happened to poor Raymond, especially when he'd been so kind and understanding and promised to turn over a new leaf. But I just can't help being happy. Besides, Nurse Biddlecome says it's better for the baby if I'm cheerful and don't brood.'

'She's a bit different from Miss Hensted, isn't she!' Daisy said with a laugh.

'Poor Miss Hensted. She always resented me just because I was Raymond's wife, and it must have been frightful for her when he died, nuts about him as she was. But thank heaven she's gone. Daisy, I expect your husband told you Harry and I are going to be married. It'll be very quiet, of course, just a registry office, and very soon because of the baby, but would you mind awfully being a witness?'

Daisy hesitated. An illicit liaison and a murder were hardly a good foundation for marriage. On the other hand, she didn't believe either of them was involved in the murder, and though Alec had not crossed them off his list, he seemed to be looking elsewhere. And there was the baby to think of. She had never understood why an innocent baby should suffer for the sins of the parents, but that was the way the world worked. 'If you'd really like me to,' she said.

'Bless you!' Daphne was silent for a moment, then she said, 'I do hope they catch whoever murdered poor Raymond before the wedding. I don't suppose you know whether the police have found out who it was?'

'They're not ready to arrest anyone yet, that much I know.'

'The more I think about it, the more certain I am that Raymond was ... seeing Gwen Walker. I half suspected it before I saw the address on that letter, though I can't pin down exactly why. Not that I mean to suggest she would have killed him because he told her it was all over between them.'

Since she appeared to be suggesting just that, Daisy said a trifle sceptically, 'No?'

'No. You see, Raymond implied that she, whoever she was, was going to be quite relieved. She was afraid her husband was suspicious and she was nervous about what he'd do if he found out. At least, that's the impression I got. I was in a bit of a state myself at the time, remember.'

Not what Alec would regard as evidence, Daisy thought. She'd pass it on to him, though, for what it was worth. If he took it seriously, he'd have to move the major to the top of his list.

* * *

Next morning, as Daisy emerged from the bedroom blinking and tying the cord of her dressing gown, the telephone bell shrilled in the hall below.

'I'll get it, Mummy!' Belinda dashed past, already dressed in her navy school-uniform gym slip, ginger pigtails neatly ribboned to match. Nana bounded after her.

'I must have been mad,' Daisy muttered to herself. After two blissful nights in Bel's bedroom, the puppy was thoroughly settled in. She was never going to accept being shut up downstairs again when Mrs Fletcher came back.

'It's for Daddy,' Belinda called up. 'Urgent!'

'He's in the bath.'

'Granny said never to tell—'

'No, don't. Say he can't come to the telephone just now and get a message, darling.' Daisy knocked on the bathroom door. 'Urgent phone call, Alec.'

'I just soaped my face,' came the spluttered reply. 'Who is it?'

Daisy went to the top of the stairs. 'Who is it, Bel?'

'Detective Sergeant Mackinnon. He says may he talk to you, Mummy.'

'Me? Right-o. Go and start your breakfast.' Back to the bathroom door. 'It's Mackinnon, darling. He's going to tell me what's up.'

Alec's roared 'No!' was sufficiently muffled for Daisy to decide she hadn't heard it. She hurried downstairs and picked up the apparatus.

'Sergeant? This is Mrs Fletcher. What's the matter?'

'It's Major Walker, ma'am. Their cook's just rung up to say she came down this morning and found him with his head in the gas oven.'

CHAPTER 19

When Alec pulled up behind Dr Curtis's maroon Talbot, anger lay as heavy in his stomach as the fried-egg sandwich Daisy had handed him as he dashed out of the door. He was furious with himself.

He ought to have foreseen that something like this might happen. Walker was obviously not the most emotionally stable of men. Whether Alec's persistence had aroused his suspicions or he was already aware of his wife's infidelity, he was bound to go off the deep end one way or another.

It all seemed horribly straightforward, though a few questions remained. Had the major killed himself from sheer despair at being cuckolded, or had he killed Talmadge and committed suicide in part from guilt? With any luck he'd have written a note of explanation.

A third uncertainty wrapped Alec in a miasma of sick dread: he prayed he wasn't going to find Gwen Walker murdered in her bed.

As he stepped from car to pavement, doubts began to nibble at the corners of his mind. They were driven into retreat by the arrival of the police surgeon. Ridgeway bounced out of his sporty Bugatti, black bag in hand.

'I gather you have another one for me, Fletcher. This'll tie up the last one, eh?'

'Perhaps.'

'Come, come, my dear chap, isn't it obvious? Walker discovers his Gwen is indulging in a bit of nooky with the dentist, does him in in a fit of temper, and kills himself out of remorse. I bet you a fiver he's left a note explaining it all. They nearly always do.'

'How do you know about Talmadge and Mrs Walker?' Alec asked sharply. 'Rumour, or of your own knowledge?'

Ridgeway laughed, a trifle uneasily. 'Why, of my own knowledge. Doctors don't spread rumours, you know, like policemen. I saw them at an hotel in Brighton, a discreet little place, doesn't ask awkward questions. I'm a bachelor, remember.'

'And whom did you tell?'

'No one.'

Alec stared at him.

'Well, perhaps one person. Pillow talk. You can't expect me to give you her name.'

No wonder Daisy hadn't been able to trace the rumour to its source. 'I hope I shan't be called to your house next, to find out who cut your throat with your own scalpel.'

Chastened, Ridgeway followed him to the house. Alec hoped he realized that his 'pillow talk' might well be responsible for Walker's death, possibly Talmadge's and Mrs Walker's as well.

The front door stood open, but Alec rang the bell. The daily woman came out of the front room. 'Oh, it's you, ducks, the rozzer. Come on in, do.'

'Morning, Mrs Davies.' Alec caught a whiff of coal-gas as he entered the hall. 'Have you seen Mrs Walker this morning?'

'I just got 'ere meself, ducks, and I'm that flambustigated I dunno whether I'm on me 'ead or me 'eels and that's the truth.'

The divisional DS came into the hall from the rear.

'Mackinnon, have you seen Mrs Walker?'

'No, sir, not yet. I only just got here.' Momentarily the Scot looked as if he resented the implication of inefficiency. He caught on with admirable speed. 'Och nay, ye dinna think . . . ?' He turned towards the stairs.

''Ere now, you can't go barging in on madam,' Mrs Davies protested. Then she looked from Mackinnon's grim face to Alec's, and her own paled. 'Blimey.'

'Mrs Bates hasn't seen her either?' Heads shook. 'Ridgeway, go up with Mackinnon, please,' Alec requested. 'Mrs Davies, Dr Curtis is in the kitchen, I take it?'

'Yes, and a young rozzer as the sergeant brung wiv 'im.'

'And Nora Bates?'

'In the front parlour 'ere. The doctor told 'er to go sit down wiv 'er feet up. Nasty shock she 'ad, and 'er not as young as she was. I was wiv 'er when you rung the bell.'

'Go back to her, will you? I'll need to talk to both of you in a bit. Don't say anything about . . . what may be upstairs, please.'

'Me lips is sealed,' promised Mrs Davies, 'but let's 'ope it's a false alarm.'

'Let's hope,' Alec agreed fervently. He headed for the kitchen.

Dr Curtis was just coming out. For a moment Alec couldn't work out why he looked lopsided, then he realized the old man's shirt was buttoned wrong so that his tie was awry. He must have left home in a great hurry. Alec raised his hand to his tie to make sure he hadn't done the same thing.

'Morning, Fletcher. Nothing to be done for the poor chap, I'm afraid. Sergeant Mackinnon said Ridgeway is on his way and no doubt he'll be more precise, but at a guess he's been dead seven or eight hours. Without moving him, there's nothing to suggest he did not die of coal-gas poisoning. I thought you'd want him left *in situ*.'

'Yes, thank you, Doctor. We have to consider all the possibilities.'

'And I dare say this may be connected to the other nasty business.' Curtis sighed. 'Ah well, such is life – and death. I'd better have a word with Mrs Walker before I go, though I'd say she's a lot tougher than Mrs Talmadge, less likely to be overcome by her feelings. Is she still upstairs?'

'Yes.' Alec put a hand on his arm. 'She hasn't yet been told about her husband. Dr Ridgeway has gone up. Perhaps you wouldn't mind looking in on Mrs Bates first? She's in the sitting room at the front.'

Alec was further delayed by the young uniformed constable Mackinnon had ordered to stop anyone entering the kitchen. By the time he had shown the embarrassed but determined lad his credentials, Mackinnon was hot on his heels.

'She seems to be all right, sir. This was by the bed.' In his handkerchief-wrapped hand he brandished a small white cardboard box. 'Sleeping powders, Veronal, to be taken as needed. But it's almost full, and Dr Ridgeway says she's sleeping normally, though verra soundly. Did you want him to wake her?'

'No, let's leave her in happy ignorance as long as we can. Constable, go and ask him to come down to the kitchen.'

'Softly,' cautioned Mackinnon, transferring the box to his pocket. 'Dinna wake the lady.'

'Did she and the major share a room?'

'Aye, Chief, looks like it. Two single beds.'

They went on to the kitchen. The door stood open. The smell of gas was strong in the passage, unpleasant but not choking. Alec stuck his head into the kitchen and sniffed cautiously.

'Not too bad.'

'Bearable,' Mackinnon agreed. 'Mrs Bates opened all the doors and windows before she rang up Dr Curtis.'

Alec stepped in and stopped to one side just inside the door, to survey the scene. To his right was an open door to the outside, the window beside it also wide open. Ahead, beyond a scrubbed wood table, was the sink, with another open window above it. Over the draining board was a gas hot-water geyser.

Following Alec's gaze, Mackinnon commented, 'Good job the geyser isna the kind with a pilot light, or we'd be investigating a hole in the ground.'

To their left was the stove. The oven door half concealed Major Walker, dressed in dinner jacket and black trousers, their formality in incongruous contrast to his position. His back to them, he was partly seated on a cushion, partly sprawled on the tiled floor, his head resting on another cushion inside the oven. Whatever dreadful despair drove people to gas themselves, they almost always tried to make their last moments as comfortable as possible. A cosy death.

'It's usually women who choose a gas oven,' Alec said with a frown. 'Not what I'd expect of a military man. You didn't see a note?'

'I would have showed you right away, Chief.'

'Of course. Sorry.'

'Nothing on the kitchen table. It could've blown off.'

'True. Check the floor in the passage and front hall, will you, and have your constable look around the front and back gardens. We'll hold off on a thorough search till Tring and Piper get here.'

As the sergeant left, Alec started to circle the table, scrutinizing everything he passed. The kitchen was neat and spotless, 'all shipshape and Bristol fashion', in Mrs Davies's words, except for two mugs and a small saucepan in the sink. The mugs were full of brown-scummed water, a teaspoon standing in each. The inside of the pan, also filled with water, was coated with white scum.

Bedtime cocoa, Alec thought, then he noticed the tin on the draining board. Bedtime Ovaltine, he amended. Samples of each liquid must be sent to the lab. He wished he had the 'murder bag' Tom kept muttering about, with everything necessary for collecting evidence.

Rounding the third corner of the table, he looked down on Major Francis Walker, deceased.

'She's perfectly all right.' Ridgeway's arrival startled Alec, whose thoughts were presently devoted to Gwen Walker's unfortunate husband. 'Veronal she appears to have taken. The sergeant has the remaining powders, which I'd say is most of them. It's best to let her sleep it off if you can. If you wake her, she's liable to be dopey.'

'No hurry.'

Ridgeway joined him by the stove. 'Poor devil. I'll tell you this, old man, if I ever decide to get married, I shan't choose a beauty. All right, if you've seen what you need to, let's have a look at him.'

'Don't move him yet, please, not more than you can help. I want some photos. Does his position look natural to you?'

'As natural as they ever do. They arrange themselves carefully, but as soon as they lose consciousness they slump all over the place. Not that I've seen more than two or three before, but once you've seen one, you've seen 'em all.'

Alec moved out of his way. He knelt beside the body, grasped one wrist and started muttering about ambient temperatures and the onset of *rigor*.

Mackinnon returned. 'No sign of a note on the floor, sir. Constable Jenkins is still looking outside. Shall I give him a hand?'

'No, leave him to it. It's a long shot. You can go and tell Dr Curtis that Mrs Walker is sleeping and ask him if he prescribed the Veronal. If so, see if he can remember how many doses he gave her.'

'He doesna dispense, himself, sir, but if he canna recall how many he prescribed, I'll ring up the chemist. The name is on the box.'

'Good.' The word was at once assent and approval. DS Mackinnon was turning out to be useful. 'Dr Curtis is free to leave when you've spoken to him. Tell the women I'll be in to speak to them shortly.' Alec turned back to Ridgeway. 'How long?'

'Eight hours, or thereabouts.' As he spoke, Ridgeway's hands roved about the body, palpating, raising an eyelid to peer into a staring eye, loosening tie and collar to examine the throat. 'Unofficially, around midnight. Officially, sometime between ten and two. It's not an exact science, you know.'

'I'm all too aware of the fact. In this case I doubt it matters much, but how often you fellows would solve a case for us if you could say, "He died at precisely twelve-oh-three a.m."'

'I would if I could,' said Ridgeway, 'but I can't. The pathologist might be able to help, if he'd eaten recently and someone can tell you when. Are you going to get Spilsbury?'

'I doubt it.' The brilliant Sir Bernard Spilsbury, Home Office Pathologist, was too much in demand to take on an apparently commonplace suicide. 'Not unless I can prove it's murder.'

'I thought that was the way you were leaning.'

'Not necessarily. He had ample reason for killing himself, perhaps more reason than the obvious.'

'You mean he may have done for Talmadge. Well, it looks to me like suicide. I can tell you with a fair degree of certainty that he was neither knocked on the head nor suffocated, strangled, or choked. Cherry red liver suggests carbon monoxide poisoning. There's a hint of hydrogen sulphide about the eyes. He could have been sedated with Veronal and moved here. Should show up at autopsy. Did you want me to do it?'

'Rather you than that idiot Renfrew, but you knew him, didn't you? I'll find someone else.'

'Thanks.' Ridgeway stood up. 'If there's nothing else, then, I'm off.'

'Right-o. No, don't wash your hands there, please. There's a downstairs cloakroom, I believe.'

Ridgeway looked at the mugs in the sink, nodded soberly and followed Alec out of the kitchen.

Mackinnon met them in the hall. 'Mrs Bates seems to have recovered from the shock,' he said with a grin. 'She wants to know when she can have her kitchen back.'

As Alec and Mackinnon entered the sitting room, Nora Bates

surged to her feet. 'I've my work to do,' she snapped, shocked, perhaps, but not notably distressed by her master's demise. 'And while Mrs Davies lounges about, the floors aren't getting any cleaner, and I s'pose she'll expect to be paid, same as usual.'

'Seeing it's not you as pays me,' said the charwoman indulgently, 'don't you fret your kidneys to flinders for nuffink, ducks.'

'I'm afraid there won't be any cleaning done until the house has been searched. I have a few questions to put to you, Mrs Bates.' Alec hid a smile as Mrs Davies leant back in her sling chair, crossed her ankles and prepared to enjoy her leisure and the show.

Sitting down again, Mrs Bates glared at him. 'Well?'

'I gather yesterday was your day off. What time did you get back?'

'Eleven.'

'Were the Walkers at home?'

'Yes.'

'In this room?'

'It's none of my business where they sit.'

'Come now, Mrs Bates, this isn't a vast country mansion. I'm sure you knew where they were.'

The housekeeper's lips pursed. 'She was in here. He was in his den.'

'Thank you. Did you speak to either of them? Or see or hear them speaking to each other?'

'No.'

'All right, what did you do when you got home?'

'They dined out so there wasn't any washing up. I put out the things for the major's Ovaltine and went to bed.'

'The *major's* Ovaltine?'

'Had to have it, every night, like clockwork.'

'What about Mrs Walker?'

'Not her. She used to tease him about it, said it was an old-maidish kind of nightcap. Brandy's what she likes at bedtime. Not a big one, I'll give her that, but it's not a proper bedtime drink for a lady if you ask me.'

So why the two mugs?

From the corner of his eye, Alec saw PC Jenkins come in. He went to Mackinnon, who was taking notes, and whispered something, shaking his head. Alec ignored them to concentrate on Mrs Bates, who was just beginning to warm up.

'After you went up to your room, did you hear any unusual sounds?'

'When you work hard like I do, you don't lie awake listening for bumps in the night,' she said witheringly.

Unwithered, Alec said, 'So you heard nothing till your usual time of waking? You have an alarm clock, I expect. What time does it go off?'

'Half six.'

'What did you do then?'

'Same as what everyone does when they get up.'

'Wash, dress, go downstairs. Did you notice anything unusual on your way down?'

'No.'

'No smell of gas?'

Not till I opened the kitchen door. It seals pretty tight to keep cooking smells out of the rest of the house.'

'All right, let's start there. What did you do then?'

'Closed it quick. I'm not stupid.'

Alec's patience frayed. 'I never thought you were, Mrs

Bates, except in your uncooperative attitude. This would waste a lot less of your precious time if you'd just answer my questions fully so that I don't have to dig for details. Tell me now exactly what you did from the moment you realized something was amiss until you came into this room to sit down.'

She sniffed but complied. She had opened the front door and the big window on the landing, then returned to the kitchen. Leaving the passage door open she had dashed through, holding her nose, to the back door, unbolted and flung it open, and gone out into the garden to breathe deeply. Not till her second foray to open the kitchen windows had she noticed the major.

'He looked dead as mutton,' she said with a shudder, the first sign of any emotion other than irritation. 'I had to get out and catch my breath, but I went back in and picked up his hand. Like ice it was. I knew he'd passed on, for sure, but I telephoned Dr Curtis and he said to telephone the police. Which I did. I waited in the hall for the doctor. When he came, he told me to come in here and sit down.'

'You kept your head admirably,' Alec said, 'and acted with the greatest common sense.'

Her snort suggested that she was not in the least gratified by his praise.

'At what point did you turn off the gas tap?'

She looked at him blankly. 'Turn off the gas? I don't remember doing that.'

'You musta done, ducks. Don't make no sense opening all them doors and winders if you di'n't. Where's the sense in that, I arst you?'

Alec gave Mrs Davies a be-quiet look.

'I don't remember,' the housekeeper said obstinately.

'Think it through again, Mrs Bates. Close your eyes and think back to opening the kitchen door. Imagine yourself going through each action. You opened the door, smelt the gas and . . . ?'

She ran through the whole sequence again, in almost exactly the same words.

'You was flustered, Nora, stands to reason. 'Course you don't 'member zackly every little bitty thing you done.' Mrs Davies turned to Alec and added confidentially, 'I 'specks it'll come to 'er in time, ducks, if you give 'er time to think about it.'

And it probably would. All the same, it was curious that Nora Bates recalled everything else so clearly yet was adamant about not remembering that one small thing. Oddnesses were beginning to mount up.

Alec asked her some general questions about the Walkers, whether she had ever heard them quarrelling, and if so what about. Her ignorance seemed to be genuine. She closed her ears and her mind to what she considered none of her business and had nothing useful to impart.

Mrs Davies had just, with pleasurable excitement, given her full name and address, when Tring, Piper and the ambulance all arrived. Alec sent Tom to photograph the body and fingerprint the gas taps on the stove.

'Piper, go with him and take samples of the liquids in the mugs and saucepan you'll find in the sink. Is there something in the larder he can use, Mrs Bates?'

'Oh, for a murder bag,' muttered Tom.

'There's clean jam jars. They're to be returned, mind, properly cleaned and no lids missing. Waste not, want not.'

'Quite right, ma'am,' Tom said, beaming at her. 'I'll check the mugs and pan for dabs, shall I, Mr Fletcher?'

'Yes. But do the photos first so we needn't keep these gentlemen waiting.' He indicated the two stretcher-bearers lounging in the hall. 'Take Constable Jenkins with you to fetch and carry.'

The three departed. Alec turned back to Mrs Davies.

'Cor, I'd be 'appy to 'elp you, ducks,' she said regretfully, 'but I bin rackin' me brains and I don't know nuffink I ain't already tol' you.'

'We'll just go over what you told me yesterday, for the record.'

With Mackinnon taking verbatim notes, she repeated what she had said about the discord between the Walkers, oblivious of Mrs Bates's face growing sourer and sourer. Alec recalled his feeling that she had said something useful before, but this time nothing sparked that impression. Nor did his questions elicit anything.

'All right, ladies, if you don't mind waiting in the hall for a few minutes, the sergeant and I will go over this room. Then you can come back and clean and tidy to your hearts' content.'

The sitting room held no obvious clues: nothing but bottles and glasses in the drinks cabinet; no safe behind the Cubist painting on the wall; no incriminating letters between the pages of the carelessly tossed magazines; no half-burnt papers in the grate. They went out to the hall. Mrs Davies was joking with the ambulance men while Mrs Bates looked crabbier than ever, if possible.

Alec asked the whereabouts of the major's den.

The small room was at the back of the house, the opposite

side to the kitchen. Here the major's passion for neatness held sway, along with his preference for tradition. No ultra-modern professional decorator had touched this cosy retreat with its deep armchairs and huge Victorian pedestal desk. The only picture was an equally huge and equally Victorian painting of the Battle of Waterloo. Wellington and Napoleon everlastingly faced each other on opposite hillsides above a scene of carnage.

'Very military,' Mackinnon commented.

'Very.' But Alec's gaze was on the desk. On the meticulously aligned blotter lay a folded sheet of notepaper. Reaching for it, he let out a long sigh. So much for all his vague theories. 'I think this is what we're looking for,' he said.

CHAPTER 20

Daisy saw Belinda off to catch the bus to school, then went to the kitchen. She was feeling guilty because calling the cook-housekeeper 'Mrs' was not sufficient recompense for loading her with a lot of extra work.

'Is there anything I ought to be doing, Mrs Dobson?' she asked. 'I know you said you could cope without me, but Mrs Fletcher told me such a long list of chores to be done while she's away, I'm sure you can't manage everything. And I *did* listen but I simply can't remember the specifics.'

'Bless you, madam, why should you? Me and Mrs Twickle can do it all 'cepting wash Mrs Fletcher's china knickety-knacks. I wouldn't dare touch 'em for all the tea in China and today's her reg'lar day for washing the dust off 'em.'

'Oh, gosh, I wouldn't dare either.' Daisy shuddered at the thought of chipping one of the hideous, delicate and possibly valuable milkmaids or pug dogs. 'They'll just have to wait until she comes back. I'm sure it won't be more than a day or two.'

'The master's hot on the trail of that murdering devil, is he, madam?'

To judge by her language, the staid Mrs Dobson must be a secret devotee of shilling shockers. Daisy was delighted with the discovery. 'I expect he'll clap the darbies on the villain any moment,' she said. 'Well, if you truly don't need me . . .'

She went up to her writing room, sat down before her typewriter and stared unseeing out of the window. Was Alec really about to 'clap the darbies on the villain?' Did Major Walker's suicide simplify or complicate the investigation? Had he left a note confessing to the murder of Raymond Talmadge?

Alec probably knew the answers to all these questions by now. It was maddening not to be able to pop over to the Walkers' house and find out what was going on. Much too restless to concentrate on her article, Daisy decided to take Nana for a walk up Primrose Hill to get rid of the fidgets.

The puppy had no objection to this plan. It was a glorious day and for once the air was clear, so the view from the top almost came up to Wordsworth's 'Earth has not anything to show more fair'. The words did pass involuntarily through Daisy's mind. However, the poet would definitely have castigated her as dull of soul, for she scarcely spared the 'ships, towers, domes, theatres and temples' a second glance. Her thoughts were elsewhere.

What if it wasn't suicide? After all, Talmadge's death would have passed as suicide or an accident if she hadn't been there.

What if some maniac was trotting around St John's Wood doing in middle-aged men so cleverly that until now no one had suspected murder? Not that Talmadge was really middle-aged, or one would have to count Alec in the same category, which he was not.

What else did Walker and Talmadge have in common? Straying wives. If that was the maniac's criterion, then Alec was safe.

But really a murderous maniac was hardly a probable explanation. More to the point, one particular straying wife was connected with both victims: Gwen Walker. Suppose she had killed her lover when he told her their affair was over. Suppose the major then found out about the affair, or the murder, or both, and simply couldn't live with the knowledge.

Suicide seemed a cowardly way out for a military man, Daisy thought, and the gas oven a cowardly way to commit suicide. His continued use of his rank after the Armistice suggested he had been regular army. Surely the proper thing for an officer and a gentleman to do was to blow his brains out with a pistol!

One way or another, Gwen Walker was mixed up in two unnatural deaths. Suddenly Daisy was dying to know what Melanie, after that tantalizing hint, had refused to tell her about the major's wife.

'Nana, come! Time to go home.'

Nana gave her a considering look, decided she was serious, and stopped trying to climb a tree after a squirrel. They set off down the hill.

When they reached home, Daisy went straight to the telephone.

'Mrs Germond's just going out,' said the maid who answered.

'Please see if you can catch her. It's . . .' Urgent would be stretching the truth. Mel's information probably had nothing to do with the major's suicide, and even if it did, a few hours could hardly make any difference. On the other hand, Daisy had an urgent desire to know. She compromised. 'It's quite important.'

'I'll tell her, ma'am.'

Melanie's soft voice came on the line. 'Daisy? What's up? Belinda's welcome to come here after school, if you're going to be busy sleuthing?'

'No, darling, but thanks for the offer. I wondered whether you could drop in for coffee this morning.'

'I'd have loved to, but I don't think I can make it. I have a million things to do today.'

'Tea this afternoon? Bring Lizzie, of course. Or drinks before dinner, you and Robert? Why don't you both come to dinner! Though I can't be sure Alec will be home.'

Melanie laughed, but a note of caution entered her tone. 'Tea, then. But I'm not promising to tell you . . . anything. I must run. 'Bye.'

'Toodle-oo, darling, see you later.' About to hang up, Daisy paused, then depressed the hook to recall the operator. She asked for Sakari's number. Melanie might hold out against one inquisitor, but she'd surely give in to the combined efforts of two.

'"I killed Talmadge, out of jealousy," Alec read aloud. '"I know the police are closing in. They shall not take me alive." Signed, Francis Walker.'

'So it really was suicide,' sighed Ernie Piper.

His evident disappointment made Tom's moustache twitch with amusement. 'Ah,' said the sergeant ruminatively. He leant back, his massive form for once comfortably encompassed by one of the big armchairs in the major's den. 'So it would appear. Handwriting's his, Chief?'

Alec passed him the sheet of paper, and Mackinnon handed

over several other examples of the signature and writing – cancelled cheques and copies of correspondence – which they had found in the desk. Tom compared them carefully, with Piper hanging over his shoulder.

'They look the same to me,' the young DC admitted regretfully.

'Ah.'

'You don't think so, Tom?'

'I do, Chief, I do.'

'Then the Talmadge case is solved,' said Mackinnon. He too was disappointed. His chance to work with the Yard had not lasted long, and the suicide of the villain brought no one any glory.

'Ah!'

'I take it you've spotted the flaw in that argument, Tom?'

'Seems to me, Chief, we'd be foolish to take his word just because he's dead. Maybe he loved his wife so much he murdered her lover, like he says. Or maybe he loved her so much, he confessed and killed himself to save her when he discovered *she'd* murdered her lover.'

'Or maybe he convinced himself quite mistakenly that she did it. I'm afraid we still can't write off Mrs Talmadge or Lord Creighton, much as I'd like to.' If he'd been alone with Tom, Alec might have added that he couldn't be sure, either, that Daisy wouldn't dig up some new suspect from under a stone.

'At least we know it's suicide, Chief,' said Piper, 'since you found this letter in his writing.'

'It's not suicide, laddie,' Tom reproved him, ''till the Coroner says it's suicide. We have to go through the motions as if it could be homicide. The major's dabs are on the oven knob, though, Chief. 'Course, if he was knocked out first, like he must've been, she could've lifted his hand up to make 'em, but d'you reckon she'd think of it? And have the nerve?'

'All the villains know about fingerprints now,' Mackinnon pointed out, 'which isna to say they never leave 'em.'

'Mrs Walker isn't exactly your run-of-the-mill villain,' said Alec, 'but she told me she reads detective stories. Not that she's a villain at all, probably. Are his the only prints, Tom?'

'No, there's a set looks like a woman's. Probably the housekeeper's when she turned the gas off. I'd better get hers and the char's.'

'That'll give 'em a thrill,' said Piper. 'D'you want to bother with these samples I got, Chief?'

'Yes. As Tom says, we have to go through the motions. Besides, it's odd that there are two mugs when Mrs Bates says only the major ever drank Ovaltine at bedtime.' His suspicions aroused again, Alec compared the suicide note with the other papers. He'd be prepared to swear the signature was Walker's, but the lot had better go to a handwriting expert. Surely, though, it would take plenty of practice to forge a signature so neatly. Could some unknown third person be involved?

'Ernie, I want you to go through this desk and any papers we find elsewhere really thoroughly. Look in particular for evidence of relatives, and see if you can find a will or at least the name of his solicitors. Tom, get the women's fingerprints, and see if you can persuade Mrs Bates to go through her story again. The important points are whether she did in fact turn off the gas taps, and can she be quite sure the back door was bolted inside when she opened it.'

'And the front door, Chief?'

'Yes, check the front door, too. I didn't look at the lock and she didn't mention a bolt or night latch. The major could have let someone in who let himself out. Also ask what she knows of relatives. Mackinnon, you and I will continue the search.'

Of course, what he really wanted was to put a few probing questions to Mrs Walker, but he wasn't quite ready to wake her from her drugged sleep. Nor did he care to search her bedroom while she slept. He stationed PC Jenkins at the door, with instructions to keep his ears open.

'Come and tell me at once if you hear any sounds from within.'

The summons was a long time coming. They had time to search the entire house and gather in the den to discuss their gleanings.

Alec had found, in Mrs Walker's untidy boudoir to one side of the bedroom, a small writing desk, not locked. In it, amidst a jumble of bills, paid and unpaid, and dunning letters, was a letter from a cousin in Northamptonshire. The tone of the letter suggested an infrequent correspondence and a distance of sympathies as well as of miles. There was a letter from her mother in Ireland, rambling about farm matters. The only other personal paper was a brief note from Jennifer Crouch, expressing her delight that dear Gwen would come to tea on Wednesday. It was dated several weeks ago.

No letters from Raymond Talmadge. If Gwen Walker had received any, she must have destroyed them, or hidden them rather more cleverly than one might expect of such an untidy person.

Ernie Piper had had still less luck on the personal side. All the meticulously filed letters in the major's neat desk were concerned with business, including his copies of those he had written himself. His address book contained only obviously business entries except for local people whose names Alec recognized. The latter were those with whom the Walkers exchanged hospitality, mostly bridge players.

His bank book, Piper reported, showed a healthy balance. His income appeared to be sufficient for comfort if not for wild extravagance. Everything went to his wife on his death.

Mackinnon had gone over Walker's dressing room, on the other side of the bedroom from his wife's boudoir. He had found nothing of interest. However, he was left with a puzzled feeling that something was missing which ought to be there. Hard as he tried, he couldn't quite put his finger on it.

'Tom, you take a look and see if you can pin it down,' Alec said. 'But first, any luck with Mrs Bates?'

'She's sure the back door was bolted, Chief, and the catch was down on the front-door lock, so that it couldn't be opened from outside even with a key. Nor no one leaving that way couldn't have set the catch behind 'em. There's no sign of breaking and entering anywhere, either. I checked.'

'What about the gas taps?'

'She absolutely can't remember turning them off. I'd say that don't mean much, but—'

'Sir!' Constable Jenkins burst into the den. 'Mrs Walker's awake. I didn't hear nothing in the room but the housekeeper came up and said she'd rung.'

'Damn!' Alec exclaimed. 'Did Mrs Bates go in?'

'Yes, sir. You didn't say to stop her,' Jenkins said reproachfully.

'Losh, man, you're supposed to use your noddle!' cried Mackinnon, exasperated.

'No use crying over spilt milk,' said Alec, making for the

door, 'and she may not have told her her husband's dead. She's not the most forthcoming of women.'

He wanted to be there when Gwen Walker was told she was a widow, in hopes of discerning whether the news came as a surprise to her – or not.

He met Mrs Bates on the stairs. 'Did you tell Mrs Walker about her husband?'

'Of course. And that you police want to talk to her.' Of course. Why should an unsentimental woman who rather disliked her mistress hesitate to give her bad news?

'How did she take it?'

Mrs Bates shrugged. 'How would you expect her to take it? She said to tell you she'll be down in half an hour.'

Alec gave up.

Half an hour later, when Gwen Walker came down, he was ready for her. Mackinnon had orders to search the bedroom as soon as she left it. Ernie Piper sat in an inconspicuous corner of the sitting room, ready with his notebook and his usual selection of ever-sharp pencils. Tom Tring stood by with his fingerprint kit.

Alec rose as Mrs Walker came in. Her face was solemn, but not sorrowful. If tears had been shed, immaculate make-up hid the signs. She wore a navy costume with a white silk blouse and a single strand of pearls. Whatever her carelessness about her surroundings, Gwen Walker's person was as always beyond criticism.

She paused in the doorway and Alec moved to meet her. 'Allow me to express my condolences,' he said, the formal phrase once more proving its usefulness.

Her lower lip quivered, almost imperceptibly, but she spoke with outward composure. 'Thank you, Mr Fletcher.'

'I'm very sorry to trouble you at this time, but there are questions that must be asked. In view of our prior acquaintance, it's perfectly understandable if you prefer to speak to another officer. Also, you're entitled to have your solicitor with you, if you feel the need.'

'No need, and I'd rather answer your questions than a stranger's,' she said with a faint smile.

Alec bowed slightly and gestured towards a chair which would place her with the light from the window on her face, her back towards Piper. 'I'm afraid I'll have to have Detective Sergeant Tring take your fingerprints, for elimination purposes.'

Dismay was followed by resignation as Tom stepped forward. 'All right.'

'It will only take a moment, ma'am,' Tom rumbled comfortably, 'and I have a cloth here to wipe your fingers afterwards.'

He was soon done, and departed with his prize. Alec sat down. 'Would you like to tell me what happened last night?' he invited.

Again the faint smile. 'No, but I will. We dined out – with the Robinsons, actually. I understand you and Mrs Fletcher were invited but were unable to attend.'

'Daisy would have dealt with that,' Alec said hastily.

'Yes, of course. I didn't want to go, but Francis insisted. He ... he was always very conscious of what the neighbours would say, and in this case, he chose not to let them say behind our backs that we were afraid to appear.'

'Afraid to appear?'

'Come now, Mr Fletcher, give us both credit for realizing that you couldn't be hounding everyone who ever sat next to

Ray— to Raymond Talmadge at dinner. It was sufficiently obvious for poor Francis to be unable to go on pretending he didn't know about us. He had a genius for not seeing what he didn't want to see, you know.'

'So you dined out. What time did you get home?'

'We left early. The circling vultures were too much for Francis, though when it came to it, I could have faced them down forever. I suppose we reached home about ten-thirty. Needless to say, Francis was spoiling for a row, so we had one. The right was all on his side, of course. I hadn't a word to say in my own defence, except that it was all over, which he could hardly deny.'

'We'll get to that in a minute. How did your "row" end?'

Gwen Walker's lips tightened momentarily. 'With Francis weeping into his Ovaltine. I said I'd—' She stopped and turned at the sound of the door opening.

Tom Tring looked in. He knew better than to interrupt an interrogation for anything unimportant, so Alec excused himself and went to the door.

'Her dabs are on the oven gas tap,' Tom said in a low voice. 'Also on the handle of the pan and one of the mugs in the sink. And ...' He beckoned Alec out to the hall, where Mackinnon was gingerly holding a Mauser by the barrel. 'And DS Mackinnon found this in the drawer of the bedside table between their beds. It has Mrs Walker's fingerprints on it too.'

CHAPTER 21

Alec couldn't for the life of him see where the pistol came in. He would have liked to discuss the matter with Tom and Mackinnon, but Mrs Walker was talking and she might decide at any moment to stop. She had already admitted to a row with her husband. Whatever the rest of her story, he didn't want to give her too much time to think about it.

Returning to the sitting room, he found her twisting the damp cloth Tom had given her between nervous fingers, though her face remained calm. Her hands stilled as he sat down.

'Go on,' he said.

'Where was I?'

'Ovaltine.'

'Oh yes. I can't say I care for the stuff myself, but Francis always drank it at bedtime. Last night I thought it might calm him down if I had some too. I even went so far as being frightfully wifely and made it for him. I poured half mine down the sink, though. He was still sitting there at the kitchen table staring gloomily into his mug, so I went up to bed.'

'And straight to sleep?'

'Straight to sleep. It had been a rather exhausting day.'

Perhaps alerted by something in Alec's face, she went on, 'No, wait, I think I took a powder. I sometimes do. Not a good habit, I know, and they're as bad as too much to drink for wrecking one's memory.'

Brilliant, Alec thought with reluctant admiration. Anything she 'forgot' to tell him could be blamed on the Veronal.

'You know the rest,' she said. 'I woke up very late, in desperate need of coffee. I rang for Bates, and when she came she told me . . . about poor Francis. He was pretty cut up last night, but I never for a moment imagined . . . Did he leave a letter for me?'

'We found nothing addressed to you. Tell me, how do you make Ovaltine?'

'Why, just the same as cocoa. Francis likes . . . liked it made with milk.'

'Heated in a saucepan on the top of the stove?'

'Yes, of course.'

'Then why are your fingerprints on the oven gas tap?'

Her lip-rouged mouth opened but for a moment nothing came out. Then she laughed shakily. 'Oh, I suppose I must have touched it when I was trying to find the right one. I'm not at all familiar with the stove. In fact, I'd go so far as to say I can't recall ever having attempted to cook on it before.'

Alec could all too easily picture himself doing exactly the same. He dropped that line, for the moment at least. 'Did the major have any other worries?'

'Besides an errant wife whose lover had just been murdered?' This time her laugh was bitter. 'I suppose everyone does, but nothing he talked about.'

The fact that she didn't credit her husband with a host of worries, thus making suicide more likely, impressed Alec.

Was she clever enough to see that overdoing it might backfire? The Veronal excuse for forgetfulness was clever, but then again, her pathetic alibi for Raymond Talmadge's death suggested the opposite.

'I went to see Miss Jennifer Crouch,' he said.

'So you know I was nowhere near Raymond's house when he died.'

'On the contrary, Miss Crouch said she had not seen you this week.'

'Jenny says I wasn't there? How could she! She must have muddled the day. She has so much on her mind with her mother to care for. Or perhaps it was her pride speaking. I took her out to lunch in the village, and she doesn't like to talk about it because she can't reciprocate.'

'I see,' he said dryly. It was the first outright lie she had told but Alec didn't bother to contradict her. If he kept her much longer – a beautiful bereaved widow with no one to support her – any good barrister would make hay with insinuations of undue pressure, especially as he had not given her the Judges' Rules warning.

There was one more question he simply had to ask, though he couldn't see what it had to do with the case. 'My men found a loaded pistol in your bedside table, with your fingerprints on it, Mrs Walker. Do you have a licence?'

'I've no idea. It's Francis's, of course. He calls it a souvenir of the war.'

'And the fingerprints?'

She hesitated, then shrugged and said with a sigh, 'It can't hurt him now. One night last week we were woken in the small hours by a noise. I thought it was a cat knocking something over in the garden, but Francis was sure it was a burglar downstairs. I'm afraid his reaction was to hide his head under the bedclothes. I took the pistol and went down, but no one was there. It must have been a cat outside after all. When I returned to the bedroom, poor Francis was under the bed.'

Shell-shock, Alec assumed. Trying to conceal it might explain the major's excessively military bearing and unwarranted continued use of his rank. It must have been hard on his wife. Plenty of people considered the mental damage caused by the horrors of war to be shameful.

Alec did not presume to judge. His war had been fought far from the mud and blood of the trenches, floating among the clouds in a winged crate made of sailcloth, balsa wood and piano wire.

'Thank you, Mrs Walker.' He stood up. 'That will be all for now, but I shall probably have some more questions for you.'

She jumped up and clutched his sleeve in a sudden panic. 'Don't go! What am I supposed to do? He's not . . . he's not still in the kitchen, is he? What about the funeral? And his will? I have very little money. I don't know what to do.'

'He's gone,' Alec said gently.

'Yes, of course. Bates made me coffee. How horrible!' She shuddered.

'I suggest you get in touch with his solicitor.'

'I don't know . . .'

'DC Piper found his name in the major's desk.'

Ernie Piper, with his phenomenal memory for names and numbers, was already writing down the information. He tore off the sheet and gave it to Mrs Walker.

'You'd better ring him up right away,' Alec advised.

'I will.' Pulling herself together with a visible effort, she attempted a smile. 'Thank you, Mr Fletcher. You've been very kind.'

After which, Alec reflected, it was going to be damned difficult to arrest her. The letter with her husband's signature seemed to let her out of that death, but she was still very much in the picture where Talmadge was concerned.

The little Austin staggered as Tom Tring took his seat beside Alec. 'I think I got it, Chief,' he announced.

'Got it?' Alec pressed the self-starter, wondering whether the Yard would pay for new springs when they wore out prematurely beneath Tom's weight.

'The missing factor,' said Mackinnon from the back seat, where he and Piper cradled the evidence.

'The something missing from Walker's dressing room?'

'Right, Chief, and not just the dressing room. He don't seem to own a single regimental tie. And there's no photos of army buddies, none of him in his dress uniform, none of the stuff you'd expect someone who still calls himself Major to treasure.'

'Odd!' said Alec. Come to think of it, he'd never seen the major in a regimental tie. Not that many men wore them, but as Tom said, Walker still called himself Major six years after the end of the war.

'No discharge papers in the desk,' said Piper, 'I didn't notice when I was looking, but I'd remember if I'd seen 'em. And no licence for the Mauser, though lots of ex-servicemen don't have one, seeing they think of it as a souvenir, not a weapon.'

'If in fact he was a serviceman,' Alec mused. 'Damned if I

can see what it means, or whether it has anything to do with our investigation.'

'It ties in, though, doesn't it, Chief?' Piper said eagerly. 'I mean, with what she was telling you about him hiding under the bed.'

'What?' asked the two sergeants in chorus.

'Tell 'em, Ernie,' said Alec, negotiating his way past a slow moving brewer's dray pulled by four massive cart horses.

'The chief asked Mrs Walker about her dabs on the pistol, and she said she went downstairs with it last week when they thought they heard a burglar, because the major hid under the bed.'

'Shows she has the nerve for anything,' Mackinnon opined.

'Ah.' Tom ruminated. 'What it could be is her making up a story to account for a military man putting his head in the oven instead of shooting himself.'

'Or maybe she just made up the story to account for the dabs, Sarge. She might've picked up the Mauser thinking she'd shoot him, and Talmadge too maybe, but didn't know how to fire it, or decided it'd be too messy.'

'Now that's an idea, laddie,' said Tom.

'Yes, we mustn't lose sight of her as a suspect in Talmadge's death.' Alec pulled into the forecourt of Marylebone Station and stopped. 'It seems more likely than that she killed her husband, given that letter. Let me see it again.'

Piper passed over the suicide note along with the papers for comparison. Alec and Tom contemplated them.

'It's his signature all right,' said Tom. 'The rest looks kind of shaky. She could've found a blank sheet with his signature on it.'

'Possibly. But a man's handwriting may well be shaky

when he's contemplating putting an end to his existence, whereas his signature comes so naturally as to be firm in spite of it. Barring evidence to the contrary from the experts, I'm inclined to think he wrote this and killed himself. On the other hand, I know she's lying about her whereabouts when Talmadge died.' Alec took an envelope from his pocket. 'Ernie, here's the typed statement of what Miss Crouch told me. Hop on a train and get it signed.'

'Right, Chief.' Piper opened the car door.

'Charm her, Ernie. If that fails, you can ask her to accompany you to Scotland Yard.'

Piper grinned. 'That'll do the trick, Chief.' He disappeared into the crowds that constantly swarmed around even the smallest of the great London termini.

'Right-o,' said Alec, 'let's get that stuff to the fellows who can tell us what it all means.'

Daisy regarded the laden tea table with dismay. Expecting the ladies this time, Mrs Dobson had done them proud: thin-sliced brown bread and butter, crustless; three kinds of biscuits besides Daisy's favourite macaroons; a Dundee cake and a jam sponge. How was she supposed to resist?

The girls had their own spread in the dining room, and the leftovers from both would keep re-appearing for days. The fashionable figure of her dreams receded ever further before her.

Once again Sakari picked up Melanie and fetched the three girls from school in her chauffeured car, so they all arrived together. Greetings over and the children settled at the table, Daisy and her friends retired to the sitting room. Daisy poured the tea, China with lemon for Melanie, Indian with milk for herself and Sakari, and passed the bread and butter.

'Thank you,' said Sakari, to whom she had hinted on the phone about her intention of pumping Mel for information. 'Are we to pretend this is an ordinary social occasion? Shall we talk about the weather, or the children?'

'Has Alec discovered something new?' Mel asked, looking unhappy. 'Something connecting . . . someone with Talmadge's death, I mean.'

'Loads of things, I'm sure, but that's not what I wanted to talk to you about, darling. Haven't you heard about Major Walker?'

Mel gasped. 'No! I've been busy all day.'

'I heard that the police were at the Walkers' house this morning,' Sakari said, 'but I was in town this afternoon. They are known to be suspects. Has the major been arrested?'

'No. If you two haven't heard perhaps it isn't generally known. You'd better not say anything unless someone else mentions it first.'

'I, for one, cannot say anything, Daisy, because you have told us nothing. Speak, before I expire from curiosity. What has happened?'

'Major Walker was found this morning with his head in the gas oven.'

'Dead?' whispered Melanie, very pale.

Sakari reached over and took her hand in a comforting clasp. 'The major killed himself to escape prosecution for killing Talmadge?' she asked.

'I don't know,' Daisy admitted. 'I haven't seen or heard from Alec since he left this morning. But I do think, Mel, that he needs to know whatever it is that Robert told you about Gwen Walker.'

'I can't see why. It can't have anything to do with what's happened.'

'You can't be sure. Even if it's just a contributing factor to his decision to commit suicide, Alec ought to know.'

'Surely having murdered Talmadge is reason enough for that!' Mel exclaimed.

'But I don't know that he did kill Talmadge.'

'Daisy is correct,' said Sakari. 'One must not withhold information from the police in a murder case, whether one sees its usefulness or not.'

'Robert told me in confidence.'

Daisy sighed. 'Yes, you're right, I shouldn't press you. I'll just tell Alec that Robert knows something about Mrs Walker which he ought to know. I expect he'll think of a way to ask Robert without letting him guess how he found out.'

'Oh no! He's sure to work out that I must have told you.'

'It will be better,' Sakari said, 'if you tell Daisy what is this tantalizing tidbit, and she tells Alec, and Robert does not come into the picture at all.'

'At least, not if it's not useful. And if it *is* useful in solving a murder,' Daisy pointed out, 'then obviously it was right to tell Alec.'

'But Robert will still be furious,' Mel wailed.

'I don't see that you need come into it at all, darling. Alec certainly wouldn't tell Robert how he found out. If he has to go to him for confirmation, he'll just say that he uncovered a clue to whatever it is in the course of his investigation.'

'So it is better if you tell Daisy the whole story, dear Melanie, rather than have Alec go to Robert in search of he knows not what.'

'Especially as in that case Robert, being a bank manager,

might not tell him, so we'd be back to Alec lacking information which could prove vital to the case. Although at this stage I bet I could make a good guess as to what it's all about. You wouldn't be making all this fuss if Mrs Walker had simply overdrawn her account, however vast the amount.'

'And if she had held up a bank with a gun, as in the American films, she would now be in prison.'

Melanie yielded to *force majeure*. 'All right, if you're going to start guessing, I'd better tell you. But swear, both of you, that you won't so much as breathe a word to anyone but Alec. It's not just Robert being angry with me, he could lose his job if anyone found out he'd told me.'

Daisy and Sakari promised. Melanie swallowed the rest of her cup of tea as if to give herself courage, looked nervously over her shoulder, then leant forwards. The others leant towards her, all agog.

'She forged the major's signature,' Mel whispered, 'on a cheque for quite a large amount. Robert says it was a brilliant forgery. They never would have caught it if the major hadn't come in and made a fuss. Of course, when they realized it was Mrs Walker who'd done it, he wanted it hushed up.'

'It had to be something on those lines.'

'Thus speaks the expert sleuth,' Sakari proclaimed.

'You see, Daisy, it can't possibly have any bearing on Talmadge's death or the major's suicide. It's no earthly use to Alec.'

'That's for him to decide,' Daisy said firmly. 'More tea? And do have some cake.'

CHAPTER 22

Daisy was still not hungry when Alec came home, just in time to say good night to Belinda. She joined him for dinner but toyed with her food.

Alec ate ravenously for several minutes, then gave her an anxious look. 'You've hardly eaten a thing. Are you feeling all right, love?'

'Oh yes. Sakari and Melanie came to tea and I ate too much. I have absolutely no willpower, darling,' she confessed mournfully. 'I think I'd better start walking Nana every day.'

'Can't hurt,' he said with abominable cheerfulness. 'Can't hurt either of you.'

'No, and it's not as if we don't both enjoy it.'

'But you're still down in the dumps. Is something else worrying you?'

The truth was, she was feeling guilty about bullying Mel into betraying a confidence. At least Mel had known from the first that her story would be passed on to Alec, so Daisy herself would not be betraying a confidence.

But they had a pact not to talk about his cases during dinner, so she said only, 'Later, darling.'

He groaned, knowing perfectly well what that meant. As they retired to the sitting room after rhubarb tart with top of the milk – another sweet to be finished off! She'd have to have a word with Mrs Dobson – he said, 'Don't tell me you've found me another suspect?'

'Are you satisfied with the ones you have?'

'Not very,' he admitted. 'They're all extraordinarily slippery. Who is it?'

'It's not. Sorry, I misled you.' Daisy poured coffee from the flask Mrs Dobson had left for them. The delicate, flower patterned demitasses were a wedding present she hadn't dared use before. (Mrs Fletcher would have strongly objected to ousting the perfectly good china she'd been using for years.) 'It's a bit of information about one of your existing suspects. Darling, I can't tell you who told me, but you're bound to guess. Will you promise not to—'

'Daisy, you know I can't promise.'

'Right-o, then, just promise to *try*, if it's a useful snippet and you have to go to the source for confirmation, just try to suggest you got it somewhere else.'

'Is this another rumour?'

'No, not at all. It's a very reliable source I trust absolutely. I was told that Gwen Walker forged her husband's signature to a large cheque, so cleverly the bank didn't catch it.'

'Great Scott!' Alec's coffee cup stopped halfway to his lips. He put it down with care. 'The note's been our biggest stumbling block.'

'Tell me?' Daisy coaxed.

He sighed. 'You know so much already, I don't see why not.' He gave her one of his brief but all-encompassing résumés of what they had learnt at the Walkers' house. 'Since then,' he went on, 'we've heard from the pathologist that the major died of coal-gas poisoning. He also had Veronal in his system, and the lab says there are traces of Veronal in the sample from the mug he must have drunk from, the one without her prints. There are no signs, though, no bruising, to show he was manhandled to the oven.'

'If the Veronal put him to sleep, she could have taken her time about moving him.'

'Exactly. We're still waiting to hear from the handwriting expert, but whatever he says, if your story's confirmed, the suicide note could well be a forgery. Then there's her alibi for Talmadge's death. Ernie Piper got a signed statement negating that.'

'It does look bad,' said Daisy.

'Unless the errand boy recognizes her, there's nothing really conclusive though,' Alec said in exasperation. 'If she comes up with a better story about where she was, one we can't disprove, the rest could be demolished by a good barrister for the defence. I shall apply for an arrest warrant tomorrow morning, but I'll try to get a confession before I use it.'

'Does she strike you as someone who's likely to cave in and confess?'

'Yes, frankly. She's not half as cool and collected as she tries to appear. Well, I'm done in.' He stood up, yawning and stretching. 'Coming to bed, love?'

'I'll be right up, darling.'

She carried the coffee tray through to the kitchen and washed up the cups, not wanting to leave them to Mrs Twickle's tender mercies in the morning. As she dried the second, she wondered why Mrs Walker had not at least rinsed out the Ovaltine mugs, if she had drugged the major.

She should have wiped her fingerprints off the oven knob,

too. Presumably she had not been thinking clearly, under-standable in the circumstances. Yet she was calm enough to think of arranging cushions to add to the appearance of suicide, calm enough to forge the major's signature. Odd! What was infinitely more horrible, she must have been calm enough in Talmadge's surgery to watch him die and remove the evidence.

Curiouser and curiouser, thought Daisy. But Alec was waiting for her in bed and she didn't pursue the thought.

The next day was Mrs Dobson's day off. After breakfast, she gave Daisy detailed instructions for heating and browning the shepherd's pie she'd left in the larder. Then she put on a hat with a distressing resemblance to a dead crow and departed.

Mrs Twickle had been given the day off, too. 'Might as well,' Mrs Dobson had said, 'seeing Mrs Fletcher isn't here to chivvy her while I'm out, and you busy with your writing, madam. She won't get much done without someone stands over her, and that's a fact.'

So Daisy was alone in the house. Driven as much by Mrs Dobson's expectations as anything else, she went up to her writing room. She made a note about the cook-housekeeper's opinion of the daily help, but she couldn't concentrate on working out how it fitted into her article. After a restless half hour with nothing accomplished, she fetched Nana from the back garden and took her for a walk in Regent's Park.

It was another perfect spring day. Daisy did her best to enjoy it and not to think about the two unnatural deaths Alec was investigating. For once he had told her everything. He was about to arrest Gwen Walker. Apparently he had solved the case, so it was too maddening to be troubled by niggling doubts.

Still, she didn't know Mrs Walker at all well, and what she knew of her was the reverse of admirable: unfaithful to her husband and forging his signature! No doubt Alec would resolve all the inconsistencies in the evidence before hauling her off to prison.

And then he would have to ring up his mother to tell her it was safe to come home. Daisy heaved such a huge and melancholy sigh that Nana looked up at her and whined. Or perhaps she whined because Regent's Park was not the sort of park where one could let the dog off the lead to run free?

'We'll go to Primrose Hill tomorrow,' Daisy promised.

When they reached home, Daisy could hear the telephone bell ringing through the front door. Naturally she fumbled with the key, but it rang on and on, a desolate, pleading sound in the empty house.

At last she reached the apparatus and snatched it up. 'St John's Wood 2351.'

'Mrs Fletcher? Mrs Alec Fletcher?' A woman's voice she didn't recognize, urgent yet uncertain.

'This is Daisy Fletcher. Would you mind holding on just a moment?' Nana, still attached to her wrist by the lead, was pulling her towards the kitchen. Daisy unclipped her and she dashed off to find her water bowl. 'Sorry, I got a bit entangled with the puppy. Who is it?'

'Thank heaven you're home. I've been trying all morning.' A pause so long she thought they'd been disconnected was followed by a sort of gasp, then, 'This is Gwen Walker.'

'I'm afraid my husband isn't at home.'

'No, he's probably on his way to arrest me.' Now, beneath

a veneer of bravado, she sounded frightened. 'Mrs Fletcher, I want to talk to you. I want to explain. I heard you went to see Mrs Talmadge – you're the only person she'll see. I must tell someone what happened or I'll go mad. Oh, please, let me come and see you. Please!'

Daisy thought fast. Curiosity and even a touch of sympathy urged her to agree. Caution pulled the other way. Alec believed Mrs Walker to be a murderer, and except for the puppy, who wouldn't be the slightest use as a protector, Daisy was alone in the house. She could ask Sakari and Mel to join her, but they might not arrive before Mrs Walker.

On the other hand, why on earth should Mrs Walker want to kill Daisy? It couldn't help her. Both Talmadge's and the major's deaths – if he hadn't killed himself – were emotional crimes. That was what was wrong with them, what clashed with the cold, unemotional carrying out.

'I'm sorry,' Gwen Walker said dully. 'I shouldn't have asked.'

'No, wait! You took me by surprise. I'll come to you.'

'You will? It's very kind of you.' The formal phrase sounded odd.

'I'll be there shortly,' said Daisy, and hung up.

Her mind still raced. The Walkers' servant would be there, and the friendly charwoman Alec had told her about. But supposing they had been given the day off? Supposing Mrs Walker wanted to strike at Alec through Daisy, or simply lost her temper and attacked?

Daisy dialled Sakari's number. If Sakari and Mel, or at least one of them, couldn't go with her, she'd just ring back and say she'd changed her mind. If she arrived with them and Mrs Walker didn't want to talk, so be it.

'Mrs Prasad, please. This is Mrs Fletcher.'

It seemed forever before Sakari spoke. 'Daisy? I am on my way out. You have found another clue?'

'Maybe a confession. I don't know exactly. But can you come with me, right away?'

'But of course. This I will not miss for all the tea in China. Or India. I will cancel my appointment and pick you up in a few minutes.'

Melanie required more explanation and was much more hesitant. By the time Daisy had persuaded her to go along, the chauffeur Kesin was ringing the doorbell.

'We'll fetch Mrs Germond next,' Daisy said to him as he opened the car door for her.

'Melanie comes with us?' Sakari asked. 'Splendid! Where are we going?'

Daisy laughed. 'Suppose I told you Bourton-on-the-Water?'

'Then I would say, I hope you can tell Kesin how to get there. What an adventure.'

'Just to the Walkers' house,' Daisy said, sobering. 'She wants to talk to me, and I don't feel quite comfortable going alone.'

'Aha. I cannot blame Mrs Walker if she prefers to confess to you rather than to Alec. He can be quite formidable, I think.'

'Yes, he can. But I don't know that she intends to confess. She may want to convince me that she's not guilty, perhaps in the hope that I can persuade Alec. And she may decide not to speak at all with you and Mel present.'

'That would be a pity.'

'Yes. I expect it's silly of me, only I'll feel safer with you there.'

'I am certain you are wise to bring us with you,' Sakari said with a smile, 'if only to appease Alec.'

They picked up Melanie and drove on to the Walkers' house. The cook-housekeeper opened the door.

'Mrs Walker is expecting me,' Daisy told her.

'*You*, madam.' The woman glowered at Sakari and Mel.

'Mrs Fletcher!' Gwen Walker, her face pale and unpowdered but still beautiful, came into the hall. She caught sight of the others. 'Oh!'

'I hope you don't mind my bringing my friends. You know Melanie Germond and Sakari Prasad, don't you?' Daisy was pretty sure the Walkers' house was one the Prasads were invited to.

The polite, commonplace words seemed to calm Mrs Walker. 'Of course. Do come in.'

'Coffee, madam?'

'Yes. No. Perhaps later.' She led the way into the sitting room and looked rather helplessly around. 'Do sit down.'

A burning cigarette, balanced on the edge of an ashtray, showed where she had been sitting. Melanie, murmuring 'Don't let us intrude,' firmly led Sakari to the other end of the room. Daisy chose a chair far enough from Mrs Walker's not to be smothered in cigarette smoke but close enough to hear if she spoke softly.

Gwen Walker sat down and stubbed out the smouldering end, then picked up a cigarette box and offered it to Daisy.

'No thanks.'

'You don't? How wise. They turn everything yellow, fingers, teeth . . . Raymond wouldn't touch them. I didn't smoke while . . .' She put the box down on the low glass table and pushed it away from her. 'You know about us?'

'Yes.'

'I didn't kill him! I swear I didn't.'

'Why can't you tell Alec where you really were that lunchtime? If you have a good reason for keeping quiet about it, he'll keep it confidential.'

'Good reason? Yes, the best of reasons. I went to see Raymond.'

'Oh dear!'

'He wrote saying he had to talk to me, and I was to go in the back way. We didn't usually meet in his house, but I'd done it once before, when we first ... I knew the way, through the alley and the garden. He was waiting at the door, and he hurried me into his surgery. What a place to be told you're not wanted any longer!'

'Why didn't he just write to tell you it was over?'

'He wanted to see me one last time. He was really rather keen on me. I liked him a lot, and we had lots of fun together, but on my part it wasn't exactly a grand passion. I suppose that makes it worse, in a way.'

Daisy's agreement remained tactfully unspoken. 'Fun' didn't seem to her an adequate excuse for infidelity. 'What happened?' she asked.

'He was in a bit of a dither, because he'd had some difficult patients and the last had only just left. He kept telling me to speak quietly because he wasn't sure whether the nurse was still in the waiting room, and the servants might come downstairs at any moment. Of course, they could have seen me coming up the garden path – he hadn't thought of that.' She shrugged. 'Actually, he was pretty upset about having to say goodbye, so I dare say he wasn't thinking too clearly at all.'

'*Having* to say goodbye?'

'His wife was going to have a baby. Is going to. Ray said he had to stand by her, it was the only decent thing to do. That was all right with me. All good things come to an end. But poor Ray was frightfully hangdog about the whole business, so I thought it might make it easier for him if I wasn't too kind and understanding. I told him in no uncertain terms that I'd had enough of him and never wanted to see or hear from him again.' She bit her upper lip. 'And I never did. I flounced out, and he must have gone straight to his "cheerer-upper".'

'His . . . ?'

'That's what he called that damned gas.' Her voice rose. Her back was slightly turned towards the other two, and she seemed to have forgotten their presence. Daisy could see Sakari, who was listening avidly, but not Mel, who was no doubt trying not to listen. Gwen Walker continued, more and more agitated. 'When I heard he was dead, I hoped it was an accident but I was afraid he'd killed himself. Why do they think he was murdered?'

'They have evidence,' said Daisy. This was not the moment to boast that she had discovered the evidence.

'I never even dreamt it was murder until your husband started asking questions. After that, Francis couldn't pretend any longer that he didn't know about Raymond and me. I told him it was all over before Ray died, and that was when he convinced himself that I'd killed him. He wouldn't believe me.' She bowed her head and covered her face with her hands. 'He wouldn't believe me, so why should anyone else? I can't prove I didn't.'

'It's a pity you lied to the police. It makes it harder for them to believe anything you tell them now.'

'I realize that now. I haven't been able to think straight for days. But lying about where I was is the least of it.' She reached for the cigarette box, took one out and lit it, then left it to die in the ashtray. 'I've been abysmally stupid.'

Stupid seemed a peculiar way to describe murdering one's husband. 'What have you done?' Daisy asked.

The sitting-room door opened. In came Mrs Bates with a tray. 'Coffee, madam.'

'But—'

'I asked if you wanted coffee and you said yes, madam.' She set the tray on the table and departed.

Blast the woman, Daisy thought, hoping the interruption was not going to put an end to the flow of confidences.

CHAPTER 23

Exasperated, Gwen Walker rolled her eyes at Daisy. 'It's no earthly use arguing with the woman. She never listens to a word I say unless she wants to. If she thinks I ought to offer my guests coffee, coffee they shall have. Will you have a cup, Mrs Fletcher? Mrs Prasad, Mrs Germond, may I offer you coffee?'

The four cups on the tray had reminded Mrs Walker of the other two, and there wasn't much chance now that her apparent frankness would continue. Daisy swallowed a sigh as Sakari joined them eagerly, Melanie reluctantly. At least Mel was far too polite to refuse to accept coffee from someone she knew to be a forger and suspected of being a murderer. A snub would turn the probability of no new revelations into a certainty.

Pouring coffee, dealing with sugar and hot milk, Mrs Walker was the complete gracious hostess. She passed a plate of simply delicious, crisp, orange peel-flavoured biscuits, homemade. Daisy decided Mrs Bates had her good points after all, but for the next few minutes the talk was all of unsatisfactory servants.

Listening, Daisy made mental notes of one or two points for her article, despite her impatience. She was beginning to despair, though, when the front doorbell rang.

Mrs Walker stopped with a gasp in the middle of a sentence and turned so pale Daisy was afraid she might faint. They sat in stiff silence, the word 'Police' unspoken on everyone's lips.

The housekeeper took her time answering the bell. At last they heard her footsteps in the hall. The front window was open, and through it came a man's voice. 'Snyder, miss, of the *Daily Graphic.* Now, you look like an intelligent woman. I expect you can tell me all about what's going on here.'

Mrs Bates said not a word but the door closed with a thud. Definitely she had her good points.

Melanie moved swiftly to the window, closed it, and pulled the orange-and-black jazz-print curtains across, then turned on the electric light. As she returned to her seat, Gwen Walker started to cry.

Sakari reached over to pat her hand. 'It is better to get it off your chest,' she advised, 'if I have the correct idiom.'

'Francis refused to believe I hadn't killed Raymond.' The words came fast now, punctuated by sniffs. 'We were sitting in the kitchen, drinking that ghastly Ovaltine he's . . . he was so keen on, and he said he was too upset to sleep. He asked for one of my sleeping powders. He wanted to take it in his Ovaltine, so I went up and got one for him. Then I went back up to bed.'

'Did you take a powder?' Daisy asked.

'Not then. I don't like to take them too often, and I was so exhausted I felt sure I'd sleep without. I did go to sleep quickly, but not soundly. You know how it is when you have bad dreams and you keep half waking, not quite sure if you're still dreaming? That's how it was. Then I did wake up, completely, and looked at the clock. It has luminous hands.

It was well past one and the light on the landing showed under the door.'

'You had turned it off?'

'No, I left it on for Francis, but he'd have turned it off when he came to bed. Electricity costs money.' Her mocking tone suggested she was quoting an oft-repeated and much-despised dictum. 'In spite of which, I turned on the bedside lamp. His bed was empty. I tried to go to sleep again, but then I thought maybe he'd taken the powder and fallen asleep at the kitchen table. It seems silly now, but I worried about what Mrs Bates would think when she found him in the morning.'

'You English!' Sakari exclaimed. 'Always worrying about what the servants will think. It is futile.'

'Yet one does,' said Mel.

The Indian attitude towards servants might add an interesting sidelight to her article, Daisy thought.

'Francis would have been mortified,' said Mrs Walker, 'and he was difficult enough to live with already. So I went down. I opened the kitchen door. You've all smelt gas. You can't imagine what it's like to breathe in a lungful. Somehow I managed to slam the door shut. For a while, I don't know how long, I couldn't do anything but choke and wheeze.'

Involuntarily, Daisy raised her hand to her throat as if she were having trouble breathing. So did Mel and Sakari. They exchanged rueful glances. If Mrs Walker was lying, she was doing it very well.

'I wasn't thinking very clearly,' she went on, 'as you can imagine. I don't remember wondering what had happened.'

'It didn't cross your mind that the major was committing suicide?' Daisy asked, more than a trifle incredulous.

Mrs Walker shook her head. 'All I could think about was that the more gas kept pouring into the kitchen, the more likely the whole house would blow up. I had to turn it off. I'd read somewhere about tying a wet cloth over one's mouth and nose in case of fire. I don't know if it's of any use against gas, but that's what I did. I soaked one of the hand towels in the downstairs cloakroom you know the sort, linen with one corner embroidered. With that across my face, I dashed into the kitchen, holding my breath, and turned off the gas tap.'

'And saw the major.'

'Yes, I saw him, of course. Should I have tried to help him? I barely got myself out of there. I breathed some more gas and went through the whole choking thing again, nausea too. I *couldn't* go back in. It was much too late for him, anyway. For the room to be so full of gas, he must have been breathing it for an age.' She was silent for a long moment. 'Until he stopped breathing.'

Silence again.

'What's hard to understand,' said Daisy, 'is why he'd choose that way out. He was so very soldierly. Why didn't he shoot himself?' *Like an officer and a gentleman*, she thought but didn't say.

Horribly, Gwen Walker started to laugh. There was more than a touch of hysteria in her laugh, and more than a touch of bitterness. 'Soldierly!' she spat out. 'He fooled everyone, didn't he? Me too, for long enough to marry the war hero. Francis never saw a battlefield in his life. Army Service Corps, he was. He never even crossed the Channel. And somehow he succeeded in going into the war poor and coming out well off.'

This time the shocked silence was filled with half-incredulous disgust. Melanie broke it.

'He sold military supplies?' she asked tentatively, as if she thought she must have misunderstood.

'"Diverted" them. That's how he put it. He couldn't resist boasting to me, knowing I wouldn't give him away. But he never really believed he'd got away with it, hence the penny-pinching. And thence' – she looked at Melanie – 'my expertise in forging his signature.'

'So you did write the suicide note,' said Daisy.

'Oh yes. I knew, from the cushions he'd taken into the kitchen to make himself comfortable, that he'd been to his den. When I recovered enough to move, I went in there and found the note he'd written. He said he was doing it because I had betrayed him and murdered my lover and he couldn't stand the disgrace. The bastard!'

The ugly word broke on a sob and she started crying in earnest. Daisy pressed a handkerchief into her hand and looked at the others. Mel seemed stunned; it was all too much for her gentle nature. Sakari's dark eyes were alight with speculation.

She caught Daisy's glance and said softly, 'Well, sleuth-hound, what is your opinion?'

By unspoken consent, they both rose and moved to the far end of the room.

'I think she's telling the truth,' said Daisy. 'What she's said answers so many odd questions which needed explaining. Alec may be able to pick holes in her story, but I can't see any at present.'

'So the major killed himself. Did he also kill Talmadge?'

'As she wrote in her note?'

'Oh, did she?'

'Alec told me so. But I think it was a bit of tit-for-tat and mostly to satisfy the police. I doubt she believes it, or she would have made a point of it to us.'

'This sleuthing is very complicated,' Sakari complained.

'Alec would say I'm just theorizing wildly. The major as murderer just doesn't feel right to me. I can't even see him as brave enough to confront Talmadge, let alone kill him. He shot his bolt when he stole the supplies bound for our men in the trenches.'

'Thus it seems to me also.'

'Who do you think did it, then, Sakari?'

'From the start I have theorized wildly. Shall I tell you who was my first guess?'

'Yes, who?'

Sakari glanced at the others. 'I do not wish to malign an innocent person. I will whisper the name.' She leant close and whispered.

Daisy stared at her, sinking into the nearest chair as the leftover pieces of the jigsaw puzzle fell neatly into place. At last the picture was complete.

'It seems so obvious now, darling.' Daisy had inveigled Alec into the major's den when he arrived at the Walkers'.

'What does?' he demanded impatiently, and Tom Tring's moustache twitched.

Ernie Piper's murmur was not quite sotto voce: 'Whatever it is, it's bound to be right.'

'As Sakari says, it's the only solution that is psychologically sound.'

This time Tom snorted audibly, but whether in amusement

or scepticism Daisy wasn't sure. Ernie looked rather dismayed.

Alec looked furious, his dark brows gathering in a thundercloud above hail grey eyes. 'Great Scott, Daisy, you've been discussing the case with your friends? I thought I could at least trust you not to do that!'

'I haven't told them a thing, darling,' Daisy said with perhaps not quite one hundred per cent accuracy. 'Like the rest of St John's Wood, they've read every newspaper they could lay their hands on. They know the people involved, better than I do, having lived here longer. And I thought you'd be pleased that I asked them to come with me when Mrs Walker insisted on seeing me. After all, if she'd been the murderer, I might have been done in by now.'

Gritting his teeth in a way that would have made his deceased dentist cringe, Alec said, 'So you've taken *her* under your wing now.'

'No. She's really behaved rather badly, much worse than Daphne. But I don't believe she's killed anyone. Wait till you hear her story.'

'That is what I came here for!'

'I know, darling. Just let me finish first.'

'As far as I can see, you haven't even started yet.'

'Well, you keep interrupting. Why don't you sit down and stop towering over me?'

With a resigned sigh, Alec sat and motioned to Tring and Piper to do likewise.

'Where's Sergeant Mackinnon?' Daisy asked. She wasn't exactly postponing the moment when she had to expose her theory to the experts, she just wondered.

Tom answered. 'When his super heard the chief was applying for a warrant, he found another job for him.'

'Did you get a warrant, darling?'

'Yes. There's quite enough evidence against Mrs Walker to persuade a judge. Whether it's enough for a jury, in the teeth of a good defence lawyer, I'm less certain. Which is why I have to talk to her before I serve the damn thing, and why I'm giving your ideas a hearing. Or hoping to. For pity's sake, Daisy, get on with it.'

Daisy took a deep breath. 'Right-o. First I have to tell you – with Gwen Walker's permission – that she was the veiled lady in the alley.'

'Aha!'

'The letter Talmadge wrote to her, the one Daphne saw, didn't say goodbye, it asked her to come. She says he was pretty keen on her and wanted to see her one last time. When she arrived, he was anxious because he'd just finished with a patient and wasn't sure whether Nurse Hensted was still in the waiting room and might overhear them.'

Alec sat up straight. 'Go on.'

'So he spoke quietly as he told her about Daphne and the baby. He said he had to do the decent thing, but he was frightfully upset at parting with her. She decided he might feel better if she wasn't too kind, so she told him she'd had enough of him and never wanted to hear from him again. And she's pretty sure she raised her voice when she said it.'

'Ah!' said Tom Tring.

Daisy looked round at Piper. He had taken out his notebook and was scribbling furiously.

'Don't write this down, please, Mr Piper, but I seem

to recall telling you, Alec, that Raymond Talmadge probably had to beat off applicants for the position of mistress.'

'Someone else told me something of the sort, too,' Alec admitted. 'I can't remember who, or exactly what they said, but I do recall having a feeling I'd learnt something significant and being unable to pin it down.'

'And Daphne once mentioned, in passing,' she went on, 'that Miss Hensted was "nuts on" her husband. I didn't see the significance.'

'Which was? Where does it lead you, Daisy?'

She had hooked him, but whether she could sustain his interest with what followed was another matter. 'Now, the next bit is pure speculation.' She was not surprised when his brows met again, but at least he was still listening. 'Suppose Miss Hensted overheard. Suppose she decides her chance has come. She will be his consolation! She waits till she's sure Mrs Walker has left – all she'd have to do is stick her head out of the waiting room door to the drive and watch. Then she goes through to the surgery and passionately offers her all.'

'And he rejects her,' said Alec.

Daisy frowned at him, for a change. 'In the meantime, he has settled himself in his chair and donned the mask. Another woman might be repulsed by the grotesque sight, but she sees it daily. When she declares herself, he has already turned on the gas and the oxygen and breathed a whiff. He doesn't merely reject her. He laughs at her.'

Alec slowly nodded. 'I myself saw her violent reaction when Hilda Kidd laughed at her.'

Tom focused on the practical: 'The nurse, of all people,

knows what to do to kill with that apparatus, and where to find the bandages and sticking plaster.'

'And a nurse, of all people,' Daisy said, 'learns to watch with cool composure as someone dies.'

EPILOGUE

Daisy didn't hear the end of the story, or as near as it came to an end, till late the following Monday. In the interim, Alec told her nothing of his investigations. On Monday he came home late, having eaten in the canteen, and slumped in his favourite chair in the living room.

'Get me a whisky, love,' he asked, most unusually. 'It looks as if you were right,' he went on when she came back from adding water to the amber liquid.

Daisy sat down on the sofa with her legs curled up under her in a most unladylike pose she would not have ventured upon in her mother-in-law's presence. Nor her own mother's, come to that. 'You've arrested Nurse Hensted?'

'No such luck. She left her digs the day Creighton settled with her, although she'd paid her rent to the end of the month. Cashed his cheque and cleaned out her bank account. A nice sum, nearly two hundred pounds, saved in dribs and drabs over the years.'

'Which shows she isn't the kind of person to waste her rent money by moving out early.'

'Exactly. She gave the landlady her parents' address in Bishop's Stortford as a forwarding address. Tom went down to see them, but they hadn't heard from her since Christmas.

Kept herself to herself, they say. Respectable people. They put us on to other relatives. No one's seen hide nor hair of her.'

'What about the nurses' agency?'

'We found their name and address in Talmadge's papers. She hasn't been back since they sent her to him three years ago, nor has she approached any of the other agencies in town. Have you any idea how many nurses' agencies there are in London?'

'Not the foggiest, darling.'

'No doubt Piper could give you the exact figure. He visited them all.'

'I suppose she'd have to use her real name because of references and her registration papers.'

'Presumably, but Ernie described her anyway, without result. She had quite distinctive features.'

'Quite pretty. As far as looks go, she had no reason to despair of Talmadge's attentions.'

'Mrs Talmadge and her servants confirm that she seemed to be keen on him, and the landlady says she mentioned once or twice how handsome he was. We're assuming your theory is correct as to motive, but it's lucky that's one thing we don't have to prove. Means and opportunity she had, and her subsequent actions are definitely indicative of guilt.'

'She's completely disappeared? Surely you'll find her sooner or later.'

'Oh, we know where she went.'

'Where? Is this tit for tat, darling?'

Alec grinned. 'Of course not. Such childishness is beneath me. I'm just telling it as it happened. When Ernie drew a blank at the last agency, the woman suggested Brenda

Hensted might have found a job through the agony column in *The Times*. We went through the back numbers. You'd be amazed at how many elderly invalids in comfortable circs are urgently in need of nursing care, other staff kept.'

'No, I wouldn't. I imagine there's quite a high attrition rate, invalids being notoriously crabby. Nurse Hensted swore she'd rather go back to hospital work than be at an invalid's beck and call.'

'Yes, Ernie has it down in black and white. Yet she didn't even try for a hospital position, which the agency said she would have found at once, registered nurses being in short supply. So *The Times* adverts were worth a try.'

'Don't tell me you talked the editor of *The Times* into violating the sacred secrecy of the Box Number?' asked Daisy, awed.

'Rather than try, we started by ringing up the few advertisers who gave telephone numbers. It was late Saturday afternoon by then, though, and hard to get hold of people. As it turned out, the chap we wanted had gone down to his constituency.'

'A Member of Parliament?'

'Whose invalid mother-in-law departed on Thursday to take the waters in Baden-Baden. In a wheelchair pushed by Miss Hensted.'

'She's gone abroad! Oh, Alec! I'm surprised she had a passport.'

'As an MP he was able to get her one in a couple of days. She rang up about the job on Monday evening.'

'A few hours after Talmadge's death!'

'She went for an interview and was hired on Tuesday, a few hours after Creighton paid her off and wrote a reference for her. They caught the boat train on Thursday and by now they'll be in Baden-Baden.'

'Surely the German police can arrest her for you, darling?'

'Germany's in too much of a mess these days to count on anything. I'm told France hasn't actually made a grab for that bit of the country, at least not yet, though Baden-Baden's not far from the French frontier. It's supposed to be safe from the chaos because the spa earns so much foreign currency no one can afford to muck about with it. But it's easy enough for anyone to disappear into the surrounding area, and thence who knows where. Our MP just received a desperate cable from mama-in-law saying please send a new nurse. Miss Hensted has vanished.'

'Oh, darling!'

'Not one of my greatest successes,' Alec said wryly. 'There were too many obvious suspects. I never even looked at the nurse.'

'More whisky?'

He laughed. 'No, it's not bad enough to drive me to drink. Let's go to bed.'

On the way up the stairs, Daisy said, 'I went to see Daphne Talmadge today.'

'Yes? You're not going to change your mind and tell me she or Creighton did it!'

'No, darling. Apparently the baby-to-be is out of danger. They're so happy about it, she and Lord Henry.' She slipped her arm through his. 'Alec, what would you think about giving Belinda a little brother or sister?'

'Suits me,' said Alec.

10.99

OXFORD STUDENT

Series Editor: Steven Croft

City and Isl¹

Geoffrey Chaucer

The Wife of Bath

Edited by Steven Croft

Oxford University Press

OXFORD
UNIVERSITY PRESS

Great Clarendon Street, Oxford OX2 6DP

Oxford University Press is a department of the University of Oxford.
It furthers the University's objective of excellence in research, scholarship,
and education by publishing worldwide in

Oxford   New York

Auckland   Cape Town   Dar es Salaam   Hong Kong   Karachi
Kuala Lumpur   Madrid   Melbourne   Mexico City   Nairobi
New Delhi   Shanghai   Taipei   Toronto

With offices in

Argentina   Austria   Brazil   Chile   Czech Republic   France   Greece
Guatemala   Hungary   Italy   Japan   South Korea   Poland   Portugal
Singapore   Switzerland   Thailand   Turkey   Ukraine   Vietnam

Oxford is a registered trade mark of Oxford University Press
in the UK and in certain other countries

British Library Cataloguing in Publication Data
Data available

ISBN: 978-019-832572-7

5 7 9 10 8 6

Typeset in Goudy Old Style MT
by Palimpsest Book Production Limited, Grangemouth, Stirlingshire

Printed and bound by CPI Group (UK) Ltd., Croydon, CR0 4YY

The publishers would like to thank the following for permission to reproduce
photographs: P3: Mary Evans Picture Library; p6: Mary Evans Picture Library; p7: Mary
Evans Picture Library; p10: Alamy; p110: Mary Evans Picture Library; p115: Mary Evans
Picture Library; p116: Heritage Image Library; p117: Mary Evans Picture Library; p121:
Mary Evans Picture Library; p136: Mary Evans Picture Library.

Contents

Acknowledgements   v

Foreword   vi

The Wife of Bath's Tale in Context   1

The Wife of Bath's Tale   13
The Wife of Bath's portrait: General Prologue   13
The Wife of Bath's Prologue   14
The Wife of Bath's Tale   40

Notes   53
The Wife of Bath's portrait: General Prologue   53
The Wife begins her prologue: Lines 1–34   55
The Wife develops her arguments to support her position:
    Lines 35–114   57
The Wife's 'biological' argument: Lines 115–162   61
The Pardoner interrupts her: Lines 163–192   63
The Wife speaks about her first three husbands and how she
    handled them: Lines 193–284   64
The Wife describes further her techniques for dealing with her
    husbands: Lines 285–361   68
The Wife achieves dominance: Lines 362–451   71
The Wife's fourth husband: Lines 452–502   75
The Wife tells of Jankyn, her fifth husband: Lines 503–626   77
The Wife marries Jankyn and the problems begin:
    Lines 627–787   81
The Wife and Jankyn have their last argument:
    Lines 788–856   88
The Wife begins her tale: Lines 857–881   91
The knight commits his crime and is given his quest:
    Lines 882–982   92
The knight receives his answer in return for a request:
    Lines 983–1108   96
The knight receives lectures on nobility, poverty, and respecting
    the old: Lines 1109–1216   100

The old woman gives the knight a choice and he makes his
    decision: Lines 1217–1264   104

Interpretations   107
Genre   107
Characterization   109
Themes   118
Language and style   134
Narrative techniques   140
The unity of prologue and tale   142
Critical views   143

A Note on Chaucer's English   145

A Note on Pronunciation   153

Essay Questions   155

Chronology   158

Further Reading   160

Glossary   162

Acknowledgements

The publishers and editor would like to thank Professor Peter Mack for permission to adapt his sections entitled *A Note on Chaucer's English* and *A Note on Pronunciation* for this edition of *The Wife of Bath's Tale*.

The text is taken from *The Riverside Chaucer*, Third Edition, edited by Larry D. Benson, copyright © 1987 by Houghton Mifflin Company.

Acknowledgements from Steven Croft

I would like to thank Sandra Haigh for all her help and support in the preparation of this text. I am also grateful to Jan Doorly for her encouraging comments and sensitive editing of the manuscript.

Editor

Steven Croft holds degrees from Leeds and Sheffield universities. He has taught at secondary and tertiary level and is currently head of the Department of English and Humanities in a tertiary college. He has 25 years' examining experience at A level and is currently a Principal Examiner for English. He has written several books on teaching English at A level, and his publications for Oxford University Press include *Literature, Criticism and Style*, *Success in AQA Language and Literature* and *Exploring Language and Literature*.

Foreword

Oxford Student Texts, under the founding editorship of Victor Lee, have established a reputation for presenting literary texts to students in both a scholarly and an accessible way. The new editions aim to build on this successful approach. They have been written to help students, particularly those studying English literature for AS or A level, to develop an increased understanding of their texts. Each volume in the series, which covers a selection of key poetry and drama texts, consists of four main sections which link together to provide an integrated approach to the study of the text.

The first part provides important background information about the writer, his or her times and the factors that played an important part in shaping the work. This discussion sets the work in context and explores some key contextual factors.

This section is followed by the poetry or play itself. The text is presented without accompanying notes so that students can engage with it on their own terms without the influence of secondary ideas. To encourage this approach, the Notes are placed in the third section, immediately following the text. The Notes provide explanations of particular words, phrases, images, allusions and so forth, to help students gain a full understanding of the text. They also raise questions or highlight particular issues or ideas which are important to consider when arriving at interpretations.

The fourth section, Interpretations, goes on to discuss a range of issues in more detail. This involves an examination of the influence of contextual factors as well as looking at such aspects as language and style, and various critical views or interpretations. A range of activities for students to carry out, together with discussions as to how these might be approached, are integrated into this section.

At the end of each volume there is a selection of Essay Questions, a Further Reading list and, where appropriate, a Glossary.

We hope you enjoy reading this text and working with these supporting materials, and wish you every success in your studies.

Steven Croft *Series Editor*

The Wife of Bath's Tale in Context

Chaucer's life

There is much uncertainty surrounding Geoffrey Chaucer's exact date of birth, although it seems likely that he was born some time in the early 1340s (1343 is often given as the likely year) in London. The date of his death can be identified with more certainty. Records show that he died towards the end of 1400, the date of 25 October being accepted by many scholars.

Chaucer's father, John, was a prosperous London wine merchant. He had served in the military campaigns of 1327 and 1329 and was the deputy to the king's chief butler from 1347 to 1349. This gave him a minor connection with the court, and his wealth was increased by his inheritance of several properties. He died in 1366. Chaucer's mother had also inherited several properties, so the young Chaucer grew up in an affluent household with some links to the royal household.

There is little concrete evidence of the kind of education Chaucer received, and there is no record of whether he attended school. It is generally thought likely that he did, and he might have attended one of several prestigious schools in the area of London in which he lived. Equally, he could have been educated at home, either by his parents or private tutors.

Whatever form it took, it is certain that Chaucer received an education typical of his social standing and one that provided him with the necessary skills for entry into a career of civil or court service. As part of his education, Chaucer would have learned Latin and would have gained some knowledge of Latin texts such as the writings of Virgil, Ovid and the fables of Aesop. French would also have been an important part of his education. In the fourteenth century, French was the language of the court and of all legal documents and proceedings; it was the standard language spoken by the middle and upper classes. It is also clear that Chaucer was familiar with Italian, and his writings reveal a knowledge of Italian authors of the period such as Dante, Petrarch and Boccaccio.

By 1357, Chaucer was a member of the court of Elizabeth, Countess of Ulster and wife of Lionel, the son of King Edward III. It is generally assumed that Chaucer was a page in Elizabeth's household, and as such he would have travelled around the country with her entourage. Pages were normally aged between 10 and 17 and performed a variety of functions including the duties of personal servants. They were not paid, and so needed the support of their families, but they were given board, lodging and clothing by their employer. While in service, they were educated in the manners and customs of upper-class society and their position also gave them the opportunity to meet and possibly impress influential people who could advance their careers by giving them promotion or patronage.

Certainly employment in Elizabeth's household would have given Chaucer access to literature, both in written and oral form. Written books were scarce as, before the invention of printing, they all had to be copied out by hand, and consequently only wealthy households possessed them. It was common for literature to be heard rather than read, with someone reading to a group of people gathered together. In Chaucer's time, the oral tradition in literature was still very strong.

In 1359, Chaucer became one of Prince Lionel's attendants, and he went to France on military service in September 1359 as a yeoman. He was captured in France in 1360 and ransomed for £16, which was a comparatively large sum. The king himself contributed to the ransom, and this suggests that Chaucer was considered of some value. He returned to France again in the autumn of 1360 carrying letters back to England from Lionel.

Little is known of Chaucer's life between 1360 and 1367, although we know that his father died in 1366. It seems that Chaucer was abroad again during part of this period and, towards the end of the 1360s, John of Gaunt became an important figure in his life. John of Gaunt was Duke of Lancaster and was, at that time, considered the wealthiest man in England. In 1369 Chaucer was once more on a military campaign in France with John of Gaunt. In 1372–1373 he was sent abroad to Genoa and Florence as part of important trade negotiations, possibly on behalf of the king.

On his return he was made, in 1374, the Controller of the Customs for wool, later adding skins and hides to his responsibilities. This was a very lucrative civil service appointment, but there are some indications that further promotions between 1377 and 1389 may have been blocked, possibly by enemies of the king. He was elected MP for Kent in 1386 but only remained in office a year, and ceased to be Controller of Customs in 1386.

A woodcut based on a portrait of Chaucer from the Ellesmere manuscript of *The Canterbury Tales*

3

However, when Richard II assumed power in 1389, Chaucer seems to have regained favour and was given new jobs, one of which involved being responsible for the maintenance of the king's palaces. Later he was given the royal appointment of deputy forestership of North Petherton in Somerset. In 1399, Richard II was deposed by John of Gaunt's son, Henry Bolingbroke, who became Henry IV. Chaucer continued in favour under the new king and moved to a house in the garden of Westminster Abbey, where he lived until his death in October 1400. He was buried in Westminster Abbey.

Language in Chaucer's time

During Chaucer's life, three languages were important in English society:

- Latin – this was the language of the Church and of scholarship and learning. The ordinary people recognized those who used Latin as being educated and learned.
- French – in the early part of Chaucer's life this was the everyday language of the educated and cultured members of society. It was descended from the Norman French, which was introduced after the conquest of England by William in 1066. This was the language of the royal court and of legal proceedings.
- English – this was the everyday language spoken by the people.

During Chaucer's time the importance of French as the language of the educated classes had begun to decline, and in 1362 for the first time Parliament was opened by a speech from the throne delivered in English. In the same year, for the first time, law proceedings were allowed to be conducted in English.

The literary context

As time went on, more and more French works were translated into English, including philosophical and religious works. Other literature appearing in English included ballads and romances. Romances were stories usually about love or adventure, involving characters from the upper end of society. These stories, such as *The Knight's Tale* in *The Canterbury Tales*, featured courtly and noble behaviour.

Fabliaux were also popular. These were bawdy tales about ordinary people, and usually involved sex and trickery of some kind, such as that seen in *The Miller's Tale*.

In addition to the works written in Latin already mentioned, and works written in French such as the French romance, *Le Roman de la Rose*, Chaucer would also have been familiar with Italian literature. Works such as Dante's *Divine Comedy*, Boccaccio's *Decameron* (a collection of tales about nobles escaping the Black Death), and the works of Petrarch all influenced Chaucer's writings in various ways.

Chaucer's works

One of the important features of Chaucer's work is that he drew on the French and Italian literature he knew well, both in terms of themes, ideas and stylistic and technical approaches, in order to create a new poetry in English which was entirely his own. The dating of some of Chaucer's works is not certain, but one of the most important of his early pieces was a translation of *Le Roman de la Rose*. His first major poem, *The Book of the Duchess*, which was written in 1369 or 1370, shows clearly the influence of French literature. The poem was written to commemorate the death of John of Gaunt's wife, Blanche, the Duchess of Lancaster. This is written as a dream-vision and is the first of four poems in which he wrote about dreams. It was followed by *The House of Fame*, *The Parliament of Fowls* and *The Legend of Good Women*.

Several of Chaucer's poems then began to show an Italian influence. One of them, the narrative poem *Troilus and Criseyde*, is considered by many to be his greatest single poem. It is a poem about courtly love embodying the idea of idealized love, a theme which he was to return to in *The Knight's Tale* in *The Canterbury Tales*.

The Canterbury Tales

Chaucer's greatest work, *The Canterbury Tales*, was written in the later years of his life, although it is possible that some parts of it had been written earlier. The poem centres on 29 pilgrims who meet by chance at the Tabard Inn in Southwark, London, before setting out on a pilgrimage to the shrine of Saint Thomas Becket at Canterbury. The pilgrims agree to tell each other tales on their journey to pass the time. Chaucer's original scheme was to have

The Canterbury pilgrims setting out

KNIGHT.

The illustration of the Knight, the highest-ranking pilgrim, from the Ellesmere manuscript

each of his pilgrims tell two tales on the way to Canterbury and two tales on the return trip to London. A prize of a free supper was to be given to the teller of the best story as judged by the Host, Harry Bailey.

As the pilgrims start their journey, the tales begin. It is decided that the Knight, the highest in rank of the party, should tell the first tale. After several tales have been told the Host asks the Parson to tell them a tale. However, the Shipman immediately objects, saying he does not want to be preached to, and so the Wife of Bath tells her tale next.

This forum gives the Wife plenty of scope to air her views on men, love and marriage, based firmly on her extensive experience of all three. Her lively personality and her frankness are given full reign in her prologue, and her ideas would either amuse or infuriate the pilgrims in the company depending on who they were and their attitudes to life.

Chaucer died before he was able to complete his ambitious scheme, which would have meant at least 116 tales. Before his death he had only written tales for 23 of the pilgrims, and even some of these are unfinished.

Chaucer's overall scheme, therefore, is much more than simply a collection of stories. The setting within the context of a pilgrimage to Canterbury allows him to bring together a group of characters representing a whole cross-section of medieval society. The characters are introduced in the *General Prologue* and this is an important part of Chaucer's scheme as he uses this introduction to give vivid portraits of each character in turn. They are drawn from all walks of life: the Knight and his son the Squire come from the ranks of the aristocracy; there are devout religious characters such as the Parson and the Nun, and those with rather more dubious morals such as the Pardoner and the Summoner, who use the power invested in them by the Church to exploit others and line their own pockets.

In addition, Chaucer also introduces a variety of other pilgrims from all echelons of society, from the wealthy, middle-class Franklin to the rough and ready Miller and the lowly Ploughman. The various characters are also given a range of motivations for embarking on the pilgrimage. There are those whose motive is entirely spiritual, such as the Parson; and those who see it as an interesting and pleasurable outing, such as the Wife of Bath herself.

The status of women in the Middle Ages

The society of the Middle Ages was very much male dominated, and the status and rights of women were quite different in many ways from those of modern times.

- Both within the Church and in law, women had no legal or

political power and were expected to be obedient (outwardly at least) to their fathers or husbands.

- Marriages were usually arranged (particularly among the aristocracy and middle classes).
- Often the younger daughters of the wealthy were put into convents to train as nuns. They usually were sent to the convent at the age of 14.
- Women of lower status with some kind of skill or trade, such as the Wife and her weaving, could earn a good living. In her case, though, she clearly obtained much of her wealth from her string of elderly but rich husbands.
- The Church was one area in which a small number of women could achieve status and power in their own right. Those who became prioresses, in charge of the nunneries, became responsible for running large and lucrative estates and achieved some power and influence, becoming women of wealth and standing.
- When men were away fighting – in the crusades, for example – women ran their husbands' estates, and lower down the social order they took on tasks normally performed by men such as brewing, leather working, baking and other trades.

Although the society was so heavily male-dominated, it was possible for individual women to achieve a degree of independence, of both thought and action, as the Wife of Bath demonstrates.

Marriage

Arranged marriages were the norm in the Middle Ages at most levels of society. A father would look for the most attractive potential son-in-law, both from a financial and a status point of view, to marry his daughter. The Wife herself tells us that she was first married at the age of 12, presumably a marriage arranged by her father.

Once married all the woman's possessions belonged to her

husband; legally she had no possessions of her own and looked to her husband for all she needed. Wives were expected to be obedient to their husbands but, of course, in practice, personal relationships between women and men took many forms; as we can see from the Wife's account of her life with her husbands, men did not always have things their own way.

The Church's view of marriage was that it was undesirable but necessary. The ideal state was to remain single and live a celibate life, as advocated by St Paul, St Jerome and the Greek philosopher Theophrastus, but the Church recognized that this was not possible for all (and in fact, the human race would soon come to an end if everyone achieved this). Marriage was the acceptable alternative.

St Helen's in Kelloe, County Durham: throughout the Middle Ages, local parish churches played a large role in people's lives

Anti-feminism

In the Middle Ages the opinion that women were inferior to men in all respects, including intellectually, was strongly held by many. This view had several origins.

- Women were seen as symbolizing the temptations and evils of the flesh.
- The Church view was that women were the root cause of all human suffering and misery, based on the biblical account of Eve succumbing to the temptation that led to the Fall of Man and the banishment of Adam and Eve from the Garden of Eden.
- Over the centuries these ideas had given rise to a wealth of anti-feminist writings of the kind that the Wife makes reference to in her prologue and which her fifth husband, Jankyn, was so fond of reading to her.
- The key ideas that are referred to in the prologue relate to St Paul's view, as expressed in the New Testament, that celibacy is the preferred state but if people cannot restrain themselves, marriage is preferable to promiscuity.
- A second source for these ideas is the writings of the Greek philosopher Theophrastus, who depicts wives as being nagging, complaining and suspicious of their husbands. In her prologue the Wife tells how she turned these arguments around and used them against her old husbands.
- A third anti-feminist writer who is referred to in the Wife's prologue is St Jerome. He believed that all forms of physical appetite were to be condemned, including the sexual appetite. When a monk named Jovinian suggested that married people and celibate people were equal in the eyes of God, St Jerome attacked him harshly in his *Letter Against Jovinian*. This tract became a favourite source of inspiration for men who wished to condemn women as inferior and sinful.

There were many versions of a story where an old woman with a voracious sexual appetite entraps an unsuspecting younger male. Chaucer himself, as we have seen, had already translated from the French the story *Le Roman de la Rose*, in which an old prostitute, La Vieille, spends most of her time trying to get the better of men in one way or another, and gives advice on how to outwit them. It is possible that Chaucer used some of these ideas to shape the character of the Wife.

The Church's attitude towards women was necessarily ambiguous to some extent as the Virgin Mary, the mother of Christ, was a woman. Mary was regarded as embodying all that was good and holy; she fulfilled the ideal of virginity and therefore was not corrupted by the sins of the flesh, yet was also a mother – the other role for which women could be respected. But the Wife of Bath does not fit, or wish to fit, into either of these categories.

The Wife of Bath's Tale

The Wife of Bath's portrait: General Prologue

445   A good WIF was ther OF biside BATHE,
But she was somdel deef, and that was scathe.
Of clooth-makyng she hadde swich an haunt
She passed hem of Ypres and of Gaunt.
In al the parisshe wif ne was ther noon
450 That to the offrynge bifore hire sholde goon;
And if ther dide, certeyn so wrooth was she
That she was out of alle charitee.
Hir coverchiefs ful fyne weren of ground;
I dorste swere they weyeden ten pound
455 That on a Sonday weren upon hir heed.
Hir hosen weren of fyn scarlet reed,
Ful streite yteyd, and shoes ful moyste and newe.
Boold was hir face, and fair, and reed of hewe.
She was a worthy womman al hir lyve:
460 Housbondes at chirche dore she hadde fyve,
Withouten oother compaignye in youthe –
But thereof nedeth nat to speke as nowthe.
And thries hadde she been at Jerusalem;
She hadde passed many a straunge strem;
465 At Rome she hadde been, and at Boloigne,
In Galice at Seint-Jame, and at Coloigne.
She koude muchel of wandrynge by the weye.
Gat-tothed was she, soothly for to seye.
Upon an amblere esily she sat,
470 Ywympled wel, and on hir heed an hat
As brood as is a bokeler or a targe;

A foot-mantel aboute hir hipes large,
And on hir feet a paire of spores sharpe.
In felaweshipe wel koude she laughe and carpe.
475 Of remedies of love she knew per chaunce,
For she koude of that art the olde daunce.

The Wife of Bath's Prologue

The Prologe of the Wyves Tale of Bathe.

'Experience, though noon auctoritee
Were in this world, is right ynogh for me
To speke of wo that is in mariage;
For, lordynges, sith I twelve yeer was of age,
5 Thonked be God that is eterne on lyve,
Housbondes at chirche dore I have had fyve –
If I so ofte myghte have ywedded bee –
And alle were worthy men in hir degree.
But me was toold, certeyn, nat longe agoon is,
10 That sith that Crist ne wente nevere but onis
To weddyng, in the Cane of Galilee,
That by the same ensample taughte he me
That I ne sholde wedded be but ones.
Herkne eek, lo, which a sharp word for the nones,
15 Biside a welle, Jhesus, God and man,
Spak in repreeve of the Samaritan:
"Thou hast yhad fyve housbondes," quod he,
"And that ilke man that now hath thee
Is noght thyn housbonde," thus seyde he certeyn.
20 What that he mente therby, I kan nat seyn;
But that I axe, why that the fifthe man
Was noon housbonde to the Samaritan?

How manye myghte she have in mariage?
Yet herde I nevere tellen in myn age
25 Upon this nombre diffinicioun.
Men may devyne and glosen, up and doun,
But wel I woot, expres, withoute lye,
God bad us for to wexe and multiplye;
That gentil text kan I wel understonde.
30 Eek wel I woot, he seyde myn housbonde
Sholde lete fader and mooder and take to me.
But of no nombre mencion made he,
Of bigamye, or of octogamye;
Why sholde men thanne speke of it vileynye?
35   Lo, heere the wise kyng, daun Salomon;
I trowe he hadde wyves mo than oon.
As wolde God it leveful were unto me
To be refresshed half so ofte as he!
Which yifte of God hadde he for alle his wyvys!
40 No man hath swich that in this world alyve is.
God woot, this noble kyng, as to my wit,
The firste nyght had many a myrie fit
With ech of hem, so wel was hym on lyve.
Yblessed be God that I have wedded fyve!
44A [Of whiche I have pyked out the beste,
Bothe of here nether purs and of here cheste.
Diverse scoles maken parfyt clerkes,
And diverse practyk in many sondry werkes
Maketh the werkman parfyt sekirly;
44F Of fyve husbondes scoleiyng am I.]
45 Welcome the sixte, whan that evere he shal.
For sothe, I wol nat kepe me chaast in al.
Whan myn housbonde is fro the world ygon,
Som Cristen man shal wedde me anon,
For thanne th'apostle seith that I am free
50 To wedde, a Goddes half, where it liketh me.

He seith that to be wedded is no synne;
Bet is to be wedded than to brynne.
What rekketh me, thogh folk seye vileynye
Of shrewed Lameth and his bigamye?
55 I woot wel Abraham was an hooly man,
And Jacob eek, as ferforth as I kan;
And ech of hem hadde wyves mo than two,
And many another holy man also.
Wher can ye seye, in any manere age,
60 That hye God defended mariage
By expres word? I pray yow, telleth me.
Or where comanded he virginitee?
I woot as wel as ye, it is no drede,
Th'apostel, whan he speketh of maydenhede,
65 He seyde that precept therof hadde he noon.
Men may conseille a womman to been oon,
But conseillyng is no comandement.
He putte it in oure owene juggement;
For hadde God comanded maydenhede,
70 Thanne hadde he dampned weddyng with the dede.
And certes, if ther were no seed ysowe,
Virginitee, thanne wherof sholde it growe?
Poul dorste nat comanden, atte leeste,
A thyng of which his maister yaf noon heeste.
75 The dart is set up for virginitee;
Cacche whoso may, who renneth best lat see.
    But this word is nat taken of every wight,
But ther as God lust gyve it of his myght.
I woot wel that th'apostel was a mayde;
80 But nathelees, thogh that he wroot and sayde
He wolde that every wight were swich as he,
Al nys but conseil to virginitee.
And for to been a wyf he yaf me leve
Of indulgence; so nys it no repreve

85 To wedde me, if that my make dye,
    Withouten excepcion of bigamye.
    Al were it good no womman for to touche –
    He mente as in his bed or in his couche,
    For peril is bothe fyr and tow t'assemble;
90 Ye knowe what this ensample may resemble.
    This is al and som: he heeld virginitee
    Moore parfit than weddyng in freletee.
    Freletee clepe I, but if that he and she
    Wolde leden al hir lyf in chastitee.
95   I graunte it wel; I have noon envie,
    Thogh maydenhede preferre bigamye.
    It liketh hem to be clene, body and goost;
    Of myn estaat I nyl nat make no boost,
    For wel ye knowe, a lord in his houshold,
100 He nath nat every vessel al of gold;
    Somme been of tree, and doon hir lord servyse.
    God clepeth folk to hym in sondry wyse,
    And everich hath of God a propre yifte –
    Som this, som that, as hym liketh shifte.
105   Virginitee is greet perfeccion,
    And continence eek with devocion,
    But Crist, that of perfeccion is welle,
    Bad nat every wight he sholde go selle
    Al that he hadde, and gyve it to the poore,
110 And in swich wise folwe hym and his foore.
    He spak to hem that wolde lyve parfitly;
    And lordynges, by youre leve, that am nat I.
    I wol bistowe the flour of al myn age
    In the actes and in fruyt of mariage.
115   Telle me also, to what conclusion
    Were membres maad of generacion,
    And of so parfit wys a [wright] ywroght?
    Trusteth right wel, they were nat maad for noght.

Glose whoso wole, and seye bothe up and doun
120 That they were maked for purgacioun
Of uryne, and oure bothe thynges smale
Were eek to knowe a femele from a male,
And for noon oother cause – say ye no?
The experience woot wel it is noght so.
125 So that the clerkes be nat with me wrothe,
I sey this: that they maked ben for bothe;
That is to seye, for office and for ese
Of engendrure, ther we nat God displese.
Why sholde men elles in hir bookes sette
130 That man shal yelde to his wyf hire dette?
Now wherwith sholde he make his paiement,
If he ne used his sely instrument?
Thanne were they maad upon a creature
To purge uryne, and eek for engendrure.
135   But I seye noght that every wight is holde,
That hath swich harneys as I to yow tolde,
To goon and usen hem in engendrure.
Thanne sholde men take of chastitee no cure.
Crist was a mayde and shapen as a man,
140 And many a seint, sith that the world bigan;
Yet lyved they evere in parfit chastitee.
I nyl envye no virginitee.
Lat hem be breed of pured whete-seed,
And lat us wyves hoten barly-breed;
145 And yet with barly-breed, Mark telle kan,
Oure Lord Jhesu refresshed many a man.
In swich estaat as God hath cleped us
I wol persevere; I nam nat precius.
In wyfhod I wol use myn instrument
150 As frely as my Makere hath it sent.
If I be daungerous, God yeve me sorwe!
Myn housbonde shal it have bothe eve and morwe,

Whan that hym list come forth and paye his dette.
An housbonde I wol have – I wol nat lette –
155 Which shal be bothe my dettour and my thral,
And have his tribulacion withal
Upon his flessh, whil that I am his wyf.
I have the power durynge al my lyf
Upon his propre body, and noght he.
160 Right thus the Apostel tolde it unto me,
And bad oure housebondes for to love us weel.
Al this sentence me liketh every deel' –
    Up stirte the Pardoner, and that anon;
'Now, dame,' quod he, 'by God and by Seint John!
165 Ye been a noble prechour in this cas.
I was aboute to wedde a wyf; allas!
What sholde I bye it on my flessh so deere?
Yet hadde I levere wedde no wyf to-yeere!'
    'Abyde!' quod she, 'my tale is nat bigonne.
170 Nay, thou shalt drynken of another tonne,
Er that I go, shal savoure wors than ale.
And whan that I have toold thee forth my tale
Of tribulacion in mariage,
Of which I am expert in al myn age –
175 This is to seyn, myself have been the whippe –
Than maystow chese wheither thou wolt sippe
Of thilke tonne that I shal abroche.
Be war of it, er thou to ny approche;
For I shal telle ensamples mo than ten.
180 "Whoso that nyl be war by othere men,
By hym shul othere men corrected be."
The same wordes writeth Ptholomee;
Rede in his Almageste, and take it there.'
    'Dame, I wolde praye yow, if youre wyl it were,'
185 Seyde this Pardoner, 'as ye bigan,
Telle forth youre tale, spareth for no man,

And teche us yonge men of youre praktike.'
  'Gladly,' quod she, 'sith it may yow like;
But yet I praye to al this compaignye,
190 If that I speke after my fantasye,
As taketh not agrief of that I seye,
For myn entente nys but for to pleye.
  Now, sire, now wol I telle forth my tale.
As evere moote I drynken wyn or ale,
195 I shal seye sooth; tho housbondes that I hadde,
As thre of hem were goode, and two were badde.
The thre were goode men, and riche, and olde;
Unnethe myghte they the statut holde
In which that they were bounden unto me.
200 Ye woot wel what I meene of this, pardee!
As help me God, I laughe whan I thynke
How pitously a-nyght I made hem swynke!
And, by my fey, I tolde of it no stoor.
They had me yeven hir lond and hir tresoor;
205 Me neded nat do lenger diligence
To wynne hir love, or doon hem reverence.
They loved me so wel, by God above,
That I ne tolde no deyntee of hir love!
A wys womman wol bisye hire evere in oon
210 To gete hire love, ye, ther as she hath noon.
But sith I hadde hem hoolly in myn hond,
And sith they hadde me yeven al hir lond,
What sholde I taken keep hem for to plese,
But it were for my profit and myn ese?
215 I sette hem so a-werke, by my fey,
That many a nyght they songen "Weilawey!"
The bacon was nat fet for hem, I trowe,
That som men han in Essex at Dunmowe.
I governed hem so wel, after my lawe,
220 That ech of hem ful blisful was and fawe

To brynge me gaye thynges fro the fayre.
They were ful glad whan I spak to hem faire,
For, God it woot, I chidde hem spitously.
    Now herkneth hou I baar me proprely,
225 Ye wise wyves, that kan understonde.
Thus shulde ye speke and bere hem wrong on
      honde,
For half so boldely kan ther no man
Swere and lyen, as a womman kan.
I sey nat this by wyves that been wyse,
230 But if it be whan they hem mysavyse.
A wys wyf, if that she kan hir good,
Shal beren hym on honde the cow is wood,
And take witnesse of hir owene mayde
Of hir assent. But herkneth how I sayde:
235   "Sire olde kaynard, is this thyn array?
Why is my neighebores wyf so gay?
She is honoured overal ther she gooth;
I sitte at hoom; I have no thrifty clooth.
What dostow at my neighebores hous?
240 Is she so fair? Artow so amorous?
What rowne ye with oure mayde? Benedicite!
Sire olde lecchour, lat thy japes be!
And if I have a gossib or a freend,
Withouten gilt, thou chidest as a feend,
245 If that I walke or pleye unto his hous!
Thou comest hoom as dronken as a mous,
And prechest on thy bench, with yvel preef!
Thou seist to me it is a greet meschief
To wedde a povre womman, for costage;
250 And if that she be riche, of heigh parage,
Thanne seistow that it is a tormentrie
To soffre hire pride and hire malencolie.
And if that she be fair, thou verray knave,

Thou seyst that every holour wol hire have;
255 She may no while in chastitee abyde,
That is assailled upon ech a syde.
    Thou seyst som folk desiren us for richesse,
Somme for oure shap, and somme for oure
        fairnesse,
And som for she kan outher synge or daunce,
260 And som for gentillesse and daliaunce;
Som for hir handes and hir armes smale;
Thus goth al to the devel, by thy tale.
Thou seyst men may nat kepe a castel wal,
It may so longe assailled been overal.
265   And if that she be foul, thou seist that she
Coveiteth every man that she may se,
For as a spanyel she wol on hym lepe,
Til that she fynde som man hire to chepe.
Ne noon so grey goos gooth ther in the lake
270 As, sëistow, wol been withoute make.
And seyst it is an hard thyng for to welde
A thyng that no man wole, his thankes, helde.
Thus seistow, lorel, whan thow goost to bedde,
And that no wys man nedeth for to wedde,
275 Ne no man that entendeth unto hevene.
With wilde thonder-dynt and firy levene
Moote thy welked nekke be tobroke!
    Thow seyst that droppyng houses, and eek
        smoke,
And chidyng wyves maken men to flee
280 Out of hir owene houses; a, benedicitee!
What eyleth swich an old man for to chide?
    Thow seyst we wyves wol oure vices hide
Til we be fast, and thanne we wol hem shewe –
Wel may that be a proverbe of a shrewe!
285   Thou seist that oxen, asses, hors, and houndes,

They been assayed at diverse stoundes;
Bacyns, lavours, er that men hem bye,
Spoones and stooles, and al swich housbondrye,
And so been pottes, clothes, and array;
290 But folk of wyves maken noon assay,
Til they be wedded – olde dotard shrewe! –
And thanne, seistow, we wol oure vices shewe.
   Thou seist also that it displeseth me
But if that thou wolt preyse my beautee,
295 And but thou poure alwey upon my face,
And clepe me 'faire dame' in every place.
And but thou make a feeste on thilke day
That I was born, and make me fressh and gay;
And but thou do to my norice honour,
300 And to my chamberere withinne my bour,
And to my fadres folk and his allyes –
Thus seistow, olde barel-ful of lyes!
   And yet of oure apprentice Janekyn,
For his crispe heer, shynynge as gold so fyn,
305 And for he squiereth me bothe up and doun,
Yet hastow caught a fals suspecioun.
I wol hym noght, thogh thou were deed tomorwe!
   But tel me this: why hydestow, with sorwe,
The keyes of thy cheste awey fro me?
310 It is my good as wel as thyn, pardee!
What, wenestow make an ydiot of oure dame?
Now by that lord that called is Seint Jame,
Thou shalt nat bothe, thogh that thou were wood,
Be maister of my body and of my good;
315 That oon thou shalt forgo, maugree thyne yen.
What helpith it of me to enquere or spyen?
I trowe thou woldest loke me in thy chiste!
Thou sholdest seye, 'Wyf, go wher thee liste;
Taak youre disport; I wol nat leve no talys.

320 I knowe yow for a trewe wyf, dame Alys.'
We love no man that taketh kep or charge
Wher that we goon; we wol ben at oure large.
  Of alle men yblessed moot he be,
The wise astrologien, Daun Ptholome,
325 That seith this proverbe in his Almageste:
'Of alle men his wysdom is the hyeste
That rekketh nevere who hath the world in honde.'
By this proverbe thou shalt understonde,
Have thou ynogh, what thar thee recche or care
330 How myrily that othere folkes fare?
For, certeyn, olde dotard, by youre leve,
Ye shul have queynte right ynogh at eve.
He is to greet a nygard that wolde werne
A man to lighte a candle at his lanterne;
335 He shal have never the lasse light, pardee.
Have thou ynogh, thee thar nat pleyne thee.
  Thou seyst also, that if we make us gay
With clothyng, and with precious array,
That it is peril of oure chastitee;
340 And yet – with sorwe! – thou most enforce thee,
And seye thise wordes in the Apostles name:
'In habit maad with chastitee and shame
Ye wommen shul apparaille yow,' quod he,
'And noght in tressed heer and gay perree,
345 As perles, ne with gold, ne clothes riche.'
After thy text, ne after thy rubriche,
I wol nat wirche as muchel as a gnat.
  Thou seydest this, that I was lyk a cat;
For whoso wolde senge a cattes skyn,
350 Thanne wolde the cat wel dwellen in his in;
And if the cattes skyn be slyk and gay,
She wol nat dwelle in house half a day,
But forth she wole, er any day be dawed,

To shewe hir skyn and goon a-caterwawed.
355 This is to seye, if I be gay, sire shrewe,
I wol renne out my borel for to shewe.
  Sire olde fool, what helpeth thee to spyen?
Thogh thou preye Argus with his hundred yen
To be my warde-cors, as he kan best,
360 In feith, he shal nat kepe me but me lest;
Yet koude I make his berd, so moot I thee!
  Thou seydest eek that ther been thynges thre,
The whiche thynges troublen al this erthe,
And that no wight may endure the ferthe.
365 O leeve sire shrewe, Jhesu shorte thy lyf!
Yet prechestow and seyst an hateful wyf
Yrekened is for oon of thise meschances.
Been ther none othere maner resemblances
That ye may likne youre parables to,
370 But if a sely wyf be oon of tho?
  Thou liknest eek wommenes love to helle,
To bareyne lond, ther water may nat dwelle.
Thou liknest it also to wilde fyr;
The moore it brenneth, the moore it hath desir
375 To consume every thyng that brent wole be.
Thou seyest, right as wormes shende a tree,
Right so a wyf destroyeth hire housbonde;
This knowe they that been to wyves bonde."
  Lordynges, right thus, as ye have understonde,
380 Baar I stifly myne olde housbondes on honde
That thus they seyden in hir dronkenesse;
And al was fals, but that I took witnesse
On Janekyn, and on my nece also.
  O Lord! The peyne I dide hem and the wo,
385 Ful giltelees, by Goddes sweete pyne!
For as an hors I koude byte and whyne.
I koude pleyne, and yit was in the gilt,

Or elles often tyme hadde I been spilt.
Whoso that first to mille comth, first grynt;
390 I pleyned first, so was oure werre ystynt.
They were ful glade to excuse hem blyve
Of thyng of which they nevere agilte hir lyve.
Of wenches wolde I beren hem on honde,
Whan that for syk unnethes myghte they stonde.
395   Yet tikled I his herte, for that he
Wende that I hadde of hym so greet chiertee!
I swoor that al my walkynge out by nyghte
Was for t'espye wenches that he dighte;
Under that colour hadde I many a myrthe.
400 For al swich wit is yeven us in oure byrthe;
Deceite, wepying, spynnyng God hath yive
To wommen kyndely, whil that they may lyve.
And thus of o thyng I avaunte me:
Atte ende I hadde the bettre in ech degree,
405 By sleighte, or force, or by som maner thyng,
As by continueel murmur or grucchyng.
Namely abedde hadden they meschaunce:
Ther wolde I chide and do hem no plesaunce;
I wolde no lenger in the bed abyde,
410 If that I felte his arm over my syde,
Til he had maad his raunson unto me;
Thanne wolde I suffre hym do his nycetee.
And therfore every man this tale I telle,
Wynne whoso may, for al is for to selle;
415 With empty hand men may none haukes lure.
For wynnyng wolde I al his lust endure,
And make me a feyned appetit;
And yet in bacon hadde I nevere delit.
That made me that evere I wolde hem chide,
420 For thogh the pope hadde seten hem biside,
I wolde nat spare hem at hir owene bord,

For, by my trouthe, I quitte hem word for word.
As helpe me verray God omnipotent,
Though I right now sholde make my testament,
425 I ne owe hem nat a word that it nys quit.
I broghte it so aboute by my wit
That they moste yeve it up, as for the beste,
Or elles hadde we nevere been in reste;
For thogh he looked as a wood leon,
430 Yet sholde he faille of his conclusion.
        Thanne wolde I seye, "Goode lief, taak keep
How mekely looketh Wilkyn, oure sheep!
Com neer, my spouse, lat me ba thy cheke!
Ye sholde been al pacient and meke,
435 And han a sweete spiced conscience,
Sith ye so preche of Jobes pacience.
Suffreth alwey, syn ye so wel kan preche;
And but ye do, certein we shal yow teche
That it is fair to have a wyf in pees.
440 Oon of us two moste bowen, doutelees,
And sith a man is moore resonable
Than womman is, ye moste been suffrable.
What eyleth yow to grucche thus and grone?
Is it for ye wolde have my queynte allone?
445 Wy, taak it al! Lo, have it every deel!
Peter! I shrewe yow, but ye love it weel;
For if I wolde selle my *bele chose*,
I koude walke as fressh as is a rose;
But I wol kepe it for youre owene tooth.
450 Ye be to blame, by God! I sey yow sooth."
        Swiche manere wordes hadde we on honde.
Now wol I speken of my fourthe housbonde.
        My fourthe housbonde was a revelour –
This is to seyn, he hadde a paramour –
455 And I was yong and ful of ragerye,

Stibourn and strong, and joly as a pye.
How koude I daunce to an harpe smale,
And synge, ywis, as any nyghtyngale,
Whan I had dronke a draughte of sweete wyn!
460 Metellius, the foule cherl, the swyn,
That with a staf birafte his wyf hir lyf,
For she drank wyn, thogh I hadde been his wyf,
He sholde nat han daunted me fro drynke!
And after wyn on Venus moste I thynke,
465 For al so siker as cold engendreth hayl,
A likerous mouth moste han a likerous tayl.
In wommen vinolent is no defence –
This knowen lecchours by experience.
        But – Lord Crist! – whan that it remembreth me
470 Upon my yowthe, and on my jolitee,
It tikleth me aboute myn herte roote.
Unto this day it dooth myn herte boote
That I have had my world as in my tyme.
But age, allas, that al wole envenyme,
475 Hath me biraft my beautee and my pith.
Lat go. Farewel! The devel go therwith!
The flour is goon; ther is namoore to telle;
The bren, as I best kan, now moste I selle;
But yet to be right myrie wol I fonde.
480 Now wol I tellen of my fourthe housbonde.
        I seye, I hadde in herte greet despit
That he of any oother had delit.
But he was quit, by God and by Seint Joce!
I made hym of the same wode a croce;
485 Nat of my body, in no foul manere,
But certeinly, I made folk swich cheere
That in his owene grece I made hym frye
For angre, and for verray jalousye.
By God, in erthe I was his purgatorie,

490 For which I hope his soule be in glorie.
For, God it woot, he sat ful ofte and song,
Whan that his shoo ful bitterly hym wrong.
Ther was no wight, save God and he, that wiste,
In many wise, how soore I hym twiste.
495 He deyde whan I cam fro Jerusalem,
And lith ygrave under the roode beem,
Al is his tombe noght so curyus
As was the sepulcre of hym Daryus,
Which that Appelles wroghte subtilly;
500 It nys but wast to burye hym preciously.
Lat hym fare wel; God yeve his soule reste!
He is now in his grave and in his cheste.
    Now of my fifthe housbonde wol I telle.
God lete his soule nevere come in helle!
505 And yet was he to me the mooste shrewe;
That feele I on my ribbes al by rewe,
And evere shal unto myn endyng day.
But in oure bed he was so fressh and gay,
And therwithal so wel koude he me glose,
510 Whan that he wolde han my *bele chose*;
That thogh he hadde me bete on every bon,
He koude wynne agayn my love anon.
I trowe I loved hym best, for that he
Was of his love daungerous to me.
515 We wommen han, if that I shal nat lye,
In this matere a queynte fantasye:
Wayte what thyng we may nat lightly have,
Therafter wol we crie al day and crave.
Forbede us thyng, and that desiren we;
520 Preesse on us faste, and thanne wol we fle.
With daunger oute we al oure chaffare;
Greet prees at market maketh deere ware,
And to greet cheep is holde at litel prys:

This knoweth every womman that is wys.
525   My fifthe housebonde – God his soule blesse! –
Which that I took for love, and no richesse,
He som tyme was a clerk of Oxenford,
And hadde left scole, and wente at hom to bord
With my gossib, dwellynge in oure toun;
530 God have hir soule! Hir name was Alisoun.
She knew myn herte, and eek my privetee,
Bet than oure parisshe preest, so moot I thee!
To hire biwreyed I my conseil al.
For hadde myn housebonde pissed on a wal,
535 Or doon a thyng that sholde han cost his lyf,
To hire, and to another worthy wyf,
And to my nece, which that I loved weel,
I wolde han toold his conseil every deel.
And so I dide ful often, God it woot,
540 That made his face often reed and hoot
For verray shame, and blamed hymself for he
Had toold to me so greet a pryvetee.
        And so bifel that ones in a Lente –
So often tymes I to my gossyb wente,
545 For evere yet I loved to be gay,
And for to walke in March, Averill, and May,
Fro hous to hous, to heere sondry talys –
That Jankyn clerk, and my gossyb dame Alys,
And I myself, into the feeldes wente.
550 Myn housebonde was at Londoun al that Lente;
I hadde the bettre leyser for to pleye,
And for to se, and eek for to be seye
Of lusty folk. What wiste I wher my grace
Was shapen for to be, or in what place?
555 Therfore I made my visitaciouns
To vigilies and to processiouns,
To prechyng eek, and to thise pilgrimages,

To pleyes of myracles, and to mariages,
And wered upon my gaye scarlet gytes.
560 Thise wormes, ne thise motthes, ne thise mytes,
Upon my peril, frete hem never a deel;
And wostow why? For they were used weel.
    Now wol I tellen forth what happed me.
I seye that in the feeldes walked we,
565 Til trewely we hadde swich daliance,
This clerk and I, that of my purveiance
I spak to hym and seyde hym how that he,
If I were wydwe, sholde wedde me.
For certeinly – I sey for no bobance –
570 Yet was I nevere withouten purveiance
Of mariage, n'of othere thynges eek.
I holde a mouses herte nat worth a leek
That hath but oon hole for to sterte to,
And if that faille, thanne is al ydo.
575   I bar hym on honde he hadde enchanted me –
My dame taughte me that soutiltee –
And eek I seyde I mette of hym al nyght,
He wolde han slayn me as I lay upright,
And al my bed was ful of verray blood;
580 "But yet I hope that ye shal do me good,
For blood bitokeneth gold, as me was taught."
And al was fals; I dremed of it right naught,
But as I folwed ay my dames loore,
As wel of this as of othere thynges moore.
585   But now, sire, lat me se what I shal seyn.
A ha! By God, I have my tale ageyn.
    Whan that my fourthe housebonde was on beere,
I weep algate, and made sory cheere,
As wyves mooten, for it is usage,
590 And with my coverchief covered my visage,
But for that I was purveyed of a make,

I wepte but smal, and that I undertake.
　　To chirche was myn housebonde born a-morwe
With neighebores, that for hym maden sorwe;
595　And Jankyn, oure clerk, was oon of tho.
As help me God, whan that I saugh hym go
After the beere, me thoughte he hadde a paire
Of legges and of feet so clene and faire
That al myn herte I yaf unto his hoold.
600　He was, I trowe, twenty wynter oold,
And I was fourty, if I shal seye sooth;
But yet I hadde alwey a coltes tooth.
Gat-tothed I was, and that bicam me weel;
I hadde the prente of seinte Venus seel.
605　As help me God, I was a lusty oon,
And faire, and riche, and yong, and wel bigon,
And trewely, as myne housebondes tolde me,
I hadde the beste *quoniam* myghte be.
For certes, I am al Venerien
610　In feelynge, and myn herte is Marcien.
Venus me yaf my lust, my likerousnesse,
And Mars yaf me my sturdy hardynesse;
Myn ascendent was Taur, and Mars therinne.
Allas, allas! That evere love was synne!
615　I folwed ay myn inclinacioun
By vertu of my constellacioun;
That made me I koude noght withdrawe
My chambre of Venus from a good felawe.
Yet have I Martes mark upon my face,
620　And also in another privee place.
For God so wys be my savacioun,
I ne loved nevere by no discrecioun,
But evere folwede myn appetit,
Al were he short, or long, or blak, or whit;
625　I took no kep, so that he liked me,

How poore he was, ne eek of what degree.
    What sholde I seye but, at the monthes ende,
This joly clerk, Jankyn, that was so hende,
Hath wedded me with greet solempnytee,
630 And to hym yaf I al the lond and fee
That evere was me yeven therbifoore.
But afterward repented me ful soore;
He nolde suffre nothyng of my list.
By God, he smoot me ones on the lyst,
635 For that I rente out of his book a leef,
That of the strook myn ere wax al deef.
Stibourn I was as is a leonesse,
And of my tonge a verray jangleresse,
And walke I wolde, as I had doon biforn,
640 From hous to hous, although he had it sworn;
For which he often tymes wolde preche,
And me of olde Romayn geestes teche;
How he Symplicius Gallus lefte his wyf,
And hire forsook for terme of al his lyf,
645 Noght but for open-heveded he hir say
Lookynge out at his dore upon a day.
    Another Romayn tolde he me by name,
That, for his wyf was at a someres game
Withouten his wityng, he forsook hire eke.
650 And thanne wolde he upon his Bible seke
That ilke proverbe of Ecclesiaste
Where he comandeth and forbedeth faste
Man shal nat suffre his wyf go roule aboute.
Thanne wolde he seye right thus, withouten doute:
655   "Whoso that buyldeth his hous al of salwes,
And priketh his blynde hors over the falwes,
And suffreth his wyf to go seken halwes,
Is worthy to been hanged on the galwes!"
But al for noght, I sette noght an hawe

660 Of his proverbes n'of his olde sawe,
Ne I wolde nat of hym corrected be.
I hate hym that my vices telleth me,
And so doo mo, God woot, of us than I.
This made hym with me wood al outrely;
665 I nolde noght forbere hym in no cas.
Now wol I seye yow sooth, by Seint Thomas,
Why that I rente out of his book a leef,
For which he smoot me so that I was deef.
He hadde a book that gladly, nyght and day,
670 For his desport he wolde rede alway;
He cleped it Valerie and Theofraste,
At which book he lough alwey ful faste.
And eek ther was somtyme a clerk at Rome,
A cardinal, that highte Seint Jerome,
675 That made a book agayn Jovinian;
In which book eek ther was Tertulan,
Crisippus, Trotula, and Helowys,
That was abbesse nat fer fro Parys,
And eek the Parables of Salomon,
680 Ovides Art, and bookes many on,
And alle thise were bounden in o volume.
And every nyght and day was his custume,
Whan he hadde leyser and vacacioun
From oother worldly occupacioun,
685 To reden on this book of wikked wyves.
He knew of hem mo legendes and lyves
Than been of goode wyves in the Bible.
For trusteth wel, it is an impossible
That any clerk wol speke good of wyves,
690 But if it be of hooly seintes lyves,
Ne of noon oother womman never the mo.
Who peyntede the leon, tel me who?
By God, if wommen hadde writen stories,

As clerkes han withinne hire oratories,
695 They wolde han writen of men moore
wikkednesse
Than al the mark of Adam may redresse.
The children of Mercurie and of Venus
Been in hir wirkyng ful contrarius;
Mercurie loveth wysdam and science,
700 And Venus loveth ryot and dispence.
And, for hire diverse disposicioun,
Ech falleth in otheres exaltacioun.
And thus, God woot, Mercurie is desolat
In Pisces, wher Venus is exaltat,
705 And Venus falleth ther Mercurie is reysed.
Therfore no womman of no clerk is preysed.
The clerk, whan he is oold, and may noght do
Of Venus werkes worth his olde sho,
Thanne sit he doun, and writ in his dotage
710 That wommen kan nat kepe hir mariage!
But now to purpos, why I tolde thee
That I was beten for a book, pardee!
Upon a nyght Jankyn, that was oure sire,
Redde on his book, as he sat by the fire,
715 Of Eva first, that for hir wikkednesse
Was al mankynde broght to wrecchednesse,
For which that Jhesu Crist hymself was slayn,
That boghte us with his herte blood agayn.
Lo, heere expres of womman may ye fynde
720 That womman was the los of al mankynde.
Tho redde he me how Sampson loste his heres:
Slepynge, his lemman kitte it with hir sheres;
Thurgh which treson loste he bothe his yen.
Tho redde he me, if that I shal nat lyen,
725 Of Hercules and of his Dianyre,
That caused hym to sette hymself afyre.

35

No thyng forgat he the care and the wo
That Socrates hadde with his wyves two,
How Xantippa caste pisse upon his heed.
730 This sely man sat stille as he were deed;
He wiped his heed, namoore dorste he seyn,
But "Er that thonder stynte, comth a reyn!"
Of Phasipha, that was the queene of Crete,
For shrewednesse, hym thoughte the tale swete;
735 Fy! Spek namoore – it is a grisly thyng –
Of hire horrible lust and hir likyng.
Of Clitermystra, for hire lecherye,
That falsly made hire housbonde for to dye,
He redde it with ful good devocioun.
740 He tolde me eek for what occasioun
Amphiorax at Thebes loste his lyf.
Myn housbonde hadde a legende of his wyf,
Eriphilem, that for an ouche of gold
Hath prively unto the Grekes told
745 Wher that hir housbonde hidde hym in a place,
For which he hadde at Thebes sory grace.
Of Lyvia tolde he me, and of Lucye:
They bothe made hir housbondes for to dye,
That oon for love, that oother was for hate.
750 Lyvia hir housbonde, on an even late,
Empoysoned hath, for that she was his fo;
Lucia, likerous, loved hire housbonde so
That, for he sholde alwey upon hire thynke,
She yaf hym swich a manere love-drynke
755 That he was deed er it were by the morwe;
And thus algates housbondes han sorwe.
Thanne tolde he me how oon Latumyus
Compleyned unto his felawe Arrius
That in his gardyn growed swich a tree
760 On which he seyde how that his wyves thre

Hanged hemself for herte despitus.
"O leeve brother," quod this Arrius,
"Yif me a plante of thilke blissed tree,
And in my gardyn planted shal it bee."

765 Of latter date, of wyves hath he red
That somme han slayn hir housbondes in hir bed,
And lete hir lecchour dighte hire al the nyght,
Whan that the corps lay in the floor upright.
And somme han dryve nayles in hir brayn,

770 Whil that they slepte, and thus they had hem slayn.
Somme han hem yeve poysoun in hire drynke.
He spak moore harm than herte may bithynke,
And therwithal he knew of mo proverbes
Than in this world ther growen gras or herbes.

775 "Bet is," quod he, "thyn habitacioun
Be with a leon or a foul dragoun,
Than with a womman usynge for to chyde.
Bet is," quod he, "hye in the roof abyde,
Than with an angry wyf doun in the hous;

780 They been so wikked and contrarious,
They haten that hir housbondes loven ay."
He seyde, "A womman cast hir shame away,
Whan she cast of hir smok"; and forthermo,
"A fair womman, but she be chaast also,

785 Is lyk a gold ryng in a sowes nose."
Who wolde wene, or who wolde suppose,
The wo that in myn herte was, and pyne?
    And whan I saugh he wolde nevere fyne
To reden on this cursed book al nyght,

790 Al sodeynly thre leves have I plyght
Out of his book, right as he radde, and eke
I with my fest so took hym on the cheke
That in oure fyr he fil bakward adoun.
And he up stirte as dooth a wood leoun,

795 And with his fest he smoot me on the heed
That in the floor I lay as I were deed.
And whan he saugh how stille that I lay,
He was agast and wolde han fled his way,
Til atte laste out of my swogh I breyde.
800 "O! hastow slayn me, false theef?" I seyde,
"And for my land thus hastow mordred me?
Er I be deed, yet wol I kisse thee."
    And neer he cam, and kneled faire adoun,
And seyde, "Deere suster Alisoun,
805 As help me God, I shal thee nevere smyte!
That I have doon, it is thyself to wyte.
Foryeve it me, and that I thee biseke!"
And yet eftsoones I hitte hym on the cheke,
And seyde, "Theef, thus muchel am I wreke;
810 Now wol I dye, I may no lenger speke."
But atte laste, with muchel care and wo,
We fille acorded by us selven two.
He yaf me al the bridel in myn hond,
To han the governance of hous and lond,
815 And of his tonge, and of his hond also;
And made hym brenne his book anon right tho.
And whan that I hadde geten unto me,
By maistrie, al the soveraynetee,
And that he seyde, "Myn owene trewe wyf,
820 Do as thee lust the terme of al thy lyf;
Keep thyn honour, and keep eek myn estaat" –
After that day we hadden never debaat.
God helpe me so, I was to hym as kynde
As any wyf from Denmark unto Ynde,
825 And also trewe, and so was he to me.
I prey to God, that sit in magestee,
So blesse his soule for his mercy deere.
Now wol I seye my tale, if ye wol heere.'

Biholde the wordes bitwene the
Somonour and the Frere.

The Frere lough, whan he hadde herd al this;
830 'Now dame,' quod he, 'so have I joye or blis,
This is a long preamble of a tale!'
And whan the Somonour herde the Frere gale,
'Lo,' quod the Somonour, 'Goddes armes two!
A frere wol entremette hym everemo.
835 Lo, goode men, a flye and eek a frere
Wol falle in every dyssh and eek mateere.
What spekestow of preambulacioun?
What! amble, or trotte, or pees, or go sit doun!
Thou lettest oure disport in this manere.'
840 'Ye, woltow so, sire Somonour?' quod the Frere;
'Now, by my feith I shal, er that I go,
Telle of a somonour swich a tale or two
That alle the folk shal laughen in this place.'
'Now elles, Frere, I bishrewe thy face,'
845 Quod this Somonour, 'and I bishrewe me,
But if I telle tales two or thre
Of freres er I come to Sidyngborne
That I shal make thyn herte for to morne,
For wel I woot thy pacience is gon.'
850 Oure Hooste cride 'Pees! And that anon!'
And seyde, 'Lat the womman telle hire tale.
Ye fare as folk that dronken ben of ale.
Do, dame, telle forth youre tale, and that is best.'
'Al redy, sire,' quod she, 'right as yow lest,
855 If I have licence of this worthy Frere.'
'Yis, dame,' quod he, 'tel forth, and I wol heere.'

Heere endeth the Wyf of Bathe hir Prologe.

The Wife of Bath's Tale

Heere bigynneth the Tale of the Wyf of Bathe.

In th'olde dayes of the Kyng Arthour,
Of which that Britons speken greet honour,
Al was this land fulfild of fayerye.
860 The elf-queene, with hir joly compaignye,
Daunced ful ofte in many a grene mede.
This was the olde opinion, as I rede;
I speke of manye hundred yeres ago.
But now kan no man se none elves mo,
865 For now the grete charitee and prayeres
Of lymytours and othere hooly freres,
That serchen every lond and every streem,
As thikke as motes in the sonne-beem,
Blessynge halles, chambres, kichenes, boures,
870 Citees, burghes, castels, hye toures,
Thropes, bernes, shipnes, dayeryes –
This maketh that ther ben no fayeryes.
For ther as wont to walken was an elf
Ther walketh now the lymytour hymself
875 In undermeles and in morwenynges,
And seyth his matyns and his hooly thynges
As he gooth in his lymytacioun.
Wommen may go saufly up and doun.
In every bussh or under every tree
880 Ther is noon oother incubus but he,
And he ne wol doon hem but dishonour.
And so bifel that this kyng Arthour
Hadde in his hous a lusty bacheler,
That on a day cam ridynge fro ryver,
885 And happed that, allone as he was born,
He saugh a mayde walkynge hym biforn,

40

Of which mayde anon, maugree hir heed,
By verray force, he rafte hire maydenhed;
For which oppressioun was swich clamour
890 And swich pursute unto the kyng Arthour
That dampned was this knyght for to be deed,
By cours of lawe, and sholde han lost his heed –
Paraventure swich was the statut tho –
But that the queene and other ladyes mo
895 So longe preyeden the kyng of grace
Til he his lyf hym graunted in the place,
And yaf hym to the queene, al at hir wille,
To chese wheither she wolde hym save or spille.
    The queene thanketh the kyng with al hir myght,
900 And after this thus spak she to the knyght,
Whan that she saugh hir tyme, upon a day:
'Thou standest yet,' quod she, 'in swich array
That of thy lyf yet hastow no suretee.
I grante thee lyf, if thou kanst tellen me
905 What thyng is it that wommen moost desiren.
Be war, and keep thy nekke-boon from iren!
And if thou kanst nat tellen it anon,
Yet wol I yeve thee leve for to gon
A twelf-month and a day, to seche and leere
910 An answere suffisant in this mateere;
And suretee wol I han, er that thou pace,
Thy body for to yelden in this place.'
    Wo was this knyght, and sorwefully he siketh;
But what! He may nat do al as hym liketh.
915 And at the laste he chees hym for to wende
And come agayn, right at the yeres ende,
With swich answere as God wolde hym purveye;
And taketh his leve, and wendeth forth his weye.
    He seketh every hous and every place
920 Where as he hopeth for to fynde grace

To lerne what thyng wommen loven moost,
But he ne koude arryven in no coost
Wher as he myghte fynde in this mateere
Two creatures accordynge in-feere.

925 Somme seyde wommen loven best richesse,
Somme seyde honour, somme seyde jolynesse,
Somme riche array, somme seyden lust abedde,
And oftetyme to be wydwe and wedde.
Somme seyde that oure hertes been moost esed
930 Whan that we been yflatered and yplesed.
He gooth ful ny the sothe, I wol nat lye.
A man shal wynne us best with flaterye,
And with attendance and with bisynesse
Been we ylymed, bothe moore and lesse.

935 And somme seyen that we loven best
For to be free and do right as us lest,
And that no man repreve us of oure vice,
But seye that we be wise and no thyng nyce.
For trewely ther is noon of us alle,
940 If any wight wol clawe us on the galle,
That we nel kike, for he seith us sooth.
Assay, and he shal fynde it that so dooth;
For, be we never so vicious withinne,
We wol been holden wise and clene of synne.

945 And somme seyn that greet delit han we
For to been holden stable, and eek secree,
And in o purpos stedefastly to dwelle,
And nat biwreye thyng that men us telle.
But that tale is nat worth a rake-stele.
950 Pardee, we wommen konne no thyng hele;
Witnesse on Myda – wol ye heere the tale?
    Ovyde, amonges othere thynges smale,
Seyde Myda hadde, under his longe heres,
Growynge upon his heed two asses eres,

955 The whiche vice he hydde as he best myghte
Ful subtilly from every mannes sighte,
That, save his wyf, ther wiste of it namo.
He loved hire moost, and trusted hire also;
He preyede hire that to no creature
960 She sholde tellen of his disfigure.
    She swoor him, 'Nay'; for al this world to
        wynne,
She nolde do that vileynye or synne,
To make hir housbonde han so foul a name.
She nolde nat telle it for hir owene shame.
965 But nathelees, hir thoughte that she dyde
That she so longe sholde a conseil hyde;
Hir thoughte it swal so soore aboute hir herte
That nedely som word hire moste asterte;
And sith she dorste telle it to no man,
970 Doun to a mareys faste by she ran –
Til she cam there hir herte was afyre –
And as a bitore bombleth in the myre,
She leyde hir mouth unto the water doun:
'Biwreye me nat, thou water, with thy soun,'
975 Quod she; 'to thee I telle it and namo;
Myn housbonde hath longe asses erys two!
Now is myn herte al hool; now is it oute.
I myghte no lenger kepe it, out of doute.'
Heere may ye se, thogh we a tyme abyde,
980 Yet out it moot; we kan no conseil hyde.
The remenant of the tale if ye wol heere,
Redeth Ovyde, and ther ye may it leere.
    This knyght, of which my tale is specially,
Whan that he saugh he myghte nat come therby –
985 This is to seye, what wommen love moost –
Withinne his brest ful sorweful was the goost.
But hoom he gooth; he myghte nat sojourne;

The day was come that homward moste he tourne.
And in his wey it happed hym to ryde,
990　In al this care, under a forest syde,
Wher as he saugh upon a daunce go
Of ladyes foure and twenty, and yet mo;
Toward the whiche daunce he drow ful yerne,
In hope that som wysdom sholde he lerne.
995　But certeinly, er he cam fully there,
Vanysshed was this daunce, he nyste where.
No creature saugh he that bar lyf,
Save on the grene he saugh sittynge a wyf —
A fouler wight ther may no man devyse.
1000　Agayn the knyght this olde wyf gan ryse,
And seyde, 'Sire knyght, heer forth ne lith no wey.
Tel me what that ye seken, by youre fey!
Paraventure it may the bettre be;
Thise olde folk kan muchel thyng,' quod she.
1005　　'My leeve mooder,' quod this knyght, 'certeyn
I nam but deed but if that I kan seyn
What thyng it is that wommen moost desire.
Koude ye me wisse, I wolde wel quite youre hire.'
　　'Plight me thy trouthe heere in myn hand,' quod
　　　she,
1010　'The nexte thyng that I requere thee,
Thou shalt it do, if it lye in thy myght,
And I wol telle it yow er it be nyght.'
　　'Have heer my trouthe,' quod the knyght, 'I
　　　grante.'
　　'Thanne,' quod she, 'I dar me wel avante
1015　Thy lyf is sauf, for I wol stonde therby;
Upon my lyf, the queene wol seye as I.
Lat se which is the proudeste of hem alle
That wereth on a coverchief or a calle
That dar seye nay of that I shal thee teche.

1020 Lat us go forth withouten lenger speche.'
Tho rowned she a pistel in his ere,
And bad hym to be glad and have no fere.
   Whan they be comen to the court, this knyght
Seyde he had holde his day, as he hadde hight,
1025 And redy was his answere, as he sayde.
Ful many a noble wyf, and many a mayde,
And many a wydwe, for that they been wise,
The queene hirself sittynge as a justise,
Assembled been, his answere for to heere;
1030 And afterward this knyght was bode appeere.
   To every wight comanded was silence,
And that the knyght sholde telle in audience
What thyng that worldly wommen loven best.
This knyght ne stood nat stille as doth a best,
1035 But to his questioun anon answerde
With manly voys, that al the court it herde:
   'My lige lady, generally,' quod he,
'Wommen desiren to have sovereynetee
As wel over hir housbond as hir love,
1040 And for to been in maistrie hym above.
This is youre mooste desir, thogh ye me kille.
Dooth as yow list; I am heer at youre wille.'
In al the court ne was ther wyf, ne mayde,
Ne wydwe that contraried that he sayde,
1045 But seyden he was worthy han his lyf.
And with that word up stirte the olde wyf,
Which that the knyght saugh sittynge on the
      grene:
'Mercy,' quod she, 'my sovereyn lady queene!
Er that youre court departe, do me right.
1050 I taughte this answere unto the knyght;
For which he plighte me his trouthe there,
The firste thyng that I wolde hym requere

He wolde it do, if it lay in his myghte.
Bifore the court thanne preye I thee, sir knyght,'
1055 Quod she, 'that thou me take unto thy wyf,
For wel thou woost that I have kept thy lyf.
If I seye fals, sey nay, upon thy fey!'
  This knyght answerde, 'Allas and weylawey!
I woot right wel that swich was my biheste.
1060 For Goddes love, as chees a newe requeste!
Taak al my good and lat my body go.'
  'Nay, thanne,' quod she, 'I shrewe us bothe two!
For thogh that I be foul, and oold, and poore
I nolde for al the metal, ne for oore
1065 That under erthe is grave or lith above,
But if thy wyf I were, and eek thy love.'
  'My love?' quod he, 'nay, my dampnacioun!
Allas, that any of my nacioun
Sholde evere so foule disparaged be!'
1070 But al for noght; the ende is this, that he
Constreyned was; he nedes moste hire wedde,
And taketh his olde wyf, and gooth to bedde.
  Now wolden som men seye, paraventure,
That for my necligence I do no cure
1075 To tellen yow the joye and al th'array
That at the feeste was that ilke day.
To which thyng shortly answeren I shal:
I seye ther nas no joye ne feeste at al;
Ther nas but hevynesse and muche sorwe.
1080 For prively he wedded hire on morwe,
And al day after hidde hym as an owle,
So wo was hym, his wyf looked so foule.
  Greet was the wo the knyght hadde in his
        thoght,
Whan he was with his wyf abedde ybroght;
1085 He walweth and he turneth to and fro.

His olde wyf lay smylynge everemo,
And seyde, 'O deere housbonde, benedicitee!
Fareth every knyght thus with his wyf as ye?
Is this the lawe of kyng Arthures hous?
1090 Is every knyght of his so dangerous?
I am youre owene love and youre wyf;
I am she which that saved hath youre lyf,
And, certes, yet ne dide I yow nevere unright;
Why fare ye thus with me this firste nyght?
1095 Ye faren lyk a man had lost his wit.
What is my gilt? For Goddes love, tel it,
And it shal been amended, if I may.'
    'Amended?' quod this knyght, 'Allas, nay, nay!
It wol nat been amended nevere mo.
1100 Thou art so loothly, and so oold also,
And therto comen of so lough a kynde,
That litel wonder is thogh I walwe and wynde.
So wolde God myn herte wolde breste!'
    'Is this,' quod she, 'the cause of youre unreste?'
1105 'Ye, certeinly,' quod he, 'no wonder is.'
    'Now, sire,' quod she, 'I koude amende al this,
If that me liste, er it were dayes thre,
So wel ye myghte bere yow unto me.
    'But, for ye speken of swich gentillesse
1110 As is descended out of old richesse,
That therfore sholden ye be gentil men,
Swich arrogance is nat worth an hen.
Looke who that is moost vertuous alway,
Pryvee and apert, and moost entendeth ay
1115 To do the gentil dedes that he kan;
Taak hym for the grettest gentil man.
Crist wole we clayme of hym oure gentillesse,
Nat of oure eldres for hire old richesse.
For thogh they yeve us al hir heritage,

1120 For which we clayme to been of heigh parage,
Yet may they nat biquethe for no thyng
To noon of us hir vertuous lyvyng,
That made hem gentil men ycalled be,
And bad us folwen hem in swich degree.
1125   'Wel kan the wise poete of Florence,
That highte Dant, speken in this sentence.
Lo, in swich maner rym is Dantes tale:
"Ful selde up riseth by his branches smale
Prowesse of man, for God, of his goodnesse,
1130 Wole that of hym we clayme oure gentillesse";
For of oure eldres may we no thyng clayme
But temporel thyng, that man may hurte and
      mayme.
    'Eek every wight woot this as wel as I,
If gentillesse were planted natureelly
1135 Unto a certeyn lynage doun the lyne,
Pryvee and apert thanne wolde they nevere fyne
To doon of gentillesse the faire office;
They myghte do no vileynye or vice.
    'Taak fyr and ber it in the derkeste hous
1140 Bitwix this and the mount of Kaukasous,
And lat men shette the dores and go thenne;
Yet wole the fyr as faire lye and brenne
As twenty thousand men myghte it biholde;
His office natureel ay wol it holde,
1145 Up peril of my lyf, til that it dye.
    'Heere may ye se wel how that genterye
Is nat annexed to possessioun,
Sith folk ne doon hir operacioun
Alwey, as dooth the fyr, lo, in his kynde.
1150 For, God it woot, men may wel often fynde
A lordes sone do shame and vileynye;
And he that wole han pris of his gentrye,

For he was boren of a gentil hous
And hadde his eldres noble and vertuous,
1155 And nel hymselven do no gentil dedis
Ne folwen his gentil auncestre that deed is,
He nys nat gentil, be he duc or erl,
For vileyns synful dedes make a cherl.
For gentillesse nys but renomee
1160 Of thyne auncestres, for hire heigh bountee,
Which is a strange thyng to thy persone.
Thy gentillesse cometh fro God allone.
Thanne comth oure verray gentillesse of grace;
It was no thyng biquethe us with oure place.
1165   'Thenketh hou noble, as seith Valerius,
Was thilke Tullius Hostillius,
That out of poverte roos to heigh noblesse.
Reedeth Senek, and redeth eek Boece;
Ther shul ye seen expres that it no drede is
1170 That he is gentil that dooth gentil dedis.
And therfore, leeve housbonde, I thus conclude:
Al were it that myne auncestres were rude,
Yet may the hye God, and so hope I,
Grante me grace to lyven vertuously.
1175 Thanne am I gentil, whan that I bigynne
To lyven vertuously and weyve synne.
   'And ther as ye of poverte me repreeve,
The hye God, on whom that we bileeve,
In wilful poverte chees to lyve his lyf.
1180 And certes every man, mayden, or wyf
May understonde that Jhesus, hevene kyng,
Ne wolde nat chese a vicious lyvyng.
Glad poverte is an honest thyng, certeyn;
This wole Senec and othere clerkes seyn.
1185 Whoso that halt hym payd of his poverte,
I holde hym riche, al hadde he nat a sherte.

He that coveiteth is a povre wight,
For he wolde han that is nat in his myght;
But he that noght hath, ne coveiteth have,
1190 Is riche, although ye holde hym but a knave.
Verray poverte, it syngeth proprely;
Juvenal seith of poverte myrily:
"The povre man, whan he goth by the weye,
Bifore the theves he may synge and pleye."
1195 Poverte is hateful good and, as I gesse,
A ful greet bryngere out of bisynesse;
A greet amendere eek of sapience
To hym that taketh it in pacience.
Poverte is this, although it seme alenge:
1200 Possessioun that no wight wol chalenge.
Poverte ful ofte, whan a man is lowe,
Maketh his God and eek hymself to knowe.
Poverte a spectacle is, as thynketh me,
Thurgh which he may his verray freendes see.
1205 And therfore, sire, syn that I noght yow greve,
Of my poverte namoore ye me repreve.
    'Now, sire, of elde ye repreve me;
And certes, sire, thogh noon auctoritee
Were in no book, ye gentils of honour
1210 Seyn that men sholde an old wight doon favour
And clepe hym fader, for youre gentillesse:
And auctours shal I fynden, as I gesse.
    'Now ther ye seye that I am foul and old,
Than drede you noght to been a cokewold;
1215 For filthe and eelde, also moot I thee,
Been grete wardeyns upon chastitee.
But nathelees, syn I knowe youre delit,
I shal fulfille youre worldly appetit.
    'Chese now,' quod she, 'oon of thise thynges
        tweye:

1220 To han me foul and old til that I deye,
And be to yow a trewe, humble wyf,
And nevere yow displese in al my lyf,
Or elles ye wol han me yong and fair,
And take youre aventure of the repair
1225 That shal be to youre hous by cause of me,
Or in som oother place, may wel be.
Now chese yourselven, wheither that yow liketh.'
　　This knyght avyseth hym and sore siketh,
But atte laste he seyde in this manere:
1230 'My lady and my love, and wyf so deere,
I put me in youre wise governance;
Cheseth yourself which may be moost plesance
And moost honour to yow and me also.
I do no fors the wheither of the two,
1235 For as yow liketh, it suffiseth me.'
　　'Thanne have I gete of yow maistrie,' quod she,
'Syn I may chese and governe as me lest?'
　　'Ye, certes, wyf,' quod he, 'I holde it best.'
　　'Kys me,' quod she, 'we be no lenger wrothe,
1240 For, by my trouthe, I wol be to yow bothe –
This is to seyn, ye, bothe fair and good.
I prey to God that I moote sterven wood,
But I to yow be also good and trewe
As evere was wyf, syn that the world was newe.
1245 And but I be to-morn as fair to seene
As any lady, emperice, or queene,
That is bitwixe the est and eke the west,
Dooth with my lyf and deth right as yow lest.
Cast up the curtyn, looke how that it is.'
1250 　　And whan the knyght saugh verraily al this,
That she so fair was, and so yong therto,
For joye he hente hire in his armes two.
His herte bathed in a bath of blisse.

A thousand tyme a-rewe he gan hire kisse,
1255 And she obeyed hym in every thyng
That myghte doon hym plesance or likyng.
And thus they lyve unto hir lyves ende
In parfit joye; and Jhesu Crist us sende
Housbondes meeke, yonge, and fressh abedde,
1260 And grace t'overbyde hem that we wedde;
And eek I praye Jhesu shorte hir lyves
That noght wol be governed by hir wyves;
And olde and angry nygardes of dispence,
God sende hem soone verray pestilence!

Heere endeth the Wyves Tale of Bathe.

Notes

The Wife of Bath's portrait: General Prologue

In *The General Prologue*, Chaucer gives a description of each of the pilgrims, often not only describing their physical appearances but also hinting at some features of their characters. In his description of the Wife of Bath, Chaucer begins by drawing attention to the fact that the Wife is somewhat deaf, and we learn the cause of this later in her prologue.

She is a skilled cloth-maker and the quality of her cloth surpasses that of Ypres and Ghent. He gives us a hint as to her character when he tells us the coverchiefs she wears to attend church on a Sunday are very extravagant and that if another woman tries to beat her to the offertory she becomes very cross and loses all her charitable feelings. Clearly going to church is important to her for the opportunity to show off her social standing rather than for religious devotion. She is finely dressed in bright red, gartered stockings and her fashionable shoes are made of soft leather; she wears wimples and a broad hat. She has a ruddy complexion, wears a riding habit and spurs and sits comfortably on her horse. She has been on many pilgrimages, but again it seems likely that she is motivated more by a desire for excitement and meeting new people than by religious needs. Chaucer also draws attention to her amorous nature, signified by her gap-teeth and her knowledge of love-potions and experience of the 'art of love'. The overall impression that he creates of her is of a strong, extrovert, sociable, adventurous character.

445 **good Wif**   a term referring to a woman of independent means and of some standing in the community (the feminine of 'goodman').
biside Bathe   close to Bath – thought to be a settlement just outside the north gate, St Michael-without-the-North-Gate or St Michael juxta Bathon.

446 **deef** deaf (she relates how this deafness came about in her prologue).

that was scathe that was a pity.

447 **haunt** skill.

448 **She passed** she surpassed (perhaps a boast on the Wife's part, as Ypres and Ghent were the chief centres of the Flemish woollen trade in the fourteenth century).

449–52 Much social prestige was attached to the order of precedence in which parishioners went forward to give their offerings in church. It is significant that the Wife would not countenance anyone going before her, and if they did it put her in a really bad mood.

453 **coverchiefs** large headscarf-like head coverings. The Wife's were particularly elaborate and flamboyant.

ful fyne weren of ground the ground was the cloth base for the coverchief, and the Wife's were finely decorated with lace and embroidery.

454 **weyeden ten pound** the Wife's coverchiefs were so elaborately decorated they must have weighed ten pounds.

456 **hosen** in Chaucer's time women's hose were made of wool or linen and came up to just above the knee. They were held in place by garter. Note that the Wife's hose are a flamboyant scarlet, of the best quality and perfectly held up.

457 **shoes ful moyste and newe** shoes were supple and new (again, the fact that she is comfortably off is evident in the quality of her clothing).

459 **worthy** in this sense, meaning wealthy and respectable.

460 **at chirche dore** in fourteenth-century marriages it was customary for the ceremony to be conducted at the church door. The party then went into the church itself and Mass was held at the altar.

fyve it was not unusual (despite the views of the Church) for a well-off woman to re-marry, perhaps several times, if widowed. In fact, it was difficult for a wealthy widow to remain unmarried. The Wife, though, needs no encouragement to marry again.

461 **oother compaignye** i.e. lovers before she married.

462 **as nowthe** for the moment.

463–6 The Wife had been on many pilgrimages and visited many

holy shrines. Apart from any religious significance,
pilgrimages offered the opportunity for safer travel and the
opportunity to meet people and socialize.

468 **Gat-tothed**   gap-toothed (i.e. with a gap between the front
teeth). This was supposed to indicate the desire to travel and
also a lecherous nature.

469 **amblere**   an ambler was a horse trained to walk putting both
feet forward on the same side at once, and therefore giving a
more comfortable ride. This was particularly comfortable for
women (who rode side-saddle) on long journeys.

470 **Ywympled**   a wimple was made of either fine linen or silk
and was worn around the neck and chest with the ends drawn
up on either side of the face and pinned to the hair on top of
the head, and then covered with a veil or hat.

471 **bokeler or a targe**   these are kinds of shields.

472 **foot-mantel**   a cloth covering the feet to keep them warm
while riding side-saddle.

473 **paire of spores**   pair of spurs. This presents some
discrepancy, as the *foot-mantel* indicates her riding side-saddle,
but wearing a pair of spurs suggests she is riding astride the
horse. The depiction of her in the Ellesmere manuscript (see
page 110) portrays her riding astride.

476 **the olde daunce**   the old game (i.e. the game of love).

The Wife begins her prologue: Lines 1–34

The Wife opens her prologue by stating what her topic will be –
namely the *wo that is in mariage*. She tells us that she has had five
husbands and they were all respectable men. She first married at
the age of 12, and when each of her husbands died she re-
married again. She questions whether the Church would
recognize all her marriages, and points to the possible
contradictions of the Church's point of view. Christ attended
only one marriage, but she questions whether that indicates that
people should marry only once. On the other hand she says that

people are told elsewhere in the Bible to 'go forth and multiply'. She says that she does not know anywhere in the Bible where a definitive figure is given for the number of husbands a woman should have.

1   **auctoritee**   authoritative texts accepted by all, and often quoted, such as the Bible or texts written by highly respected religious or philosophical writers.

1–2   **though noon auctoritee/ Were in this world**   even if no textual authority could be quoted. The Wife immediately shows she is prepared to challenge authority (here, the Church).

4–6   **sith I twelve yeer... I have had fyve**   the Wife first married when she was 12 and has had five husbands altogether.

7   If my marriages might be considered valid. The Church argued that second and subsequent marriages were not recognized in the eyes of God. Church teachings suggested that widows should remain chaste after the death of their first husband.

8   **alle were worthy men in hir degree**   all were respectable men in their own way.

9   But I was certainly told not long ago.

10–11   **That sith that Crist ne wente nevere but onis/ To weddyng** that since Christ only went once to a wedding.
  in the Cane of Galilee   in Cana in Galilee. A reference to St John's Gospel 2:1, which tells how Christ performed his first miracle by turning water into wine at the wedding feast.

12   **ensample**   example.

13   That I should marry only once.

14–16   Hear also the sharp words which Jesus, beside a well, spoke to reprove the Samaritan. This refers to St John's Gospel 4:6, which relates the story of the Samaritan woman whom Jesus met by a well on his way to Galilee. In his attempt to convert the Samaritan, Jesus told her to go and fetch her husband. When she replied that she had no husband, Jesus replied 'You are right in saying that you have no husband, for although you have had five husbands, the man with whom you are living is not your husband'.

20   The Wife is unsure what Jesus meant by this.

21–3 She asks why the fifth man was not the Samaritan woman's husband, and how many she was allowed to have in marriage. According to the medieval Church, marriage was sacred and a woman was only allowed to marry once; any further marriages were not recognized by the Church or God. The Wife is questioning this belief and asking where it is supported by the Bible or any other authority.

24–5 She has never, in all her life, heard a definite number given.

26 **devyne and glosen**   guess and explain.

27 **But wel I woot, expres**   but I really know, definitely.

28 God bade us to increase and multiply (see Genesis 1:28 'and God said unto them, Be fruitful, and multiply').

29 **gentil text**   noble, or excellent, text.

30 **Eek wel I woot**   also I well know.

30–1 **he seyde myn housbonde/ Sholde lete fader and mooder and take to me**   he said my husband should leave his father and mother and take me (see Matthew 19:5, 'For this cause shall a man leave father and mother, and shall cleave to his wife: and they twain shall be one flesh'.)

32–3 But he made no mention of any number (of husbands) or of bigamy or octogamy.

34 Why should marrying more than once be said to be a discreditable thing?

The Wife develops her arguments to support her position: Lines 35–114

The Wife uses examples from the Bible to support her views and cites Solomon, who had more than one wife, and she thanks God that she has had five husbands, and welcomes the sixth whenever he comes along. She cites Abraham and Jacob, who also had more than one wife, and she asks if anyone can provide evidence from anywhere that God forbade marriage or commanded virginity. She argues that if there was no procreation there would be no virgins. She accepts that St Paul was a virgin, and that he felt that virginity was the preferred state, but he only recommended it and gave leave for people to marry because he recognized that the flesh is weak. The Wife accepts that she is not suited to virginity herself, although she recognizes that it is good for those whom it suits.

Lines 44A–44F are generally accepted by scholars as genuine late insertions to the manuscript by Chaucer.

35–6 Consider the example of the wise King Solomon; I believe he had more than one wife. (*Lo, heere* – literally 'look, listen' – is a colloquial phrase often used when citing an authority.)

37–8 Would that God was willing to give me a fresh spouse half so often as he. (According to the Bible, Soloman had 'seven hundred wives, princesses, and three hundred concubines', I Kings 11:3).

39 What a gift from God he had with all his wives.

40 No man alive has such a gift.

41 **God woot** God knows.
as to my wit to my way of thinking, or as I believe.

42 **a myrie fit** a merry time.
so wel was hym on lyve so good it was for him to be alive.

44B **nether purs** literally, lower purse (i.e. scrotum).

44C **Diverse scoles** different schools.
parfyt clerkes perfect scholars.

44D **practyk** practice.
sondry werkes different works (i.e. a range of works).

44E **sekirly** certainly.

44F **scoleiyng** schooling (the Wife is talking about the 'schooling' she has experienced from having had five husbands and the influence they have had on her and her attitudes).

45 Welcome to the sixth, whenever he may come.

46 For truly I will not keep myself entirely celibate.

47 **fro the world ygon** i.e. dead.

49–52 See Corinthians 7:8, St Paul's First Epistle to the Corinthians, in which he said 'I say therefore to the unmarried and widows, It is good for them if they abide even as I. But if they cannot contain, let them marry: for it is better to marry than to burn.'

53 **What rekketh me** what does it matter to me.

53–4 **thogh folk... bigamye?** if people speak ill of wicked Lameth and his bigamy – see Genesis 4:19–23, which tells how Lameth 'took unto him two wives'. (Note the blurring of the discussion here – marrying again after the spouse has died is different from being married to two at the same time.)

55–6 **Abraham, Jacob** the biblical patriarchs.

56 **as ferforth as I kan** as far as I know.

57 **mo** more.

59 **in any manere age** at any time in history.

60 **hye God** God on high.

61 **expres** explicit.

63 **it is no drede** there is no doubt.

64 **Th'apostel** i.e. St Paul.
maydenhede virginity.

65 See I Corinthians 7:6, where St Paul gives his advice but points out that it is not based on divine authority.

66 Men may advise women to be one (i.e. a virgin, remain single).

67 Advising is not commanding.

68 He left it to our discretion.

69–70 For if God had commanded virginity, by doing so he would have condemned marriage.

71–2 And certainly, if no seed were sown, where would virginity grow from?

73 **Poul dorste nat comanden** Paul dared not command.
atte leeste literally at the least, i.e. 'this much at least is certain', or 'at all events'.

74 **his maister** his master, i.e. Christ.

75 There is a prize to be won for virginity (see I Corinthians 9:24, where Paul speaks of the prize for virginity by using the metaphor of a race).

76 Win it whoever can, let's see who runs the best.

77 **word** advice or counsel.

78 But it pleased God to give it through his great power.

79 I know well that the apostle (i.e. St Paul) was celibate.

80 **nathelees** nevertheless.
wroot wrote.

81 He would that everyone was such as he (i.e. he wanted everyone to be like him).

82 **Al nys but conseil** it's nothing but advice.

83–4 **he yaf me leve/ Of indulgence** he has given me permission (referring back to St Paul giving permission for those who found the life of celibacy too hard to re-marry).

85 To marry if my mate dies.

86 Without being accused of bigamy.

87 Even if it were a good thing not to touch a woman (see I Corinthians 7:1 'It is good for a man not to touch a woman').

88 **He mente as**   what he meant was.

89 For it is dangerous to bring together fire and flax.

90 You know what this example means.

91 **This is al and som**   this is the sum total (of what he said).

92 **weddyng in freletee**   marrying because the flesh is weak (i.e. unable to resist sexual urges).

93 **Freletee clepe I**   frailty I call it.

93–4 **but if that he and she... in chastitee**   if he and she (the married couple) led all their lives in chastity.

95 **I graunte it wel**   I am willing to accept this.
I have noon envie   I have no ill-will.

96 If abstinence takes precedence over marrying again.

97 It pleases them to be pure, body and soul (referring to lines 93–94).

98 With regard to my own position I will not make such a boast.

99–100 **a lord... al of gold**   a lord does not have every vessel in his household made of gold.

101 **been of tree**   are made of wood.
and doon hir lord servyse   and still give good service to their lord.

102 God calls people to him in various ways.

103 And everyone has a particular gift of his own from God.

104 **as hym liketh shifte**   as it pleases him to provide.

106 **continence eek with devocion**   abstinence also when undertaken out of religious devotion.

107 **that of perfeccion is welle**   that is the source of perfection.

108–10 Did not command every man should go and sell everything he had and give it to the poor and in such a way follow in his footsteps.

111 He spoke to those who wished to live perfect lives.

113–14 I will devote the prime of my life to the pleasures of sexual fulfilment in marriage.

The Wife's 'biological' argument: Lines 115–162

The Wife now asks why we are endowed with reproductive organs, and argues it could be said that they were made for both the discharge of urine and in order to tell male from female, and for no other reason. Her own experience tells her that this is not so. She says that they were made for both practical use and to experience the delights of intercourse, in such ways as do not displease God (she adds this so as not to offend the clerics). She is quick to point out that she is not advocating that all should feel obliged to indulge in the delights of marriage. She says that respect should be given to chastity, and she in no way wants to speak ill of virginity. She, however, will have a husband, although she will retain power over her own body and not relinquish it to her husband – rather, her husband will be her slave.

115–16 **to what conclusion... of generacion**   for what purpose were the reproductive organs made.

117   And human beings made in such a perfect way.

119   Interpret whoever will and argue whichever way. *Glose* literally means 'interpret the scriptures'. The Wife is making a point about scholars who interpret the scriptures to support their own arguments.

120–1 **That they.../ Of uryne**   that they were made for the discharge of urine.

121   **and oure bothe thynges smale**   that both our little things.

122   Were also created to tell a female from a male.

124   Experience knows well it is not so.

125   **clerkes**   clerics or scholars.
   wrothe   angry.

127–8 **for office and for ese/ Of engendrure**   for purging urine and the pleasure of procreation.

129–30 Why else should men write down in their books that a man should yield to his wife and her debt? (i.e. he should pay her what he owes her). See I Corinthians 7:3, 'Let the husband render unto the wife due benevolence'.

131 Now with what should he make his payment.

132 **sely instrument**   blessed tool (i.e. penis). In Chaucer's time *sely* had several meanings including 'innocent', 'simple', 'humble'. The Wife's use of it here can create an affectionate, approving tone towards the *sely instrument*. The associated meanings of 'blessed' and 'innocent' suggest her view that there is nothing morally wrong with sexual intercourse.

133–4 Therefore they were made as part of human beings not only to pass urine but also for procreation (intercourse).

135–7 But I do not say that every person who has such equipment as I just mentioned must go and use it for procreation.

138 If that were the case we would show chastity little regard.

139 **mayde**   virgin.

140 **sith that**   since.

142 I will feel no ill-will towards virginity.

143–4 Let them (i.e. virgins) be like bread made from pure wheat flour, and let us wives be called barley-bread (barley-bread was a coarse, less refined bread but nevertheless nutritious).

145 **Mark**   St Mark (a confusion of reference – it is St John who refers to barley loaves).

146 **refresshed**   fed.

147 In such estate as God has called us to.

148 **precius**   precious, fastidious, overly refined.

149 **In wyfhod**   literally, in wifehood – i.e. as a wife.
instrument   i.e. her sexual parts (see line 132).

150 **frely**   freely, without restriction, generously.

151 **daungerous**   reluctant, unwilling, aloof (the modern sense of 'dangerous' did not develop until later).

152 **eve and morwe**   night and day.

153 **Whan that hym list come forth**   when it pleases him to come.
and paye his dette   see line 130.

154 **I wol nat lette**   I will not give way.

155 Who shall be both my debtor and slave.

156–7 **tribulacion.../ Upon his flessh**   tribulations of the flesh (see I Corinthians 7:28 'But and if thou marry, thou hast not sinned; and if a virgin marry, she hath not sinned. Nevertheless such shall have trouble in the flesh...').

158–9 I have the power over his own body during my life, and not he.

The Wife is referring to St Paul, I Corinthians 7:4, in which he says 'The wife hath not power of her own body, but the husband: and likewise also the husband hath not power of his own body, but the wife'. Note how the Wife uses her references to the scriptures very selectively. She conveniently ignores the first part of the reference.

160 **Right thus**   just as.
161 And commanded our husbands to love us well (see Ephesians 5:25, 'Husbands, love your wives'.
162 This opinion is very much to my liking.

The Pardoner interrupts her: Lines 163–192

The Pardoner interrupts the Wife and tells her that he had intended to marry soon but having heard the Wife speak of how she will have her husband as a slave, he has been put off the idea of marriage. She tells him to listen to what she has to say; she has not yet begun her tale of the tribulation that is to be found in marriage. She continues, asking the rest of the company not to be offended, as she is only speaking to entertain.

163 Up leapt the Pardoner, there and then.
165 **Ye been**   you are.
    in this cas   on this subject.
166 **wedde a wyf**   marry a woman. In Middle English the word *wyf* can sometimes mean wife, sometimes woman.
167 Why should I pay such a high price for it?
168 I would rather have no wife to marry this year (i.e. I would rather not marry at all).
169 **Abyde!**   wait.
170 **drynken of another tonne**   drink of another barrel.
171 **Er that I go**   before I've finished.
    savoure wors than ale   taste worse than ale.
172 **toold thee forth**   carried on telling you.
174 **expert in al myn age**   expert all my life.

175 **myself have been the whippe**   I have held the whip hand.

176 **maystow**   you can (literally 'may thou').
chese   choose.

176–7 **wheither thou... shal abroche**   whether you wish to sip
more from the cask I shall broach.

178 **Be war**   be wary, be careful.
er thou to ny approche   before you get too close.

179 **ensamples**   examples or illustrations.
mo than ten   more than ten (i.e. more than just a few).

180–1 The general sense of this proverb from Ptolemy is 'He who
will not be warned by the mistakes of others shall, by his own
mistakes, serve as an example to others'.

182 **Ptholomee**   Ptolemy (renowned astronomer and geographer
who lived in Alexandria in the second century AD).

183 **Almageste**   Ptolemy's best-known work on astronomy.
take it there   learn the lesson there.

186 Tell us your tale and spare nothing because of any man.

187 And teach us young men from your practical experience.

188 **sith it may yow like**   since it may please you.

190 **after my fantasye**   as the inclination takes me.

191 Don't take offence at what I say.

192 For my intention is simply to entertain.

The Wife speaks about her first three husbands and how she handled them: Lines 193–284

The Wife now begins to tell of her first three husbands. These
were rich, old and 'good', although they had difficulty in
fulfilling their obligations to her, by which she means having
sexual intercourse with her. They doted on her but she treated
them badly, constantly quarrelling with them. She then goes on
to tell how she handled them and the techniques she used to keep
them in their place, and catalogues all the things she accused
them of in order to put them on the defensive.

194–5 **As evere... seye sooth**   literally, as ever may I drink wine or ale I shall speak the truth (i.e., if she does not tell the truth, may she never by able to drink wine or ale again).

195 **tho**   those.

198–9 They were hardly able to fulfil the obligation by which they were bound to me (i.e. their sexual obligation in marriage).

200 **woot**   know.
pardee!   by God (from the French 'par Dieu').

202 **swynke**   work or toil (i.e. in bed).

203 **by my fey**   by my faith.
I tolde of it no stoor   I set no store by it (i.e. she did not care how they felt).

204 They had given me their land and wealth.

205 There was no further need to take any trouble.

206 **doon hem reverence**   be respectful to them.

208 **ne tolde no deyntee**   did not set much value on.

209 **wol bisye hire evere in oon**   will busy herself completely.

210 **ther as she hath noon**   when she has none.

211 **hoolly in myn hond**   completely in my hand.

213 Why should I take the trouble to please them.

214 Unless it was for my profit or pleasure?

215 **I sette hem so a-werke**   I set them so to work.

216 **songen**   sang (or wailed).
Weilawey   alas.

217–18 The bacon was not for them, I'm sure, that some men have at Dunmow in Essex. This is a reference to the old custom in the village of Dunmow, near Chelmsford in Essex, that a side of bacon is awarded to a married couple who have been married a year and can swear that they have never quarrelled or regretted marrying their partner.

219 **governed**   managed.
after my lawe   in my own way.

220 **ful blisful was and fawe**   was only too happy, eager.

221 **gaye thynges**   nice things.
fayre   fair or market.

222 **faire**   pleasantly.

223 **God it woot**   God knows.
spitously   spitefully, cruelly, relentlessly.

224 **herkneth**   listen.

hou I baar me proprely   how well I handled things.

225 **that kan understonde**   who know what I mean.

226 You should make false charges against them (i.e. the Wife is suggesting that one of her techniques for handling husbands is to put them in the wrong).

227–8 There is no man who can swear (i.e. make false oaths) and lie like a woman can.

229 **by wyves**   about wives.

230 Except when they have acted misguidedly.

231 **if that she kan hir good**   if she knows what's good for her (i.e. what is in her best interests).

232 Deceive him into believing the *cow* (chough) is *wood* (mad). The Wife is referring to a popular story where a wife is unfaithful to her husband in front of a bird (a chough) that can talk. The bird tells the husband of his wife's unfaithfulness but the wife manages to convince her husband that the bird is lying and is mad.

233–4 **And take... hir assent**   and call her own maid as witness.

235 **kaynard**   fool.
is this thyn array?   is this how you carry on (i.e. is this how you treat me).

236 **gay**   smartly dressed (note that this word can be used in several different senses).

237 **overal ther she gooth**   everywhere she goes.

238 **I have no thrifty clooth**   I have no decent clothes.

239–41 Note how the Wife is illustrating how she puts her husband in the wrong. Here she is insinuating that he is interested in other women.

239 **dostow**   do you.

240 **Artow**   are you.

241 **What rowne ye**   why are you whispering.
Benedicite!   a common exclamation with the sense of 'God bless us' or 'heaven bless us'.

242 **lecchour**   lecher.
lat thy japes be!   give up your tricks.

243 **gossib**   friend (to gossip with).

244 Without my doing anything to deserve it you scold me like the devil.

245 If I walk or stroll towards his house.

247 **on thy bench** benches were the normal form of seating.
   with yvel preef! may evil take you.
248 **greet meschief** a great misfortune or disadvantage.
249 **for costage** because of the expense (a poor woman would have no dowry).
250 **heigh parage** high rank or birth.
251 **seistow** you say.
   tormentrie torment or torture.
252 **malencolie** melancholy or moods.
253 **verray knave** complete scoundrel.
254 **every holour wol hire have** every lecher wants to have her.
255 She won't stay chaste very long.
256 When she is assailed on every side.
258 **shap** shape (i.e. a pleasing figure).
   fairnesse beauty.
259 **outher** either.
260 **gentillesse** refined manners.
   daliaunce playful love-making.
262 And so we all go to the devil according to you.
263–4 You say that nobody can hold a castle wall when it is been attacked from all sides for so long.
265 **foul** ugly.
266 **Coveiteth** covets (wants).
267 **as a spanyel** like a spaniel.
268 **hire to chepe** to do business with her.
269–70 There is no goose so grey on the lake, according to you, who will do without a mate.
271 **for to welde** to control.
272 Something that no man would willingly keep hold of.
273 **lorel** rogue, wretch.
275 **that entendeth unto** who intends to go to.
276 **wilde thonder-dynt** violent clap of thunder.
   firy levene fiery lightning.
277 May your withered neck be broken.
278 **droppyng houses** leaking houses.
279 **chidyng** nagging.
280 **a** an exclamation similar to 'ah!'.
281 What ails such an old man to complain so much?
282 **vices** defects.

283 **Til we be fast**   until we have made ourselves secure (through marrying).

284 **Wel may that be**   that might well be.
   a proverbe of a shrewe   a saying of a wicked man.

The Wife describes further her techniques for dealing with her husbands: Lines 285–361

There follows a list of the things that the Wife accused her old husbands of unfairly charging her with, such as not being happy unless her beauty is constantly praised, she is well-dressed, a big fuss is made over her birthday, and so forth. She also accused them of unjustly being suspicious that she is attracted to the young clerk, Jankyn. The Wife also complained that they hid from her the keys to their money chests, and told them that they can have control of their money or her body but not both. It is obvious, though, that she did not intend to let them have control over either. She liked to go out nicely dressed and accused them of spying on her and trying to prevent her from socializing.

285 **hors, and houndes**   horses and hounds.

286 **assayed at diverse stoundes**   tried out at different times (i.e. before buying).

287 **Bacyns, lavours**   different kinds of basin.

288 **al swich housbondrye**   all such household goods.

289 **pottes**   household crockery.
   clothes   cloth, material (rather than clothing).
   array   clothing.

290–1 **But folk… be wedded**   but wives are not tested until they are married.

291 **olde dotard shrewe!**   you critical old fool.

292 **seistow**   you say.

293–6 You also say that it displeases me if you do not praise my beauty and always gaze intently at my face and call me 'gracious madam' wherever we go.

297-8 **And but thou make... I was born**   and unless you give me a
party on my birthday.

298 **make me fressh and gay**   possibly meaning making her feel
young and happy, or perhaps, a reference to providing her
with new, bright clothes to wear.

299 **And but thou do**   and if you don't.
norice   nurse.

300 **chamberere**   chambermaid.
bour   bedroom, or private room.

301 **fadres folk**   father's relatives.
allyes   friends or associates.

303 **oure apprentice Janekyn**   we shortly learn that Jankyn
became her fifth and latest husband.

304 **crispe heer**   curly hair.

305 **squiereth me bothe up and doun**   escorts me everywhere.

306 You have become falsely suspicious.

307 I wouldn't want him even if you were to die tomorrow.

308 **why hydestow**   why do you hide.
with sorwe   a mild curse similar in meaning to 'may sorrow
take you' or 'may the devil take you' or 'blast you'.

310 **my good as wel as thyn**   my property as well as yours.

311 **wenestow make an ydiot of oure dame?**   do you suppose
you can make a fool of me. *Oure dame* is the lady of the
house – the Wife is referring to herself here.

312 **Seint Jame**   St James. His shrine at Compostella was one of
the four major medieval centres of pilgrimage. We are told in
the *General Prologue* (line 466) that the Wife had visited this
shrine.

313 **Thou shalt nat bothe**   you will not be both.
thogh that thou were wood   even though you may be mad.

314 Be master of my body and my property.

315 **That oon thou shalt forgo**   you will give up one of them.
maugree thyne yen   in spite of your eyes (i.e. no matter how
closely you watch me).

316 What does it help to ask questions about me or spy on me?

317 **trowe**   believe.
loke   lock.
chiste   chest or strong-box.

318 **wher thee liste**   wherever you wish.

319 **Taak youre disport**   take your amusement.
    leve   believe.
    talys   ales or gossip.

320 **Alys**   an abbreviation of her name, Alisoun (see line 804).

321 **taketh kep or charge**   watches carefully.

322 **we wol ben at oure large**   we like to be free to act as we
wish.

324 **Daun**   master.

324–5 **Ptholome... Almageste**   see notes to lines 182–3.

327 Who doesn't care who holds the world in his hand (i.e. in
terms of wealth).

329 If you have enough, what should you care.

330 How well other people are doing.

332 **queynte**   a term used by Chaucer and his contemporaries for
the female sexual parts, or vagina. Chaucer's term did not
have the same shock value as the modern English four-letter
word related to this *queynte*; in modern British English, the
slang term 'fanny' may provide a parallel here. The Wife
certainly intends to make a clear sexual reference and the
word would undoubtedly have surprised, if not slightly
shocked, her fellow pilgrims.

333–4 He is too great a miser who would refuse to allow another
man to light a candle in his lantern.

335 **He shal have never the lasse light**   he won't have any less
light.

336 If you have enough there is no need to complain.

337 **make us gay**   get dressed up.

338 **precious array**   fine adornments.

339 **is peril of oure chastitee**   puts our chastity in danger.

340 **thou most enforce thee**   you have to push your point.

341 **the Apostles**   St Timothy's. See I Timothy 2:9: '... that
women adorn themselves in modest apparel, with
shamefacedness and sobriety; not with broided hair, or gold,
or pearls, or costly array'.

342 **habit**   clothing.

343 **apparaille yow**   dress yourself.

344 **in tressed heer**   with braided hair.
    gay perree   bright jewellery.

345 **ne**   nor.

346–7 Neither to your text nor your rubric will I give so much as a gnat.

349–50 For if someone would singe a cat's skin (fur) then the cat will stay at home.

351 **slyk and gay**   sleek and attractive.

353 **er any day be dawed**   before the day has dawned.

354 To show off her fur and go caterwauling (howling and looking for a mate).

356 I will run out to show off my clothes. *Borel* is a coarse woollen cloth not at all in keeping with the kind of clothes the Wife is referring to. It is likely that she is being sarcastic here.

357 **what helpeth thee**   how does it help you, what use is it to you.

358 **Argus**   in Greek mythology a huge creature with a hundred eyes who was sent by Zeus to guard his mistress, Io.

359 **warde-cors**   bodyguard.

360 **he shal nat kepe me but me lest**   he shall not restrain me unless it pleases me.

361 **Yet koude I make his berd**   yet I could outwit him.
so moot I thee!   literally, so may I prosper.

The Wife achieves dominance: Lines 362–451

The Wife continues with her description of how she achieved dominance over her husbands. She kept them in hand by telling them things they said when they were drunk, such as comparing a woman's love to hell and wild fire and that a wife destroys a husband just as insects destroy a tree. She had made all this up, though, in order to put them in the wrong. She harried them constantly and refused them in bed until they had given her whatever it was she wanted. She tells the others that she always came off best in the end and got her way.

364 **no wight may endure the ferthe** nobody can endure the fourth (see Proverbs 30:21).

365 **Jhesu shorte thy lyf!** may Christ shorten your life.

366 **Yet prechestow** yet you still preach on.

367 Is reckoned to be one of these misfortunes.

368 Are there no other kinds of comparison.

369 **likne** compare.

370 Other than a poor wife be one of them.

372 To barren land where water cannot last.

373 **wilde fyr** wild fire (a fierce, raging fire).

375 **that brent wole be** that will be burnt (i.e. that is inflammable).

376 **right as wormes shende a tree** just as insects destroy a tree.

378 **been to wyves bonde** are bound to wives.

380 I firmly kept my old husbands in hand.

381 **in hir dronkenesse** in their drunkenness.

382–3 And it was all false but I got Jankyn and my niece to say they had heard it.

385 **Ful giltelees** although they were innocent.
    pyne pain or suffering.

386 **byte and whyne** literally bite and whine (i.e. the Wife would show irritation and snap at her husbands or whine for attention).

387 **pleyne** complain.
    and yit was in the gilt and yet I was in the wrong.

388 Or else often I would have been ruined.

389–90 The Wife liked to get her complaint in first.

390 **werre** literally, war (i.e. argument).
    ystynt ended.

391 **ful glade to excuse hem blyve** very glad to excuse themselves quickly.

392 **nevere agilte hir lyv** had never been guilty in their lives.

393 I would accuse them of having other women.

394 **for syk** because of illness.
    unnethes myghte they stonde they could hardly stand up.

395 **tikled I his herte** delighted his heart (note how the Wife switches from talking about her husbands in the plural to talking about one in particular).

396 **Wende** believed.

I hadde of hym so greet chiertee!   I had so great an affection for him.

398 **dighte**   had sexual relations with.

399 **colour**   pretence.

hadde I many a myrthe   I had many a laugh.

400 **al swich wit**   all such cunning (or ingenuity).

401 **spynnyng**   the art of spinning wool. Spinning and ale-making were two key occupations of unmarried, middle-class women in the Middle Ages – hence the term 'spinster'. It is worth noting, however, that some interpret this as meaning 'spinning' tales.

401–2 **God hath yive... they may lyve**   God has given to women as part of their nature.

403 **o**   one.

avaunte me   boast.

404 In the end I got the better of them in every way.

405 **By sleighte, or force**   by cunning or force.

406 **continueel murmur or grucchyng**   continual muttering or grumbling.

407 **Namely abedde**   particularly in bed.

hadden they meschaunce   they had a bad time of it.

408 **do hem no plesaunce**   give them no pleasure.

409 **abyde**   stay.

411 **maad his raunson**   paid his ransom.

412 **suffre hym do his nycetee**   allow him to have his treat.

414 **Wynne whoso may**   make whatever profit you can.

al is for to selle   everything is for sale.

415 You cannot lure a hawk with an empty hand.

416 **For wynnyng**   for (my own) profit.

417 And pretend to be sexually aroused.

418 Even though I never did enjoy bacon (the Wife is using a euphemism expressing her distaste for the sexual relations she had with her old husbands).

419 **evere I wolde hem chide**   would go on and on nagging them (her distaste for them sexually caused her ill-tempered nagging).

420 Even if the Pope had sat beside them.

421 I would not spare them even at their own table.

422 **quitte hem word for word**   answered them back.

424 **testament**   will and testament.

425 I do not owe them a word that has not been repaid.

426 **by my wit**   by my ingenuity.

427 **moste yeve it up**   had to give it up.

428 Or we would have never been at rest.

429 **wood leon**   mad lion.

430 **faille of his conclusion**   not get his way.

431 **Goode lief**   a term of endearment such as 'darling' or 'my love'.

    taak keep   look or take note.

432 **How mekely looketh**   how docile looks (the Wife is suggesting to her husband that he should be as docile as their sheep, Wilkyn).

433 **ba**   kiss.

435 **sweete spiced conscience**   a scrupulous sense of doing what is right.

436 The Wife is scornfully telling her husband that he should practise what he preaches.

437 **Suffreth alwey**   be resigned to your suffering.

438 **And but ye do**   and if you don't (literally: unless you do).

439 **it is fair to**   it's a fine thing to.

440 **moste bowen, doutelees**   must certainly give way.

442 **ye moste been suffrable**   you must be the most tolerant.

443 **grucche thus and grone**   grumble and groan.

444 Is it because you want to keep my body all to yourself.

445 **every deel**   every part of it.

446 **Peter!**   by Saint Peter.

    shrewe   curse.

447 *bele chose*   pretty thing (another euphemism for her sexual parts). This time, the phrase has a courtly, more refined tone to it in contrast to the vernacular *queynte* of line 444.

447–8 The Wife is saying that if she sold her sexual favours (i.e. became a prostitute) she could walk around as fresh and bright as a rose (i.e. finely dressed).

449 But I will keep it for your own private appetite.

450 **to blame**   in the wrong.

451 Such was the kind of arguments we had between us.

**CITY AND ISLINGTON
SIXTH FORM COLLEGE
283-309 GOSWELL ROAD**

The Wife's fourth husband: Lines 452–502

The Wife now tells of her fourth husband. He was very different from her first three husbands as he enjoyed the good life and had a mistress. She remembers that she was young, stubborn and full of hot passion and loved to dance and sing and drink wine. However, she was very jealous because her husband enjoyed himself with other women and she made his life hell. He died when the Wife returned from Jerusalem and she didn't waste much money on his funeral.

453 **revelour** reveller (someone who enjoys a dissolute, high-living lifestyle).

454 **paramour** mistress.

455 **ful of ragerye** highly sexed.

456 **Stibourn and strong** stubborn and strong-willed.

joly as a pye merry as a magpie.

457 **harpe smale** a small harp (held on the lap rather than placed on the floor).

458 **ywis** indeed.

460 **cherl** ugly brute.

swyn pig.

461 That beat his wife to death with a stick (*biraft* literally means 'robbed').

462 **For** because.

463 He would not have frightened me away from drink.

464 **Venus** the goddess of love (i.e. after wine, sex was foremost in the Wife's mind).

465 **al so siker** just as surely.

engendreth brings forth.

466 **likerous** lecherous (lechery is one of the seven deadly sins).

467 When women are drunk they have no defence (against lecherous seducers).

470 **jolitee** vivacity. Again there are sexual overtones.

471 It warms me to the bottom of my heart.

472 **it dooth myn herte boote** it does my heart good.

473 That I have enjoyed life to the full in my time.

474 **al wole envenyme**   poisons everything.

475 **me biraft**   robbed me of.
pith   vigour.

476 **Lat go**   let it go.

478 **bren**   bran.

479 **fonde**   try.

481 **I hadde in herte greet despit**   my heart was full of anger.

482 **of any oother had delit**   had enjoyed sexual relations with
other women.

483 **quit**   repaid.
Seint Joce   Judocus, a Breton saint.

484 Literally, I made him a cross of the same wood (i.e. a
proverbial phrase similar to our expression 'I gave him a taste
of his own medicine').

485 **Nat of my body**   not with my body.

486 **I made folk swich cheere**   I made myself attractive to other
people.

487 **grece**   fat. Another proverbial phrase like the one in line 484
– similar to 'I made him stew in his own juice'.

488 **verray jalousye**   sheer jealousy.

489 **in erthe**   on earth (i.e. while he was alive).

490 **his soule be in glorie**   his soul is in heaven.

491 **God it woot**   God knows.
song   cried out (as in pain).

492 Whenever his shoe pinched him painfully (i.e. when his
marriage caused him pain).

493 **no wight**   nobody.

494 **wise**   ways.
soore   sorely or grievously.
twiste   tormented.

496 **lith ygrave**   lies buried.
roode beem   the cross-beam in a church.

497 **Al**   although
curyus   ornate.

498 **Daryus**   Darius, King of Persia in the ancient world.

499 **Appelles**   a Jewish craftsman who is thought to have built
the tomb of Darius.
subtilly   very skilfully.

500 **It nys but wast** it would have been a waste.
 preciously at great expense.
502 **cheste** coffin.

The Wife tells of Jankyn, her fifth husband: Lines 503–626

She says that he was the most unkind of all her husbands and he used to beat her and yet she loved him best of all, because it was not easy to make him love her. She reflects on how women long for the thing that is not easily had and explains how she fell in love with him while her fourth husband was still alive. He had once been a scholar at Oxford, and she was immediately physically attracted to the young man, who was half her age. Shortly afterwards her fourth husband died and she was left free to pursue her flirtation with Jankyn. She briefly interrupts her story with an account of her horoscope, which, she say, explains her lusty and volatile nature.

505 **the mooste shrewe** the most cruel (of all five husbands).
506 **al by rewe** one by one.
508 **fressh and gay** energetic and lively.
509 **therwithal** moreover.
 glose flatter.
510 *bele chose* see note to line 447.
511 That even though he had beaten me on every bone.
512 **anon** straight away.
513 **trowe** believe.
 for that just because.
514 Was hard for me to please as a lover.
516 **queynte fantasye** strange idea.
517 Whatever thing we cannot easily have.
518 We will cry and crave for all day long.
519 **thyng** something.
520 **Preesse on us faste** press something on us insistently.
521 Show us indifference and out will come all our merchandise.

522 **Greet prees**   a big crowd.

maketh deere ware   makes expensive wares (i.e. pushes the prices up).

523 **to greet cheep**   too great a bargain.

holde at litel prys   held at little value.

526 **no richesse**   not for his wealth (the reason she had married her other husbands).

527 **som tyme**   at one time.

clerk of Oxenford   scholar at Oxford.

528 **scole**   university.

wente at hom to bord   moved in as a boarder or lodger.

529 **gossib**   close friend.

531 **myn herte**   my innermost thoughts.

my privetee   my private affairs.

532 **Bet**   better.

533 **biwreyed**   divulged.

my conseil al   all my secrets.

538 **toold his conseil every deel**   told every little bit of his secret.

540 **made his face often reed and hoot**   often made him blush hotly.

541 **For verray shame**   out of sheer shame.

543 **so bifel**   so it happened.

in a Lente   at Lent (a time for religious contemplation and abstinence).

545 For I always loved to be merry and enjoy myself.

547 **to heere sondry talys**   to hear all the gossip.

548 **That Jankyn clerk**   that student, Jankyn.

Alys   short for Alisoun, the name of her friend.

551 **leyser**   opportunity.

pleye   to enjoy myself.

552 And to see and be seen.

553 **Of lusty folk**   by lively folk (the implication being that the Wife wants to be seen by lively, fun-loving young men).

553-4 **What wiste... shapen for to be**   how could I know where my good luck (in meeting a lover) was going to come.

555 **I made my visitaciouns**   I went on trips.

556 **vigilies**   vigils. These were meant to be solemn, religious events involving fasting and keeping watch all night. However, they were often turned into occasions for merrymaking and

socializing – hence their attraction for the Wife.

processiouns processions.

557 **prechyng** sermons.

pilgrimages such as the one she is on at the moment.

558 **pleyes of myracles** miracle plays. These dramatized key episodes from the Bible and were performed in the open air in spring and summer. They were very popular in the Middle Ages.

mariages weddings would obviously hold many attractions for the Wife and would give her a great opportunity to socialize and enjoy herself.

559 **wered** wore.

gaye scarlet gytes bright scarlet gowns.

560 **wormes** grubs.

motthes moths.

mytes mites.

561 **Upon my peril** on my oath (i.e. on peril of my soul).

frete hem never a deel consumed them not one bit (i.e. the moths never had a chance to eat her best clothes because she was always wearing them, going out and socializing).

562 **wostow why?** do you know why.

565 **swich daliance** such flirtatious banter.

566 **my purveiance** my future plans.

567 **seyde hym** told him.

568 **wydwe** widow.

569 **for no bobance** not wanting to boast.

570 I was never without some plan for the future.

572 **I holde** I believe.

573 **sterte to** run to. The Wife clearly likes to keep her options open.

574 **faille** fail (or is unavailable).

is al ydo all is lost.

575 **I bar hym on honde** I led him to believe.

he hadde enchanted me he had bewitched me (by means of a love-potion).

576 **My dame** possibly a reference to Dame Alisoun, her friend, or possibly her mother, or Venus.

soutiltee trick or tactic (literally: subtlety).

577 **mette** dreamt.

578 **He wolde han slayn me** he was going to kill me.
upright flat on my back.

581 **bitokeneth** signifies. A popular belief in the Middle Ages
was that there was a symbolic association between blood and
gold – a reminder of the Wife's wealth.

582–3 All this was completely untrue, I didn't dream it at all, I was
following my Dame's teaching. By telling Jankyn of this
fictitious dream she is employing the tricks and tactics taught
to her by her 'Dame'.

585 **what I shal seyn** what I was going to say.

587 **beere** bier (the moveable frame a coffin is placed on).

588 **algate** continuously.
made sory cheere behaved as if I was grieving.

589 As wives must do because it is customary.

590 **coverchief** cloth head covering.
visage face.

591 But because I was already provided with another mate.

592 **smal** little.
I undertake I assure you.

593 **born a-morwe** carried the next day.

594 **for hym maden sorwe** mourned for him.

595 **tho** those.

598 **clene and faire** shapely and attractive.

599 That I gave my heart to him completely.

600 **trowe** believe.
twenty wynter oold twenty years old.

602 **I hadde alwey a coltes tooth** I still had my youthful nature
and desires (*coltes tooth* is the first set of teeth in a young
horse).

603 **Gat-tothed** gap-toothed (with widely spaced front teeth).
This feature is mentioned in the *General Prologue*, line 468,
and was believed to indicate a lecherous nature.

604 I had the print and seal of Saint Venus. The Wife's references
reflect a blend of Christian and pagan beliefs popular in the
Middle Ages. They are based on medieval beliefs about
astrology, that the positions of planets and stars determine
the characters of individuals. The Wife's ruling planet was
Venus, to which her desires and lecherousness are attributed,
but Mars is also present (see lines 610 and 612–613), which is

seen as a malignant influence giving rise to her difficult, aggressive moments.

606 **wel bigon**   well provided for.

608 *quoniam*   you know what (another of the Wife's euphemisms).
myghte be   there could be.

609 **al Venerien**   entirely under the influence of Venus.

610 **Marcien**   influenced by Mars.

611 **my lust, my likerousnesse**   my desire and lecherousness.

612 **sturdy hardynesse**   obstinate boldness.

613 The Wife was born when the sign of Taurus, which is one of the houses of Venus, was in the ascendant, but Mars was also in the sign at that time (see note to line 604).

615 **ay**   always.

616 According to my horoscope.

617 **I koude noght withdrawe**   I could not withhold.

618 **My chambre of Venus**   my chamber of Venus – another of the Wife's euphemisms for her sexual parts.

619 **Martes mark upon my face**   the mark of Mars on my face; a ruddy complexion (see *General Prologue* line 458), which was thought to be due to the influence of Mars.

622–3 I was never discreet in my love-making but always followed my appetite.

624 **Al were he**   whether he be.

625 **I took no kep**   I did not mind.
so that   as long as.

626 **degree**   social rank.

The Wife marries Jankyn and the problems begin: Lines 627–787

Within a month of her fourth husband's death the Wife had married Jankyn and she had signed over to him all her land and possessions. However, their relationship was a stormy one and he once struck her so hard on the head for tearing a page out of one of his books that she became deaf in one ear. He constantly read out parts from his anti-feminist books about 'wicked wives' and how the fall of mankind is all the fault of women.

628 **joly** this word can have a variety of meanings e.g. merry, cheerful, spirited, playful, lusty, amorous, attractive. All of these meanings capture the flavour here.

hende another word that can have a variety of meanings e.g. courteous, gracious, pleasant, lovely, as well as having sexual connotations in the sense of 'handy'. It was a term often used to describe young men who were well-practised in paying court to ladies.

629 **with greet solempnytee** with an elaborate formal ceremony and celebration.

630 **lond and fee** land and possessions.

631 That had ever been given to me previously.

632 **repented me ful soore** I regretted it bitterly.

633 He would not allow me to have any of the things I wanted.

634 **smoot** hit.

lyst ear (note the difference in meaning from line 633).

635 **For that** because.

rente tore.

leef page.

636 **strook** blow.

myn ere wax al deef my ear became totally deaf (the Wife's deafness is mentioned in the *General Prologue*, see line 446).

637 **Stibourn** stubborn.

638 **jangleresse** a female chatterbox and gossip.

639 **And walke I wolde** and I would walk.

640 **although he had it sworn** although he had sworn that I should not.

641 **often tymes wolde preche** would often preach.

642 And lecture me from Roman history.

643 **Symplicius Gallus** this story and the following one are from the writings of Valerius Maximus.

644 **for terme of al his lyf** for the rest of his life.

645 **Noght but for** only because.

open-heveded bare-headed (literally: open headed).

646 **upon a day** one day.

648 **someres game** a summer game (a summer festival).

649 **wityng** knowledge.

651 **That ilke** that particular.

652 **comandeth and forbedeth faste**   orders and strictly forbids.

653 **go roule aboute**   go wandering about.

655 **salwes**   willow branches.

656 **priketh**   spurs on.
falwes   open fields (fallow ground).

657 **go seken halwes**   go on pilgrimages (literally: go visiting shrines).

658 **Is worthy to been**   deserves to be.
galwes   gallows.

659 **But al for noght**   but all for nothing (i.e. Jankyn was wasting his time).
I sette noght an hawe   I didn't give so much as a *hawe* (literally, a hawthorn berry, used here as a symbol of worthlessness). A modern equivalent might be 'I didn't give a fig'.

660 **n'of his olde sawe**   nor of his old sayings.

661 Nor was I willing to be corrected by him.

662 **that my vices telleth me**   that tells me of my faults.

663 And so, God knows, do more of us than just me.

664 **with me wood al outrely**   absolutely furious with me.

665 I would not give in to him in any way.

666 **seye yow sooth**   tell you truthfully.
Seint Thomas   Saint Thomas (i.e. St Thomas Becket of Canterbury – the destination of the Wife and other pilgrims).

670 **desport**   amusement.

671 **cleped**   called.
Valerie and Theofraste   both are anti-marriage texts.

672 **he lough alwey ful faste**   he always laughed.

673 **somtyme**   once.

674 **highte**   was called.
Seint Jerome   an early Christian scholar.

675 Who wrote a treatise against Jovinian. His epistle against Jovinian attacks Jovinian's claim that the merits of married people were not necessarily inferior to those of virgins. Jerome's condemnation of women and marriage provided fuel for the anti-feminists.

676 **Tertulan**   Tertullian, an early Christian writer who wrote several treatises extolling the virtues of chastity and monogamy.

677 **Crisippus** another writer mentioned by Jerome in his epistle.
Trotula lived in Salerno in the eleventh century and was
believed to have been a doctor or midwife. She wrote a
number of treatises, one on women's passion and one on
cosmetics.
Helowys Heloise, a distinguished scholar who lived in
France in the twelfth century. She is famous, however, for her
love affair with the renowned philosopher and theologian
Peter Abelard. The affair caused a great scandal and Heloise's
uncle, canon of Notre Dame, Paris, ordered Abelard to be
attacked and castrated for the perceived insult he had given to
their family. Abelard entered a monastery and Heloise became
a nun and eventually prioress. In Chaucer's time the story was
used by anti-feminists as an example of someone of great
promise whose seduction by a woman had caused him great
shame and suffering.

679 **the Parables of Salomon** the Book of Proverbs.

680 **Ovides Art** Ovid's *Ars Amatoria*, which gives advice on
succeeding in love.

681 **in o volume** in a single volume.

683 **leyser and vacacioun** leisure and spare time.

684 **worldly occupacioun** practical matters.

686 **of hem mo legendes and lyves** more stories and
biographies about them.

687 Than there are of good women in the Bible.

688 **trusteth wel** believe me.

690 **But if it be** unless it be.

691 **never the mo** never at all.

692 **leon** lion. The fable by Aesop refers to a painting (in some
versions a sculpture) which depicts a man overcoming a lion.
Looking at it, a lion says that if lions could paint, the lion
would be shown overcoming the man. The Wife explains the
point of her reference in lines 693–695.

694 As scholars have within their private rooms. Originally the
oratory was a small room set aside for private prayers or
meditation. The Wife's comment suggests that she feels they
are shut away from everyday life and experiences.

696 **al the mark of Adam** all men made in the image of Adam.
may redresse could make up for.

697 Those born under the planets of Mercury and Venus
(Mercury was believed to produce scholars; Venus, lovers).

698 Are completely contrary in their beliefs and behaviour.

700 **ryot and dispence**   debauchery and extravagant living.

701 And because of their different natures.

702 The influence of one planet weakens when the other becomes dominant.

703 **desolat**   dejected.

704 In Pisces, where Venus is dominant.

705 And when Venus falls (i.e. loses her influence) Mercury is ascending (i.e. assumes power).

706 **of no clerk is preysed**   is praised by any scholar.

708 **Of Venus werkes**   the works of Venus (i.e. love-making).
worth his olde sho   i.e. his attempts at performing the 'works of Venus' are not worth an old shoe.

709 **writ in his dotage**   writes in his old age. The Wife's implication here is that the writings that she objects to are the product of old scholars writing when they are past it and senile.

710 **kan nat kepe hir mariage**   cannot keep to their marriage vows.

711 After another digression the Wife returns to the story again.

713 **Upon a nyght**   one night.
oure sire   head of the house (her apparent deference to Jankyn as her 'lord and master' is clearly ironic).

717 **For which that**   which was the reason why.

718 **herte blood**   heart's blood, i.e. life.

719 **heere expres of womman**   here explicitly stated about women.

720 **was the los of al mankynde**   brought about the ruin of all mankind.

721 **Tho redde he me**   then he read to me.
how Sampson loste his heres   how Samson lost his hair (see Judges 16:4–22).

722 **lemman**   lover.
kitte   cut.
sheres   scissors or shears.

723 **treson**   treachery.
yen   eyes.

85

725–6   Chaucer may have drawn on Ovid or Boethius for the story of Hercules and Deianira, which tells of how Deianira, the wife of Hercules, unwittingly caused his death by giving him a tonic soaked in poison. In his agony he threw himself onto a fire and died.

727   **No thyng forgat he**   he forgot nothing of.
     care   worry.

728   **Socrates**   a philosopher in ancient Greece (469–399 BC).

729   **Xantippa**   the wife of Socrates, who has become notorious for the bad temper she showed towards him.

730   **sely**   unfortunate.

731   **namoore dorste he seyn**   no more dare he say.

732   **But**   except.
     thonder stynte, comth a reyn   before the thunder stops, down comes the rain.

733   **Phasipha**   Pasiphae, the wife of Minos, King of Crete. In legend, her love affair with a bull led to the birth of the Minotaur – half man, half bull.

734   **For shrewednesse**   as an example of wickedness.
     hym thoughte the tale swete   he thought this was a pleasing tale.

735   **grisly**   dreadful or awful.

736   **likyng**   pleasure or desire.

737   **Clitermystra**   Clytemnestra, in Greek mythology the wife of Agamemnon, King of Mycenae and the Greek leader in the Trojan War. During his absence at the war she had a lover, Aegisthus. When Agamemnon returned from the war she pretended to welcome him but then murdered him in his bath.

738   **falsly**   treacherously.

739   **good devocioun**   great devotion.

740   **for what occasioun**   in what circumstances.

741   **Amphiorax**   Amphiaraus. In Greek mythology his wife Eriphyle was bribed with a gold clasp to give away her husband's hiding place and persuade him to join the expedition against Thebes. The expedition resulted in his death.

743   **Eriphilem**   Eriphyle, wife of Amphiaraus.
     ouche   this term has a wide variety of meanings involving mounted gemstones, e.g. clasp, brooch, necklace, etc.

744 **prively**   secretly.

746 **sory grace**   misfortune (i.e. he was killed).

747 **Lyvia**   influenced by her lover Sejanus to poison her husband Drusus in 23 AD.

Lucye   Lucilia, the wife of the poet Lucretius (first century BC).

750 **on an even late**   late one evening.

751 **Empoysoned**   poisoned.

752 **likerous**   lecherous or full of desire.

753 **for**   so that.

sholde alwey upon hire thynke   should always think about her.

754 **yaf**   gave.

swich a manere love-drynke   such a powerful love potion.

755 **er it were by the morwe**   before the next morning.

756 **algates**   always.

757 **oon Latumvus**   someone called Latumius.

758 **felawe**   friend.

761 **for herte despitus**   from a broken heart (perhaps suggesting that they had killed themselves because their lives were so full of bitterness and pain).

763 **Yif**   give.

765 **Of latter date**   from later times.

767 **lete**   allowed.

lecchour   lover.

dighte hire   to lie with her.

768 While the corpse lay stretched out on the floor.

770 **and thus they had hem slayn**   and in this way they killed them.

771 **han hem yeve**   had given them.

772 **harm**   malice.

than herte may bithynke   than can be imagined.

775 **Bet is**   it is better.

775–7 See Ecclesiasticus 25:23, 'And there is no anger above the anger of a woman. It will be more agreeable to abide with a lion and a dragon than to dwell with a wicked woman.'

777 **usynge for to chyde**   in the habit of nagging.

778 **hye in the roof abyde**   to live high in the loft.

780 **contrarious**   contrary or perverse.

781 They always hate whatever their husbands love.
784 A beautiful woman, unless she be chaste also.
787 **wo** misery.
     pyne pain or distress.

The Wife and Jankyn have their last argument: Lines 788–856

The Wife can bear Jankyn's stories no longer and she tears three pages out of his favourite book and hits him in the face so hard that he falls backwards into the fire. He jumps up and hits the Wife so hard that she lies still on the floor and he thinks that he has killed her. She asks for a last kiss, and as he bends to kiss her and beg her forgiveness she hits him again. In the end they are reconciled and she makes him burn his book there and then. At last she has achieved sovereignty over him; from that day on they never argued again and she was kind and true to him.

She is now ready to begin her tale, but first the Friar laughs as the Wife's prologue has been so long. This provokes an argument with the Summoner, who does not like the Friar, but the Host intervenes and quietens them so that the Wife can begin her tale.

788–9 **fyne/ To reden on** stop reading from.
  790 **Al sodeynly** all of a sudden.
     leves pages.
     plyght torn.
  792 **fest** fist.
     so took hym on the cheke punched him on the cheek so hard.
  793 **fil bakward adoun** fell down backwards.
  794 **up stirte** leapt up.
     wood leoun a furious (mad) lion.
  798 **agast** horrifed.
     fled his way run away.
  799 **swogh** swoon.
     breyde started.

803 **faire**   gently.

804 **suster**   sister (his way of addressing her expresses his concern for her).

806 **it is thyself to wyte**   it was your own fault (literally: it is yourself to blame).

807 **Foryeve it me**   forgive me for it.
biseke   beseech.

808 **eftsoones**   again.

809 **thus muchel am I wreke**   this much am I revenged.

811 **atte laste**   in the end.

812 We came to an agreement between the two of us (i.e. we agreed to make up).

813 **bridel**   bridle. The Wife is speaking metaphorically here; the bridle controls the horse, and so Jankyn has handed control to the Wife.

814 **governance**   control.

816 **brenne**   burn.
anon right tho   straight away, there and then.

818 **By maistrie**   by proving superiority.
soveraynetee   authority (over her husband).

820 **Do as thee lust**   do as you please.

821 **Keep thyn honour**   keep charge of your honour
and keep eek myn estaat   and also take care of my reputation.

822 **debaat**   disagreement.

824 **Ynde**   India.

829 **Frere**   Friar. In the first part of the thirteenth century, friars lived by simple rules of poverty, humility and self-sacrifice in the name of their religion. However, these ideals eventually became corrupted, and by Chaucer's time their reputation had been damaged by their increasing corruption, greed and immorality.

830 **so have I joye or blis**   as I may have joy or bliss (i.e. in heaven).

832 **Somonour**   Summoner, another of the Wife's fellow pilgrims. A summoner was not a cleric but a minor official of the ecclesiastical courts. His main task was to deliver summonses issued by the bishop or archdeacon. Many summoners, however, were corrupt and abused their position, resorting to

blackmail or extortion to extract money from their victims. In Chaucer's time they were disliked and discredited. There is much animosity between Chaucer's Summoner and Friar (as can be seen from their exchange here).

gale   cry out.

833 **Goddes armes two**   by God's two arms.

834 **entremette hym everemo**   forever interfere.

835–6 **a flye... eek mateere**   a fly and also a friar will fall into every dish and everything that is going on (i.e. friars, like flies, are everywhere and will interfere where they are not wanted).

837 **preambulacioun**   the Summoner picks up on the Friar's use of the word *preamble* and creates this word from his half-understood knowledge of Latin. He tries to sound impressive but actually shows his ignorance.

838 **amble, or trotte, or pees, or go sit doun**   wander about, or walk, or shut up, or go and sit down.

840 **Ye, woltow so**   oh yes, is that how you feel about it. (Outwardly the Friar appears charming and affable, but his unpleasant side begins to show here.)

843 **alle the folk shal laughen in this place**   all the people (i.e. the other pilgrims) here will burst out laughing.

844 **bishrewe**   curse.

847 **Sidyngborne**   Sittingbourne.

848 **make thyn herte for to morne**   make you very sorry (literally: make your heart mourn).

849 **woot**   know.

thy pacience is gon   you have lost your temper.

850 **Hooste**   host (Harry Bailey, the landlord of the Tabard Inn, who was elected as leader of the party of pilgrims, organized the story telling and kept everyone in order).

Pees! And that anon!   be quiet at once.

852 **Ye fare**   you are behaving.

that dronken ben of ale   that are drunk with beer.

853 **Do, dame**   go on, madam.

854 **right as yow lest**   as it pleases you.

855 **licence**   permission. Her request for the 'worthy' Friar's permission is likely to be tongue-in-cheek. He has just criticized her *preamble* for being overly long.

The Wife begins her tale: Lines 857–881

She begins her tale in the style of a traditional romance, setting it in the far distant past, in the time of the legendary King Arthur. However, she quickly gets in some thinly veiled insults about the nature of friars and their reputation for dubious morals.

857 **Kyng Arthour**   in legend, he was the British king and head of the Knights of the Round Table. He figures in several medieval romances.

858 **Britons**   possibly Britons, the ancient Celtic British, or a reference to Bretons (again a Celtic people). Various stories, known as the Breton Lays, had Arthurian links and involved lovers who underwent some kind of trial, usually involving supernatural elements, in order to prove their love. *The Franklin's Tale* is an example.

859 **Al**   entirely.
fulfild   filled with.
fayerye   fairies. There was a popular belief in Chaucer's time that fairies existed and possessed magical powers that allowed them to interfere in human affairs.

860 **elf-queene**   the queen of the fairies (Chaucer uses the term 'elf' and 'fairy' interchangeably).

861 **ful**   very.
mede   meadow.

862 **as I rede**   as I understand it.

866 **lymytours**   limiters – friars with a licence to beg for donations for the upkeep of their Dominican, Augustinian, Franciscan or Carmelite orders, within a certain area or district.

867 **serchen**   visit (literally: search).

868 **motes**   specks of dust.

869 **Blessynge**   the Wife's use of the word here is ironical – the friars' main concern was getting as much money out of people as possible.
boures   private rooms.

870 **burghes**   towns.
hye toures   high towers.

871 Villages, barns, cattlesheds and dairies. The Wife's long list of the places friars can be found amusingly emphasizes that they are everywhere, and how intrusive they are.

872 **This maketh that ther ben** this is the reason why there are (literally: this brings it about that there are).

873 For where an elf used to walk.

875 **undermeles** late mornings (from 9 to 12). The meaning of this word changed over time, however, and some interpret it as meaning 'afternoons' here, given its use with *morwenynges* (mornings).

876 **hooly thynges** devotions.

877 **lymytacioun** allotted district.

878 The Wife is being ironical here – by Chaucer's time, friars had developed a reputation for immorality.

880 **incubus** in popular folklore an evil male spirit, believed to have sexual intercourse with sleeping women. This always resulted in the woman becoming pregnant. The Wife is also making a tongue-in-cheek remark about the activities of friars in Chaucer's time and their reputation for immorality.

881 The Wife's implication here is that the friars bring dishonour to the women they seduce.

The knight commits his crime and is given his quest: Lines 882–982

A knight rapes a young maiden, is caught and is taken to the court of King Arthur to be put to death. However, the queen asks for him to be handed over to her and her ladies for punishment. She sets him a quest of finding out what it is that women most desire. He must return in a year and a day and give the correct answer, or he will be executed. The knight sets out on the quest and asks many people, but cannot find two people who agree on the answer. The Wife is able to give her assessment of the answers offered, and so enters the debate herself. She says that the idea that women love to be flattered comes close to the truth.

883 **lusty**   pleasure-loving.
  bacheler   young and inexperienced knight or young squire
  waiting to be knighted. The term indicates his status in the
  chivalric hierarchy and has no reference to his marital
  status.

884 **fro ryver**   from the river. The word *ryver* has falconry
  associations and the phrase could be interpreted as meaning
  the young man was returning from the river where he had
  been hawking for waterfowl.

885 **happed**   it happened.
  allone as he was born   alone as he was borne by his horse
  (i.e. he was riding alone).

886 **hym biforn**   ahead of him.

887 **anon**   immediately.
  maugree hir heed   against her will (literally: in spite of her
  head).

888 **verray force**   violent force.
  rafte   robbed.
  maydenhed   virginity.

889 **oppressioun**   violation (i.e. rape).
  swich clamour   such a clamour (outcry).

890 **pursute**   petition. An obsolete meaning of the word 'pursuit',
  indicating that the people who were outraged petitioned or
  entreated the king to take action against the offender.

891 That the knight should be condemned to death.

893 **Paraventure**   perhaps (literally: by chance).
  swich was the statut tho   such was the law at that time.

894 **But that**   had not.

895 **So longe preyeden**   at such length begged.
  grace   mercy.

896 **in the place**   on the spot.

897 **yaf**   gave.
  al at hir wille   completely at her will (i.e. to do whatever she
  wanted to with him).

898 **chese**   choose.
  spille   put to death.

901 One day when she saw that the time was right.

902–3 You still stand in such a position that you have no guarantee
  that you will keep your life.

906 **Be war** be careful.
    iren axe.
907 **anon** immediately.
908 **yeve thee leve for to gon** give you permission to go.
909 **seche and leere** seek and learn (i.e. to go and find out).
910 A satisfactory answer in this matter.
911 **suretee** pledge.
    er that thou pace before you set off.
912 You will yield up your body in this place (i.e. you will return here and give yourself up).
913 **Wo** sad.
    siketh sighed.
914 **But what!** but then.
    He may nat do al as hym liketh he could not do just as he liked.
915 **he chees hym for to wende** he chose to go off.
917 **as God wolde hym purveye** as God would provide him with.
920 **fynde grace** have the good luck.
922 **he ne koude arryven** he could not find (*arryven* literally means 'arrive at').
    in no coost anywhere (literally: at no coast or country).
924 **accordynge in-feere** in agreement.
925 **richesse** wealth or riches.
926 **honour** respect.
    jolynesse having fun.
927 **riche array** expensive clothes.
    lust abedde sexual pleasures of the bed.
928 And to be widowed and married again often.
929 **oure hertes been moost esed** our hearts are most satisfied.
930 **yflatered and yplesed** flattered and paid attention.
931 **He gooth ful ny the sothe** he goes very near the truth (i.e. the person who says that women love flattery and attention).
933 **attendance** attention.
    bisynesse solicitude.
934 **ylymed** caught.
    bothe moore and lesse i.e. women of all kinds and ranks.
936 **do right as us lest** do just as we please.
937 **repreve us of** reproach us for.
    vice faults or weaknesses.

938 **and no thyng nyce**   and in no way foolish.

939 **ther is noon of us alle**   there is not one among us.

940 **wol clawe us on the galle**   scratch us on a sore place.

941 **That we nel kike**   that we will not kick.

for he seith us sooth   for telling the truth about us.

942 Let him try it and he will find it to be so.

943 For whatever our secret vices.

944 **We wol been holden**   we want to be regarded as.

946 **stable**   faithful.

eek secree   also discreet.

947 **o purpos stedefastly to dwelle**   to keep firmly to one thing at a time.

948 **biwreye**   betray or reveal.

949 **rake-stele**   rake handle (i.e. not worth much).

950 **Pardee**   by God.

konne no thyng hele   can keep nothing secret.

951 **Myda**   Midas.

952 **Ovyde**   Ovid (see line 680).

thynges smale   small matters.

952–82 This is the Wife's version of the story of King Midas as told by Ovid. In Ovid's original, Midas does not reveal his secret to his wife but to his barber. It seems likely that Chaucer made this adaptation to make it better suit the Wife's purpose.

953 **heres**   hair.

954 **eres**   ears.

955 **vice**   deformity.

956 **Ful subtilly**   very skilfully.

957 **ther wiste of it namo**   there was nobody else who knew about it.

960 **disfigure**   disfigurement.

961 **for al this world to wynne**   for the whole world.

962 **nolde**   would not.

vileynye   dishonourable or shameful behaviour (in the Middle Ages the term *vileyn* was applied to someone of low birth, and had disparaging connotations).

963 **so foul a name**   so bad a name.

965 **natheless**   nevertheless.

hir thoughte that she dyde   she thought she would die.

966 If she had to keep the secret for long.
967 It seemed to swell so hard about her heart (i.e. the burden of carrying this secret was unbearable).
968 That necessarily some word must burst out of her.
969 **sith** since.
   dorste dared.
   no man no one.
970 **mareys faste by** nearby marsh.
972 **bitore bombleth** bittern booms (a bittern is a large wading bird that frequents marshland and has a low booming call).
973 She put her mouth down into the water.
977 **al hool** entirely healed.
978 I could not have kept it (the secret) any longer, without a doubt.
979 **thogh we a tyme abyde** though we wait for some time.
980 **Yet out it moot** yet it must come out.
981 **remenant** rest. In Ovid's story the reeds grow and repeat what they have heard, thus revealing Midas's secret.

The knight receives his answer in return for a request: Lines 983–1108

The knight's year has almost ended and he still does not have his answer, but on his way back to Arthur's court he comes across an old woman in the forest. She is unimaginably ugly, but he asks her for help as he is desperate. She agrees to tell him the answer to his question provided he grants her one request. He agrees and they go together to King Arthur's court. There he reveals that the thing that women desire most is to have mastery over men. The court approves of this answer and the knight's life is saved. The old woman then makes her request – that he marries her. He begs to be excused this, but she will not hear of it and he has to marry her and take her to the bridal bed. However, he is revolted by her ugliness, old age and lack of nobility.

983 **specially** particularly concerned.

984 **he myghte nat come therby** he could not come by it.

986 **goost** spirit.

987 **sojourne** linger.

989 **And in his wey** and on his way.

990 **In al this care** with all his worries.

     forest syde edge of a wood or forest.

991–2 Where he saw 24 ladies or more taking part in a dance.

993 **drow** drew.

     ful yerne very eagerly.

996 **nyste** did not know.

997 **bar** bore.

998 **wyf** woman.

999 **wight** person.

     devyse imagine.

1000 **gan ryse** rose to meet.

1001 **heer forth ne lith no wey** this way forward leads nowhere.

1002 **by youre fey** by your faith.

1003 **Paraventure** perhaps.

1004 **kan muchel thyng** know many things.

1005 **My leeve mooder** my dear mother (a general term of address for an older woman of low social class).

1006 **nam but deed** am nothing but dead (i.e. am as good as dead).

     but if that unless.

1008 **Koude ye me wisse** if you could tell me.

1009 **Plight me thy trouthe** give me your solemn word of honour. The medieval concept of *trouthe* here is closely linked to ideas of honour and trust. The promise is completed here, as it is and in the modern marriage service, with a joining of hands. The practice of shaking hands to seal a deal or agreement comes from the same origin.

1010 **requere thee** ask you.

1011 **myght** power.

1012 **er** before.

1013 **I grante** I agree.

1014 **I dar me wel avante** I dare to boast openly.

1015 **sauf** safe.

     I wol stonde therby I will stand by it.

1017 **Lat se**   let us see (i.e. show me).
1018 Who wear a head-scarf or a headdress (the *coverchief* covered the head completely; the *calle* was a small netted cap for the hair, often decorated with small ornaments).
1019 **dar seye nay**   dare deny.
1020 **withouten lenger speche**   without any more talk.
1021 **Tho rowned she a pistel**   then she whispered some piece of information (i.e. the answer to his question).
1024 **holde his day**   kept his promise to return on the appointed day.
　　 hight   promised.
1027 **for that they been wise**   because they are wise (note how the Wife is reinforcing her status as a 'wise' woman here).
1028 **justise**   judge.
1030 **bode appeere**   commanded to appear.
1032 **in audience**   to the assembled people (i.e. publicly).
1033 **worldly**   of this world (i.e. material).
1034 **stille**   silent.
1037 **My lige lady**   my liege lady. The formal address reflects the formality of the court setting and the deference shown by the knight to the queen. The word *lige* became applied to the lord that the 'liege-men' served.
1038 **sovereynetee**   dominion (i.e. authority or power).
1039 **love**   lover.
1040 **for to been in maistrie hym above**   to have mastery over him.
1041 **mooste**   greatest.
　　 thogh ye me kille   though you kill me (i.e. for saying it).
1042 **as yow list**   as you please.
1044 **contraried**   contradicted.
1045 **worthy han**   worthy to have (i.e. worthy to keep).
1046 **up stirte**   up jumped.
1047 **Which that**   whom.
1055 **unto**   for.
1056 **thou woost**   you know.
1057 **sey nay**   deny it.
　　 upon thy fey   upon your faith.
1059 **swich was my biheste**   such was my promise.
1060 **as chees a newe requeste**   choose another request.

1061 **good**   goods (i.e. possessions).
   lat my body go   let my body go (i.e. release me).
1062 **I shrewe us bothe two**   I curse the pair of us.
1063 **foul**   ugly.
1064 **I nolde**   I would not want.
   al the metal, ne for oore   all the metal or the ore (i.e. precious metal).
1065 That is buried under the earth or lying above.
1066 Unless I were your wife and also your beloved.
1067 **dampnacioun**   damnation (notice how quickly the knight has forgotten that the old woman has saved his life).
1068 **nacioun**   family.
1069 **so foule disparaged be**   be so dreadfully disgraced (i.e. by marrying someone so lowly).
1071 **Constreyned was**   was forced.
   he nedes moste hire wedde   he needs must marry her (i.e. he had to marry her).
1074 **for my necligence**   out of neglect.
   I do no cure   I do not take the trouble.
1075 **al th'array**   all the rich display (i.e. the banquets, celebrations etc.)
1076 **feeste**   festivities.
   ilke   same.
1077 **To which thyng**   to the criticism that she has neglected to describe the joyous celebrations.
1078 **nas no joye**   was no joy.
1079 **Ther nas but**   there was nothing but.
   hevynesse   heaviness of heart (i.e. depression and despondency).
1080 **prively**   privately.
   on morwe   in the morning.
1082 **So wo was hym**   he was so miserable.
1084 **abedde ybroght**   brought to bed (by the guests after the wedding).
1085 **walweth**   tossed about restlessly.
1086 **everemo**   all the time.
1088 **Fareth**   behaves.
1090 **dangerous**   indifferent (she is complaining that he is not forthcoming in showing his love for her).

1092 **which that**   who.
1093 **certes**   certainly.
 unright   wrong.
1094 **fare**   behave.
1095 **lyk a man had lost his wit**   like a man who has gone out of his mind.
1097 **amended**   put right.
1100 **loothly**   loathsome.
1101 And, moreover, you come from such lowly stock.
1102 **walwe and wynde**   toss and turn about.
1103 Would to God my heart would burst (i.e. I wish God would let me die).
1107 **If that me liste**   if it pleased me.
 er it were dayes thre   before three days had passed.
1108 So satisfactorily, that you would behave respectfully towards me.

The knight receives lectures on nobility, poverty, and respecting the old: Lines 1109–1216

The old woman lectures the knight on nobility, telling him that it has nothing to do with birth but is to do with how a person behaves. Real nobility comes from God alone, and cannot be handed down simply because of social position. She then reproaches him for his attitude to her poverty. She reminds him that Jesus chose to lead a life of poverty and that to be poor and happy is an honest way to live. Finally, she reminds him that he should respect older people.

1109 **gentillesse**   nobility.
1110 **old richesse**   ancestral wealth.
1111 **That therfore sholden**   that because of this you should be (considered as).
 gentil   noble.
1113 **Looke who**   whoever.

1114 **Pryvee and apert** in private and in public.
  and moost entendeth ay and is always most concerned.
1117 Christ wants us to claim from him our noble qualities.
1118 Not from our ancestors for their inherited wealth.
1119 **yeve** give.
1120 **heigh parage** noble lineage.
1121–4 Yet they cannot bequeath in any way to any one of us their
  virtuous way of living, which caused them to be called
  'gentlemen', and bade us follow them in the same fashion.
1126 **highte Dant** called Dante (the Italian poet, 1265–1321,
  whose major work was the *Divine Comedy*, a long poem which
  portrays hell, purgatory and paradise).
1127 **in swich maner rym is Dantes tale** Dante's comments are
  expressed in rhyme in this manner.
1128–9 **Ful selde... of man** seldom by small branches does man's
  moral integrity (*Prowesse*) rise up. The quotation is from
  Dante's *Purgatoria*, VII, 121.
1130 Wills that we claim our nobility from him.
1132 Except temporal things, that can be damaged or maimed.
1134 **planted natureelly** implanted by nature.
1135 Into the heredity of a family lineage.
1136 **thanne wolde they nevere fyne** then they would never cease.
1137 To do all moral actions of nobility.
1138 **vileynye or vice** villainy or wickedness.
1139 **Taak fyr** take fire.
  ber it in carry it in.
1140 **the mount of Kaukasous** the Caucasus mountains (suggests
  somewhere a long way away).
1141 **go thenne** go away.
1142 **lye and brenne** blaze and burn.
1143 As if twenty thousand men were watching it.
1144 It will hold its natural properties.
1145 **Up peril of my lyf** I swear on my life.
1146 **genterye** noble conduct.
1147 **nat annexed to possessioun** not connected to wealth.
1148–9 **ne doon hir operacioun/ Alwey** do not always behave.
1149 **in his kynde** in its true nature.
1152 **he that wole han pris of his gentrye** he who wants to be
  respected for his high rank.

1153 Because he was born from a noble family.
1155 **nel hymselven**   will not himself.
     do no gentil dedis   do noble deeds.
1156 **Ne folwen**   nor follow.
     deed   dead.
1158 Because villainous and sinful deeds make him a churl. In the
     Middle Ages the terms *vileyn* and *cherl* had two distinct
     meanings. A *vileyn* was tenant in the service of the lord of the
     manor, and was bound to his lord. He was, therefore, low
     down on the social scale. However, the term was often used in
     the more general sense of a low-born person lacking in
     manners, a scoundrel or rascal, and was used as a
     contemptuous form of address. A *cherl* was a more general
     term meaning a person lacking in refinement, education, and
     morals; generally a base and ignorant person.
1159–61 For nobility is but your ancestors' reputation, earned by their
     great virtue, which is foreign to your personality.
1163 **verray gentillesse**   true nobility.
1164 **no thyng**   in no way.
     biquethe us with oure place   bequeathed to us with our
     social position.
1165 **Thenketh**   think.
1166 **thilke**   that.
     Tullius Hostillius   one of the legendary kings of Rome, said
     to have risen from humble origins.
1168 **Reedeth**   read (i.e. study).
     Senek   Seneca (a Roman philosopher who died in 65 AD).
     Boece   Boethius (another philosopher, executed in 525 AD).
1169 **expres**   clearly.
     that it no drede is   that there is no doubt.
1170 That he is noble who does noble deeds (i.e. only he who lives
     his life in a noble way can be considered noble).
1171 **leeve**   dear.
1172 **Al were it that**   although.
     rude   lacking refinement.
1175 **Thanne am I gentil**   then I am (will be) considered a
     gentlewoman (i.e. when I begin to live virtuously and refrain
     from sin).
1176 **weyve**   refrain from.

1177 **And ther as**   and as for.
of poverte me repreeve   reproaching me for being poor.
1179 **wilful**   voluntary.
chees   chose.
1180 **certes**   certainly.
1182 **vicious lyvyng**   shameful way of living.
1183 **Glad**   contented.
an honest thyng   a worthy way to live.
1185 **halt hym payd**   is satisfied with.
1186 **al hadde he nat a sherte**   although he had no shirt.
1187 **coveiteth**   covets.
povre wight   poor person.
1188 For he would have that which it is not in his power to have.
1189 **noght hath**   has nothing.
ne coveiteth have   nor wants anything.
1190 **although ye holde hym but a knave**   even though you may regard him as a peasant.
1191 True poverty sings by its very nature (i.e. true poverty is a naturally joyous condition).
1192 **Juvenal**   a Roman writer of the first century AD.
myrily   jokingly.
1193 **goth by the weye**   goes along the road.
1194 **pleye**   relax.
1195 **hateful good**   both good and bad (i.e. it is not pleasant to be poor but it has spiritual benefits).
1196 A great incentive to hard work.
1197 **amendere**   improver.
sapience   wisdom.
1198 **taketh it in pacience**   accepts it patiently.
1199 **seme alenge**   may seem miserable.
1200 **Possessioun**   a possession (i.e. a thing).
no wight wol chalenge   that no person will challenge you for (i.e. that no one wants to take from you).
1201 **lowe**   humble.
1202 Makes him know his God and also himself.
1203 **a spectacle**   spectacles, eye-glasses.
as thynketh me   so it seems to me.
1204 Through which he may see who his true friends are.
1205 **syn that I noght yow greve**   since I am not doing you any harm.

1206 Do not reproach me any more about my poverty.

1207 **elde** old age.

1208–9 **thogh noon... no book** though there are no authoritative ideas to be found in books.

1209 **ye gentils of honour** you gentlemen of honour.

1210 **doon favour** treat respectfully.

1211 **clepe** call.

for youre gentillesse out of courtesy.

1212 **auctours** authorities (i.e. writers).

as I gesse I should think.

1214 Then you have no fear of being a cuckold.

1215 **filthe** foulness (literally: dirtiness).

eelde old age.

also moot I thee as I hope to thrive.

1216 **wardeyns upon** guardians of.

The old woman gives the knight a choice and he makes his decision: Lines 1217–1264

The old woman then gives the knight a choice. She tells him he could either have her ugly and old but a faithful and humble wife to him, or he could have her young and fair, but take a chance on her faithfulness. The knight thinks about his choice but in the end asks the old woman to choose which of the two would be most pleasant and honourable for both of them. Whatever pleases her will please him. She asks him if that means that she has mastery over him, and he agrees. She asks him to kiss her, and when he pulls the curtain aside he sees that the old woman has been transformed into a young and beautiful woman. They live in perfect joy for the rest of their lives.

1217 **syn I knowe youre delit** since I know what pleases you (i.e. in a sexual sense).

1218 **fulfille youre worldly appetit** satisfy your worldly appetite.

1219 **oon of thise thynges tweye** one of these two things.

1220 **han** have.

1224 **aventure** chance.

repair frequent visits (i.e. of men, because of her infidelity).

1226 **may wel be** it could well be.

1227 **chese yourselven** choose for yourself.

wheither that yow liketh whichever you like.

1228 **avyseth hym** considers carefully (literally: consults with himself).

sore siketh sighs deeply.

1231 I put myself under your wise governance (control).

1232 **moost plesance** most pleasurable.

1233 **moost honour** most honourable.

1234 It doesn't matter to me which of the two.

1235 For whatever you like is sufficient for me.

1236 **gete** got (i.e. achieved).

of yow maistrie dominance over you.

1237 **governe as me lest** govern as I please.

1238 **holde it best** consider it best.

1239 **wrothe** angry.

1241 **ye** yes.

1242 **moote sterven wood** may die insane.

1243 If I am not as good and true to you.

1244 **syn that the world was newe** since the world began.

1245 **And but I be** and if I am not.

to-morn tomorrow.

1246 **emperice** empress.

1249 **Cast up the curtyn** throw open the curtain. Note the dramatic effect created.

1250 **verraily** really.

1251 **therto** also.

1252 **hente** seized.

1254 **a-rewe** in succession.

gan hire kisse kissed her.

1260 **grace t'overbyde** luck to outlive.

1263 **nygardes of dispence** misers.

1264 **verray pestilence** the plague itself.

Interpretations

In the opening section of this book, we examined the setting and overall context of *The Wife of Bath's Prologue and Tale*. In this section we will discuss in more detail the key elements that you will need to consider in preparing yourself for examination questions on the text.

Exactly what kind of text Chaucer presents us with here will be discussed in the opening section. We will then go on to look at the techniques Chaucer uses to present his characters, the ways in which he uses language to achieve his effects, and the themes and ideas explored through the text. Throughout there are activities for you to think about, each followed by a discussion of some of the ideas that they raise. The section concludes with a consideration of critical views, which present a variety of interpretations by other readers.

Genre

The prologue

The Wife of Bath's Prologue differs from the prologues of all the other characters in *The Canterbury Tales*. One obvious difference is its length; at 856 lines, it is much longer than any of the others. However, it also differs in the purpose to which the Wife puts it. First, she uses it to present her audience with a kind of autobiography, and secondly this autobiography takes the form of the medieval *confessio* – a kind of confession.

Activity

Note the ways in which *The Wife of Bath's Prologue* is autobiographical, and the ways in which it could be said to present a kind of 'confession'.

Discussion

In one obvious way the prologue is, in part at least, autobiographical in the sense that in it the Wife tells her audience about her life, particularly her marriages, her attitude towards her husbands, and her attitude to life in general. In Chaucer's time the idea of an autobiography, in terms of someone telling his or her life story, did not exist as a concept. The closest to what we would recognize as autobiography was the medieval concept of the *confessio* – a kind of confessional in a religious sense, in which writers confessed to the unsatisfactory way they had lived their lives and ended with a submission to the will of God and an undertaking to reform and live according to God's will. It is clear, though, that the Wife's prologue does not serve this purpose. Far from admitting that her views and way of life are not acceptable, she revels in them and certainly has no intention of changing them. This readiness to admit her 'sins' but also to delight in them is, of course, central to the humorous nature of Chaucer's presentation of her character.

The tale

The Wife's tale is in many ways a complete contrast to her prologue and belongs to a genre that contains elements of folk tale, fairy tale and romance.

Activity

What elements of folk tale, fairy tale and romance can you identify in the Wife's tale?

Discussion

- The setting of the tale in *th'olde dayes of the Kyng Arthour,/ Of which that Britons speken greet honour* (lines 857–858) places it firmly in the context of the folk tale and all its associations with Arthurian myth and legend.
- The description of this time as one in which fairies abound gives the tale a fairy-tale background – it was a time when *Al was this land fulfild of fayerye* and *The elf-queene, with hir joly*

compaignye,/ Daunced ful ofte in many a grene mede (lines 859–861).

- The 'magic' of the transformation of the ugly old woman into a beautiful young woman at the end of the tale reinforces this impression.
- The tale itself has elements of the traditional romance throughout. For example, the knight is sent on a quest, and the time allotted for him to complete his task is a year and a day, the traditional time for a quest in romantic literature. The ending of the tale also presents the traditional ending of a romance, with the knight and lady very much in love and set to *lyve unto hir lyves ende/ In parfit joye* (lines 1257–1258).

Characterization

The portrait of the Wife

Our first impression of the Wife of Bath is gained through Chaucer's portrait of her in the *General Prologue*. This initial impression is developed further through the very forthright way she expresses some contentious views in her prologue which, in turn, are supplemented by the tale itself.

Activity

Look at the description of the Wife of Bath from the *General Prologue* (page 13). Make a list of the things you learn about her from this description.

Discussion

- We are told that *A good WIF was ther OF biside BATHE*. In other words, she comes from a place close to Bath rather than from Bath itself. This may seem a minor detail, but it could be that Chaucer uses this touch to add realism to his description.
- She is rather deaf, which the narrator says is a pity (we later learn that the reason for this was the blow that she received from Jankyn when she tore a page from his book).

WIFE OF BATH.

The illustration of the Wife of Bath in the Ellesmere manuscript

- She was extremely skilled in cloth-making, so much so that she surpasses the weavers of Ypres and Ghent.
- No other woman in the parish can go before her in making her offering in church (if someone does, she becomes very angry and, ironically, loses all sense of charity).
- Her head coverings are made of the finest material, and the ones she wears on a Sunday are particularly fine and heavy with ornamentation.
- She wears bright red stockings neatly tied, and her shoes are of new and supple leather.
- Her face is bold, attractive and ruddy in complexion.
- She has been married five times, in addition to knowing other young men in her youth (the implication being that she knew quite a few men in her youth).
- She has been on three pilgrimages to Jerusalem and has crossed many foreign rivers. She has also been to Rome, Boulogne, the shrine of St James at Compostella, and Cologne.
- She has a gap between her front teeth, sits comfortably on her horse, and wears a wimple and a broad-brimmed hat and warm

coverings over her broad hips. She also wears sharp spurs. (See the illustration of her from the Ellesmere manuscript, opposite.)
* She jokes and chatters with the other pilgrims, knows all about love-potions and knows all the tricks of the 'old game' of love.

Overall, this description reveals a strong woman of spirit with a sense of adventure and a real lust for life. She is clearly a gregarious and sociable character who loves the chance to mix with a wide variety of people that results from going on pilgrimages. It is, of course, a good way to meet men, and she certainly has a wide experience of men and matters of love.

Many of the features of the Wife's character that we see in this introductory description are developed further through her prologue, where we gain an insight into her character and her views on life, love, relationships, marriage, and how to handle husbands. Unlike the portrait from the *General Prologue*, however, where we learn about her through the narrator's description, in her prologue she addresses her audience directly and we learn about her through what she says herself.

The Wife's prologue

Activity

What do you think her purpose is in the prologue, and which of her characteristics do you think come over most strongly here?

Discussion

One of her main purposes in her prologue is to justify to her audience her belief in marriage (indeed, multiple marriages) and her arguments for the dominance of women over men within marriage. Several features of her personality are revealed through her comments.

* She believes that experience of relationships and marriage is important in qualifying her to make comments on the topic, and challenges some accepted beliefs. She questions whether

authority on these issues is to be found through experience, or in books and learned writings. Obviously she has a wealth of experience of life and so it is no surprise that she rates experience more highly than authority.

> Experience, though noon auctoritee
> Were in this world, is right ynogh for me
> To speke of wo that is in mariage   (1–3)

- She has had five husbands (and is ready for the sixth whenever he may come along) and so believes firmly in the institution of marriage: *An housbonde I wol have – I wol nat lette* (line 154).
- She also believes in the *maistrie* of women in marriage and that they should:

> … han the governance of hous and lond,
> And of his tonge, and of his hond also   (814–815)

- She appears a confident and strong woman who almost seems to revel in the torment that she causes her husbands:

> Ther was no wight, save God and he, that wiste,
> In many wise, how soore I hym twiste   (493–494)

- She shows little feeling for her husbands (with the exception of the fifth). In speaking of her fourth husband it is clear she is happy with the way that she made him suffer, feeling that he got what he deserved:

> … in his owene grece I made hym frye
> For angre, and for verray jalousye.
> By God, in erthe I was his purgatorie   (487–489)

- Her earlier marriages were to old men whom she did not love but who were wealthy and could keep her well. Her fifth marriage, however, was for love and this relationship reveals a different and softer side to her character.

In addition to what we learn about the Wife's views and attitudes towards marriage, love and her husbands from what she tells us herself, she is explicit in her assessment of her own character and, as with everything else, she has strong views on herself. She bases these ideas firmly on medieval beliefs in astrology and physiognomy.

Activity

Look carefully at lines 603–626: *Gat-tothed I was, and that bicam me weel... How poore he was, ne eek of what degree.*

What does the Wife tell us about the effects that:
1 her physical characteristics
2 her astrological influences
had on her character?

Discussion

1   She tells us that *Gat-tothed I was* and that this was very appropriate to her. In Chaucer's time physical features were believed to give a significant indication of character (the theory of 'physiognomy'). A gap between the front teeth was believed to show a strong sexual appetite, a bold, irreverent and unfaithful nature, and a desire for travel. These features describe the Wife's character very well.

She also mentions that she has the mark of Mars on her face, meaning that she has a ruddy or red complexion. This was believed to indicate an argumentative and aggressive nature. This reflects one aspect of the Wife's character, and she is certainly not easily pacified until she has her own way.

A third physical feature mentioned is the birthmark she has in a *privee place*. In the Middle Ages it was believed that birthmarks had astrological links and were the consequence of some factor prevailing in the stars at the time of birth.

2   The Wife tells us that she has the *prente of seinte Venus seel* (line 604) upon her (referring to the birthmark mentioned earlier), and therefore her ruling planet is Venus. This was regarded as a positive influence, giving her a gregarious and pleasure-seeking

attitude to life, and as she says herself she is a *lusty oon* (line 605). She regards herself as being completely influenced by Venus as far as her feelings go. However, she also tells us that she was born under the sign of Taurus when Mars was rising, and so she is subject to certain influences of Mars. Unlike Venus, Mars was regarded as a negative force and this gives rise to the argumentative and aggressive aspects of her nature. Typically, though, she makes even her negative features sound like positives:

> For certes, I am al Venerien
> In feelynge, and myn herte is Marcien.
> Venus me yaf my lust, my likerousnesse,
> And Mars yaf me my sturdy hardynesse   (609–612)

As she bears the marks of both Venus and Mars, this gives rise to conflicting aspects of her character: Venus gives her a desire for love-making and Mars gives her an argumentative nature, and a determination to take what she wants and get her own way.

The tale

The prologue allows us to form a vivid impression of the Wife's character but, although completely different in style and content, her tale can also throw light on her character. In her prologue she has presented at great length her ideas on marriage and her advice on how to handle husbands. She has also revealed something about her feelings for her five husbands and we have been given a detailed picture of her life with them. It may be that we would have expected a rather different kind of tale from her and there is some evidence that originally Chaucer intended her to tell the story eventually given to the Shipman. His tale is a fabliau (a coarse and humorous tale) featuring sexual betrayal and immorality, involving a monk who has sex with a merchant's wife while her husband is away.

Instead, the Wife's tale is a romance in which her highly personal voice almost disappears at first, to be replaced with the more detached tone of the conventional medieval romance opening: *In th'olde dayes of Kyng Arthour* (line 857). Tales set in the days of the legendary King Arthur and his Knights of the Round Table were popular in medieval times.

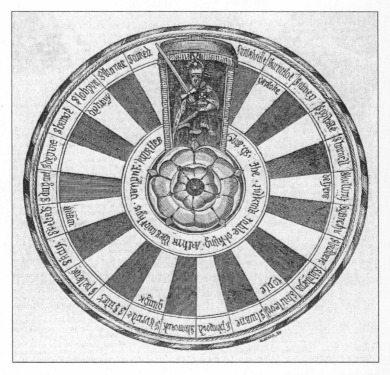

The Winchester Round Table dates from the thirteenth century, with sixteenth-century painting, and shows the places at the table

The content of the tale seems straightforward, with the knight setting out on a traditional quest, his task being to find out what women most desire. However, almost immediately we can detect the voice of the Wife coming through.

A romantic image of a knight from a fourteenth-century illustration

Activity

How does the Wife's voice come through at the beginning of her tale (lines 857–881)?

Discussion

After the conventional opening, the Wife comments on the way that friars, working on behalf of the Church, have rid the world of *elves*, representing the world of magic and superstition associated with an older, pagan religion. However, there is clear irony and irreverence in her words which, while outwardly praising the work of these *hooly freres*, describes them as *thikke as motes in the sonne-beem* (line 868). Her extensive list of places where they are to be found implies that nowhere is free of them. Her tongue-in-cheek description suggests that they have simply replaced the elves, and that the change is not necessarily for the better. Nor does she pass up the opportunity to take a further swipe at friars by introducing a strong sexual innuendo:

> Wommen may go saufly up and doun.
> In every bussh or under every tree
> Ther is noon oother incubus but he,
> And he ne wol doon hem but dishonour.   (878–881)

The Wife is making fun here of the rather dubious reputation that friars had acquired by Chaucer's time, and hinting that although women might be safe from elves, they were certainly not safe from the attentions of the numerous friars who roamed the country. One of her audience of pilgrims, of course, is a friar. In the *General Prologue* he is described as a loose-living character who clearly enjoys worldly pleasures. He is on particularly good terms with wealthy women and carries many ornamental pins that he can give to pretty women he comes across. He is far better acquainted with taverns and barmaids than with the poor, disadvantaged people he is supposed to give aid and comfort to. This stereotypical image of the friar who is more concerned with feeding his physical appetites than fulfilling spiritual needs is one that is still preserved today in popular versions such as the 'Friar Tuck' figure of the Robin Hood stories. Here, though, the Wife also suggests that friars are well known to be seducers of women, by linking the friar to the idea of the incubus.

FRIAR.

The illustration of the Friar in the Ellesmere manuscript

Themes

Marriage

The Wife's prologue and tale form part of a broader discussion of marriage that Chaucer develops in *The Canterbury Tales* involving, among others, the Clerk, the Merchant and the Franklin. The Wife certainly has very clear ideas about how the relationship between husband and wife should be conducted. She begins by making it completely clear where she stands on the topic of marriage and re-marriage.

Activity

Look at the opening of the Wife's prologue up to line 142. What arguments concerning marriage versus virginity does the Wife put forward here?

Discussion

She opens by directly stating her intention to speak about the *wo that is in mariage* and making clear her credentials to speak with authority on the topic: *Experience.*

She states that she has had five husbands, being first married at the age of 12. Each time she had been widowed she has re-married. However, she does suggest that not everyone might accept all these to be 'proper' marriages: *If I so ofte myghte have ywedded bee* (line 7). She mentions the *chirche door* as if to prove that these marriages had the approval of the Church, in order to counter a view often held at the time that to marry more than once in a lifetime was a form of *bigamye*. As we have seen, in theory at least chastity was the ideal state in the eyes of the Church. Marriage was considered greatly inferior to virginity. It was accepted that many people would not achieve this 'ideal' spiritual state, but sexual relationships within marriage were supposed to have the divine aim of procreation, and not be undertaken merely for physical gratification.

Having started by stating the importance of her experience she then goes on to cite various 'authorities' to support her ideas. She says that she has never heard of a specific number being given in the Bible to indicate the number of husbands women may have, or that God anywhere commanded virginity:

> For hadde God comanded maydenhede,
> Thanne hadde he dampned weddyng with the dede.
> And certes, if ther were no seed ysowe,
> Virginitee, thanne wherof sholde it growe? (69–72)

She cites the examples of King Solomon, Abraham and Jacob, all of whom had more than one wife, and she blesses God that she has had five husbands and looks forward to marrying the sixth, whenever that might be.

She challenges established thinking, asking where God expressly forbade marriage and commanded virginity, and she says that even when St Paul recommended chastity he did not command it. As she comments, advising is not the same as commanding, and St Paul accepted that although virginity is the preferred state the flesh is weak and not everyone is capable of attaining this perfect state. The Wife is the first to admit that she is not, declaring:

> I wol bistowe the flour of al myn age
> In the actes and in fruyt of mariage. (113–114)

She then raises the question of what the reproductive organs are for and goes on to answer her own question by saying that they were made for both the practical purpose of the *purgacioun/ Of uryne* and for the pleasure of intercourse (in such a way as not to displease God, she adds, to keep the religious members of the party happy):

> I sey this: that they maked ben for bothe;
> That is to seye, for office and for ese
> Of engendrure, ther we nat God displese. (126–128)

The Wife, then, robustly defends her position as a five-times married, five-times widowed woman and makes no apology for the fact that she finds sexual relationships pleasurable. She is determined to have a husband and let him pay his 'debt' to her and be her slave. However, his experience of being her husband will entail suffering as well as pleasure:

> Myn housbonde shal it have bothe eve and morwe,
> Whan that hym list come forth and paye his dette.
> An housbonde I wol have – I wol nat lette –
> Which shal be bothe my dettour and my thral,
> And have his tribulacion withal
> Upon his flessh, whil that I am his wyf.   (152–157)

She has had different experiences of marriage with her five husbands and has obviously learned much from her experiences.

Some of the pilgrims would find her words amusing but some would be quite shocked by them. She is interrupted by the Pardoner.

Activity
Look at the Pardoner's interruption (lines 163–192). How does he respond to her comments on marriage?

Discussion
The Pardoner seems to be driven to interrupt more through excitement than shock at what she has said, telling her, perhaps rather 'tongue-in-cheek', that *Ye been a noble prechour in this cas* (line 165). He tells her that he had been about to marry but her words have made him have second thoughts. This is particularly ironic and the rest of the company would be amused at his words as he is described in the *General Prologue* as a eunuch with a high, squeaky voice, no beard and long, straggly yellow hair. At the end of his own tale he has a difference of opinion with the Host, who threatens to cut off his testicles. The Pardoner's words here are likely to be designed to deflect attention from his own sexuality (or lack of it). The Wife tells him that she has not yet begun her tale and by the time she has finished it, it will taste worse than ale to him (another joke at the Pardoner's expense, as he has already had plenty of ale to drink).

PARDONER.

The illustration of the Pardoner in the Ellesmere manuscript

Activity

What kind of picture does the Wife present of her first three marriages, and how did these three marriages contrast with her fourth?

Discussion

- She does not distinguish between her first three husbands, although she does say that they were *goode* men. The other features that they all had in common was that they were rich and old. They had difficulty in fulfilling the terms of their commitment to her (i.e. having sexual intercourse with her), presumably because of their age. She has to laugh when she thinks back to how piteously she made them work at night in bed, but she admits that she couldn't care less how they felt.
- As they had already handed over to her all their land and wealth, it was not necessary for her to gain their love or show them any respect. She had them *hoolly in myn hond* (line 211) and there was no need for her to please them unless it was for her profit or pleasure.

- She had her own way to such an extent that they were really pleased when she spoke to them pleasantly – they were so used to her nagging at them relentlessly. She also reveals the techniques she used to keep them in their place and to maintain dominance over them. Even when she was in the wrong she made it appear that it was her husbands who were at fault. Getting in first with her own complaint deflected the husband from whatever legitimate grievance he may have had:

  > For as an hors I koude byte and whyne.
  > I koude pleyne, and yit was in the gilt,
  > Or elles often tyme hadde I been spilt.   (386–388)

  This tactic got her out of trouble on many occasions and forced her husbands to apologize for things they had never been guilty of in the first place.

- Her fourth husband was a complete contrast to the first three. He was a rake and had a mistress, and the Wife felt full of malice towards him when she thought of him enjoying himself with other women. But she paid him back in full, not by going with other men herself, but by making herself so attractive to other men that she made him jealous:

  > ... he was quit, by God and by Seint Joce!
  > I made hym of the same wode a croce;
  > Nat of my body, in no foul manere,
  > But certeinly, I made folk swich cheere
  > That in his owene grece I made hym frye
  > For angre, and for verray jalousye.   (483–488)

Her fifth husband, Jankyn, stands out from the rest. Her attitude towards him is completely different because she fell in love with him first. He was half her age (he was 20 and she was 40) and this time it was she who had the land and money and he who had little. It is significant that he is the only one of her husbands that she refers to by name.

Activity

Look at the Wife's account of her life with Jankyn (lines 503–827). Make a list of the ways in which this marriage differs from her previous ones.

Discussion

- Her first words in relation to her fifth husband give a good indication of how she felt about him: *God lete his soule nevere come in helle!* (line 504). She clearly cared about him.
- Despite her feelings about him she tells us that he was the most unkind of all her husbands and that he beat her. Even so he could easily win her love back again and he could flatter her so easily that he could make love to her whenever he wanted to. She admits that she believes that she really loved him and that these feelings were spurred on by the fact that he did not make a fuss of her and it was difficult to make him love her:

  > I trowe I loved hym best, for that he
  > Was of his love daungerous to me.   (513–514)

  She says that women always want what they cannot easily have.

- She had fallen in love with him while her fourth husband was still alive, and the vocabulary she uses to describe this 'courtship' again reveals her feelings towards him. For example, there is no mention of 'love' with regard to her first four husbands but Jankyn she *took for love, and no richesse* (line 526). She met him in spring, with all its associations of new beginnings, life and vitality. She completely lost her heart to Jankyn and can still remember how the sight of his legs made her feel at her fourth husband's funeral:

  > ... me thoughte he hadde a paire
  > Of legges and of feet so clene and faire
  > That al myn herte I yaf unto his hoold.   (597–599)

- By the end of the month after the death of her fourth husband she had married Jankyn. The words she uses to describe him here, *joly* and *hende*, reveal her positive attitude towards him, although she came to regret her haste as he submitted her to physical abuse – he hit her – and mental abuse, constantly bombarding her with quotations from his favourite anti-feminist books.

- In the end, though, she gained the upper hand and the *maistrie* over him that was essential for them to live in love and harmony with one another.

Ideas associated with sex, power and dominance are at the heart of both the prologue and the tale.

Sexuality

In the prologue the Wife's awareness of her own sexuality is immediately evident, and she spends a good deal of time in the first part of the prologue arguing against the view that virginity is a more blessed state than marriage. Although she concedes, to give greater respectability to her argument, that virginity is the purest state, she also argues that celibacy does not suit everyone. She backs this up with her debate on what the sexual organs are for if not for pleasure as well as procreation.

Activity

Make a list of the things that the Wife says that suggest sex is something to be enjoyed.

Discussion

> Lo, heere the wise kyng, daun Salomon;
> I trowe he hadde wyves mo than oon.
> As wolde God it leveful were unto me
> To be refresshed half so ofte as he!
> Which yifte of God hadde he for alle his wyvys!   (35–39)

The Wife does not simply use the fact that Solomon had a number of wives to support her argument but comments on the fun he must have had with them. Her use of the word *refresshed* in one sense suggests that she wishes God would let her have a new spouse half as often as Solomon had, but it also carries the possible innuendo of the refreshment provided by sexual satisfaction.

> God woot, this noble kyng, as to my wit,
> The firste nyght had many a myrie fit
> With ech of hem, so wel was hym on lyve.   (41–43)

The idea of the pleasure of sex is clearly at the forefront of the Wife's mind here, as she imagines the fun that Solomon must have had on so many wedding nights.

> Yblessed be God that I have wedded fyve!
> …
> Welcome the sixte, whan that evere he shal.
> For sothe, I wol nat kepe me chaast in al.   (44–46)

The Wife is glad to have had the opportunity to have five husbands and looks forward to the sixth whenever he may come along.

> Al were it good no womman for to touche –
> He mente as in his bed or in his couche,
> For peril is bothe fyr and tow t'assemble;
> Ye knowe what this ensample may resemble.   (87–90)

Here she comments on the words of St Paul when he warned against the sexual desire that is ignited when man and woman come together, observing the inevitability of the mixing of the two. Her tone here seems to be more one of approval than condemnation.

> I graunte it wel; I have noon envie,
> Thogh maydenhede preferre bigamye.
> It liketh hem to be clene, body and goost;
> Of myn estaat I nyl nat make no boost.   (95–98)

Again acknowledging the accepted view of virginity being the preferred state, the Wife makes it quite clear where she stands – she will make no boast of being a virgin (the implication of 'and nor would I want to' is as clear as if she had spoken it).

> I wol bistowe the flour of al myn age
> In the actes and in fruyt of mariage. (113–114)

The *fruyt* the Wife speaks of here refers to the sexual enjoyment she intends to have, not children. There is no indication at any point that motherhood was an aspect of marriage that interested her.

> Telle me also, to what conclusion
> Were membres maad of generacion
> …
> I sey this: that they maked ben for bothe;
> That is to seye, for office and for ese
> Of engendrure, ther we nat God displese. (115–128)

This discussion of sexual parts and their function increases the focus on the physical aspects of sexuality, culminating in the Wife's conclusion that they were created both for practical use and also *for ese*, in other words pleasure. Whenever she refers to her own sexual organs she does so with a kind of affectionate pride, using a variety of euphemisms such as *my queynte*, *my bele chose* and *chambre of Venus*.

> In wyfhod I wol use myn instrument
> As frely as my Makere hath it sent.
> If I be daungerous, God yeve me sorwe!
> Myn housbonde shal it have bothe eve and morwe,
> Whan that hym list come forth and paye his dette. (149–153)

The Wife proudly declares that she will readily engage in sex with her husband, having turned the chastity argument on its head. It now appears, according to her logic, that by giving herself freely to her husband at every available opportunity she is carrying out the will of God and allowing her husband to *paye his dette* to her. According to her argument here she is not only happy to readily engage in sexual activity but has an obligation to do so.

Power

In both the Wife's prologue and her tale the ideas on marriage and sex are inextricably linked to the idea of power.

Activity

How are sex and power linked in the Wife's prologue?

Discussion

In the prologue the Wife presents her relationships with all her husbands as a kind of power struggle in which she strives to achieve the upper hand. In this struggle the Wife is quite prepared to use sex as a weapon in her armoury. For example, with her first three husbands she often gained power over them and made them do as she wanted by withdrawing her sexual favours until she got her own way:

> Namely abedde hadden they meschaunce:
> Ther wolde I chide and do hem no plesaunce;
> I wolde no lenger in the bed abyde,
> If that I felte his arm over my syde,
> Til he had maad his raunson unto me;
> Thanne wolde I suffre hym do his nycetee.   (407–412)

Further she taunts them by asking them why they grumble and groan so much. Is it that they want her body all to themselves? She hints that she could buy the fashionable new clothes and other things she wants by selling her body, but instead she is going to keep it for her husband's own private pleasure, thereby both putting him in the wrong for denying her the things she wants and also planting in his mind the unsettling thought of what might happen if he does not let her have her own way:

> What eyleth yow to grucche thus and grone?
> Is it for ye wolde have my queynte allone?
> Wy, taak it al! Lo, have it every deel!
> Peter! I shrewe yow, but ye love it weel;
> For if I wolde selle my *bele chose,*

> I koude walke as fressh as is a rose;
> But I wol kepe it for youre owene tooth.
> Ye be to blame, by God! I sey yow sooth. (443–450)

Her fourth husband was a completely different proposition. He was a *revelour* and had a mistress, but the Wife again used sex as a way of getting even with him. She paid him back in kind, not, as she is quick to point out, by doing anything indecent but by making herself as attractive as possible in order to make him jealous:

> I made hym of the same wode a croce;
> Nat of my body, in no foul manere,
> But certeinly, I made folk swich cheere
> That in his owene grece I made hym frye
> For angre, and for verray jalousye. (484–488)

Activity

How is the idea of sex and power presented in the tale?

Discussion

- The tale takes its starting point from a sexual act, the rape, in which the knight exerts his power over the maid.
- Because of her rank, the queen has power over the knight and she and the ladies set him a quest.
- The old woman has power over the knight by virtue of the fact that she knows the answer to the question – an answer that will save his life.
- The knight's wedding night, usually a time of celebration and anticipation at the thought of sexual delight, is blighted by his wife's ugliness:

> Greet was the wo the knyght hadde in his thoght,
> Whan he was with his wyf abedde ybroght;
> He walweth and he turneth to and fro. (1083–1085)

- Sexual pleasure is only granted to him after he relinquishes power to his wife.

Dominance

The ideas of *maistrie* and *soveraynetee* are of central importance in both the prologue and tale. In her prologue, the Wife describes how, in all her marriages, her main objective was to achieve *maistrie* over her husbands: in other words, to get the upper hand in the relationship and thereby gain mastery. The tale that she tells is an exemplum or example of this theme, as ultimately the old woman gains mastery over her husband, the knight.

The Wife gives us an indication of how she sees the ideal relationship between husband and wife working out early in the prologue, when she tells us that her husband should be both her debtor and her slave, and how he will *have his tribulacion withal/ Upon his flessh, whil that I am his wyf* (lines 156–157). She also makes it clear that she wants to have complete power over his body:

> I have the power durynge al my lyf
> Upon his propre body, and noght he. (158–159)

She found it relatively easy to achieve *maistrie* over her first three old husbands, and she:

> ... governed hem so wel, after my lawe,
> That ech of hem ful blisful was and fawe
> To brynge me gaye thynges fro the fayre.
> They were ful glad whan I spak to hem faire,
> For, God it woot, I chidde hem spitously. (219–223)

Fortunately for them they seem to have acquiesced in her belief that in order to live in peace one or the other must give way, and as a man is more reasonable and tolerant it is better for the man to give in:

> ... it is fair to have a wyf in pees.
> Oon of us two moste bowen, doutelees;
> And sith a man is moore resonable
> Than womman is, ye moste been suffrable. (439–442)

Her fourth husband was more of a challenge, but she maintained her struggle to achieve dominance with him too, and *in erthe I was his purgatorie* (line 489).

> ... he sat ful ofte and song,
> Whan that his shoo ful bitterly hym wrong.
> Ther was no wight, save God and he, that wiste
> In many wise, how soore I hym twiste.   (491–494)

However, the Wife's struggle for *maistrie* moves to a new level with her marriage to her fifth husband, and she and Jankyn become engaged in a long struggle to gain the advantage over each other. This struggle for dominance reaches its climax in the quarrel they have when she tears the pages out of his book and he strikes her. However, in the end they come to an agreement in which Jankyn gives complete control to the Wife:

> He yaf me al the bridel in myn hond,
> To han the governance of hous and lond,
> And of his tonge, and his hond also   (813–815)

At last she had *geten unto me,/ By maistrie, al the soveraynetee* (lines 817–818).

With domination achieved, peace can ensue and Jankyn promises to let her do as she pleases for the rest of her life. After that they lived in peace with each other and he was kind and loving towards her.

The Wife's tale reflects the message that in order for a marriage to flourish and for husband and wife to live in happiness the wife must achieve *maistrie* over her husband. This is the answer to the question that the knight seeks, and it is the answer that the old woman gives him to repeat in front of the queen and the court:

> 'My lige lady, generally,' quod he,
> 'Wommen desiren to have sovereynetee

As wel over hir housbond as hir love,
And for to been in maistrie hym above.'   (1037–1040)

The knight, like Jankyn, only achieves real happiness when he hands over power to his wife to make the decisions:

'My lady and my love, and wyf so deere,
I put me in youre wise governance;
Cheseth yourself which may be moost plesance
And moost honour to yow and me also.
I do no fors the wheither of the two,
For as yow liketh, it suffiseth me.'   (1230–1235)

Having gained *maistrie* over her husband the old woman is transformed into a beautiful young woman, and like Jankyn and the Wife they live the rest of their lives in *parfit joye*.

The closing lines of the tale sum up the Wife's philosophy and the importance of achieving dominance in marriage:

... Jhesu Crist us sende
Housbondes meeke, yonge, and fressh abedde,
And grace t'overbyde hem that we wedde;
And eek I praye Jhesu shorte hir lyves
That noght wol be governed by hir wyves;
And olde and angry nygardes of dispence,
God sende hem soone verray pestilence!   (1258–1264)

Gentillesse

The idea of *gentillesse* was a very important concept in the Chaucer's time. It encapsulated the essence of noble, honourable and virtuous behaviour in all its forms. *Gentillesse* was normally associated with the behaviour of the nobility and the higher ranks in society (although not all people of high rank displayed it). However, Chaucer raises the possibility on several occasions in *The Canterbury Tales* of people of lower status displaying *gentillesse*. The Wife does not mention the idea of *gentillesse* in her prologue, but in the tale the old woman has quite a lot to say about it and her words have a vital part to play in the development of the rest of the action of the tale.

Activity

Look at the section of the tale from *Greet was the wo the knyght hadde in his thoght* (line 1083) to *To lyven vertuously and weyve synne* (line 1176). What points does the old woman make to the knight here about *gentillesse*?

Discussion

- The old woman begins by questioning why the knight is behaving so badly to her on their wedding night, particularly as she has just saved his life. The knight responds that it is because she is so old and ugly, and in addition is of such low birth.
- This leads the old woman to tell him a few truths about the nature of *gentillesse*. She points out to him that it is nothing but his own arrogance that persuades him good manners and noble behaviour were passed on to him through birth and rank, and that he should see himself as a gentleman. *Gentillesse* cannot be inherited, she tells him; it is something that can only be manifested through virtuous and noble behaviour.

> Looke who that is moost vertuous alway,
> Pryvee and apert, and moost entendeth ay
> To do the gentil dedes that he kan;
> Taak hym for the grettest gentil man. (1113–1116)

- The old woman tells him that it is from Christ that we claim our *gentillesse* and not from our forebears, because of their *old richesse* or *heigh parage*. They cannot bequeath to us *vertuous lyvyng*, and she quotes from Dante to support her argument:

> Ful selde up riseth by his branches smale
> Prowesse of man, for God, of his goodnesse,
> Wole that of hym we clayme oure gentillesse (1128–1130)

- She argues that if *gentillesse* were passed down through lineage, those people to whom it passed would always act in a virtuous way and it would be impossible for them to do anything bad. As she points out, in fact it is not uncommon to find a lord's son behaving badly even though he was born of a noble house. He who is of noble birth but does not behave nobly is no gentleman but a churl:

> And he that wole han pris of his gentrye,
> For he was boren of a gentil hous
> And hadde his eldres noble and vertuous,
> And nel hymselven do no gentil dedis
> Ne folwen his gentil auncestre that deed is,
> He nys nat gentil, be he duc or erl,
> For vileyns synful dedes make a cherl.   (1152–1158)

- The old woman reiterates that *gentillesse* comes from God alone, and therefore she concludes that although her own ancestors were low-born she hopes that God has granted her the grace to live virtuously and that thereby she will show the qualities of *gentillesse*.

> ... I thus conclude:
> Al were it that myne auncestres were rude,
> Yet may the hye God, and so hope I,
> Grante me grace to lyven vertuously.
> Thanne am I gentil, whan that I bigynne
> To lyven vertuously and weyve synne.   (1171–1176)

The old woman's words on the nature of *gentillesse*, and the speech on poverty which she goes on to give, have a clear effect on the knight and he sees the error of his ways. He puts himself in her hands, a decision which leads to his own salvation and the future happiness of the couple.

Language and style

Verse form

Like most of Chaucer's *Canterbury Tales*, the Wife of Bath's prologue and tale are written in iambic pentameter. This means each line consists of five metrical feet (or iambs) each made up of an unstressed and a stressed syllable. Each line therefore contains ten syllables:

> Experience, though noon auctoritee
> Were in this world, is right ynogh for me
> To speke of wo that is in mariage   (1–3)

This verse pattern is noted for using a rhythm very close to that of normal English speech, and so allows Chaucer to create a natural tone to his verse. He does not adhere rigidly to iambic pentameter, but uses it flexibly where necessary, so not all lines have ten syllables. He also uses rhyming couplets, which add a further sense of rhythm and movement to his lines.

Imagery

Imagery is used quite extensively by the Wife in her prologue to describe herself, her husbands and the kinds of relationships she has with them. The imagery that Chaucer has the Wife use falls into two main types. Many of her images are to do with animals, while a second kind of imagery is based upon notions of business, trade or goods and possessions.

Activity

How does the Wife use animal imagery in her prologue and what effect does it create?

Discussion

The Wife uses animal imagery of various kinds. For example, when criticizing one of her old husbands for wanting to limit her scope for dressing up in finery and going out, she says that he compared her to a cat, a creature traditionally associated with vanity. It was said that if one singed a cat's fur it would stay at home:

> Thou seydest this, that I was lyk a cat;
> For whoso wolde senge a cattes skyn,
> Thanne wolde the cat wel dwellen in his in;
> And if the cattes skyn be slyk and gay,
> She wol nat dwelle in house half a day   (348–352)

When describing the ways in which she made her husbands suffer she likens herself to a horse that bites and whinnies:

> O Lord! The peyne I dide hem and the wo,
> Ful giltelees, by Goddes sweete pyne!
> For as an hors I koude byte and whyne.   (384–386)

When she remembers her youth and the way that she could sing she compares herself to a nightingale:

> How koude I daunce to an harpe smale,
> And synge, ywis, as any nyghtyngale   (457–458)

When she remembers how lively she was in her youth she tells us she was *joly as a pye* (line 456), bringing immediately to mind the chattering, striking and bold magpie.

She accuses her husbands of saying that a woman will desire every man she sees and *For as a spanyel she wol on hym lepe* (line 267) and that there is no goose on the lake so grey as to be unable to find a mate:

> Ne noon so grey goos gooth ther in the lake
> As, sëistow, wol been withoute make.   (269–270)

Although the husbands are said to use the images of cats, spaniels and geese, she sees herself as a rather more assertive creature, saying that: *Stibourn I was as is a leonesse* (line 637).

Unlike the lion which St Jerome tamed through his goodness, the lioness that the Wife has in mind is not one that will be tamed by any man.

Although the majority of the animal imagery that the Wife uses refers to women, she sometimes uses animal imagery to refer to men. The effect is rather different in their case, however. For example, she accuses her old husbands of coming home *as dronken as a mous* (line 246).

She also suggests that her old husbands should behave as meekly towards her as sheep:

> Thanne wolde I seye, 'Goode lief, taak keep
> How mekely looketh Wilkyn, oure sheep!
> Com neer, my spouse, lat me ba thy cheke!
> Ye sholde been al pacient and meke…'   (431–434)

The medieval view of the world was that God created man in his own image, then created woman, and then the various kinds of animals in descending order. This placed women close to the animals in the hierarchy, and they were often compared to animals in an unfavourable way. The Wife, however, as with so much else, turns convention on its head and is happy to compare herself (or women in general) to animals as they represent her sensual, freedom-loving attitude towards life and a challenge to the authorities which oppose her views.

The Nuremberg Chronicle, 1493, depicts God creating Eve while Adam lies sleeping

Activity

Make a list of some of the images related to business, trade, goods or possessions that the Wife uses in her prologue, and explain the effects created.

Discussion

We perhaps should not be surprised that the Wife uses so much imagery based on the idea of trade to describe marriage and relationships, because marriage in the Middle Ages was very much a commercial proposition. As we have already discussed, mostly marriages were arranged, with the prime considerations being either political or economic advantage or both. Here are some examples of the use of such imagery.

- When discussing the merits of virginity over marriage, the Wife makes the point that people of all kinds can perform a valuable service:

      For wel ye knowe, a lord in his houshold,
      He nath nat every vessel al of gold;
      Somme been of tree, and doon hir lord servyse.   (99–101)

- She makes the same point again, this time using the image of bread made of the purest flour as opposed to barley bread. Of virginity she says:

      Lat hem be breed of pured whete-seed,
      And lat us wyves hoten barly-breed;
      And yet with barly-breed, Mark telle kan,
      Oure Lord Jhesu refresshed many a man.   (143–146)

- She refers to her husband having intercourse with her as him paying his 'debt' to her:

      Myn housbonde shal it have bothe eve and morwe,
      Whan that hym list come forth and paye his dette.   (152–153)

- She describes her relationship with her old husbands in terms of profit and gain:

  > But sith I hadde hem hoolly in myn hond,
  > And sith they hadde me yeven al hir lond,
  > What sholde I taken keep hem for to plese,
  > But it were for my profit and myn ese?   (211–214)

- In order to get her own way the Wife does not let her old husband have his way in bed until he has paid his 'ransom' to her (line 411).

- She says that people should make what profit they can, for everything is for sale: *Wynne whoso may, for al is for to selle* (line 414). She even suggests the profit she could make if she sold her *bele chose:*

  > For if I wolde selle my *bele chose,*
  > I koude walke as fressh as is a rose.   (447–448)

- Commenting on the nature of women and how, faced with indifference from a man they will attract attention elsewhere, the Wife uses the image of the market-place:

  > With daunger oute we al oure chaffare;
  > Greet prees at market maketh deere ware,
  > And to greet cheep is holde at litel prys   (521–523)

  This again creates the impression of a woman 'selling her wares'.

- The idea of 'selling' is also used when she describes herself now that she is older. The best 'flour' is gone so she must make the most of 'selling' the 'bran' that is left:

  > The flour is goon; ther is namoore to telle;
  > The bren, as I best kan, now moste I selle   (477–478)

Various other kinds of images are also used by the Wife. For example, there are images associated with food and drink, as might be expected from the Wife, who clearly enjoys comfortable living; and the idea of fire is used symbolically in the prologue.

Activity

Discuss the use of fire as a symbol in the prologue.

Discussion

Fire is used in one way to represent the heat and destructive power of sexual passion. One of the things that one of her old husbands used to say was to compare a woman's love to a wild fire that destroyed everything:

> Thou liknest eek wommenes love to helle,
> To bareyne lond, ther water may nat dwelle.
> Thou liknest it also to wilde fyr;
> The moore it brenneth, the moore it hath desir
> To consume every thyng that brent wole be.   (371–375)

The danger of sexual passion being ignited by the bringing together of man and woman had been noted earlier too, when the Wife was speaking of the St Paul's teachings:

> Al were it good no womman for to touche –
> He mente as in his bed or in his couche,
> For peril is bothe fyr and tow t'assemble;
> Ye knowe what this ensample may resemble.   (87–90)

Fire is also a factor in the climax of the struggle for *maistrie* between the Wife and Jankyn, as he falls backwards into the fire when she strikes him and this prompts him to hit her hard. However, the final victory of the Wife as she achieves power over him is symbolized in her making him *brenne his book anon right tho* (line 816).

Narrative techniques

Chaucer uses a variety of techniques to create his effects in the Wife's prologue and tale; there is a strong sense of the Wife's personal voice and of her speaking to her audience.

Activity

Make a list of the narrative and dramatic techniques that Chaucer uses to create his effects and give a strong impression of the Wife's character.

Discussion

- The Wife uses a variety of techniques to put forward her arguments. One key technique is that she cites *auctoritees* to support her views, but often her examples and quotations are selective and even distorted to suit her ends and make them appear to support her more effectively. For example, she says:

  > God bad us for to wexe and multiplye;
  > That gentil text kan I wel understonde.   (28–29)

  However, her use of the reference here is questionable. The quotation is concerned with procreation, and not the accumulation of husbands.

  A little later, she uses the idea that Solomon had more than one wife to support her position of having had five husbands:

  > Lo, heere the wise kyng, daun Salomon;
  > I trowe he hadde wyves mo than oon.
  > As wolde God it leveful were unto me
  > To be refresshed half so ofte as he!   (35–38)

  She is humorously understating the situation here, as Solomon had a thousand wives and concubines, but she is also ignoring the awkward implications of Solomon's polygamy, again twisting the reference to suit her own purposes.
- She turns around the arguments of some of the anti-feminist writers that she cites to use their arguments against them.

Sometimes, ironically, she uses the same techniques of glossing biblical quotations to suit her purposes as do the writers she is criticizing or attempting to counter.

- She digresses at various points, sometimes to the point where she briefly loses the thread of what she was saying. For example, shortly after she has begun to tell us about Jankyn (line 525) she digresses and reminisces about her friend Alisoun, and then returns to her story:

> But now, sire, lat me se what I shal seyn.
> A ha! By God, I have my tale ageyn.   (585–586)

At the beginning of her tale she digresses again in order to make some humorous and not very complimentary comments about friars (lines 864–881).

- She is interrupted twice during her prologue, first by the Pardoner and secondly by the Friar and Summoner. This allows interplay between the characters, reminding us, of course, of the context of the tales but at the same time developing the dramatic depth by showing responses to the Wife's words.
- At various points the Wife addresses her audience directly. She asks questions of them:

> But that I axe, why that the fifthe man
> Was noon housbonde to the Samaritan?
> How manye myghte she have in mariage?   (21–23)

She keeps them informed as to what she is talking about by signalling she is about to embark on a new subject: *Now of my fifthe housbonde wol I telle* (line 503).

- She brings scenes from the tale to life through dramatic description:

> He saugh a mayde walkynge hym biforn,
> Of which mayde anon, maugree hir heed,
> By verray force, he rafte hire maydenhed;
> For which oppressioun was swich clamour
> And swich pursute unto the kyng Arthour
> That dampned was this knyght for to be deed,
> By cours of lawe, and sholde han lost his heed   (886–892)

She also uses direct speech to enliven her tale:

'My leeve mooder,' quod this knyght, 'certeyn
I nam but deed but if that I kan seyn
What thyng it is that wommen moost desire.
Koude ye me wisse, I wolde wel quite youre hire.'
'Plight me thy trouthe heere in myn hand,' quod she,
'The nexte thyng that I requere thee,
Thou shalt it do, if it lye in thy myght,
And I wol telle it yow er it be nyght.'   (1005–1112)

The unity of prologue and tale

As mentioned earlier, the tale that the Wife tells comes, perhaps,
as a surprise in some ways after what we have seen of her
character in the prologue. We may have expected the type of
bawdy fabliau that it is thought Chaucer may have originally
intended for her, rather than the romance that she tells. However,
although the tale is very different from the prologue in its
language, style and presentation, the two link together in several
ways.

Activity
What links can you see between the Wife's prologue and her tale?

Discussion
- In many ways the tale can be seen as an 'exemplum' or example
  that serves to illustrate or reinforce the argument and views
  expressed in the prologue. It illustrates the Wife's view that the
  woman gaining *soveraynetee* by achieving *maistrie* leads to
  marital bliss.
- The happiness the Wife eventually achieves with Jankyn is
  reflected in the happiness eventually achieved between the
  knight and the old/young woman.
- The sermon about *gentillesse* may seem detached from the
  prologue, which does not overtly deal with this theme, but some

critics have argued that it reflects another side to the Wife's character in that behaviour and not breeding determines what we are.

- It has also been suggested that the old woman becoming young and beautiful again reflects the desire that the Wife has to recapture the life and vitality of her youth, which she so wistfully describes in the prologue.

Critical views

The Wife's prologue and tale have been viewed in a variety of ways through a variety of critical approaches.

1 **The context.** Historical criticism looks at the text as a work within the historical context in which it was written. These critics see the Wife and her tale as inseparable, linked to the political and socio-economic factors of the fourteenth century. They argue that we can only really understand the ideas and views that the character expresses when seen in this context, and focus on the status of women and views on marriage of the time. This has given rise to a wide variety of ways of looking at the text, some seeing a knowledge of the history of the time as vital in understanding the position of the Wife in society, and the ways in which she challenges accepted assumptions and the attitude of the Church. Other critics have seen the work as making satirical points about women in general, pointing out that the Wife herself shows evidence of many of the bad qualities said to be in women by the anti-feminist writers quoted in her prologue. Some have moved away from the idea of it being about 'a Wife of Bath' at all and see the text as an allegory of the problems faced by King Richard II during his reign.

2 **The feminist viewpoint.** There has been much focus on the Wife's prologue and tale in terms of the misogynistic views

that she attacks. Opinion is divided, however, as to what exactly this reveals and whether Chaucer meant the character of the Wife to challenge or support views that were critical of women. The character of the Wife has sometimes been seen as an early feminist fighting against a male-dominated society, but others see her as destined to failure because by attempting to achieve equality she uses the tactics of men and assumes the role of a male 'dominator'. Other critics point to the fact that she is the fictitious construct of a male writer, and as such can never genuinely represent the feminine viewpoint.

3   **The Wife and religion.** Some critics have looked at the presentation of the Wife's prologue and tale from the perspective of religion, examining the biblical texts that she cites in support of her arguments and the ways in which she manipulates them to support and reinforce her views.

4   **The Wife and social class.** Some critics, such as those adopting a Marxist approach, see the Wife's prologue and tale from the point of view of what they reveal about class differences and the relationships between classes. They see the Wife in terms of her position within the medieval social hierarchy and the ways in which she uses her limited power to achieve her ends. This approach has also led to some debate as to Chaucer's intentions as a writer and whether, through the character of the Wife, he is criticizing or satirizing the established views of society.

A Note on Chaucer's English

Chaucer's English has so many similarities with Modern English that it is unnecessary to learn extensive tables of grammar. With a little practice, and using the glosses provided, it should not be too difficult to read the text. Nevertheless, it would be foolish to pretend that there are no differences. The remarks which follow offer some information, hints and principles to assist students who are reading Chaucer's writings for the first time, and to illustrate some of the differences (and some of the similarities) between Middle and Modern English. More comprehensive and systematic treatments of this topic are available in *The Riverside Chaucer* and in D. Burnley, *A Guide to Chaucer's Language*.

1 Inflections

These are changes or additions to words, usually endings, which provide information about number (whether a verb or a noun is singular or plural), tense or gender.

a) Verbs

In the **present** tense most verbs add –e in the first person singular (e.g. *I rede*), –est in the second person singular (e.g. *thou biwreyest*), –eth in the third person singular (*he clymbeth*) and –en in the plural. This can be summarized as follows:

	Middle English	Modern English
Singular	1 I telle 2 Thou tellest 3 He/She/It telleth	I tell You tell He/She/It tells
Plural	1 We tellen 2 Ye tellen 3 They tellen	We tell You tell They tell

As you can see, Middle English retains more inflections than Modern English, but the system is simple enough. Old English, the phase of the language between around 449 AD, when the Angles first came to Britain, and about 1100, had many more inflections.

In describing the **past** tense it is necessary to begin by making a distinction, which still applies in Modern English, between strong and weak verbs. **Strong verbs** form their past tense by changing their stem (e.g. I sing, I sang; you drink, you drank; he fights, he fought; we throw, we threw), while **weak verbs** add to the stem (I want, I wanted; you laugh, you laughed; he dives, he dived).

In the past tense in Middle English, strong verbs change their stems (e.g. *sing* becomes *sang* or *song*) and add –e in the second person singular (e.g. *thou songe*) and –en in the plural (e.g. *they songen*). Weak verbs add –de or –te (e.g. *fele* becomes *felte*, *here* becomes *herde*) with –st in the second person singular (e.g. *thou herdest*) and –n in the plural (e.g. *they felten*). The tables below and on the next page compare the past tense in Middle and Modern English for strong and weak verbs.

Strong verbs		
	Middle English Present stem: 'sing'	**Modern English**
Singular	1 I sange (or soonge) 2 Thou songe 3 He/She/It sange	I sang (or sung) You sang He/She/It sang
Plural	1 We songen 2 Ye songen 3 They songen	We sang You sang They sang

Weak verbs		
	Middle English Present stem: 'here'	**Modern English**
Singular	1 I herde 2 Thou herdest 3 He/She/It herde	I heard You heard He/She/It heard
Plural	1 We herden 2 Ye herden 3 They herden	We heard You heard They heard

The past tense can also be formed using the auxiliary verb *gan* plus the past participle (e.g. *gan ryse*: rose [1000], *gan hire kisse*: kissed her [1254]). Some verbs add initial *y* to make their past participle (e.g. *yplesed*: pampered [930], *yblessed*: blessed [323], *ystynt*: ended [390]).

b) Nouns and adjectives

Nouns mostly add –s or –es for plural (e.g. *lordynges* [4]), but notice the possessive (e.g. *Goddes* [50]). There are no apostrophes in Middle English (although modern editors sometime add one to indicate that a letter has been elided, e.g. *t'overbyde hem* [1260], *th'olde dayes* [857]). Some nouns add –en for plural (e.g. *yen*: eyes [358]) and some adjectives are converted to adverbs by the addition of –e (e.g. *faire*: courteously [222]).

c) Personal pronouns

The forms of the personal pronouns are somewhat different from those used in Modern English and are worth recording in full:

		Subject	Object	Possessive
Singular	1	I, ich	me	myn, my
	2	Thou, thow	thee	thyn, thy
	3 masculine	He	hym, him	his
	3 feminine	She	her	hir, hire
	3 neuter	It, hit	it, hit	his
Plural	1	We	us	owre, our, owres
	2	Ye	you, yow	your, youres
	3	They	hem	hire, here

Remember that the distinction between *thou* and *you* in Middle English often involves politeness and social relationship as well as number. This is similar to modern French or German. Thus *thou* forms are used with friends, family and social inferiors, *you* forms with strangers or superiors. In *The Wife of Bath's Prologue* she speaks to the Pardoner, for whom she clearly has little respect, using *thou*, and she always uses the *thou* form when giving the pilgrims an account of what she said to her husbands. When addressing the company directly she uses *you* (*Now wol I seye yow sooth* [666]), as she does when she responds to the Host's request for her to begin her tale.

2 Relative pronouns

The main **relative pronouns** found are *that* and *which*. In translating *that* it is often wise to try out a range of Modern English equivalents, such as *who*, *whom*, *which*. The prefix *ther–* in such words as *therto* and *therwith* often refers back to the subject matter of the previous phrase. *Therto* may be translated as 'in addition to all that' or 'in order to achieve that'.

148

3 Impersonal construction

With certain verbs the **impersonal construction** is quite common, e.g. *it tickleth me* (471), *it remembreth me* (469).

4 Reflexive pronouns

Many verbs can be used with a **reflexive pronoun**, a pronoun which refers back to the subject (as in modern French or German) and which may, depending on the verb employed, be translated or understood as part of the verb (e.g. *I baar me* [224], *I avaunte me* [403]).

5 Extra negatives

In Middle English extra **negatives** often make the negative stronger, whereas in Modern English double negatives cancel each other out. *I ne owe hem nat a word* (425) would now be 'I do not owe them a word'; *I ne loved nevere by no discrecioun* (622), 'I was never discreet in love'; *Ne of noon oother womman* (691), 'not of any other woman'.

6 Contraction

Sometimes pronouns merge with their associated verbs, e.g. *seistow* (= *sayest thou*): you say (251), *hydestow* (= hidest thou): you hide (308), *prechestow*: (= preachest thou): you preach (366).

7 Word order

Middle English **word order** is often freer than Modern English, and in particular there is more inversion of subject and verb (e.g. *vanysshed was this daunce* [996]) or subject and object or complement (e.g. *Gat-tothed I was* [603]). In analysing difficult sentences you should first locate the verb, then its subject, then the object or complement. (Roughly, a verb which involves activity takes an object – 'she hit the ball', 'he gave her the book' – while a verb which describes a state of affairs takes a complement – 'it was yellow', 'you look better'.) Then you should put these elements together. It should then be easier to see how the various qualifiers fit in.

In the sentence *By verray force, he rafte hire maydenhed* (888) the main verb is *rafte*. The subject is *he* and object *hire maydenhed*, with the qualifier *by verray force*.

Chaucer sometimes adds to his sentences in ways that would not be considered 'good English' today. For example, the sentence beginning in line 285, in which the Wife describes all the things that people examine carefully before buying, consists of so many clauses and phrases that if translated directly into modern English it provides a very long convoluted sentence: 'You say that oxen, asses, horses and hounds have been tried out at different times; basins, wash bowls, before men buy them, spoons and stools and all such household equipment, and so have pots, fabrics and clothing; but folk do not try out wives until they are married – senile old scoundrel – and you say that we then show our defects.' Written in modern English this one sentence would probably become two or three, but Chaucer achieves his effects by letting the sentence build up to the comic climax.

In the long sentence beginning *For, God it woot* in lines 1150–1158, the old woman is speaking to the knight about true nobility. You need to work out the connections that link together to lead to the main point, which comes in the final clause of the sentence. The key point the old woman is making comes at the end – *For vileyns synful dedes make a cherl* – and the previous eight lines build up to it. A modern translation might run:

'For, God knows, people may well often find a lord's son doing shameful and wicked things; and he who wants to have the advantages of having been born of a noble house and of his noble and virtuous elders, and yet does not himself act in a noble

A Note on Pronunciation

The Wife of Bath's Prologue and Tale, like other poems, benefits from being read aloud. Even if you read it aloud in a Modern English pronunciation you will get more from it, but Middle English was pronounced differently (the sounds of a language change at least as much as the vocabulary or the constructions) and it helps to make some attempt at a Middle English accent. The best way to learn this is to imitate one of the recordings (the tapes issued by Pavilion and Argo are especially recommended for this purpose). A few principles are given below; more can be found in *The Riverside Chaucer*.

1   In most cases you should pronounce all consonants (for example you should sound the 'k' in *knight* and the 'l' in *half*). But in words of French origin initial 'h' (as in *habitacioun* [775] for example) should not be sounded, nor should 'g' in the combination 'gn'. The combination 'gh' (as in *right* [332, 376]) is best sounded 'ch' as Scottish 'loch'.

2   In most cases all vowels are sounded, though a final 'e' may be silent because of elision with a vowel following (e.g. do not sound the 'e' in *mette of* [577]) or because of the stress pattern of the line (e.g. I would sound the final 'e' in *cheere* [588], but leave it silent in *mente* [20]).

3   Two points of spelling affect pronunciation. When 'y' appears as a vowel you should sound it as 'i' (see table on page 154). Sometimes a 'u' sound before 'n' or 'm' was written 'o' (because 'u' and 'n' look very similar in the handwriting of the time). This means that *song* and *yong* should be pronounced 'sung' and 'yung'. This also applies in *comen* and *sonne* (as in their Modern English equivalents 'come' and 'son').

4   You will not go too far wrong with combinations of vowels, such as *ai*, *eu* and *oy*, if you sound them as in Modern English. There are significant exceptions (for example *hous* [239] and many words of similar ending should be pronounced with an *oo* sound) but it is not possible to establish reliable rules purely on the basis of the spelling.

5   The principal vowel sounds differ somewhat from Modern English. They are set out in the table below (adapted from Norman Davis's table in *The Riverside Chaucer*). The table distinguishes long and short versions of each vowel. This distinction still applies in Modern English (consider the 'a' sounds in 'hat' and 'father'), but unfortunately it is often only possible to decide whether a particular vowel is long or short by knowing about the derivation of the word. Do not despair. Even a rough approximation will help you. Only experts in medieval languages have reliable Middle English accents, and even they cannot be sure that Chaucer would have approved them.

Vowel	Middle English example	Modern equivalent sound
Long 'a'	name (341), cas (165)	'a' in father
Short 'a'	nat (77, 98, 128), that (130)	'a' in hat
Long 'e'	she (1021), been (1027)	'a' in fate
Open 'e'	deed (1006), breste (1103)	'e' in there
Short 'e'	gentil (1111), wende (915)	'e' in set
Unstressed 'e'	sonne (868)	'a' in about, 'e' in forgotten
Long 'i'	I (863), tymes (544)	'i' in machine
Short 'i'	hym (513), right (2)	'i' in sit
Long 'o'	no (71), moot (361)	'o' in note
Open 'o'	hooly (690)	'oa' in broad
Short 'o'	som (104),	'o' in hot
Long 'u'	hous (239)	'oo' in boot
Short 'u'	but (80), ful (986)	'u' in put

Essay Questions

Worked questions

The two questions below are followed by some points you might address in your response.

1   **What do we learn about the Wife's attitude towards power and dominance in the *Prologue and Tale*?**

Here are some ideas you might explore in your response:

- The Wife presents her relationships with all her husbands as a struggle for power in which she constantly strives to achieve the upper hand in the relationship.
- The ideas of *maistrie* and *soveraynetee* are of key importance: the Wife describes how, in all her marriages, her main objective was to achieve *maistrie* and get the upper hand over her husbands
- She found it relatively easy to achieve *maistrie* over her earlier, old husbands, but her fourth husband was more of a challenge, although in the end she came out on top here too.
- She used a variety of techniques, all of which made her husbands suffer in various ways until they gave in.
- She believes that harmony in marriage can only be achieved when the husband has surrendered power to the wife.
- This message is reinforced through the knight and the old woman in the tale.

2   **Explore the ways in which Chaucer uses imagery in the Wife's prologue.**

Here are some ideas you might explore in your response:

- The Wife uses animal imagery to describe herself and her relationships.

- There are differences between the imagery she applies to herself and that she uses to describe her husbands.
- Various effects are created through this imagery, for example her descriptions of the vitality she had in her youth or her recommending to her husband that he should behave as meekly as their sheep.
- She uses imagery relating to trade, goods and possessions, for example when discussing the merits of virginity over marriage, and her relationships with her husbands are described in terms of profit and gain.
- She suggests that 'everything is for sale'.
- She uses the imagery of fire to describe, for example, the dangers of sexual passion.

Sample questions

The following questions are for you to try.

1   Discuss the ways in which Chaucer links the Wife of Bath's prologue to her tale.

2   Explore the ways in which Chaucer presents attitudes towards marriage in *The Wife of Bath's Prologue and Tale.*

3   Remind yourself of lines 1109–1176 (from *But, for ye speken of swich gentillesse* to *To lyven vertuously and weyve synne.*) How important is this section to *The Wife of Bath's Tale?*

4   Explore how Chaucer uses fourteenth-century views about women in *The Wife of Bath's Prologue and Tale.*

5   Discuss the ways in which the Wife argues and supports her points in her prologue.

6   In what ways is the setting of the story important in *The Wife of Bath's Tale?*

7 Examine Chaucer's presentation of the Wife of Bath in the *General Prologue*.

8 With detailed reference to **two** or **three** passages from her prologue, examine how the Wife presents her experiences of married life.

9 Explore the ways in which Chaucer ends *The Wife of Bath's Tale*. In your answer you should examine in detail the section from *'Chese now,' quod she, 'oon of thise thynges tweye'* (line 1219) to the end of the tale.

10 How does the Wife use *auctoritees* in her prologue? You should write in detail about **two** or **three** passages from the prologue in your answer.

11 How effective do you find the opening of the Wife's prologue? You should look at the section from the beginning of the prologue to *Virginitee, thanne wherof sholde it growe?* (line 72).

12 How is the medieval concept of *gentillesse* important in *The Wife of Bath's Tale*?

13 How are the ideas of *maistrie* and *soveraynetee* important in *The Wife of Bath's Prologue and Tale*?

14 Compare the Wife's presentation of her first four husbands with that of her fifth. What does this reveal about her character?

15 Explore how appropriate the Wife's tale is to her as the teller. Do we learn anything more about the Wife's character through her tale?

Chronology

c. 1340–1345   Geoffrey Chaucer born in London to John and Agnes Chaucer

1357   Chaucer becomes a page in the household of Elizabeth, the Countess of Ulster and Lionel, Earl of Ulster (second son of Edward III)

1359   September: Edward III invades France; Chaucer serves in the army and goes to France in the retinue of Lionel

1360   Chaucer is captured at Reims and ransomed for £16; carries letters from France to England for Prince Lionel

c. 1365   Chaucer marries Philippa Roet, who is employed in the Queen's household

1367   Enters service as a squire in the household of Edward III

c. 1367–1370   Translates *Romaunt of the Rose*

1369   Chaucer returns to France and serves in the army of John of Gaunt

c. 1369–1370   Writes *The Book of the Duchess* to commemorate the death of Blanche, Duchess of Lancaster

1372   Chaucer is sent to Italy on a diplomatic mission on behalf of the king

1374   Edward III appoints Chaucer Controller of the Customs for hides, skins and wool for the port of London

1376–1370   Chaucer makes several journeys to France and Flanders on important diplomatic business

1378   Travels to Milan on a diplomatic mission

c. 1378–1382   Chaucer writes *The House of Fame* and *The Parliament of Fowls*

c. 1382–1387	Writes *Troilus and Criseyde, Palamoun and Arcite* and *The Legend of Good Women*
1385–1386	Appointed Justice of the Peace for Kent
1386	Elected as a Member of Parliament and retires as Controller of Customs
1387	Chaucer's wife dies
1387–1392	Begins *The Canterbury Tales*, writing the *General Prologue* and some of the tales
1389	Appointed Clerk of the King's Works by Richard II
1391	Retires as Clerk of the King's Works and is appointed Deputy Forester of the Royal Forest of North Petherton in Somerset
1391–1392	Writes *The Treatise of the Astrolabe*
c. 1392–1400	Writes more of *The Canterbury Tales*
1400	25 October: Chaucer dies and is buried in Westminster Abbey

Further Reading

Editions

The following editions have useful notes and glossaries:

V. Allen and D. Kirkham (eds.), *The Wife of Bath's Prologue and Tale* (Cambridge University Press, 1998)

G. Cigman, *The Wife of Bath's Prologue and Tale and The Clerk's Prologue and Tale* (University of London Press, 1975)

J. Winney (ed.) *The Wife of Bath's Prologue and Tale* (Cambridge University Press, 1965)

Background reading on Chaucer and his works

I. Bishop, *The Narrative Art of the Canterbury Tales* (Everyman's Library, 1988)

P. Boitani and J. Mann (eds.), *The Cambridge Companion to Chaucer* (Cambridge University Press, 1983)

M. Bowden, *A Reader's Guide to Geoffrey Chaucer* (Thames and Hudson, 1964)

D. Burnley, *A Guide to Chaucer's Language* (Methuen, 1983)

H. Cooper, *Oxford Guides to Chaucer: The Canterbury Tales* (Oxford University Press, 1989)

S.S. Hussey, *Chaucer: An Introduction* (Methuen, 1981)

G. Rudd, *Geoffrey Chaucer* (Routledge, 2001)

Criticism

J.J. Anderson (ed.), *The Canterbury Tales: A Selection of Critical Essays* (Macmillan Casebook Series, 1974)

P.S. Lisowska, *The Wife of Bath's Tale* (Hodder and Stoughton, 2000)

N. Marsh, *The Wife of Bath's Tale* (Macmillan Master Guides, 1987)

P. Martin, *Chaucer's Women: Nuns, Wives and Amazons* (Macmillan, 1990)

J.A. Tasioulas, *The Wife of Bath's Prologue and Tale* (York Notes Advanced, Longman, 1998)

Glossary

abedde   in bed
abroche   open up
abyde   stay, wait
a-caterwawed   caterwauling
accordynge in-freere   in agreement together
adoun   down
agast   horrified, aghast
agayn   against (675), towards (1000)
al   although, everything, entirely
al hool   entirely healed, well again
al outrely   entirely, absolutely
al sodeynly   all of a sudden
al Venerian   entirely influenced by Venus
alenge   miserable, wearisome
algate   continuously
allyes   kinsmen
amblere   ambling horse
amended   put right
amendere   improver
a-morwe   next morning
anight   at night
anon   straight away
apparaille   attire
appetit   craving
a-rewe   in succession
array   adornment (338), rich display
arryven   come upon, arrive at
artow   are you
assay   trial (290)
assayed   examined (286)
asterte   escape

attendance   attention
auctoritee   authority
auctours   authoritative writers
avaunte me   boast
aventure   chance
axe   ask

ba   kiss
bacheler   young knight
bacyn   a kind of basin
bad   commanded
bathed   basked
be war   be careful
beere   bier
bele chose   beautiful thing (sexual euphemism)
beren hem on honde   accuse them
bernes   barns
best   beast
bet   beaten
bifel   happened
bigamye   marrying twice
biheste   promise
biquethe   bequeath
birafte   take away from, robbed
biseke   entreat
bishrewe   curse
biside   near
bisynesse   solicitude (933)
bithynke   imagine
bitokeneth   symbolizes
bitore   bittern
biwreye   reveal, betray
biwreyed   revealed
blisful   delighted
blyve   quickly

bobance boast
bokeler a small round shield
bombleth booms
bon bone
bonde bound, fettered
bord table
borel coarse, poor-quality cloth
bountee goodness
bour bower, bedchamber
boures bedrooms
bowen give way, give in
bren bran
brenne burn
brenneth burns
brest breast, heart
breyed started up, awoke
brydel bridle
brynne burn
burghes boroughs
but if unless
byte bite

calle hairnet, kind of headdress
care worry
carpe chatter
certes certainly
certeyn certain
chaffare wares
chalenge lay claim to
chambere chambermaid,
   personal maid
cheke cheek
chepe buy
cherl boor
chese choose
cheste coffin
chidde nagged, scolded, chided
chiertee affection
chyding nagging
clamour outcry

clene pure, well-formed
cleped called
clepeth calls
clerk scholar
clothes fabrics (289)
cokewold cuckold
colour pretence, mask
conseil secret
conseille advise
constreyned compelled
contraried contradicted, denied
contrarius opposite (698)
coost coast
costage expense
coverchiefs head-coverings
coveiteth wants, longs for
crispe heer curly hair

daliance flirtation
daliaunce socializing
daun lord or sir, master
daungerous aloof, standoffish,
   hard to get
daunted frightened
dawed dawned
dayeryes dairies
debaat disagreement
deef deaf
defended forbade
degree social rank
delit desire, pleasure
desolat dejected, powerless
desport amusement
dettour debtor
devocioun devout reverence
devyne conjecture
devyse imagine
dighte copulated with
discrecioun moderation,
   prudence

disfigure   deformity
disparaged   degraded
dispence   extravagant living
disport   entertainment
diverse stoundes   different times
dores   doors
dorste   dare, dared
dostow   do you
dotard shrewe   senile scoundrel
douteless   doubtless
dronken   drunk
droppyng   leaking, dripping
drow   drew

eek   also
eft-soones   again
engendreth   brings forth
ensample   illustration
entendeth   strives
entremette   interfere
envenyme   poison
er, er that   before
estaat   standing
everich   everyone
every deel   every bit
exaltat   elevated, exalted
expres   clearly (27); explicit (61)
eyen   eyes

fader   father
fair, faire   beautiful
faire   market
falsly   treacherously
falwes   fallow ground or fields
fare   act
fast   securely tied
fawe   eager
fee   property, possessions
feeldes   countryside
feeste   festivities

felawe   friend
felaweship   company
ferthe   fourth
fest   fist
fey   faith
feyned   pretended
fil   fell
firy levene   flaming lightning
folwe   follow
fonde   try
foore   footsteps
forbedeth faste   strictly forbids
forbere   put up with
forgo   give up
foul   ugly
freletee   infirmity, frailty
frely   generously, unrestrictedly
frere   friar
fro   from
ful   very
ful soore   most bitterly
fulfild of   thronging with, filled
   with
fynde grace   have good fortune
fyne   cease
fyr   flame, fire

gale   exclamation
galwes   gallows
gat-tothed   gap-toothed
gay   finely dressed
geestes   stories
genterye   gentility
gentillesse   manners,
   refinement, nobility
gilt   offence
glosen   interpret (26)
God list   it pleases God
goode lief   a term of
   endearment, e.g. sweetheart

goos   goose
goost   soul (97); go (273); spirit (986)
gossib   close friend
governance   control
grace   luck
grece   grease, fat
greet meschief   great misfortune
grisly   ghastly
ground   texture
grucchyng   complaining
grynd   grinds
gytes   robes, gowns

habit   clothing
happed   happened
hardinesse   boldness
harm   slander
hastow   hast thou
haukes   hawks
haunt   skill
hawe   hawthorn berry
hayl   hail
heeste   behest, command
heigh parage   high rank, high birth, noble lineage
hele   keep secret
hende   courteous
hente   seized
heres   hair
herkneth   listen
herte roote   bottom of [my] heart
hevene   heaven
hevynesse   despondency
hight   promised
highte   was called
his thankes   willingly
holden   regarded, considered
holour   lecher, whoremonger

hoold   keeping
hoolly   entirely, wholly
hors   horses
hosen   stockings
houndes   dogs
housbondrye   household goods
hydestow   do you hide

ilke   same
in honde   in control, in hand
inclinacioun   impulse, urge
iren   iron (906, i.e. executioner's axe)

jalousie   jealousy
jangleresse   chatterbox
jape   trick
joly   gay, lively
jolynesse   cheerfulness, amorousness
juggement   judgement
justise   judge

kan   know, understand
kaynard   dotard, sluggard
keep   take charge of, heed
kepe   defend (263), preserve (710)
kette   cut
knave   peasant, scoundrel
kynde   stock (1101), true nature (1149)

lavour   a kind of basin
lecchour   lecher, seducer
leere   learn
leeve   be quiet (365); dear (762)
lemman   mistress
leonesse   lioness
leon, leoun   lion

lepe pounce, leap
lettest hinder, spoil
leve allow (319); leave, permission (908)
leves pages
leyser leisure
licence permission
likerous lecherous, gluttonous
likyng preference, pleasure
limitour limiter, a friar with a specific district
list wishe, desire
litel small
lith lies; leads
lith ygrave lies buried
loke lock
lond land
long tall
loothly loathsome
lordinges gentlemen, lords
lorel rogue, scoundrel
lough laughed (672); low, base (1101)
lowe humble, wretched
lusty lively, vigorous, pleasure-loving
lye blaze
lyen lie
lyes dregs
lykene compare
lymytacioun territory
lyst ear

maad devised
maister master
maistrie mastery, getting the upper hand
make mate
malencolie sullenness, anger, moodiness

Marcien influenced by Mars
mareys marsh
mateere matter
maugree hir heed against her will (lit. in spite of her head)
mayde virgin
maydenhed, maydenhede virginity
mayme injure
maystow you can
me liste (it) pleases me
mede meadow
mekely meekly, docilely
mencioun mention
meschances calamities
mette dreamt
mirily wittily
mo more
mooder mother
mordred murdered
morne mourn
morwenynge morning
moste must
motes specks of dust
motthes moths
muchel much
murmur grumbling
mytes mites

nacioun family
nathelees nevertheless
ne eek nor (lit. not also)
nedely of necessity
never the mo in any way
nigard miser
no thing in no way
noght not (19)
noon not a
norice nurse
nyce foolish

nycetee lust, nonsense, foolishness

o one, a single
octogamye marrying eight times
office duties
old richesse inherited wealth
oore ore
open-heveded bare-headed
operacioun action
oppressioun wrong, violation
oratories chapels, private rooms
outher either
outrely completely, utterly

parage rank, birth, parentage
paramour mistress, concubine
paraventure perhaps
pardee by God
parfit perfect
pees harmony, peace
perree jewellery, precious stones
peyne pain, distress, grief
peyntede painted
pistel message
pith vigour
pitously pitiably, pathetically
plesaunce joy, happiness
pleye relax
pleyne complain
plight torn
pottes household pots
poure gaze
povre poor
preambulacioun making a preamble
precept commandment

preche preach, lecture
preciously expensively
precius overly refined, fastidious
prees crowd
preese urge, entreat
prente imprint, mark
priketh spurs on
privee private, secret
prively privately
prowesse moral excellence
pryvetee secret
purgacioun purging, discharge
pursute petitioning, suing for justice
purveiance foresight, provision
purveye provide
purveyed of provided with beforehand
pye magpie
pyne distress, suffering, anguish

queynte female sexual parts
queynte fantasye strange, curious inclination
quit, quitte repaid
quod said
quoniam 'whatsit' or 'you-know-what' (euphemism for sexual parts)

radde read
rafte robbed
ragerye wantonness
rake-stele rake handle
raunson penalty, fine, ransom
rede read
refresshed satisfied, fed
remenant rest
renne run

renomee renown
rente tore
repreve reproach
resonable rational
revelour reveller, rake
reysed raised; assumes power
richesse wealth
right naught not at all
roode beem beam supporting the cross in a church
roule wander
rowne whisper
rude lacking refinement, basic
ryot debauchery, revelry
ryver hawking for waterfowl

salwes willow branches
saufly safely
saugh saw
savoure taste
scathe pity
science learning, knowledge
scole university
seche seek
secree discreet
seistow you say
seken halwes go on pilgrimages
seketh searches
selde seldom
sely unfortunate; innocent, blessed; simple, humble
seme may seem
senge singe
seye seen
shap figure, shape
shapen formed, destined
shende destroy, ruin
sheres scissors
shette shut
shipnes stables

shrewe scoundrel, malicious person (284); curse (1062)
shrewed wicked, evil, cursed
shrewednesse malignancy
siketh sigh
sith since
sith that because
slepinge sleeping
slyke sleek, shining
smale little, slender
smoot hit, struck
sojourne linger, remain
somdel somewhat
someres summer
Somonour Summoner
sondry various
sondry talis all the news
sooth truth
soothly for to seye to tell the truth
sory grace misfortune
soun sound
soutiltee subtlety, trick
soveraynetee sovereignty, complete authority
spanyel spaniel
spectacle eyeglass
spiced scrupulous
spille put to death
spilt ruined, come to grief
spitously relentlessly
spores spurs
squireth escorts
stable constant
sterven wood die insane
stiborne stubborn, strong-willed
stille silent
stinte stops
strem river
strook blow

subtilly with great skill
suffisant satisfactory
suffrable tolerant, able to bear suffering
suffre allow
suretee security, certainty (903); pledge (911)
suspecioun suspicion
suster sister
swal swelled
swete sweet, pleasing
swich such
swinke toil
swogh swoon
swyn pig, swine
syk illness

t'assemble to bring together
t'overbyde to outlive
taak keep observe, take note
talis tales, gossip
targe a small round shield
tayl tail
testament will
ther as wherever
therto moreover
thilke that, that same
thonder dint thunder clap
thral slave
thrope village
tikled pleased, tickled
to those
tonne barrel
tormentrie torture
tow flax
tree wood
treson treachery
tresor wealth, treasure
tressed heer braided or carefully arranged hair

tribulacioun great suffering or affliction
trowe believe

undermeles see Notes, p. 92, line 875
unright wrong
up stirte leapt up
upon a day one day
upright lying down
usage custom

vacacioun spare time
verray genuine
verray force sheer violence
verray jalousye sheer jealousy
vessel utensil
vice fault, deformity (955)
vileynye shameful action
vinolent drunken
visage face

walweth tosses and turns, writhes
warde cors bodyguard
wardeyns guardians
weilawey alas
wel bigon in a good situation
welde control
wenestow do you expect
werne refuse to allow
wex became, grew
wexe increase
weyeden weighed
weylawey alas
weyve abandon
whoso whoever
whyne whine
widwe widow
wight person

wilde fyr fierce fire
wilful voluntary, willing
wiste knew
with sorwe bad luck to you, blast you
withal moreover
wittyng knowledge
wo misery (3); wretched (913)
wole desires
wood mad
woot know
worldly occupacioun practical matters
wreke avenged
wroght fashioned
wroot wrote
wrooth, wrothe angry
wyf woman (998, 1000, 1046); wife (1026)

wynde writhe
wynnyng profit
wyte blame

yaf gave
yelden surrender
yen eyes
yerne eagerly
yeven given
yflatered fawned upon
ygon gone
yif give
yifte gift
yis yes indeed
ylymed caught (as with bird-lime)
Ynde India
yplesed flattered, pampered
ywis indeed